Shot to Pieces

a novel

by Michael O'Keefe

ISBN: 978-1-4834-5327-9 (sc)
ISBN: 978-1-4834-5326-2 (hc)
ISBN: 978-1-4834-5325-5 (e)

Library of Congress Control Number: 2016909590

Lulu Publishing Services rev. date: 07/11/2016

In loving memory of my mother,
Mary Ellen O'Keefe,
who would not approve of some
of the saltier language in this book.

DEDICATION

This book is dedicated to my lovely, patient, and at all times supportive wife, Janet. *Shot to Pieces* wouldn't have been possible without her inspiration and unwavering belief in me. After boring her with my war stories for the last five years, she bought a laptop for me and told me to get to work writing them down. She had heard quite enough. I owe her a lifetime of thanks.

CHAPTER ONE

October 10, 2013
Brooklyn

Paddy Durr was sweating and thrashing around in the knotted bedsheets in his dormitory bunk. He was in the throes of another of his usual nightmares. Muttering curses at an unseen enemy, threatening violence, he hadn't hit anything yet. Given that, this would qualify as one of the more benign recurring dreams residing in Durr's REM sleep. When he finally awoke, he would be unable to describe the dream in any detail. All that would be left to him would be the flop sweats and the latent anxiety. Durr woke up most mornings this way. His state of mind would alternate randomly between an uneasy feeling of something not being quite right, and the outright certainty that everything was thoroughly wrong. So he was angry most of the time. The words most frequently used to describe him by the cops and supervisors in the 83rd Precinct were *vicious* and *prick*. Kevin White was aware of all this. He had worked at the *eight three* with Durr for the last couple of years. He knew he was surly, but he also knew he was brilliant. His brilliance was needed right now on Wilson Avenue. The last thing White wanted to be doing this morning was waking a bitter and angry detective, but the exigencies of the service demanded it.

The nudge was weak, but insistent, accompanied by a quietly repeated, "Detective." There it was again. Detective Padraig Joseph Durr roused himself enough to realize he was looking into the face of Lieutenant Kevin White, the late tour platoon commander at the 83rd precinct. It took Durr a moment to remember where he was. As his eyes focused, he saw he was in the detective's dormitory. The alarm on his cell phone hadn't gone off. So he checked it for the time, 0630 hours. As he became more alert, the detective put these items together. Something had to be seriously amiss for the uniform platoon commander to decide to come into the dorm. Things had to be totally fubar for him to wake the sleeping detective an hour and a half prior to his scheduled tour.

"What the fuck are you doing in here, Lou?" Durr barked, using the informal diminutive for the rank. Lieutenant White steeled himself for Durr's acrimony.

"We've got a shooting, likely to die, outside Angela's Diner on Wilson Avenue."

"Her son's on the job," Durr remembered. "In the *seven eight*, I think."

"We're already talking to him. He was in the restaurant this morning. He opened up with his mother. They didn't see the shooting. He said he watched the victim leave with two other guys. Nobody followed them out."

"Where are the two guys that were with the victim?"

"We got them here in the muster room."

"Is Night Watch responding?"

"Yeah, they're already at the scene."

"Okay, now for the sixty-four-thousand dollar question; if the victim isn't dead, and Night Watch is already there, why are you waking me at the crack of fucking dawn?"

"The guy is pretty well ventilated. We counted six holes, including a head shot. EMS hasn't pronounced yet, but the guy is already a ghost. Plus, I know how you like to get a jump on these things."

"That was awesome, Kevin. Did you practice that bullshit in the mirror before walking it in here? Or are you just winging it? What are you not telling me?"

"Vito Piombone is the Night Watch detective."

"Ah fuck!" Durr exclaimed.

"That's what I figured."

"Has he screwed anything up yet?"

"Not as far as I know."

"Alright, here's what we do. Have that numbnuts call the desk. We need to give him something time consuming, and meaningless to do. Tell him I am catching this case and responding. I want him to identify and interview everyone in the diner. When he's done, I need the plate numbers on all the cars parked on Flushing and Wilson, two blocks each way. That should keep the idiot busy. And whatever you do, don't let EMS remove the body till I get there."

"What are you gonna do?"

"I'm going to take a shower, put on a fresh suit, and solve this thing. Thanks for the heads-up, boss. Heading Piombone off at the pass is going to save me a lot of work."

The Night Watch in the NYPD was a squad of detectives who handled serious crimes occurring between 0100 hours and the incoming day tour. They would keep major crimes investigations warm for the catching day tour of the precinct detective squad. 0800 hours was when the regular precinct detective squad would come in for their day tour. The detective duty chart was set up with the regular squad detectives performing two *four to ones*, followed by two *eight to fours*. The six hours between the last four-by and the first day tour was called the *turnaround*. This was generally dreaded by the detectives. The problem was, six hours wasn't enough sleep to get properly rested, and it wasn't enough overtime to justify the sleep deprivation. It was also called the *marriage killer*. This was because detectives who were so inclined, would go out carousing to eat up the time between tours. Many of them would arrange affairs with women from the neighborhood. They were marriage killers because these affairs usually ended badly, and seldom in secret.

Detective Durr had his own issues and experience with infidelity, but he did not engage in any turnaround shenanigans. For the past two years, he had been trying desperately to salvage his marriage after his infidelity was exposed. It was not going well at all. His wife Mairead had evidently had enough, and had asked him to leave. She had stopped participating in couples' therapy with him, reasoning that the problem was Paddy's. The awful truth, which Durr was loath to admit, was Mairead no longer had any interest in fixing their relationship. In her mind, she had already transcended the marriage. But, as long as she hadn't served him with papers, he still had some hope. The understanding was the separation would be temporary, but as the months continued to pass with no reconciliation, it was starting to feel permanent. In any event, he had no interest in revisiting that kind of pain on Mairead, whether or not she wanted him back. He would never forgive himself for having hurt her. In fact, he hated himself for it. So if Detective Durr did not have an arrest with which to make overtime, he went to bed--alone.

Detective Vito Piombone had been in Night Watch for the past ten years. He was well known to the Squad detectives in Brooklyn North. In fact, he was legendary. There was nothing Detective Piombone could touch that wouldn't instantly turn to shit. He couldn't interview a witness without screwing up their identifying information, or totally getting wrong whatever it was they said. Anything he did, had to be redone. This was bad enough. But it had become further complicated by the department instituting the new computerized Investigative Follow-up System. The NYPD was trying to work out the bugs of the new system. The chief complaint from the detectives was their inability to remove reports from their case which were prepared in error by an outside investigator. And all of Detective Piombone's reports were in error. If you didn't catch him before he started typing, you were stuck with the misinformation coming out of his fingertips. Sometimes his stupidity, memorialized in perpetuity, was so egregious it could wreck your case. One of the most disconcerting sights a detective could encounter, was to come in to the squad in the morning to find Detective Piombone seated at one of the desks, typing into the computer terminal. Detective Durr had spoken to Piombone's supervisor about it. The sergeant was a reasonable man. So Detective Durr approached him off the record one night.

"Please Sarge, don't let that imbecile Piombone submit *fives* anymore." *Fives* was short for DD 5's, the designation of Detective Follow-up reports.

"Why not?"

"Because everything he types is so wrong. He provides the defendant with instant reasonable doubt. I'm risking my life to catch these murdering scumbags. I don't want to see them walk on Piombone's boobery."

CHAPTER TWO

October 10, 2013
Brooklyn

Detective Durr left two voicemails with his partners, telling them to get into the office forthwith. This was detective-speak for *we've got a fresh body. Get your asses in here right now.* Then after showering and dressing, he got a fresh reporter's notepad from the supply locker, along with the digital camera and the keys to a squad car. He grabbed his top coat and hat and headed to the crime scene. As Durr was descending the stairs leading to the back parking lot of the precinct, he encountered his least favorite police officer. The slovenly and obnoxious Ralph Marten had been a cop for twenty-plus years. Because of this, he thought of himself as one of Durr's peers. He imagined they were somehow equals. Durr wouldn't even acknowledge they were of the same species. Marten saw Durr and brainlessly commented.

"Here comes the white knight now. Off to avenge the wrongs of God's misbegotten children. When are you going to realize that these mutts don't deserve the shred off your balls?"

Durr looked critically at the fat cop. Then he punched Marten in the face as hard as he could. He grabbed him by the throat with his left hand and lifted him off the ground, smashing the back of his head against the wall. A rivulet of blood ran down from Marten's nostril and dripped over Durr's fist. He closed off the flow of air from Marten's trachea and waited a beat for the cop to appreciate the sense he was dying. Paddy leaned in and bit down on Marten's ear, crunching through the cartilage and drawing blood.

"If you ever speak to me again," Durr whispered in the terrified cop's bleeding ear. "If you even look at me, you're a fucking dead man. So help me God, I will end you. Is any of this unclear?"

The choking officer struggled to nod through Durr's tightening grip. Then Paddy dropped him, gasping for breath, in a heap on the floor. Durr drove his shoe into Marten's groin for emphasis. He wiped the blood from his hand on the cop's thinning hair, then spit on him and exited the stairwell, heading out to the parking lot as if nothing had occurred at all.

Number 18 Wilson Avenue was between Noll and George Streets. When Detective Durr got there, the victim was covered by an orange vinyl tarp. He asked the uniform officer who was safeguarding the scene where the tarp had come from. He told the detective it came out of the trunk of his radio car.

"Lose it. It was never here."

"We just wanted to cover the body," the young cop said.

"What the hell for?"

"So the neighbors don't get freaked out."

"How long have you been on the job, kid?"

"Just over a year and a half," he answered sheepishly.

"Don't be ashamed to admit you're new at this. I know I must look like a dinosaur to you, but I was once a rookie too. We were all shiny and unspoiled once upon a time. After a while, the job rubs the shine right off you, and a dead body becomes nothing more than a piece of rotting meat with evidence on it. Don't sweat the neighborhood either. This is Bushwick. The dead fall from the sky here. You are going to have to do this for a long time to see as many dead bodies as these people. They don't freak out easy."

The officer removed the tarp and folded it up, placing it back in the trunk of the radio-car. When he was done, he came back over to the detective. Paddy told him he was going to take some pictures and think out loud.

"Stay with me. If you see anything I haven't already mentioned, you speak up."

"I'm only a rookie. I don't know what I should look for."

"You know what normal looks like, right?"

"Yeah."

"If you see anything that doesn't look normal, you tell me about it. Can you do that, Officer Crowe?" Durr asked, reading the cop's name from the tag under his shield. But Paddy already knew who the young man was, had actually met him twenty-five years earlier when the officer was just a boy. The young cop nodded.

Detective Durr walked over to the body, snapping pictures with the digital camera. He stood next to the body and took pictures in all four directions. He walked west to the corner. Durr slowly walked back toward the body, looking down at the sidewalk. Fifteen feet from the victim he stopped and wrote something in his notepad. Then the detective started talking out loud.

"Victim is a dark-skinned Hispanic male, approximately mid-to-late thirties. He is prone, face down. His left hand is extended in front of him. There is a gunshot wound on the back of that hand. It appears to be an exit wound."

Durr turned the hand over to examine it.

"The victim has what appears to be an entry wound on the palm. Noted is the presence of stippling, starring and powder tattooing, suggesting a point-contact-wound."

Durr dropped the hand and continued to examine the body.

"The victim has a gunshot wound to the back of his head. The orientation of the protruding brain matter and bone fragments suggest an exit wound, as does the absence of starring or stippling. The victim has an additional five gunshot wounds observed on his back. His white denim jacket has very little blood around the wounds, suggesting these were entry wounds. The shape of them further suggests the shooter stood over the victim and fired straight down. There are no shell casings at the scene. The weapon was most likely a revolver. Approximately fifteen feet west of the victim, there is a large blood spatter with flecks of what appear to be bone and brain matter. There are droplets of blood leading up to the body. They are tear-drop-shaped and appear to have fallen from the victim as he moved in an easterly direction."

Detective Durr asked Officer Crowe if he noticed anything significant. The young cop pointed at the top of the wrought iron gate in front of 18 Wilson Avenue. There, in iron letters it said *The Pearly Gates*.

"Damn, he almost made it," Durr laughed. "How much you want to bet, when we find out who he is, he's in the *other* place?"

"What makes you say that?"

"Somebody wanted this man very dead. You don't get shot this many times at point blank range without having seriously pissed someone off. On top of which, the victim has tear-drop tattoos at the corner of his eye. I see three of them there under the left eye. That's a gang thing. Each tear is supposed to represent a body the wearer dropped. And if you look over here, he has a gun tattooed between his thumb and forefinger. Also a gang thing, it means he was a stickup guy. All in all, I'd say the probability is he's already burning, if you believe in that stuff."

Detective Durr pulled out two sets of heavy rubber gloves from his inside coat pocket. He tossed one set over to the rookie officer.

"What are these for?"

"You put them on your hands."

"I know where they go. Why are we wearing them?"

"We gotta flip him over and search him. Do you want to do that with bare hands?"

"Oh hell no!" the officer exclaimed, with a mixture of confusion and horror.

"Relax. I'll do most of the touching. I'll be looking for a wallet and a cell phone. You write down where I find them. You're gonna need that information when you voucher them."

Durr grabbed the victim's shoulders and told Officer Crowe to grab the victim's pants at the hips. On the count of three, they turned the body over on its side. The front of the victim's clothing was saturated in blood. More blood was copiously pooling where he had lain. In the blood, Durr noted several deformed lead bullets, definitely from a revolver.

"What do we do with those?" Officer Crowe asked.

"We leave them right where they are. Crime Scene will recover and bag them for you to voucher and send to Ballistics."

Durr then reached inside the victim's blood-soaked jacket and extracted a silver flip phone with a Mercedes Benz logo on its face.

"Inside right jacket pocket," Durr noted.

They turned the victim back over onto his belly. Durr reached into the victim's right rear jeans pocket and removed a brown leather wallet. Embossed on the wallet were the words *el hombre malo*.

"*The bad man*. If nothing else, he knew what he was. I'm gonna hold on to these until I can copy the contents. When you come into the squad with the other evidence to voucher, these will be waiting for you, along with the money in the wallet. Do you want to count it, or do you trust me?"

Officer Crowe looked uncomfortable as he stammered, not sure how to answer. Durr had a good laugh. He opened the wallet and pulled the cash from it. He quickly counted it in front of the young cop.

"Four twenties, US currency--that's eighty bucks. I hope you didn't think I would imperil my career for eighty dollars. There'd have to be two million of them to even get me to think about it. Then I'd think again, and voucher every penny. I'm not here to be a bad guy. I'm here to catch them."

The detective saw the Crime Scene Unit van pull onto the block.

"Good news, kid. Crime Scene is here. You'll be able to start the vouchering just in time to make the lunch order. Beginner's luck I guess. You wrote everything I said down, right?"

Officer Crowe had a look of abject terror on his face.

"Ahhh!" Paddy Durr said laughing at the young cop. "I'm just fucking with you. I got it all right here," he said tapping the side of his head.

CHAPTER THREE

October 10, 2013
Brooklyn

When Detective Durr got back to the squad, detectives from the Fugitive Apprehension Squad were there. They had grabbed a perpetrator wanted for a shooting by one of the other detectives.

"What's up, RJ?" Durr said to Detective Ron Johnston.

"We caught *Rabbit* this morning at his mother-in-law's crib in the 75. Matty Price has him wanted for a shooting."

"Does Matty know he's here?"

"I called him. He's on the way in."

"Where do you have the perp?"

"He's cuffed to the rail in the back interview room. He's sleeping like a baby. Being on the lam for two weeks was exhausting, I guess. Speaking of perps on the lam, are we still going to Philly this week?"

"We're going to have to put that off for a while, RJ. I just caught a fresh body."

"That's alright. We're up on the cell phone you got for him. It hasn't moved and he's calling his boys from Schaeffer Street every day. Who is the new vic?"

"I don't know yet. But I got his wallet here, so I should soon."

"We're gonna go get breakfast. We'll stop back in when Matty gets here," RJ said. "By the way, why do they call that kid *Rabbit*?"

"I guess you never saw him run."

After the warrant detectives had left, Durr started pulling the contents out of the victim's wallet, laying them out in an array on his desk. There was a New Jersey Driver's license for a Tenocencio Heriberto Milan, thirty-five-years old, from Newark. There was a Social Security card bearing the name Juan Luis Salazar. There were several credit cards using other names. The victim had five photographs. The first was of himself in front of a white Mercedes Benz. He had his arms crossed in front of his chest, and a large semi-automatic pistol sticking out of his belt at the waist. The smile on his face was more like a sneer. The second photo was of a beautiful Latina woman in her twenties. There was writing on the back which said *Euri, Te amo mi Corazon.* It was signed *Luciana.* The next photo was of the victim with a woman in her sixties. He was hugging the woman, who seemed very happy. The detective assumed it was his mother. The fourth picture was of the victim and the beautiful young woman holding an infant dressed in white. It was in front of a baptismal font. The last photo was of a tombstone. In the background could be seen palm trees in a tropical setting. The tombstone read *Herminio Roberto Betances.* Under the name it read 1969-1995. Perhaps a brother, Durr surmised. The rest of the wallet contained business cards for barbershops, mechanics, pawn shops, and car washes, along with numerous other innocuous slips of paper. There was nothing to positively identify the victim at this point.

Durr sat down at his computer terminal and began a series of name checks for the Jersey license. It turned out to be a forgery. New Jersey DMV had no record of a license for that ID number, nor for the name on the Social Security card. The detective then ran the name on the tombstone. He got a hit on that one. A Herminio Roberto Betances was the victim of a homicide in the 34th precinct in Washington Heights in 1995. The complaint report made no mention of any family notification. The victim's listed address was 508 West 164th Street, in Manhattan. An address check revealed no one else named Betances in either the complaint index or the arrest log. Hopefully, the two witnesses who were with the victim could shed light on who he was. Otherwise, the detective would have to wait for Missing Persons to take the stiff's finger prints at the morgue tomorrow. Durr could conceivably have to wait two days for the prints to come back, costing him precious time.

Detective Joseph Furio was the first of Durr's partners to arrive. He came bursting into the squad, out of breath, as if he had run all the way from his home on Staten Island. He had a box of pastries in his hand and wanted to know what was going on with the case before he even took his coat and hat off. This was typical Furio, all energy and excitement-- and anger. Furio was always angry about something. Everything was an emergency. If he didn't think others shared his sense of urgency, he could snap. Paddy Durr was his perfect counterpoint. He had the ability to calm his partner without robbing him of his energy. Paddy slowed everything down for Joe. Which was good, because when Furio slowed down and was able to focus his considerable investigative skills, he was as good as any detective on the force.

"Take your coat off, Joe. Get a cup of coffee, and I'll tell you what we have."

As Durr brought Furio up to speed on the case, Detective Armando Gigante came into the squad. Paddy had worked with Gigante when they were both Anti-Crime cops in the "Old 34th" Precinct. They had reconnected years later in the *eight three* Squad, but their friendship had spanned the years. Detective Gigante was proud to call himself a Mexican-American, but he really wasn't one. He was of half Mexican descent on his father's side, but those Mexicans came here four generations ago. His mother was a New York Sicilian. Gigante grew up in Whitestone Queens. By the time he had told you his name, he had exhausted all the Spanish he knew. While Gigante was an excellent detective, his greatest asset was his cutting sense of humor. He was an incessant ball-buster. This was surprisingly effective in relieving the enormous tension surrounding a homicide investigation. He had the ability to take the edge off by allowing everyone else to laugh at themselves. But, there was no one he enjoyed giving the needle to more than his friend and partner, Joe Furio.

"What's in the cake box, fat boy?" he said to Furio.

"You see what I have to deal with?" Furio asked Durr, as if he hadn't watched this show play out for the last ten years. "Why don't you waddle your fat Mexican ass over here and see?"

Gigante had a good laugh. Then he joined his partners at the table in the coffee room, where the detectives discussed the case, and developed an investigative plan.

After finishing their coffee and briefing, it was decided Durr and Furio would interview the witnesses separately, and then compare notes. Meanwhile, Gigante would handle the phones, make notifications and do record checks based on whatever information Durr and Furio ascertained from the witnesses.

CHAPTER FOUR

October 10, 2013
Brooklyn

Miguel Baez was a thirty-two-year-old car thief. His sheet indicated he had taken five falls for felony possession of stolen property over the last ten years. He had managed to combine these cases into one concurrent conviction. He got three to five years. He did the three, and finished his remaining two years on Parole. It did not appear he had any contact with the justice system for the last two years. He was still involved in auto theft, but he didn't get his hands dirty anymore. He was now engaged in the storage, transport and delivery of the product. This was more lucrative, and involved less exposure. In spite of this, he was no more comfortable speaking to the police than if he was still boosting cars. Miguel decided to employ the most common strategy of people in his position. He was going to lie his ass off--about everything. Detective Durr entered the interview room with a legal pad, the victim's cell phone and a legal folder of papers. After introducing himself, Durr asked Miguel what he did for a living.

"I sell cars."

"I see that from your sheet. But they're not yours. Are they, Miguel?"

"Seriously, I'm legit."

"That's comforting to know. What would be even more comforting to know would be who the guy was who got smoked this morning outside Angela's."

"I don't know him. I was walking to my car on George Street," Miguel said.

"You're gonna be that guy, aren't you? You're going to make me deconstruct your bullshit for the next six hours before you realize you don't have any reason to lie to me. Is that who you want to be today?"

"On my mother's grave, I wasn't with anybody."

"I really wish you hadn't done that. It's just going to make you feel foolish when I break you. For now, you think you have a role to play here. If you're determined to play it, go ahead. Tell me about your night. Leave nothing out. I want to know who you were with, where you were, what you were doing."

Miguel told Durr he was out at a club in Manhattan, *Las Vegas* on Dyckman Street. He met a girl there from Bushwick, named Marisol. She invited him to breakfast with her friends. That's how he ended up in Angela's. After breakfast, and saying goodbye to Marisol, he was walking to his car around the corner on George Street. There were two guys walking about a half a block in front of him. He saw a guy in a dark hoodie jump out from between two parked cars and start shooting. Miguel said he dove under a car as soon as he heard the first shot. The police found him there when they showed up a minute later. He said it was dark. He didn't see the shooter, who was too far away. He never saw the two guys who were getting shot at before. He insisted that was all he had to offer. Durr regarded Miguel with heavy-lidded eyes.

"I have a record of the 911 callers on this shooting," Durr told Miguel, waving a computer printout in front of him. "The first three calls are from residents on the block who heard the shots. Those calls were made at the same time, 0630 hours. The next call was a minute later from a cell phone where the caller was recounting what had just happened. He further described the two males who had been walking with the victim as arguing over something. The first uniform officers told the dispatcher they were present at the scene at 0632 Hours. I talked to the officer. He told me he saw you arguing with the other guy as they were pulling onto the block. His partner hit the siren. Only then did you run and dive under a car. Is he lying?"

"Maybe he was confused."

"May I look at your cell phone?"

Miguel handed Durr his phone. He started going through the contacts and recent calls, jotting down notes on his legal pad. When he was done, he looked up at Miguel and smiled. Then he hit the dial button for the last call and put the phone on speaker-mode. A moment later, the voice of Detective Furio answered.

"Who is this?"

"It's Paddy. Is that the other witnesses' phone you answered?"

"Yeah."

"Ask him whose phone just called him."

"I showed him the phone when it rang. He says it's his cousin, Miguel."

"Okay, that's all for now."

Durr ended the call and looked matter-of-factly across the table at Miguel Baez. Then he went back into the phone and hit the dial key again. The victim's phone started ringing this time. On the screen the caller ID verified the call was coming from Miguel Baez.

"*Dominican Luis* is in your contacts. He knows you by name. Are these just interesting coincidences?"

"Okay, I had breakfast with my cousin and his friend. But the rest is true. I was a block behind them coming out of the diner. I had stopped to talk to a girl. When I heard the shots, I dove under the car. I wasn't close enough to see the shooter."

"Before I tell you why that's a load of bullshit, I noticed you had a contact listed only as *Mami*. When I dial that number, is your mother going to answer the call from beyond the grave, or is she going to be very much alive, and thrilled to hear from her son?"

"Alright, I lied about my mother being dead. But the rest is true."

"Do you know what that pink shit is all over your jacket and shirt? That's blood and brain matter. Now for you to have what we call the *pink mist* all over you, you would have had to be to the right of the victim, and just a step or two behind him. If you persist in trying to jerk me off, I'm going to take those clothes and send them to the lab, and send you home naked. Is that what you want?"

"No."

"Then stop lying to me. You were directly in front of the shooter. You looked him right in the face."

"I don't want to get in trouble with Parole."

"Now you're just stalling. You haven't been on parole for two years. You don't want to, but you can id this guy. I'll accept that you might not know him. But when I figure out who he is, and I show you his picture, you are going to recognize him. And when I grab him and put him in a line-up in this very room, you're gonna identify him."

"It was too dark. I didn't see his face."

"The sun was already coming up, and that corner is right under a streetlight. It was as bright as a movie set. You saw his face. You looked right at it."

Durr took a minute to glare at Miguel. His stare was regarded in Brooklyn North as something otherworldly. It was often called *a thousand yard stare*. But Durr's thousand yard stare was something else entirely. If you were the target of it, you would think he was peering into your soul from the ninth ring of hell, and if you weren't careful, he would drag you back there with him. Miguel kept trying to avoid the detective's piercing eyes. He was fidgety, and nervous, and kept trying to look away. Every time he looked up, Durr was still there burning holes through him with his terrible glare. Finally, Miguel couldn't stand it anymore.

"What do you want from me, Detective?"

"It's not about what I want. It's about the truth. Do you understand what that is? Because, I'm not convinced you do. Here is what's going to happen; I'm going to give you one more chance. You are going to answer all of my questions, completely and truthfully, or else."

"Or else what?"

"Ordinarily I don't care about auto crime. It bores me, to be honest. I don't have the time to dedicate to it, what with all the shooting and murder. I tend to prioritize those. But if you lie to me again, I'm going to get real interested in *your* business. I'll make the time. You will be my only priority. When I'm done with you, you'll think a building fell on you. Now, this is your last shot. Don't fuck it up."

Miguel slumped in his seat, defeated. Then he told the detective how he knew the victim. He had sold him a Mercedes Benz several months ago. He only knew him as Luis. Luis had his niece buy the car for him, at least on paper. He said he couldn't register the car under his name because he was here illegally from the Dominican Republic. He didn't remember the niece's name off hand, but he had paperwork on the transaction. Of course he would be happy to share it with the police. Since selling Luis the car, he had been going to clubs around Brooklyn and Manhattan with him. He had never been to Luis' crib, but he believed Luis lived in Williamsburg. Durr asked Miguel if there was anything he remembered about Luis that seemed out of the ordinary.

"One night we were in a club uptown. Luis saw a bunch of Dominican guys he knew. These guys looked like serious guys. They had all the flashy gold, expensive clothes, and the attitude, you know?"

"No. What do you mean?"

"They looked at everybody like they were trying to figure out if they were going to have to kill them or not. They were scary like that. They kept calling Luis *Yuri.* After they left, I asked Luis why these guys kept calling him that. Was he Russian or something?"

"What did he say?"

"He told me to mind my own fucking business."

"Did you?"

"You bet your ass I did."

CHAPTER FIVE

October 10, 2013
Brooklyn

Meanwhile in the other interview room, Detective Furio was having a relaxed and productive conversation with Robert "Bobby" Ruiz. Bobby, as he liked to be called, was a twenty-four-year-old union plasterer. He told Detective Furio he was arrested once for smoking marijuana when he was seventeen.

"I see that. I'm curious why I can."

"I pled guilty at arraignment and got probation."

"Who told you to do that?"

"My lawyer. He told me I could get a year in jail if I went to trial."

"Legal Aid?"

"Yeah."

"Even for free, you got fucked."

"What do you mean, Detective?"

"You were a seventeen-year-old with no previous record. You got caught with a half a joint, no other weed or drugs recovered. Do I have that right?" Bobby nodded.

"If you had pled not guilty, you would have been ROR'd. That means released on your own recognizance. The DA would have offered you a violation, disorderly conduct for instance. No mention of the weed, you could have paid a fine. A year later the case would have been expunged from your record. Your lawyer screwed you over to clear his case load. If you help us with this murder, I can get that shit off your record."

"Hell yeah, I'll help. That was fucked up, what that guy did to Luis."

Bobby went on to tell Furio he met Luis for the first time last night. He was a friend of his cousin, Miguel. They met him at the club in Manhattan. He said his cousin described Luis as a cool guy, but shady. Bobby thought Miguel was a little afraid of the guy. Bobby said he didn't give it too much thought. He was out to have a few drinks and meet some girls. He wasn't looking to buy someone else's trouble. He said he didn't hang out all that much with Miguel for that very reason. When Furio asked him to expound upon that, Bobby's phone started ringing. The caller id read Miguel Baez. Bobby saw it and said it was from his cousin's phone. Furio answered the phone.

"Who is this?" Furio demanded. Then he said "Yeah." And finally, "I showed him the phone when it rang. He says it's his cousin Miguel." Then Furio hung up.

"What was that all about?"

"I can only assume your cousin is trying to lie to my partner. About now, Durr is blowing his story out of the water. He should stop lying. At least he shouldn't lie to Durr. That Irish lunatic will nail him to the cross, and keep him alive just to prolong his suffering. You should talk some sense into your cousin. I've grown up with Sicilians who couldn't hold a grudge like Paddy Durr. I think he lives for that shit."

They got back to Bobby's recounting of the night and morning's events. He said after the club closed, the three of them agreed to meet at Angela's for breakfast. He went in Miguel's car. They parked on George Street and walked to the restaurant. When they got inside Angela's, Luis already had a booth. He insisted on sitting where he could face the door. Miguel grabbed the seat across from him, so Bobby sat next to Luis. They had breakfast and talked about the night. They didn't have any problems with anyone. But Bobby said something odd happened. Since the shooting, he was starting to think it may have something to do with it.

"What happened?"

"This guy came into the restaurant. He looked right at Luis and made a face, like he was surprised to see him. Luis glared back at him. The guy turned around and left, so I didn't pay it any more mind."

"Could this have been the shooter?"

"No. The shooter was a smaller guy. This guy was a big fat mess. He had to weigh close to four hundred pounds. He was wearing a filthy, yellowed tee shirt. As cold as it was this morning, the guy was sweating bullets and breathing heavy. He had those orthopedic shoes that make your feet look like clubs. And he was messed up looking. He had giant ears. His hair looked like a greasy crew cut that grew out a little. He had one of those Frankenstein foreheads that stuck way out. His face was all fat and pinched together, with tiny little eyes. When he turned around to leave, he had those rolls of fat on the back of his neck that look like a pack of hot dogs. It's weird, but he kind of looked like an elephant. Does that sound crazy?"

"That actually makes perfect sense," Furio said as he went over to the computer terminal in the room. He accessed the Arrest Photo system and ran the name Erik Vasquez. The computer screen was filled with a picture of a fat-faced young man who looked strangely like an elephant.

"That's the guy from the diner!"

"That's Erik Vasquez. He is from the crew of Latin Kings who run the drugs on Starr Street and Knickerbocker Avenue. I can almost guarantee the confrontation in the diner had something to do with the shooting. Erik might not be the shooter, but I bet he knows who is. By the way, Erik Vasquez' nickname is *Elephant Boy*."

Bobby went on to describe how the three of them left the diner and were walking on Wilson Avenue toward George Street.

"All of a sudden, this guy in a navy blue hoodie jumps out from between two parked cars. He sticks this big black gun in our faces. What do they call it, a revolver? One of those. The guy doesn't even look at me and Miguel. He's only interested in Luis. He yells, "*Negro! Morir, hijo de puta!*" Then he shoots Luis in the face, right through his hand."

"What is that?" Furio asked. "Negro, *Morir hijo de puta?*"

"I think *Negro* is a name. It means black. The rest is Spanish for *Die, son of a whore.*

"What happened then?

"Luis tried to run past the guy. He only got three steps before he fell on his face. The guy paid me and Miguel no mind. He walked over to Luis, stood over him, and shot him in the back five more times. Then the guy runs out into Wilson Avenue without looking. He gets hit by a car, a rust colored livery cab I think. He rolled up on the hood and bounced off the windshield. He jumped off the car and ran up Wilson. The driver of the cab got out. He took the gun off of the hood of the car where the shooter had dropped it. He looked around like he wasn't sure what to do with it. Then he got in his car and drove down Wilson, toward Flushing."

"Can you describe the shooter?"

"He was a light-skinned Puerto Rican guy, like me. He was in his early twenties, brown eyes, short brown hair, and clean shaven. He was kind of little, maybe five six, 130 pounds, skinny. He had that navy hoodie I told you about, and black baggy jeans."

"Do you think you can ID him?"

"Oh yeah, I'll never forget that guy's face."

Furio left the room for a few minutes. When he came back in he gave a business card to Bobby.

"This is my friend, Danny Kirk. He used to be a DA in Brooklyn. Now he does criminal defense, but he's still a good guy. He didn't drink the cool-aid. Tell him you're working with me and Paddy Durr on a homicide. Then tell him you need the weed beef off your record. He'll know what to do."

"Is he expensive? I don't have a lot of money."

"He owes us a couple of favors. He's got a nephew who keeps screwing up. Paddy and I have come to the rescue a few times. He'll only make you pay for the filing fees, and they're not expensive."

"I don't know how to thank you, Detective."

"You don't have to thank me. You're a good kid, and it's what should have been done in the first place. But you do have to do me one favor."

"Anything."

"Stop hanging out with your knucklehead cousin. Guys like him are a magnet for trouble. If the shooter had more sense, you and he would be lying on slabs at the morgue next to Luis.

CHAPTER SIX

October 10, 2013
Brooklyn

Durr and Furio regrouped with Gigante in the squadroom. The detectives shared what each of them had discovered. Gigante told them he had pulled the 911 calls for the shooting. There were four callers. Three of them lived on the block and heard the shots, but didn't see anything. But the fourth caller saw the whole thing from beginning to end.

"He's a nineteen-year-old college student. His name is Albert Alvarez. He had just dropped his mother off at work at the Boar's Head plant on Morgan Avenue. The kid was sitting at the light at Flushing and Wilson. He saw the shooter jump out in front of the three guys and shoot the one in the middle. Albert says the shooter walked over to the victim and emptied the gun into his back."

"Did he recognize him?"

"No. But get this. The kid says the shooter runs out into the street and gets hit by a livery cab. He dropped the gun on the cab's hood, bounced off and ran up Wilson towards Myrtle. The cabby got out and grabbed the gun before driving away."

"Does he know the cabby?"

"No, but the guy drove right by him. The kid wrote the plate down. He's got it in his car."

"Did you run the plate?"

"I don't have it yet. I got the kid on his cell phone. He's in the middle of a chemistry mid-term at St. Johns. He's coming here as soon as he's done." Gigante told them.

"Didn't you go to St. Johns?" Furio asked Gigante.

"Yeah."

"That's a school for the mentally impaired, isn't it?"

"Big talk from a fat guy with a GED," Gigante laughed.

"Alright, that's enough," Paddy told them. "You can beat each other up later. Let's focus on the work at hand. Did you notify the Homicide Squad, Armando?"

"Yeah, but they're going to be detained. They caught a triple in the *seven five.*"

"That's fine. The three of us have this covered for now. What do you have, Joe?"

Furio told him what Bobby had said. He thought his story was forthcoming and credible.

"The kid is an innocent. He's freaked out about seeing that guy get smoked. He really wants to help."

"What's with the weed beef?" Durr asked.

"It shouldn't be there. Legal Aid convinced him to plea at arraignment. I put him onto Danny Kirk to get it sealed."

"Maybe we should have dangled that until he gave us something," Durr suggested.

"No need. He's already helping. I've got him looking at photos to see if he can id the shooter. Whoever it turns out to be, he's probably from Starr Street."

"Why is that?"

"Bobby id's *Elephant Boy* as trading hard looks with the *vic* in the diner. Then *EB* splits. Twenty minutes or so later, the victim walks into an ambush. I'm not inclined to believe it was a coincidence."

"That's good stuff. Now, if we can get this victim identified, we can figure out who he had a beef with. Chances are it's over drugs. The drug set on Starr Street is run by the Latin Kings. The *vic* looks to be Dominican. Maybe it's a territory issue."

"How are you making out with the other guy?" Joe asked.

"We have an understanding, but I had to break him first. He's cooperative while he's here, but he's not going to be our star witness. He's basically a shitbird. I have him writing his statement now as punishment. He'll id. But I'm only going to let him look at a line-up when we get the perp. The less we have to deal with this douchebag, the better."

CHAPTER SEVEN

October 10, 2013
Brooklyn

At around 1000 hours, Detective Matty Price came strolling into the squad-room. Tall, thickly muscled, with a severe high and tight crew-cut, Price looked every bit the Marine Drill Instructor he had once been. In spite of the fact that he had come in on his day off to handle his shooting case, he was immaculately dressed. It wasn't the fanciness or the expense of his suit which drew attention. His clothes were actually quite inexpensive and pedestrian. But you could shave with the creases in his pants and shirts. His sport jacket was an off the rack number from The Men's Warehouse. But it fit him so well, you would think it was custom tailored. In spite of his seemingly all business appearance, Detective Price was in fact the most easygoing detective in the 83 Squad. Nothing seemed to bother him. He had a dry, understated sense of humor, with an ear for the ironic, and a deep appreciation for conundrums. He also enjoyed mispronouncing difficult words like hyperbole and ennui, which he would pronounce for his own amusement as *hyper-bowl*, and *enn-you-eye* respectively. He described his state of mind as being one of perpetual bemusement. He never tired of twisting the intellectually and emotionally unkempt. Unless you were genuinely in need of help, then he was a tireless advocate on your behalf. But if you were one of those people who tried to enlist the police to clean up your messes, he made sure you wished you hadn't.

"Good morning, Paddy. I heard you caught a fresh one. Is this your victim?" Matty asked, looking at the license on the desk in front of Durr.

"That's him. But his eyes had a somewhat more vacant look to them when I met him this morning."

"Is he an innocent?"

"We don't know who he is yet, but every instinct I have is suggesting to me that he is not. Even dead, he gave me *perp fever*."

"This is Bushwick. Today's witness is tomorrow's suspect, is the next day's victim. It's a ghetto-centric circle of life."

"True enough. RJ and the Fugitive Squad should be back soon. They went to breakfast about an hour or two ago. Your boy *Rabbit* is cuffed to the rail in room one."

"Outstanding," Matty said, looking out the door and down the hallway. "Here comes RJ now."

Detective Johnston entered the squadroom. He was telling Matty about the circumstances of *Rabbit's* apprehension when his attention was drawn to the driver's license on Durr's desk.

"Is that your victim?"

"That's his picture. But the name is a fake. We still don't know who he is."

"Well I do. I'll be right back," RJ said, as he turned and ran out of the office.

"It would appear Detective Johnston has some pertinent information about the identity of your victim, Paddy."

"So it would seem. But if RJ knows him, it means he's wanted for some heinous shit. He might be more of a bad guy than I suspected."

A minute later, RJ returned carrying a legal folder the thickness of a valise. He took out a federal fugitive wanted poster with an eight by ten photo of the victim. The fugitive's name was listed underneath as Euripides Luis Betances.

"Euripides; that explains where the name Yuri came from," Paddy said.

"I've been looking for this mutt for two years," RJ said. "We tracked him to Naples Florida. He did two murders there before he skipped to the Dominican Republic. The Collier County Sherriff's Office wants him bad. He shot one of their Deputies escaping the second murder down there. They want to make him ride the lightning."

"What is he wanted for in New York?"

"Do you remember those three robbery-homicides two years ago in the *nine four*?"

"Yeah," Price recalled. "They executed the store owners."

"He was the trigger man. He laid the owners face down and blew the backs of their heads out. He didn't need to. They couldn't identify him. The perps all wore masks. He killed them for the sheer meanness of it."

"How did the *nine four* get him identified?" Durr asked.

"Street Crime grabbed a guy with the gun used in all three murders. He rolled on Euripedes as the shooter. After printing the gun, they came up with his prints on the rounds and the magazine. When they looked at the video from the liquor store, it was obvious it was him, mask and all."

"Give me what you got on him," Durr said.

"His Alias is *El Asesino Negro,* the black assassin. The wanted poster has everything you need, his known addresses, and NYSID number, and such."

"I'll get that NYSID to Missing Persons. They can match those prints with our stiff's. We should have a positive id by this afternoon."

CHAPTER EIGHT

October 10, 2013
Brooklyn

At just before 1100 hours, Police Officer Thomas Crowe came into the squad carrying a handful of Crime Scene bags, and a confused and frantic look on his face. Paddy waved him over to his desk. He took the crime scene bags from the officer and put them on the unoccupied desk next to his own. An unoccupied computer terminal was already on the desk for the officer's use.

"You sit here today, Tommy," Paddy told the young cop.

"How do you know my first name?"

"I met you when you were three-years-old. I worked with your father in the *three four*. He had a couple of years on already when I showed up. I was brandy-new and clueless, just like you are now. I didn't know shit about dick. Your father was already a terrific cop. He was fearless, and he could spot a gun from a block away. He took me under his wing. He taught me how to be a cop. I was working the night in October, when he and his partner ran into that robbery team. I carried your father into the hospital. The story they tell is that he died in my arms, but that wasn't true. He was gone already. In twenty-eight years, that's still my worst day on the job."

"I remember you now. You gave my father's police hat to me at the wake."

"You said you were going to be a policeman so you could catch the guys who did this to your dad. I was going to give it to your mom, but you seemed so determined. I figured you needed it more."

"They ended up arresting everyone on the case," Tommy said.

"I know. I was at the airport when the marshals brought the last two scumbags back from the Dominican Republic. I saw you at the trial. I was impressed with your victim's impact statement at the sentencing. I thought you sounded like a cop already."

"To be honest, Detective, I don't feel like much of a cop. This stuff is all a mystery to me."

"Of course it is. You're brand new. But the great thing about mysteries is, once you figure them out, you own them. You need to find someone to help you figure them out. Who is your sergeant?"

"Sergeant Feigling."

"Oh Jesus! You'll get no help from that jerk-off."

"Everybody says that. Nobody will tell me why."

"Apart from him being a nitwit, he's a coward. When he was a housing cop in the Bronx, he and his partner responded to a 10-13 in the Edenwald Projects. As they were running up the stairs, shots rang out above them. His partner kept going and ended up getting into a gunfight with one of the perps. She poked him out. But Feigling was nowhere to be found. He had turned around and run out of the building. He didn't come out of wherever he was hiding until all the perps were either shot or in custody. His partner was understandably pissed. She trashed him to anyone who would listen. His bosses tried to bring him up on charges for cowardice, but the job wouldn't let them do it. The cops took matters into their own hands. They ostracized him. No one would work with him from that day forward. They wouldn't even speak to him unless it was to call him a coward. Of course, he ratted on every one of them. In the department's infinite wisdom, those cops got Charges and Specifications. Julian Feigling got to take the sergeant's exam. The job promoted him and put him in Brooklyn North. You can smell the shit in his pants from here. He's going to get someone killed one day. He's already jammed up a half-dozen cops."

"How did he do that?"

"He gives fucked-up orders. When they go bad, he denies ever giving them. He leaves his cops swinging in the breeze. If he even gets a whiff he might catch some heat for something, you're going right under the bus."

"What the hell am I supposed to do about that?"

"You call me," Paddy told him, as he gave him his business card with his home and cell phone numbers added to it. "I don't care if it's 0500 hours. If you have a question or a problem, you call me. I'll walk you through it."

"I don't want to be a burden."

"You are not a burden, Tommy. Everything you get on this job has already been bought and paid for by your family's sacrifice. For those of us who knew your dad, your protection and well-being are a sacred duty. As far as everyone on the job is concerned, you are my adopted son. We take care of our own here. Anything you need, you come upstairs."

"I don't know what to say, Detective."

"You can begin by calling me Paddy. Enough with the detective shit. I'm just a cop like you. And you did great today. Your father would be very proud. Just don't be in such a rush. This stuff is going to take a while to make sense. But you have an unfair advantage over the other rookies. You've got the blood of a hero cop running through your veins, and you have me as your guardian angel. Now, let's go through the vouchers."

CHAPTER NINE

October 10, 2013
Brooklyn

An hour later, Detectives Furio and Gigante returned to the squad, having dropped Miguel and Bobby at Miguel's car. While out at the scene, they took the time to conduct a canvass for video. They found cameras on the exterior of 10 Wilson Avenue. A storefront manufacturing and repair outfit named Amalgamated Industrial Equipment, they made the blades for commercial mixers. The owner, Kai Tom, was helpful to a point. When Gigante and Furio came back to the squad with a VHS videotape, they related it to Durr.

"The little prick didn't even want to talk to us. 'No time! No time!' Like if he didn't watch the machines they would slack off on him."

"How did you elicit the gentleman's cooperation, Joe?"

"I told him if he didn't make time to talk to us, I would break everything in his shop, starting with his head."

"I'll bet that got his attention."

"Even still, the cheap little bastard wouldn't part with the tape unless we gave him a replacement. Fortunately, the bodega across the street is as crooked as fuck. He gave me a tape just to get me outta there."

"What is the tape going to show us?"

"The front of 10 Wilson, next door to Angela's," Gigante informed him. "It's a twelve hour, time stamped view. We'll see the *vic* and his friends coming and going, and whether or not they were followed by anyone from the diner."

"We also should see *EB*," Furio Added.

The detectives went into the coffee room and popped the tape into the VCR. A very clear image of the front of 10 Wilson Avenue could be seen with the running time stamp on the bottom right of the screen. Furio fast forwarded the tape until the time read 0530 hours. Then they had coffee and watched the tape advance. At 0538 hours, they saw the victim pass in front of the location, walking in the direction of Angela's. At 0542 hours, they saw Miguel and Bobby pass in the same direction. At 0602 hours, they saw a battered white van they all recognized as belonging to Erik Vasquez, pull up to the front of 10 Wilson and park. They could make out a large individual moving with great difficulty inside the van from the driver's seat to the passenger door.

"What the hell is he doing in there? He looks like a monkey trying to fuck a football," Furio said.

In the next instant, the detectives saw the unmistakable, misshapen form of *Elephant Boy* fall out of the passenger door of the van and onto the sidewalk. He picked himself off the ground with great effort. Then he waddled off in the direction of Angela's.

"What was that belly flop on the sidewalk all about?" Gigante asked. "Why didn't he just get out the driver's side?"

"He had the driver's door welded shut," Paddy explained. "When I brought him in for questioning for those commercial burglaries on Knickerbocker, he told me he broke the lock on the door. It was cheaper to weld it shut than to fix it. Evidently, he doesn't mind face-planting every time he has to get out of it."

At 0604 hours, they saw *EB* moving in a way that might be characterized as running. Lumbering was a better description. He got into the van, again with great difficulty, and tore up Wilson Avenue in the direction of Starr Street. Twenty-four minutes later, they saw the victim and his friends cross in front of 10 Wilson Avenue again. Nobody followed them. Three minutes later, they saw the first marked radio cars arrive. Concluding the murder had occurred by then, they turned off the tape and removed it from the VCR.

"That's going to have to get vouchered and copied for the DA. We've gotta bring *EB* in for questioning. He won't tell us shit, but we still have to have a go at him," Paddy said.

"I'd like to have a go at him with a phone book," Furio offered.

"Me too, but we probably wouldn't get any more out of it than a sore phone book."

CHAPTER TEN

October 10, 2013
Brooklyn

Lieutenant Mariano Martino had been the Commanding Officer of the 83 Detective Squad for the last three years. In that time, he had come to realize his detectives knew more about this business than he ever desired to. It wasn't that he didn't care. It was just that the pressure being put on squad commanders at this time in the NYPD was enormous, and had nothing to do with catching criminals. Once a month, squad and precinct commanders were summoned to Police Plaza at the crack of dawn. There they were humiliated and berated for the crimes which occurred within their precincts. As if they were committing those crimes themselves. Martino quickly saw what it took to emerge unscathed in such an environment. To succeed he would have to be the king of *chickenshit*. The memorization of impertinent information superseded the importance of actual police work. He reasoned if he could help his detectives out in any way with the difficult task of investigating violent crime, it was to insulate them from this land of make believe, and give them the room to do what they were skilled at.

In this regard, Lieutenant Martino counted himself as fortunate to have a veteran squad of accomplished investigators who not only knew their business, but relished it. Most of his detectives had more time on the job than he did. The majority of them had spent their whole careers in the violent precincts of Brooklyn North. They had come to appreciate, if not quite love the people in their communities. They respected the struggle of the good people trying to scrape out a living in these blighted neighborhoods. And, the detectives were almost maniacal in their zeal to punish the savages who preyed upon them. Lieutenant Martino knew that he had something special in the 83 Squad. And he was determined to protect it.

Martino got the call at home at 0800 hours, this Friday morning. Durr apologized for waking him up on his day off. He gave him a quick synopsis of the case to that point, including how he intended to investigate it. Durr told the lieutenant he didn't need to come in if he didn't want to. Paddy and his partners had it covered. Paddy said he just wanted him apprised in case the Chief of Detectives decided to bother him at home. Martino told Paddy they both knew that was a certainty. The lieutenant said he would come in. That way he could deflect the bureaucratic nonsense, so Paddy and his team could do their work unfettered by the innumerable functionaries at headquarters who all felt they needed to know what was going on. In that way Martino thought, they were like lawyers. They had a theoretical understanding of law enforcement and criminal investigation, but no practical experience with its application. Martino decided to feed them just enough information to make them feel like they were a part of the solution, instead of the encumbrance he knew they were.

When Martino came into the squad, he found Durr going through a cell phone with what looked like dried blood on it. He was scrolling through the contacts and writing information on a legal pad.

"Good morning, Paddy. Anything new since we spoke last?"

"We got the victim tentatively ID'd. Turns out he's a straight-up mutt."

"Really? How bad?"

"The guy is a mass-murderer. Fugitives was looking for him for those three robbery-homicides in the *nine four* a couple of years ago, where he executed the store owners. He was wanted for two more murders in Naples Florida, plus the shooting of one of their deputies. And that's only what we know about. I was going to try and figure out who had motive to off this guy, but now it's starting to look like that list is going to stretch around the block. It will be easier to figure out who *didn't* want him dead."

"Are we going to have to eat this one?" the lieutenant asked.

"Nah, boss. We got a lot of meat on the bone. We have reason to believe this may go back to Starr Street and the Latin Kings. We got *Elephant Boy* at the scene, and then diddying up Wilson a minute later. A witness tells us *EB* and the *vic* eye-fucked each other in the diner. Twenty or so minutes later the victim walks into an ambush. The shooter is seen running up Wilson toward Starr after the fact. So we have a place to start looking."

"Is Gang notified?"

"Notified, and I sent them a copy of the unusual. Dave Molinari, the Latin King guy said he'll reach out to his CI's for us."

"Where are Joe and Armando?"

"They're looking for *EB*. We're going to sweat him."

"You think he'll give it up?"

"Not a chance. But you know I never get tired of fucking with that miscreant. Worst case scenario, we can still use him to lock down our timeline and make a circumstantial connection to Starr Street."

"Good work so far. Keep me posted."

After Lieutenant Martino went into his office to begin making notifications and fielding inquiries, the precinct receptionist came into the squad. He informed Detective Durr he had an Albert Alvarez downstairs asking to see him. Durr informed the young cop Alvarez was a witness, so he could send him right up.

He was back a minute later with a clean-cut young man, neatly dressed in khakis, a plaid button-down shirt and black penny loafers. Albert Alvarez completed the squared away look with a fresh haircut. As impressive as his appearance was, he was more so because of his confident, respectful manner. He introduced himself to Durr, making direct eye contact with him as he offered a firm handshake.

"I'm Detective Durr. Thank you for coming to see me."

"I hope I can be of assistance."

Paddy led Albert back to the interview room. He was already impressed with the young man, but his estimation of him grew as he talked to him. Albert Alvarez was a sophomore at St. John's University in Queens, majoring in Biology. He was also a member of the school's ROTC program. He had already pledged his post-graduate service to the Army. After which, he either hoped to go to medical school or join the NYPD. Paddy was almost giddy. This young man was turning into a *Super Witness*. In a case where everyone so far was at least a little damaged, Albert Alvarez seemed like a gift from God. Paddy asked him to tell his story.

Albert told Durr he had just dropped his mom off at work at the Boar's Head plant at Morgan and Flushing Avenues. He was returning home to get ready for school. He was waiting at the red light on Wilson and Flushing, when he witnessed what he had already told Detective Gigante. He wasn't sure if he could id the shooter, estimating he was approximately seventy-five yards away. But he said he would like to try. Alvarez called 911 on his cell phone immediately after the shooting. He stayed at the scene for a few minutes to talk to the police. He told a detective with black hair and glasses that he was a witness. The detective told him he didn't have time for him, and for him to move his car. He said he was going to come in after class anyway, but he was relieved when Detective Gigante called him. Then Albert described the ensuing accident with the shooter and the livery cab. He produced an envelope from his pocket with the livery's plate number, T19415C. He said he saw the cabby take the gun off of the hood after the shooter ran off. The guy looked like he was trying to find someone to give the gun to, but the cops hadn't come yet. So he got in his car and drove to Flushing Avenue and parked. He went over and talked to the same detective Albert had.

"I don't know what the detective told him, but a minute later he got back in his car and drove off."

"This detective, was he tall and kind of dumpy?"

"Yeah."

"Did he have a big bushy head of hair like Elvis, and thick glasses?"

"You know him then?"

"Unfortunately, I do."

"I hope I didn't get him in trouble," Albert said.

"I wouldn't worry about it. He's so incompetent that nobody expects anything from him."

"Why is he a detective?"

"Do you golf, Albert?"

"A little. It's expensive and time consuming. But I know the game."

"You know how really good golfers have to give a few strokes to lesser golfers sometimes? That's called a handicap. Well, that guy is ours."

CHAPTER ELEVEN

October 10, 2013
Brooklyn

"This is bullshit!" *Elephant Boy* said, as he was being led into the 83 Squad by Detectives Furio and Gigante.

"Shut your pie-hole, fat boy," Furio told him.

"Yeah," Gigante added. "Save it for Detective Durr. He's the one who wants to talk to you."

"Oh fuck! Not him again."

Furio and Gigante led *EB* into the coffee room where Paddy Durr was waiting. He had the video from 10 Wilson Avenue already cued up in the VCR. They sat *EB* in front of the TV. Paddy kept replaying the portion of the tape from when Erik Vasquez pulled up in his white van, until he could be seen speeding away toward Starr Street. They paused to laugh at him each time the tape showed *EB* falling on his face as he burst from the passenger door.

"Are you that lame? Or do you just like the taste of concrete?" Durr asked.

"I have bad feet."

"Those aren't feet, *Gordo*," Gigante said. "They're hooves. And you don't know how to walk on them without falling on your face."

"Have your toes started falling off yet?" Durr asked him.

"That's not funny. I have diabetes."

"You're right, fatso," Furio contributed. "It's not funny. It's fucking hysterical."

Erik Vasquez elected to sullenly brood, rather than incur further abuse from the detectives, who clearly did not like him. After Durr had enough of watching *EB's* face hit the pavement, he led him back to the interview room.

"You have the right to remain silent and refuse to answer questions, yada, yada, yada. You understand all of that, dipshit?"

"I didn't do nuthin," *EB* protested.

"You don't know how to do nothing. You are a busy little cancer cell. Here's what we know. You live, hang out, and sell drugs on Starr Street between Knickerbocker and Irving Avenue. That's a Latin King set, of which you are a member. You like for people to call you *King Erik,* but no one ever does. You're just plain old *Elephant Boy.* Everybody laughs at you behind your back. Except me, I laugh at you right in your fat, ugly face. You are a disgusting piece of human excrement who can't pass four consecutive hours without committing a crime. Ordinarily, they are non-violent drug or property crimes. But this morning, you dipped your rancid foot into the deep end of the pool. Now you have my attention. As you already know, things start to go bad for people I become interested in."

"I don't know what you're talking about," *EB* claimed.

"No, you don't know yet if *I* know what I'm talking about. There's a difference. Allow me to enlighten you. At about 0540 hours, a guy you know as *El Asesino Negro,* or just *Negro* for short, shows up at Angela's diner for breakfast. About twenty minutes later you show up in that shitbox van of yours. You do that little trick you do, diving on the sidewalk. Then you go into Angela's. A handful of people see you have a stare-down with *Negro.* Then you book out of there and head back to Starr Street. What I want to know is, who did you tell that Negro was in the diner?"

"I didn't talk to anyone. And I don't know anyone named *Negro.*"

"You're lying. Why did you leave the diner in such a hurry?"

"I forgot I didn't have any money."

"Hey Armando," Paddy asked Detective Gigante. "How much money is this cretin holding right now?"

"He's got three thousand, four hundred and sixty dollars in twenties, tens, fives and some crumpled ones," Armando said.

"So, you would have us believe that in the seven and a half hours since you were penniless at Angela's, you managed to accumulate almost four grand?"

"I sold a car," *EB* claimed.

"You've never owned a car. All you have is that shitbox van. And no one is going to give you three cents for that piece of garbage. Want to try again?"

"I want to talk to a lawyer," *EB* declared.

"Good. Because the lying has grown tiresome. Before we release you back into the wild, here's what you should know. This murder today is going to be the centerpiece of a vast federal Latin King RICO prosecution. We're going to start flipping cooperators. No deal for you though. You're going down as a co-conspirator. You're gonna get thirty years. But don't sweat it. You won't do half of that. Because of your own sloth and bad diet, you're going to start disappearing one gangrenous inch at a time. Until finally, there won't be enough of you left to do time. So, good luck with that, diabetes boy. Now, you may get the fuck out of my sight."

"Aren't you going to give me a ride back to Starr Street?" *EB* asked.

"You've got a better shot at hitting the lottery. You get to hobble your fat ass home."

"It's almost twenty blocks!" *EB* exclaimed.

"So you better get started. And by all means, feel free to have a massive heart attack on your way."

"That ain't fair!"

"*EB*, don't make me kick you down those fucking stairs."

Elephant Boy was pointed in the direction of the exit, and sent on his way. Gigante made sure *EB* left the building. He wanted to be certain *EB*, who didn't have a cell phone, wasn't able to use the public phone in the precinct lobby to call a cab.

After Erik Vasquez was gone, Lieutenant Martino came out of the viewing area attached to the interview/line-up room, having watched and listened to the conversation with *EB*. He couldn't help from laughing.

"Do me a favor, Paddy. If I ever do something to piss you off, give me a chance to apologize?"

"Fair enough, Lou."

"Are you really going to try to take this case federal?"

"Hell no. I don't work with those people unless I have to. They can't be trusted. Besides, Dave Molinari from Gangs already has a case going with the FBI on this set. They can use this murder as a count in their RICO, after I solve it. I am going to find a way to charge *Elephant Boy* as an accessory in this case, though."

"Why do you hate him so much?" Martino asked.

"I don't hate him. I dispassionately and professionally dislike him with the white hot intensity of a thousand suns."

"I get that. Why?"

"Six years ago, when Erik Vasquez was twenty, he was giving his three-year-old nephew a bath. At some point, *EB* decided to anally rape him. He split him right up the back. The mother, *EB's* sister, heard the boy's screams, and came into the bathroom, interrupting it. Otherwise he would have killed the kid. Adding insult to injury, he gave his nephew syphilis."

"That's sodomy 1. How come he's not in prison?"

"Because the only swearable witness to the abomination was his sister, and she refused to testify,"

"She chose her brother over her son?"

"She didn't give a shit about her brother. He was already a big shot on Starr Street. He paid her twenty-five grand to keep her mouth shut. The case washed out in the grand jury."

"That's awful."

"I still have nightmares. Ever since, I've made it my business to make *EB's* life a living hell whenever I get the opportunity. Mark my words, if I ever catch him with a gun, I'll send that motherfucker straight to hell."

"Understood," Martino said.

CHAPTER TWELVE

October10, 2013
Brooklyn

Detective Durr was at his desk going through the victim's cell phone. In the contacts, he had found a listing for an *Esposa*. He ran the number through a reverse directory on his computer. The number came back to a Luciana Morales at 94 Morgan Avenue, in Greenpoint. Paddy then ran the name and address for anything he could find. There was nothing. No arrests, no complaints, no warrants, no domestic incidents, not even a car registered to the address. Durr realized he would just have to visit the building. He didn't want to call the number cold until he was sure of the victim's identity. Paddy knew there was no telling how Ms. Morales might react. If she decided to lose her shit, it wouldn't do for Durr not to have his facts in order.

As he was coming to this conclusion, the phone on his desk rang. Detective Carmella Del La Fuente from the Missing Persons Squad was on the line. Durr enjoyed working with Detective Del La Fuente. She was energetic, competent, and most importantly, motivated. All of these attributes were in short supply in the Missing Persons Squad. The problem was MPS had turned into a dumping-ground in the Detective Bureau. Most of the detectives were put there without volunteering. The vast majority of Missing Persons detectives were either misfits who could not assimilate into a regular squad, or were placed at the MPS because they had run afoul of a boss with the juice to punish them. Neither situation provided much incentive.

Carmella Del La Fuente was not one of those detectives. She had been a uniform police officer at the 83rd Precinct. She came on the job with a degree in Mortuary Science, and years of experience working with the dead in her family's funeral home. She became a police officer with the specific goal of working at the Medical Examiner's Office one day. Given the dearth of applicants for the job, that day came sooner than she had expected. She had just passed her third anniversary with the department when she received a notification to report to Missing Persons for an interview. She was excited for the opportunity, but mystified about how it came to pass. She had meant to put in a Detective Bureau Application, but hadn't gotten around to it yet. However it may have happened, she was determined to take advantage of her good fortune. She would figure out who to thank for it later.

The next day she put on her best, most conservative suit, and reported to the Missing Persons Squad at one Police Plaza. The commanding officer of the unit was waiting for her in his office. Lieutenant Phil Baker greeted Carmella and had her sit across from his desk. He offered her coffee, and surprised her when he fixed it himself. She hadn't seen the coffee bar on the window sill when she came in, and wouldn't have anticipated the CO of the unit would make her a cup even if she had. She thanked the lieutenant sheepishly when he handed her the coffee and sat down at his desk.

"I'm Phil Baker," the CO said by way of introduction. "I'm the new boss here at Missing Persons, and I'm looking for some new blood. The detectives here don't seem to have much enthusiasm for their jobs. I need detectives who do. This isn't a dumping-ground, or at least it won't be when I get through with it. I have it on good authority that you have mortuary education and experience, and a desire to work in the ME's Office. What do you anticipate your duties would be there, Officer Del La Fuente?"

"I imagine I would liaise with the Medical Examiner on behalf the detectives and the families of the deceased."

"Liaise, what does that mean?"

"I mean I would make sure the detectives on homicide and missing persons cases would be kept informed of what the ME was doing. I would see that any evidence recovered during an autopsy would be safeguarded and quickly reported to the assigned detectives. In the case of unidentified DOAs, I would participate in any procedures to identify them, like fingerprinting the deceased or taking dental impressions, or following up on DNA examinations. I believe I would also be escorting family members for official identifications and viewing of the deceased. That was my primary responsibility in my parent's funeral home. So I'm well acquainted with that particular duty."

"Wow! Best answer ever! Most people in your chair mumble something about wanting to be a detective. When what they mean is, they want a gold shield without having to get shot at or work very hard. Not you, you're all about the work. You're hired. I filled out your Detective Bureau Application and your UF 57. Sign them. Take the 57 back to your CO. He'll be expecting you. Inspector Sheridan is a friend. He also thinks highly of you. Have him sign the 57 and then you fax it right back to me. I want you here by the end of the week. Any questions?"

"As much as I want the job, and I do, very much, I never applied for this. How did you even know I existed?"

"I have ESP," Baker joked. "Actually, your name came up when I was talking to two of my old partners. You were the first officer on a homicide last year on Halsey Street. You handed the detectives a pristine crime scene. In addition, you kept following up with them to see if there was anything else you could do for the case. Paddy Durr and Armando Gigante don't forget, or let good work go unnoticed. They recommended you to me as soon as I got this posting. They actually did your DB interview for you at the Ashford Arms, over beers. If I didn't take you, they'd never let me hear the end of it. I have no complaints. After meeting you, you are all they said you were."

"Thank you very much, Lieutenant. I won't disappoint you."

A week later Police Officer Carmella Del La Fuente was transferred to the Missing Persons Squad and assigned to the Medical Examiner's Office in the basement of Kings County Medical Center, as dismal, dank and awful smelling a place as existed on this side of hell. Carmella was delighted. She applied her acumen and experience to her new assignment, and thrived at it. The Medical Examiners loved her, as she was always available and enthusiastic to assist with the autopsies and any other procedure. She was fantastic with the families of the dead. She had tact and a natural and sincere empathy for people, as she ushered them through a very traumatic and painful experience. She was particularly appreciated by the squad detectives. Carmella was professional, knowledgeable and available. This was not usually the case with her forebears. Eighteen months later, she was deservedly promoted to detective. She was on the phone now to confer with Durr about this morning's homicide.

"I ran your victim's prints through SAFIS using the NYSID number you gave me. It's a slam dunk. I faxed you the official report already."

"Thanks, Carmella. You're the best."

"Doctor Tollefsen is doing the post tomorrow at 0900 hours. Are you coming?"

"You know I am."

CHAPTER THIRTEEN

October 10, 2013
Brooklyn

Number ninety-four Morgan Avenue was located on the corner of Ingraham Street, just five blocks west of Angela's diner. Detective Durr understood immediately why his computer inquiries were negative for that address. It was a fenced-in lot with various earth moving machines inside. The sign on the gate read *Preston Excavation and Foundation.* Durr remembered passing this lot many times. As it never factored into one of his investigations, the number didn't resonate with him when he saw it. It was obvious to Paddy he had the wrong address for Luciana Morales.

"We're going to have to call her," Paddy told Joe Furio.

"Unless she's a bulldozer or a crane, she don't live here," Furio observed.

"The phone number has to be legit. It came out of the victim's phone. And the picture I have of her is signed Luciana, so she's not make believe," Durr said as he dialed her number into his cell phone. A woman answered.

"Hello, this is Detective Durr from the 83 Squad. Is Luciana Morales there?"

"I'm Luciana Morales. What is this about?"

"Do you know a Euripides Luis Betances?"

"What has that animal done now?" Luciana sighed.

"This morning he managed to get himself killed."

"Oh, thank God! He didn't hurt anyone else, did he?"

"Nope," Paddy said. "He pretty much just stood there and got shot a lot. Clearly you know him. You seem to have a particular perspective we would be interested in hearing. Could I come see you? I'll fill you in on the details."

"Sure, Detective, I'll put on a pot of coffee."

"Great. I'm at 94 Morgan Avenue, and you're not. So I'm going to need your correct address."

"It's 694 Morgan, apartment 3C."

"My partner and I will see you in five minutes."

"I look forward to it."

The six-ninety block of Morgan Avenue in Greenpoint is a tree-lined residential block overlooking McCarron Park. The buildings were classic pre-war, six family apartment houses which were well maintained and beautiful in their way. The stone scroll work around the oversized windows and doors was exquisite, and gave the buildings a grace not dissimilar to the brownstones in Brooklyn Heights. The wrought iron gates and railings in front of the buildings were magnificent. If you closed your eyes, you could easily imagine you had been transported back in time, seventy or eighty years, to a time in Brooklyn when people didn't get ambushed and shot to pieces on a regular basis. Knowing what he did about Euripides Betances, Durr had a hard time picturing him living in so serene a setting.

The detectives took their time walking from the car to the front of the building. They were enjoying the pleasant and fading sunlight cascading through the trees and mixing with the fall colors of the remaining foliage this late afternoon in October. Durr had a manila envelope with an eight by ten of the victim. He had given some thought to obscuring the bullet hole in the victim's face. But after speaking to Ms. Morales, he decided against it. He thought at this point she might enjoy seeing it, along with the vacant, perplexed look in Betances' eyes. The detectives climbed the stone stairs in front of the building. A moment later, they were buzzed in.

Luciana Morales was waiting for them inside her open apartment door. She looked to be in her early thirties. She was dressed in tight jeans and a yellow V-neck tee shirt, which contrasted nicely against her coffee-brown skin. Her long hair was thick, and glimmered in the fluorescent light in the hallway. She was barefoot, revealing a floral tattoo on her right instep, and a fairly new pedicure. Durr was prepared for her beauty, having seen her pictures contained in the victim's wallet. Furio was not. When he saw her, Joe pulled up short and let out an audible breath. Ms. Morales noted the handsome detective's appreciation and smiled. The apartment was spotless, and nicely appointed. As she led them into the dwelling, she suggested they go into the living room. Durr took one look at the plush sofa with its overstuffed cushions and realized if he sat in it, he would fall right to sleep. He requested they do the interview at the kitchen table. She led them into the kitchen and offered them coffee, which they both gratefully accepted.

Durr sat opposite Ms. Morales at the table. Furio stood to the left of Durr and leaned against the kitchen counter. This gave him the opportunity to look at Luciana without seeming to stare. But that was exactly what he did. Paddy read the heat coming off of his partner. He knew the recently divorced detective was mesmerized by this witness. So, he made a point of introducing him properly.

"This is my partner, Detective Joseph Furio. He'll be assisting me with this investigation."

"How you doing?" Joe said to her, with every bit of his olive oil charm.

"Very well, thank you." Luciana wrinkled her nose, and smiled coyly at Furio. "This day just keeps getting better."

Paddy began the interview by asking Luciana the usual background questions. She was thirty-two-years old. She had received an associate's degree in business at Hostos Community College. She was employed by H&R Block on Graham Avenue as a tax preparer. She was presently working toward her bachelor's degree in accounting at Baruch College. She intended to become a CPA after she graduated. She had never been arrested, nor had she made any complaints to the police. She had a four-year-old son named Mario with Euripides Betances. Mario was presently spending the weekend at her sister's house in Park Slope.

"What is your relationship to Euripides Betances?" Paddy asked.

"Estranged."

"Good for you. Prior to that, what *was* your relationship?"

"I met him several years ago at a club. He claimed he was the manager. He dressed nice. He acted like a gentleman. Two months later we moved in together. Things were fine for a while. Then I started noticing some things which just didn't fit. He would get calls only on his cell. Sometimes he would leave the apartment to take the calls. When I asked him about it, he would claim it was business involving the club. But his schedule wasn't regular for a club manager. Sometimes he would go days without going there. Then there were the times he would disappear for as long as a week. When I would ask where he had been, he started to get nasty. He told me it was none of my business, and if I knew what was good for me, I'd stop asking him about it. I was going to leave him. He figured this out and threatened me. He told me if I left, he would track me down and kill me like a dog in the street. It was a side of him I hadn't seen before, but I believed him. Then I got pregnant with my son. I felt trapped. Soon after, Euripides started hitting me. First it was just some slapping. Then punching. He started to get rough sexually. Really cruel stuff, filthy language, and then the choking started. I drew the line at that."

"Drew the line how?"

"I'm a New York Puerto Rican, Detective. We're not famous for our passive obedience. I stabbed him in the stomach with a kitchen knife. He almost died. He was better for a while when he came home from the hospital. Then after Mario was born, the same shit started again. That's when I went back to school. It got me away from that asshole for at least a couple of hours a day. My sister watched Mario whenever I needed her."

"Why didn't you go to the police, have him arrested?" Paddy asked.

"I told him I was going to do that. He said if I went to the police, I wouldn't live long enough to see the first court date. I knew he meant it."

"So, what happened?"

"About two years ago, he just disappeared. No calls, he just vanished. It was great for Mario and me without him, but every day that passed, I would dread the next, hoping it wouldn't be the day he returned. Finally, I vowed to myself if he ever came back, I would kill him in his sleep. But he never did. When you called me today to tell me he was dead, God forgive me, I was never so relieved in my life. Not only was he out of our lives, I didn't have to kill him to accomplish it."

"I need you to identify his photo."

Paddy took out the digital photo from his envelope and laid it in front of Luciana to view. She looked at it silently for a long moment.

"Do you have any others? He looks entirely too peaceful for my taste."

"I just need to know if that is Euripides Betances."

"Yeah, that's the asshole."

"Are you free tomorrow morning? I need you to come down to the Medical Examiner's Office to formally identify him."

"I'll identify him for you, Detective, but I won't spend one penny to bury that son of a bitch. Potter's field is too good for him. I think you should just kick his rotten ass down a sewer."

"That's fine. But I have to try and find a next of kin. Does he have any family you know of?"

"He had a brother he used to talk about who was murdered uptown. That was before I knew him. He had a mother in the Dominican Republic. But she died about three years ago. I remember because he cried like a baby for a week. When I asked him why he didn't go to the funeral, he slapped me around. For whatever reason, I think he was afraid to go back to the Dominican Republic."

"Do you know where in the DR he came from?"

"He used to brag about being from San Francisco De Marcoris. He used to say that all the best shortstops in baseball, and all the best hitmen in New York came from there. I don't think he played baseball, so, you know…"

"I have a pretty good idea. I have to be at the ME's Office for the autopsy at 9. Would you like to meet me there at about 11?"

"I can pick you up at about 10:30," Furio offered. "I can bring you down there and show you those other pictures you wanted to see."

"That would be great, Detective," Luciana smiled.

"Oh boy," Paddy muttered. "Looking at dead bodies and murder porn, what a charming first date."

CHAPTER FOURTEEN

October 11, 2013
Kings County Medical Center

The Medical Examiner's Office was tucked away in the basement at the rear of the oldest building in the Kings County Medical complex. To call the facility obsolete told only a part of the story. It was downright archaic. It was so poorly ventilated, the swinging doors out to the loading dock had to remain open, irrespective of the temperature outside. As a result, you picked up the putrid aroma of formaldehyde and decomposing corpses from blocks away. The smell became stronger the closer you got. If you were lucky, the sensory overload would short circuit your ability to smell.

The worst part of attending an autopsy for Durr was the lingering odor that remained in his clothes. No matter how many times you sent them out for dry cleaning, there was the smell, faint, but ever-present. It was for that reason Durr had one of his older suits dedicated exclusively for this duty. In fact, he kept a separate locker for it in the basement corner of the precinct locker room. He'd keep the suit in a plastic garment bag. The whole thing, jacket, pants, shirt and tie, he'd wear for the all-important post-mortem. Afterwards, back at the Squad, he would shower and change into a fresh suit. The autopsy suit would be run directly to the dry cleaner, to be cleaned and deodorized. Then it was back in the plastic bag and in the locker till the next homicide. Occasionally, the uniform officers who lockered nearby would complain about the faint, but foul odor. But this corner of the locker room was where they stuck the rookies. According to NYPD culture, the rookies had to learn. To do so, Paddy knew they needed to take the short end of the stick for a while.

"Get used to it, boys" Paddy would tell them. "That's the smell of the job."

Upon entering the facility, after the stench, one noticed the poor lighting. Usually overhead fluorescent lights were exceedingly bright and garish. Not here; here they were dirty and flickered frequently, giving one the sensation of being trapped in a horror movie. There was just enough light to appreciate the vomit green ceramic wall tiles and worn linoleum floors. The overall environment could best be described as cold, rancid, and depressing. And this was even before you saw a single cadaver. In spite of all of this, Carmella Del La Fuente loved it here. She had reached what she considered was the pinnacle of her profession, in her dream job. She couldn't be happier. She was in her office when Durr came in. Carmella was wearing her standard outfit, green medical scrubs, with her long brown hair up in a high ponytail. She looked up from her computer to greet Paddy.

"I met Officer Crowe this morning for the id. He's a nice looking young man."

"I'll tell him you think so."

"I can already see him blushing. He thinks very highly of you."

"I worked with his father."

"I know. He told me all about it."

"Then you also know that he's my responsibility."

"You know, Paddy, In spite of how hard you try to convince everyone otherwise, deep down, you're a good guy."

"Let's keep that as our secret."

"I have your ballistics. There were four deformed bullets under the body on the street. We found a pristine one still in his clothes. The head shot was an in and out. I called Crime Scene. They never found that one on the street, so you got five out of six. You want me to send them to ballistics?"

"That would be great. Anything else I should know about before the post?"

"I saw two things when I removed his clothes. He has a jagged scar on the left side of his abdomen. It looks to be a couple of years old, definitely from a stabbing. The other thing is a recent tattoo over his left pectoral. It's a bleeding heart with a woman's face in it, weeping. There is a scroll underneath it that says *Beatriz, mi novia*. Does that mean anything to you?"

"I knew about the stabbing. It's not related. I don't know who Beatriz might be. That name hasn't come up. I'll have to explore that when I get back to the squad."

"Is there anything else I can do for you, Paddy?"

"There's nothing I can think of at the moment. But when his clothes dry, if you should find a note in his pocket that says *So and So killed me*, you'll let me know. Won't you?"

"There's nothing in his pockets," Carmella laughed. "You know I checked. Now let's head into the cutting room. Doctor Tollefsen likes to start promptly."

The examination room had the same bleak décor as the rest of the facility. The only difference was the modern appliances arrayed about the room. Then there were the stainless steel sinks along the back wall and the four steel-basin gurneys containing naked corpses in various states of vivisection. Finally, one noticed the hanging scales at the head of each gurney. These were to weigh the organs of the deceased. Next to the gurneys were surgical carts with various tools for the medical examiners, like rib spreaders, bone saws and scalpels.

Doctor Bjorn Tollefsen was standing next to the third gurney. The very dead Euripides Betances was laying on the gurney face up. Doctor Tollefsen was gowned up with his clear plastic eye shield on. He was holding a scalpel in his latex-gloved right hand, and he seemed anxious to start cutting. He waved his scalpel at the detectives.

"*Allo, detectives.* I was about to get started. Before I dissect the subject, would you like me to establish and chart the trajectories of the wounds?"

Detective Durr responded affirmatively, but he knew he needn't have. Doctor Tollefson had been a Medical Examiner here in Brooklyn for forty-two-years. It was standard procedure in shooting deaths to determine the angle of the entrance and exit wounds. The question was more a matter of Doctor Tollefson thinking out loud, and sharing his thoughts with the detectives. This was to Detective Durr's advantage. He took autopsies very seriously. He thought the post-mortem was critical in revealing evidence which spoke to the facts of how a murder went down, things like distance between the shooter and the victim, the trajectories of the wounds, and the time of death. You could ascertain these things by reading the ME's report later. But you couldn't know the facts and understand them in a three dimensional way unless you were present at the autopsy and paying attention. For that reason, Durr insisted upon attending every autopsy on his murder cases. He paid rapt attention, and took copious notes during the examination, so he could document the facts later on a DD5. He knew the minutia of the evidence gathered in this room might provide the impetus to gaining a confession at interrogation, and a conviction later at trial.

Doctor Bjorn Tollefsen had lived in New York since he was eleven-years-old, but somehow never was able to totally lose his Scandinavian accent. It was during his first year of pre-med at Columbia that his class made a field trip to the morgue in Manhattan. He got the opportunity to observe his first autopsy, and from that moment he was hooked. He decided to pursue a career in Forensic Pathology. He was hired by the Chief Medical Examiner of the City of New York in 1972. He was assigned as an Assistant ME in Brooklyn, by his own choosing. Brooklyn was where most of the murders were happening. And so began a lifelong love affair between Doctor Tollefsen and death, or at least the various causes of it.

Doctor Tollefson in 2013 was a sight to behold. He was five feet two inches tall, and appeared even shorter because of his stooped posture. He weighed all of a hundred pounds. His complexion was sallow, and so pale you might think he had been carved out of cream cheese. His head appeared enormous. But that was just an effect of the rest of him being so slight. He had three thin strands of white hair protruding forward over his forehead. The top of his head was bald and veiny. The sides and back were covered by a long and wild mane of white hair. He had crisp, deeply blue, mischievous eyes. These were topped by thick and unruly white brows. His small wire bifocals, which he wore precariously at the end of his large bony nose, accentuated his bemused, thin-lipped smile. Durr thought Doctor Tollefsen was adorable, and enjoyed working with him thoroughly.

In spite of his tininess, Doctor Tollefsen easily propped Euripides Betances' lifeless body on its side. The doctor then shoved a wedge of wood under it to keep it there. Tollefsen took from his surgical cart a stainless steel rod which looked like a knitting needle, only longer. He inserted it into the wound on the victim's face. He gently pushed the rod forward until it protruded through the exit wound in the upper rear of Betances' skull. He did the same thing with the five wounds through his torso. The doctor described the wounds, indicating the entrance, exit, and angle of the trajectory. He allowed Detective Del La Fuente to photograph each of them upon completion. He characterized and measured the wounds, describing any starring, stippling or tattooing he encountered. His descriptions and calculations of the wounds were identical to Detective Durr's original observations, made the day before at the crime scene.

"Time to cut," Doctor Tollefsen said, as he removed the block from under the subject's neck and placed it vertically along the lower spine. This caused the spinal column and upper body to extend to a full arch. This would stretch out the internal organs and make them more visible and accessible. Doctor Tollefsen picked up the scalpel from the surgical cart. He made his first incision from the right shoulder joint, along the collarbone, ending in the center of the victim's body, just above the breastbone. He made a duplicate cut from the left shoulder joint, meeting the other incision in the middle. At the axis point, Doctor Tollefsen made a vertical incision down the middle of the subject's torso, ending just above the pubic bone. This enormous Y-shaped laceration was bloodless. Detective Durr knew this was because without a beating heart, the fluid in the body was subject to gravity. It pooled along the bottom, finding the lowest place to come to rest. This was visible, as the lower part of the victim's body was the color of a deep bruise. This was called *lividity*. Detective Durr knew all this. He had witnessed it more than a hundred times. He understood how and why it happened. In spite of that, the bloodless incision still unnerved him. It felt somehow unnatural. Paddy laughed at himself. He found it ironic that in a process which was altogether ghoulish and unnatural, it was the absence of blood that felt peculiar.

When he was done dissecting the body, Doctor Tollefsen cleared his throat.

"The pericardium and the right ventricle of the heart are punctured in two places and have sustained massive trauma. In addition, both lungs have been punctured and are deflated. There are two puncture wounds in the left lung, and one in the right. These organs have also sustained massive trauma, from the expended energy of the bullets passing through them, as well as the expanding gasses from the close distance of the point of fire."

"We have a technical term for that in the squad, Doc. We call it *shot to shit.*"

Doctor Tollefsen chuckled softly.

"I'm ready to make a finding as to the cause of death. The gunshot wounds to the brain, the heart and both lungs all would have proved fatal on their own. If you can determine which came first, Detective, that will be the cause of death."

"All the witnesses concur. The head shot came first."

"There you have it. Of course, I will cite the additional wounds as contributing factors in my report. There is little left to do. If you want to get back to your investigation, I could always call you if I have any questions."

"That would be fine, Doc. Carmella can fax me your report when you finish it."

"Always a pleasure, Detective Durr."

Paddy and Carmella left the cutting room and returned to her office. Detective Furio and Luciana Morales were there talking and laughing and generally enjoying each other's company. They were oblivious to the arrival of the other detectives.

"Is any police work getting done here, Joe? Or is this just a social visit?"

"I showed Luciana the rest of the crime scene photos. I was waiting for Carmella to come back and do the ME's id."

"Luciana," Durr said. "This is Detective Del La Fuente. She works in the Medical Examiner's Office. She's going to take you through their id procedure."

"Hello, Luciana. You can call me Carmella. I'm going to show you a digital photograph I took this morning. Please tell me who it is."

Carmella went to her desk and pulled a digital photo of Euripides Betances from a folder. She placed the photo in front of Luciana and waited.

"That's Euripides Betances."

"And what is your relationship to him?"

"He's the father of my son."

Carmella produced an ME's affidavit of identification from the same folder. It was already filled out with the exception of the time, date and the spaces for the signatures of the identifier and the detective conducting the identification.

"The time is 1105 hours, October eleventh, two thousand thirteen," Carmella stated as she filled out the top of the form. "Would you please sign here," she said placing the form in front of Luciana. Luciana signed the form and handed it back to Carmella, who signed it herself before putting the form back in her case folder.

"Now we have to discuss who's going to take custody of the body."

"Not with me you don't," Luciana said firmly. Carmella looked questioningly at Paddy.

"Ms. Morales was not at all upset to hear about the demise of Mr. Betances. In fact, his murder was a piece of good fortune for her. Out of everyone we know about so far, Luciana had more motive than anyone to kill him. If she fit the description even a little, she would be my prime suspect," Paddy said, not really joking.

"He was a prick to you, huh?" Carmella asked.

"Yeah, he was a son of a bitch. He used to beat me, and he threatened to kill me and my son. We're not going to miss him."

"Would you like to see him all fucked-up?"

"What do you mean, *all fucked-up?* Luciana asked.

"I mean carved down the middle from his neck to his nuts, his guts scooped out, his head cut in half, and his brain removed. Would you like to see that?" Carmella asked. Luciana nodded excitedly.

"When we're done here, I'll take you into the cutting room. I'll even look the other way if you want to spit on him," Carmella suggested.

"You are not at all what I expected, Detective."

"Really? What did you expect?"

"Well, you're so pretty, and cool. When Joe told me the detectives called you the *Queen of the Dead,* I expected you to be old, and kind of creepy."

"You guys really call me that?" Carmella asked Paddy. He nodded, embarrassed.

"That's awesome! I'm going to get that tattooed on my shoulder."

CHAPTER FIFTEEN

October 11, 2013
Brooklyn

When Detective Durr got back to the 83 Squad, Detective Romeo Amodeo and Sergeant Robert McPherson from Brooklyn North Homicide were waiting for him. Evidently, the triple homicide in the 75th Precinct no longer required their assistance. Paddy brought them up to speed on the case so far. Unlike many detectives in the various precinct detective squads, Durr had an excellent working relationship with the homicide squad in general, and Romeo Amodeo in particular. Sergeant McPherson was another matter. Some detectives resented homicide's interference. Paddy never viewed it that way. He understood their only motivation was to help him solve his case. They were not there to overshadow him or steal the credit or glory from him. In the first place, there was no credit or glory to be had. This was a Brooklyn North street murder. These cases weren't considered *high profile*. In fact, they existed almost in a media vacuum. The victim's weren't prominent enough to get anyone's attention. They didn't occur in a toney Manhattan neighborhood. They couldn't serve to properly horrify the vast majority of newspaper readers, because they just couldn't relate. Violent crime in the ghetto was cliché. It was expected, and was almost mundane

This was the environment Detective Durr and the homicide squad operated in. There was no credit or glory to be had, because nobody cared but the cops themselves. The powers that be demanded one thing and one thing only. That the detectives keep a lid on the chaos in the ghetto, so it didn't boil over and splatter them, staining their pristine political cover. If it was Paddy's lot to toil in obscurity, all the better. It left him more room to operate. Besides, Paddy had experienced his share of notoriety. Not only was it highly overrated, he thought it sucked. If he never had to read his name again in the newspaper, it was fine with him.

"It looks like you've got all the bases covered so far, Paddy," Sergeant McPherson said. "What do you want to do next?"

"I want to find that cabby with the gun before he gets rid of it."

"Do you have his info?" Romeo asked.

"Yeah. Sergio Mendez, he drives car number 26 for Albatross car service on Wyckoff Avenue. He lives at 248 Stanhope Street, apartment 1L."

Paddy was approached by the Squad Police Administrative Aide. Janine Confuso was aptly named. Her appearance, her desk, the boxes upon boxes of cases she was supposed to have already filed, all looked like they had been hit by a tornado. She was sent upstairs to replace Miss Flo when she retired. Florence Tully had been the squad PAA for twenty-six years, and had become legendary for her professionalism and discretion. In fact, new squad PAAs from other precincts were sent to be trained by her. She had trained Janine Confuso, but the training wouldn't take. Miss Flo cautioned Lieutenant Martino before she left. She told him she had shown Janine everything she needed to know, but she didn't seem interested in knowing it

At this particular moment, she was in front of Detective Durr's desk, shuffling nervously from foot to foot. If Paddy didn't ask her what she wanted, she would have continued like that all day. Durr didn't have time for that.

"What do you want, Janine?"

"I couldn't help overhearing your conversation. I know I'm not supposed to listen, but I did, and well, you know…"

"The point, Janine, get to it now, please."

"Sergio Mendez called for you. Here's his number," she said, handing Paddy a yellow post-it note with a phone number on it.

"When did he call?"

"Yesterday afternoon. You were busy, so I didn't want to bother you."

"You're right, Janine. I was busy, looking for this guy. I know we've been over this a thousand times, but let's refresh anyway. When someone calls for a detective, if he is out of the office, or otherwise engaged, take the message on a post-it note with the time and date of the call. Then stick it on the computer terminal of the particular detective the message was for. It's that easy. You don't have to overthink it." Janine apologized for the mix up and scurried back to her desk.

"Is she brain damaged?" Romeo asked.

"In all honesty, I don't know if it's damaged or just chronically inactive."

Paddy called the number PAA Confuso had given him. It turned out to be a cell phone. Sergio Mendez answered on the third ring.

"*Digame*," a male voice answered.

"*Como esta?*" Paddy began in Spanish. "*Estas Sergio Mendez?*"

"*Si, Si,*" Mendez responded. "*Quien es esto?*"

"*Mucho gusto, Senor. Estoy Detective Durr, del precincto ochenta y tres. Habla inglese?*"

"*Si,* I mean yes, Detective. I've been trying to reach you since yesterday morning."

"I'm sorry about that. I just got the message. My understanding is you saw something yesterday morning on Wilson Avenue and George Street. Is that correct?"

"Yes. I have the gun. I tried to give it to a detective yesterday. He wouldn't talk to me, and chased me away. The gun has been sitting in my glove-box since."

"Where are you now?"

"I'm in Bushwick, driving my cab."

"I need you to pull over right now," Durr told him. "What corner are you on?"

"I'm on Irving Avenue and Weirfield Street. Why?"

"Because having that gun could be a problem for you if the guy who owns it comes back looking for it. I need you to get out of the car and lock it up. Wait for me on the corner. I'll be there in less than five minutes."

"Okay," Mendez said.

Paddy went into the storage room in the back of the squad. He got a brown paper bag and grabbed his coat and hat.

"Are you ready, Romeo? Let's go get that gun."

CHAPTER SIXTEEN

October 11, 2013
Brooklyn

When Durr and Amodeo arrived at Irving and Weirfield, Sergio Mendez was leaning against the building, nervously smoking a cigarette. Paddy introduced himself. Sergio was relieved when Paddy took his keys from him and removed the gun from his glove compartment, placing it in the paper bag, preserving whatever fingerprints might remain. Paddy asked Mendez if he would come back to the 83 Squad with them.

"I have a steady fare to pick up in Ridgewood at two o'clock. I can be at the precinct by two fifteen. Is that okay?"

"That's fine. Take my card. When you get to the precinct, park in one of the visitor's spots out front. Put my card on your dashboard, so the cops know you're with me. Then call me. I'll come down and get you, so you don't have to wait in the fishbowl."

Mendez left to pick up his fare. Durr and Amodeo headed back to the squad.

"Why did you let him leave?" Romeo asked.

"He's not running. He's making a living. Besides, we know where he lives, where he works, and we have his cell phone number. If he were to run, where could he hide from us?"

"I guess you're right."

"And let's not forget, he was looking for us before we were looking for him. He wants to help."

"He seemed like he knew you."

"Either that, or somebody he knows does. I don't think he knew it was my case. He was reaching out to me specifically. I don't remember him, so I must have done the right thing for someone he knows. We'll find out when he comes in."

"You mean, if he comes in."

"You've been spending too much time in Brownsville. This is Bushwick. Not *everybody* hates us here."

When they got back to the squad, Detectives Durr and Amodeo were joined by Sergeant McPherson, who had been in the lieutenant's office reading the *fives*.

"Where is the witness?" McPherson asked.

"He had a fare to pick up. He'll be in right after."

"Are you out of your fucking mind? You can't just let a homicide witness walk off."

"I didn't let him walk off. I let him drive off."

"If he doesn't come in, you're getting a Command Discipline shoved up your ass."

Durr regarded the sergeant from over the top of his reading glasses. He looked at him just long enough to make McPherson uncomfortable. Then Durr took his glasses off and smiled at the young sergeant.

"I keep forgetting how new you are to homicide investigation. This is not the *seven three*. We don't screw over our witnesses as a matter of course. We don't automatically assume they are all lying, cop-hating, scumbags. We let them do what they need to do to feed their families, because it's the right thing to do. My experience is, and I have a lot of it, treating your witnesses with respect and dignity makes for better, more compliant witnesses. They tend to get more invested in the case if they know they can trust the detective assigned to look out for them."

"I don't need a lecture from you," McPherson said, steaming.

"You wouldn't think so. I'll tell you what, boss. If he doesn't show up by 1430 hours, you can shove a whole ream of green paper up my ass," Paddy said, referring to the green forms the Command Discipline was printed on.

"Lieutenant Martino is going to hear about this."

"Good. Tell him all about how you want to fuck with his senior first grade detective in the middle of a homicide investigation. If you're lucky, he'll let you use the stairs when he throws you out of here. Now, I have things to do, and you're hogging my oxygen. Why don't you use the time to get some experience and knowledge about this stuff, instead of interfering with a detective who has been solving murders since you were hitting the bong in high school?"

"You can't talk to me like that!" McPherson said belligerently.

"And yet, I do. It must be a terrible conundrum for you."

Just then, Lieutenant Martino came in the door. He was signing into the command log when he heard the conversation between Paddy and Sergeant McPherson get heated. He decided to step in.

"That's enough. The pissing contest is over. What is this all about?"

"He's being insubordinate," McPherson whined.

"Is that so, Paddy?"

"That's a matter of semantics. You guys are supervisors," Paddy said. "I'm gonna let you two figure it out. I got a homicide to solve. So I'm going to do that. You can come out later and tell me what happens next."

Martino laughed. He waved Sergeant McPherson into his office and closed the door. Paddy started a full battery of computer checks on Sergio Mendez. If he was going to defend his decision to let Mendez come in later, he needed to be sure his witness was not wanted for a crime. Much to Durr's relief, everything came back in order. While he waited for Crime Scene to show up to dust the murder weapon for prints, Paddy contemplated the problem of Sergeant Robert McPherson. Durr knew for a fact McPherson had indeed been smoking pot in high school when Paddy was already working murders in the 83 Squad. He knew because one of the young detectives in the 81 Squad had gone to high school with him. He said he was an entitled prick even then. At this particular time, Sergeant McPherson was assigned to Brooklyn North Homicide because his uncle was the Chief of Personnel. The assignment was based on young Bobby's sole qualification. He was the son of Chief Freddie Dryden's sister. McPherson's entire twelve year career had been blessed for that same reason.

McPherson came on the job in 2002. He was assigned to the Mid-Town South Precinct out of the police academy. He spent all of three months on patrol before he was precipitously and inexplicably elevated to the plain clothes Anti-Crime unit. This was an assignment usually reserved for the more experienced and active cops in the precinct. Unless of course, your hook was a crane. In that case, you didn't need to know your ass from a hole in the ground, as Robert most definitely did not. After a year of botching things up in Anti-Crime, he was transferred to Manhattan South Narcotics as an Undercover. After eighteen months there, without executing a single successful narcotics buy, he was promoted to detective and converted to an investigator. He was equally ineffective in that capacity. So the bosses put him in charge of the prisoner van. This involved babysitting the prisoners the Buy and Bust Teams had grabbed. This gave Bobby plenty of time to study his Patrol Guide, which was the only thing related to police work for which he had shown any ability. When the department offered the test for promotion to Sergeant, Bobby passed it.

In 2006 McPherson was promoted to sergeant. He was assigned to the 1st Precinct in Manhattan. He was there for six months, just long enough to finish his sergeant's probation, before he was transferred to Brooklyn Warrants, supervising detectives. But Bobby demonstrated no more ability or acumen at supervising warrant investigations than he had at anything else. So he was *kicked up-stairs,* and given the administrative position of supervising the equipment locker and the three detectives who rotated shifts covering it. His only real responsibility was a bi-weekly inventory of the equipment, which he delegated to one of the detectives. He did that until 2012, when he was promoted to Sergeant, Supervisor of Detectives. Commonly referred to as *The Money* throughout the Detective Bureau, the promotion came as quite a surprise to Bobby's supervisors, none of whom could remember putting him in for it. This promotion, and the increase in pay grade which came with it inspired a latent ambition within McPherson. Suddenly he had the abiding desire to do some detective work, coupled with the delusion he might actually have the ability. He told his uncle he wanted to go to the homicide squad.

Bobby had meant the Manhattan South Homicide Squad, but Chief Dryden did not share his nephew's delusions of grandeur. He knew he was a horseshit detective. The media exposure in Manhattan was just too great to hide Bobby's inevitable screw-ups. So he put him in the care and protection of his friend and former partner, Lieutenant John Terrapino, the Commanding Officer of the Brooklyn North Homicide Squad. Terrapino had been warned by his friend that his nephew was a numbskull. So, for his own protection, Bobby was assigned as a second sergeant in the C-Team, Terrapino's most senior and expert squad of detectives. In spite of even this, Bobby managed to cause difficulties in every squad he visited. His chief problems were that he was stupid, combative, and oblivious to the fact that he was stupid and combative. He was one more screw-up away from being relegated to the Missing Persons Squad. That would be the end of Bobby McPherson's career trajectory. Lieutenant Phil Baker, Paddy's old partner and the CO there, did not suffer assholes for long, even ones with crane-sized hooks.

After about twenty minutes, Sergeant McPherson came out of Lieutenant Martino's office red-faced, his shoulders slumped. He would not make eye contact with Durr. Somehow, he seemed even punier than his five foot, five inch frame. He went right up to Romeo Amodeo and demanded the car keys.

"You can call for a ride. Or ask one of your new best friends in the 83 Squad to give you a ride after you're done today."

McPherson left the squadroom and was gone. Amodeo looked confused and uncomfortable. Martino addressed him directly.

"Keep doing what you're doing, Romeo. You're always welcome here. We'll get you home later." Then he pointed at Paddy.

"You, in my office now."

Paddy followed his boss. He closed the door and sat in the chair across from the desk. It was still warm from Bobby McPherson's squirming ass. He waited for the lieutenant to sit down and begin. Martino shook his head with a grin.

"Did you really tell that little twat that I would throw him out a window?"

"I might have mentioned it was a possibility."

"You know he's a loose cannon, why would you fire him up like that?"

"The cannon had already gone off. He started talking down to me like he was my father, and you know I never had any use for that asshole."

"He's still a sergeant. He said you lectured him like he was a know-nothing."

"Well…" Paddy let the rest lie.

"Did the witness come in?"

"He should be in in ten minutes. If he isn't in by then, I'll call him. But, he's coming in."

"That's good enough for me."

"Why did the wonderboy storm out of here?" Paddy asked.

"He started yelling at *me*. He actually threatened me with his uncle. I didn't have the heart to tell him the PC was going to ask for the chief's resignation this week. That boy is about to get hit with the ugly-stick."

"What did you tell him?"

"I told him to take his pimply ass out of my squad, and never darken my doorway with his shadow again. I also told him I was calling his boss to tell him that his sergeant was abusing my detectives, and interfering with my investigations. So we're never going to have to see that clown again. But Paddy, our asses are hanging in the breeze on this one if you don't break the case."

"I'll break it."

"Then get about it."

CHAPTER SEVENTEEN

October 11, 2013
Brooklyn

Sergio Mendez called Durr from the front of the precinct. Paddy checked his watch and noted the time was exactly 1415 hours. Paddy let the lieutenant know the witness had arrived, then went down to the street to get him. Sergio was outside of his cab holding a brown paper bag carefully.

"What do you have there, Sergio?"

"I got us some café con leche from *Pineda's Cuchifritos*. I got one for your partner too. I hope he likes Spanish coffee."

"Did you ever know a cop who would turn down free coffee?" Paddy asked him, leading him through the front doors of the precinct.

The entrance to the 83rd Precinct consisted of two heavy swinging doors which opened out. This was an unintended metaphor for the welcome which was most definitely *not* extended to the chronic complainers, cranks, and kooks who typically walked into police stations from off of the street. Unfortunately, people who had a legitimate reason to visit the precinct had to run this gauntlet as well, until they could be weeded out from the riffraff by the precinct receptionist, and directed to the office or person who could properly assist them. To prevent the lunatics from taking over the asylum, the department had constructed a barrier of steel and bulletproof glass from floor to ceiling in a box shape inside these double doors. Paddy was determined not to subject his witnesses to this inconvenience. So he instructed them to call him from the street so he could escort them unmolested up to his office.

The fishbowl had been constructed only one month after the precinct had moved from their pre-Civil War, decrepit and rat-infested abomination on DeKalb and Wilson Avenues. This *new* precinct was supposed to be a state of the art police facility. But the plans were drawn in the fifties, and the construction began in the seventies. Because of the dual whammy of corruption, and accepting the lowest bidder, the building wasn't completed until 1984. By then it was already obsolete. The need for the fishbowl was pointed out at the ribbon cutting ceremony by the precinct commander. No one in the Building and Maintenance Section paid him any mind when he predicted a tragedy would occur if the entrance to the precinct remained unsecured. A month later, a deranged neighborhood resident with a chemical imbalance and an AR 15 came into the precinct. He easily stepped around the wooden saw-horses that served as an impromptu barrier. He emptied his rifle, trying to shoot the cops behind the front desk. They were fortunate to find cover under the heavy oak and metal of that desk. The gunman managed to load a second magazine, and had recommenced shooting up the desk and the wall behind it, when an Anti-Crime cop who had been in the muster room came out from the back and shot and killed the assailant. Building Maintenance was at the precinct that night measuring and drawing plans for the fishbowl which was completed two days later. The splintered front desk had to be replaced as well. To this day, a very large American Flag is draped on the brick wall behind the desk. It is not there for decoration. If you looked behind the flag, you would see a wall so bullet pocked you might think it had been used for a firing squad. It very nearly was.

Durr ushered Sergio Mendez into the interview room. They were joined by Romeo Amodeo. Sergio handed out the coffees.

"How did you know I like Spanish coffee?" Paddy asked Sergio.

"You don't remember me, do you, Detective?"

"I'm Sorry, I'm afraid I don't."

"Two years ago, my brother Alfonso was having problems with his wife. She ended up with a black eye and made a police report. She was drunk. She was always drunk. The next day she tried to drop the charges.

You wanted to let her, but the black eye took the decision out of your hands."

"I remember now. Alfonso is a butcher at Western Beef. I had to lock him up."

"You had to. But you treated him with respect."

"I try and treat everyone with respect. With your brother it was easy. He had no criminal record, no previous Domestic Incidents, he was a working guy and a good father. Plus, his wife was adamant she wanted to drop the charges. Why would I want to give a guy like that a hard time?"

"You went out of your way not to. You called him up and told him you knew where he lived, where he worked, and even where he went to hide when his drunk wife was making him crazy. You let him make an appointment to come in so he didn't have to miss any work."

"I wasn't all lightness and sweetness. I threatened to drag him out of work by his hair if he missed that appointment."

"But you waited to let him keep it. When he got here, you let him sit in the interview room, not the cell. You also told him if he didn't tell you he wanted a lawyer, he was an idiot. You wouldn't let him talk about the fight with his wife, in case he said something stupid to get himself in trouble. You didn't lie to him. Everything you told him was going to happen, did."

"That sounds like me."

"I called and asked if I could visit him in the precinct. You said I could if I would pick up an order for you on the way in at Pineda's. When I got there they gave me a bag of Spanish coffees for you. They wouldn't take my money. They said you would take care of it later. When I got here, we all sat down and drank the coffees you bought. Alfonso was just finishing the dinner you got for him. He said he was never treated so well at home. That's how I knew you liked Spanish coffee."

"I remember you now, Sergio. You've put on a few pounds, lost some hair, and wear glasses."

"Life's been good. I like it here in America."

"What did you do in the Dominican Republic?" Paddy asked.

"I was a police officer in Santo Domingo, for ten years."

"I thought I got a cop vibe off of you. Why did you leave the job?"

"There was too much corruption there. My brother was already raising a family here. So I joined him and bought a cab. I have no regrets."

"How did you know this was my case?"

"I didn't until now. I didn't care whose case it was. I only wanted to talk to you. I trust you."

Paddy directed Sergio's attention to the morning before. Sergio told the story of how he saw the ambush and murder as it unfolded. He told Durr how the shooter ran in front of his cab and got rolled up on the hood. He told him how the perp left the gun on the hood of the car as he ran away up Wilson Avenue. Sergio told Paddy how he tried to tell his story to the detective at the scene. He wanted to give him the gun right then. But the detective wasn't interested and chased him away. That's when he knew he had to call Durr.

"I think that other detective is dirty," Sergio said.

"He's not corrupt, just incompetent and stupid. We try and keep him away from anything important, but he keeps showing up where he is least needed."

Paddy asked Sergio if he thought he could identify the killer. He said yes. He had seen him before many times. He also had seen the victim around the neighborhood. In fact, Sergio said, he had seen the both of them with the same girl on different occasions.

"They might have been fighting over her."

"What makes you think that?"

"She used to ride in my cab with the killer, a bunch of times. They would fight a lot. Then I started seeing her with the guy who got killed. They rode in my cab twice. She introduced him as her cousin, but I don't believe he was," Sergio surmised, with a face that communicated pure distaste.

"Why?"

"Because he was fingering her in the back seat. When I dropped them off at the restaurant on Bushwick Avenue and Beaver Street, I told him I didn't appreciate the disrespect. He leered at me in a way that was just disturbing. That was the last time I drove her anywhere. When she would call after, I would let it go to voicemail."

"Do you know her name and address?"

"Just her first name, it's Beatriz. She lives on Willoughby Avenue between Wilson and Knickerbocker, but I don't know the house number. I used to pick her up and drop her off on the avenue."

"Do you still have her phone number?"

"It's in my old phone. I can call you with it later."

"You said you know the killer from the neighborhood," Durr reminded him. "Where do you see him?"

"He sells drugs on Starr Street across from Maria Hernandez Park. Other times, I see him selling drugs on Willoughby and Cypress Avenue, in front of the Chinese restaurant. Oh, one other thing; his name might be *Casper.*"

"How do you know that?"

"Because one time when he was fighting with Beatriz in my cab, she said *'Fuck You, Casper!'* He seemed to know she was talking to him."

"You're still a cop deep down. Aren't you?"

"It's not something you can turn off like a switch."

"Don't I know it?"

Paddy had Sergio view photos on the computer. He had him view all light-skinned Hispanic males arrested in the 83rd Precinct. He additionally had Mendez view all males in the system with the first name or nickname of *Casper.* Sergio carefully and patiently viewed all the photos presented to him. He apologized to Durr when he was finished, not having seen the killer's photo. Before he could go, Paddy had to take a set of Sergio's fingerprints. These were for comparison, in case his prints were on the murder weapon. It was conceivable they might be, and explainable.

"I will keep my eyes open," Sergio promised Durr.

"Thank you. Please give me a call with Beatriz' phone number when you get home."

"I will," Sergio said before leaving the squad to finish his taxi shift.

After the witness had left, Paddy and Romeo worked the computers and phones to try and find an address and last name for Beatriz from Willoughby Avenue. When this failed to gain results, Paddy figured he would have to wait on Sergio providing Beatriz phone number to find her. Unless Romeo had better luck with the phone and cable providers, which was highly unlikely. Most Bushwick residents had unlisted phone numbers, and if they had cable TV at all, they stole it. As Paddy had predicted, Romeo struck out. They would just have to wait on Sergio Mendez.

"Did Crime Scene give you an ETA?" Paddy asked.

"They said about 1600 hours."

"It's 1700 now. Want to give them another call?"

"Hold that phone!" called a voice from down the hall.

Paddy looked up to see the smiling and somewhat ridiculous face of Detective Howie Mishkin. Howie was the senior detective in the Crime Scene Unit, and if he was coming out to Brooklyn North on a follow-up run, it was because he wanted to. Howie wasn't in the regular CSU rotation. He was the go-to-guy for all the heavies, like cop shootings, and high profile murders and sex crimes. Other than that, he got to pick and choose his jobs. He and Paddy had become close friends over the years. Between the dozens of homicides they worked together, and the fact that they both were steady lecturers at all the Detective Bureau Training Courses, seldom did a month pass that they didn't run in to each other. Like all good cop friendships, they spent as much time as they could trying to get under each other's skin.

"It's the famous Howie Mishkin. If he's here, it can only mean one of two things. Either our victim suddenly got famous, or Howie wants an Italian dinner in Greenpoint. I'm betting on the latter."

"That's unfair. When the call for the print run came in from the *eight three*, I saw it was your case, and I wanted to come out and see my old friend."

"That's heartwarming. So, where do you want to eat tonight, Frost Street?"

"That would be fine," Howie said, smiling.

Detective Durr led the large and jovial Crime Scene Detective to a card table laid out in the interview room. Paddy handed Howie the paper bag with the murder weapon in it. He stood back to watch him work. Howie opened his print kit, which was actually a folding valise. He put on latex gloves and rolled up the sleeves of his Crime Scene Unit windbreaker. Howie took out a rectangular piece of static-resistant paper and smoothed it over the top of the card table. He was ready to remove the gun from the paper bag. He did so gently, using his thumb and forefinger to pinch the butt of the gun. He placed it on the paper. Then Howie took out a bottle of white finger-print powder. He spilled out a disc-shaped pile of the dust the size of a nickel in the corner of the table. Howie set up a battery powered pendent lamp, casting the weapon in bright light. Already smudges of fingerprints were visible on the outside of the gun.

"Did any civilians or nosey cops handle this gun when it was recovered?" Howie asked.

"Just the witness who recovered it."

"Do we have his comparison prints?"

"I took a set when he was here earlier."

"I'll send them down to SAFIS with whatever I get off the gun."

"That's what I figured," Paddy said.

"This is for who picks up the check tonight. Do either of you detectives know what SAFIS stands for?"

"SAFIS stands for something?" Romeo asked.

"SAFIS is an acronym, short for *Statewide Automated Fingerprint Identification System.* Howie has been using that one to score free dinners since they instituted the system in 1989."

"How has that been working out for you?" Romeo asked.

"I think my robust physique speaks for itself on that subject," Howie grinned.

"We're all eating on the arm tonight," Paddy informed them. "The owner, Antonio let his idiot stepson take his Mercedes. He got popped by Narcotics in the *eight three* for scoring smack. Narco vouchered the car for forfeiture. I got the DA's Office to give him his car back. He's been breaking my balls to come in for a meal ever since. So tonight, we eat on Antonio."

Detective Mishkin retrieved a fingerprint brush from one of the secret compartments in his valise. The brush was ten inches long, and made of the softest horse-hair bristles. Howie turned the brush gently over the fingerprint dust in tiny circles. He applied the dust carefully to the outside of the gun, first heavily, and then continuing to brush away the dust until several partial prints began to emerge on the frame and the barrel of the gun. Howie took a large magnifying glass from the valise and bent over the table to examine the possible prints more closely.

"You are the only detective since Sherlock Holmes to use a magnifying glass. All you need to complete the picture is a deerslayer cap," Paddy said.

"Third zippered pocket on the top right," Howie directed.

Paddy went over to the valise and opened the pocket. He pulled out a beautiful brown tweed deerslayer hat. The tag inside read *The Woolmark Company, Savile Row London*. Paddy went over and placed the cap ceremoniously on Howie's balding head. He stood back to appraise his friend with admiration.

"I feel like I'm in the presence of greatness," Romeo said.

"Easy, Killer. Howie is the best in the business at what he does. But this is just detective work. We're not splitting the atom here." To Howie, he said, "Where did you get the hat, funny man?"

"Do you remember the Homicide Course when the two inspectors from the London Bobbies were there? I asked them to send me a hat. I didn't imagine they would send me *the* hat. I only wear it for people I know will appreciate it."

Detective Mishkin went back into his kit and removed a roll of clear fingerprint tape, along with several black laminate cards. He cut a piece of the tape into a four inch length. This he carefully smoothed over a now visible print on the frame of the revolver. He did this three more times, lifting another print from the frame and two from the barrel. Howie inserted a pen into the gun barrel to turn it over. He repeated the dusting and raising process on the other side. He recovered two more prints on the barrel. After securing the tape with the lifts onto the laminate cards, he turned the cards over and numbered them, as well as indicating where the prints had come from on the revolver.

"I got six partials from the outside of the revolver. They probably belong to your witness rather than the shooter. Fingerprints on a gun usually aren't very durable. Has anyone disassembled the stocks or touched the empty brass in the cylinder?"

"No. Those prints, if there are any, should belong to the owner of the gun. They might not be the shooter's prints though. The gun might be a loaner. These gangbangers pass their guns around like they were a venereal disease."

"Well, we can hope," Howie said.

The CSU detective removed a small flat-head screwdriver from his kit. He unscrewed the fastener in the wooden stocks of the revolver and pried them off the frame. Howie dusted the inside of the handle of the gun as well as the inside of the wooden stocks. Nothing like a fingerprint became visible. Another thing gangbangers were not famous for was maintaining and cleaning their firearms. So, it wasn't surprising nothing showed up. Finally, Howie opened the cylinder and ejected the empty shell casings onto the table. He dusted these and recovered prints on each of the shell casings. Howie examined them with the magnifying glass. He was of the opinion the same person left each of these prints, and they were different from the ones lifted on the outside of the weapon. Detective Mishkin lifted the prints and taped them down on a fresh black card. He numbered and annotated each of these as he did the earlier ones. Howie put the gun back together and gave it to Paddy.

"I'll drop these off at SAFIS tonight. Other than your witness, do you have a possible you want compared to these?"

"Yeah. I'm hearing Casper might have done it. Do you know him?"

"We can rule out the Casper that I know. Ghosts are spectral beings. You need skin on your fingers to leave a print."

"In that case, no possible suspects at this time. Before we go out to dinner, I need you to do one more thing for me, Howie."

"What's that?"

"Take off that ridiculous hat."

CHAPTER EIGHTEEN

October 11, 2013
Greenpoint

After a sumptuous meal of Scungilli Fra diavolo, a house specialty, the detectives relaxed over cappuccinos. Howie Mishkin could not pass up desert. He ordered the tiramisu, also a specialty. When Antonio served the cake with a flourish, Howie almost moaned. The richness of the cream filling mixed with the deep aroma of the rum and espresso. Paddy felt he might lapse into a diabetic coma if he had to smell it much longer. Howie eliminated that concern, devouring the rich Italian pastry in three bites. He sat back in his chair with the glassy-eyed relaxed look only the truly satisfied can manage. When the waiter, Marco, brought over the check, Paddy opened the leather binder to discover a note from Antonio inside. It read, *Thank you for your friendship. It was my pleasure to have you and your partners as my guests.* It was signed, *your dear friend, Antonio Primobono.* Paddy left a generous tip in the folder for Marco. The detectives found Antonio on their way out. Howie and Romeo thanked him and shook his hand. Paddy was extended the additional honor of Antonio's embrace and a kiss on each cheek. Paddy was actually uncomfortable with these traditional Italian niceties. But it was his policy to let good people like Antonio express themselves however they felt necessary, his own comfort notwithstanding.

The detectives congregated for a moment in front of the restaurant, enjoying the sweet air of Greenpoint. Paddy surmised the air quality was attributable to the fact that the neighborhood was almost saturated with Italian bakeries and restaurants. As a result, the sweet smell of powdered sugar mixed with the savory aroma of sautéed garlic to give this air a pleasant quality like no other neighborhood in New York. He breathed deeply, quietly enjoying himself as Howie and Romeo raved about the dinner. Paddy's quiet reverie was interrupted by Howie Mishkin.

"Why is the restaurant just called *Frost Street?* Why not Antonio's or something else Italian."

"When this place opened in the fifties, the neighborhood was exclusively Italian. The restaurants didn't need to be identified as such. They were just called restaurants. This one is on the corner of Frost and Humboldt. It's been called Frost Street since I was a kid. I met Antonio when we were both thirteen. I went out to eat here with my friend's family. Antonio was bussing tables for his father at the time. When I got a little older, I started bringing dates here. It was like going to *Little Italy* without having to pay *Little Italy* prices. The food was just as good. By then Antonio had graduated to waiting tables. He used to treat me like a bigshot to impress my dates. You gotta like that."

"Is there anyone in New York who doesn't want to do nice things for you?" Howie asked.

"Actually," Paddy reminded him. "There are a lot of people in New York who want to do dastardly, awful things to me."

"Yeah, but I noticed those people either end up dead or in prison. So it looks like you've got it covered."

"In the future, Howie, if you want to have dinner, all you have to do is call me. I like your company well enough. You don't have to show up to throw fingerprint dust around."

"I'll remember that, Paddy," he said as he turned to go, Howie's CSU van was parked up the block on Humboldt Street.

Paddy drove Romeo back to the homicide squad. On the way they discussed the progress of the case. At the moment they had hit a wall. The only active lead to pursue at this point was the cell phone number for Beatriz that they had to wait for Sergio Mendez to provide. Paddy would check with Sergio tonight. He intended to stay for another couple of hours to catch up on the *fives*. Tomorrow both of them were swinging out for two days. If anything broke on the case, Paddy promised Romeo he would call him and get him authorized to come in on overtime.

When Paddy got back to the 83 Squad he found Matty Price's team busy working their cases. Paddy went into the lieutenant's office to brief him. With the lieutenant was Sergeant Steve Krauss, the squad whip. He asked the supervisors if he could stick around for a couple of hours to type. Of course, they agreed. The lifeblood of the police department was, after all paper. It wouldn't do to leave it undone before the weekend.

"Do you want to come in tomorrow?" Lieutenant Martino asked him.

"If something breaks on the case, definitely. Otherwise, I've got to close my pool."

"That's late for you," Steve Krauss observed.

"I don't live there anymore. So it's not something I could just get around to doing when I had time. Now I have to make an appointment."

"It's not getting any better?" the lieutenant asked.

"No. I think she's done. I'm just waiting for the other shoe to drop."

"Does she have someone else?" Steve asked.

"God, I hope not, unless you know something I don't. I don't even want to think about it. The idea of anyone else touching her makes me physically ill."

"Hang in there, Paddy. It might work out," Martino said.

"Yeah, and I might hit the lottery, or get drafted to play for the Giants. But I'm thinking, probably not. I'm going to call the cabby now and do some typing," Paddy told them as he left the bosses' office.

Paddy dialed Sergio Mendez' number on his desk phone.

"Do you have that number for me?"

"I have some bad news. I have the phone, but the battery is dead. I'm charging it now, but I don't know if it's working. I will call you as soon as I can get into my contacts."

"I'm going to be off tomorrow. You have my cell phone number. You can call me or text me with Beatriz' number when you get it."

"I will do that," Sergio promised.

"One other thing, if the phone won't charge, hold on to it for me. I have someone who can get into the sim card. I'm heading home now. So I'll talk to you tomorrow, one way or another."

Paddy sat for a long minute trying to rub the fatigue out of his eyes and will away the tension headache that was building behind them. The suspect quality of some of the witnesses in this case was taking a toll on him. The distractions of his crumbling personal life were also of no assistance. He was looking for one break, one good thing to pan out, and some sign that might suggest it wasn't all just shoveling shit against the tide. Matty Price came over with a cup of coffee for Paddy. He had one for himself as well. He sat at the vacant desk next to Paddy's and cleared his throat. Paddy looked up to see the unflappable detective grinning at him.

"What's the matter, Paddy? When you left yesterday, it looked like you were getting ready to break this case wide open."

"I'm still going to break it. It's just that nothing is going the way it should. Everything is difficult."

"What's the problem?"

"I only have three witnesses who are even worth a rat's ass. Everyone else involved in this case I want to set fire to. That includes some of the detectives and bosses."

"Things aren't going well at home either, I take it."

"It shows, huh?"

"You have that distracted and miserable look about you. Mairead doesn't call looking for you anymore, and I can't help noticing you're in no hurry to get out of here."

"I've been out of the house for a couple of months now. There isn't much allure to a shitty one-bedroom apartment next to the railroad in Farmingdale. I have to play slalom around the passed out drunks just to get in the door. Most nights, unless I'm dead tired, I lie awake staring at the ceiling and counting my regrets. They're not exactly sheep. I might as well stay here and make overtime."

"I thought you two were working things out."

"Mairead didn't want to do any more work. I'm still going for counseling, but even he's trying to prepare me for the fall. I take her ambivalence as a harbinger of things to come."

"Are you going to be alright?"

"Define *alright*."

"Are you going to hurt yourself?"

"That would be an absurdity; a permanent solution to temporary problems. Do you remember who told me that?"

"I said that. When we talked the kid off the roof of Wyckoff Heights. I didn't think you were listening."

"That might have been the most profound thing you've ever said. And I know. I've been writing them down."

"Have you now?"

"When I retire, I'm going to make a boatload of money recycling your material for inspirational cards and posters for Hallmark."

"As long as I get my cut."

"Thanks for taking an interest, Matty. It's getting a little tiresome having no one to talk to about this shit. And keeping my own counsel is getting me nowhere. If I were that smart, I wouldn't be in this predicament in the first place."

"You can't talk to Joe or Armando?"

"They both just got divorced. They don't exactly have a lot of helpful insight into the subject."

"I forgot. Sorry about that," he laughed. "You can always call me."

"I appreciate that. Now I've got to get busy. These *fives* aren't going to type themselves."

Paddy spent the next three hours transcribing his notes on the work from today onto a series of DD5's in the complaint follow-up system. When he was done, he went into Sergeant Krauss' office to tell him the case was up to date. Krauss could now look at the case on his own computer terminal and sign off on each *five*. Paddy prepared an overtime slip and signed out.

On his way out to the parking lot, Paddy saw Lieutenant White behind the desk. He stopped over to apologize for his behavior the other morning.

"I'm sorry for the way I spoke to you the other day. There was no excuse for that kind of disrespect. I'm just dealing with a lot of shit right now. It seems to be clouding my judgement. It won't happen again."

"That's okay, Paddy. It was almost worth it. I never saw anyone wake from a dead sleep and think like that. It's like you flipped a switch and snapped into instant detective mode. I did want to talk to you about something else though."

"What's on your mind, boss?"

"Ralph Marten claims you tried to kill him in the stairwell the other morning. Any truth to that?"

"If I wanted to kill him, he would already be dead. I did give him a good beating, though."

"Care to enlighten me as to why?"

"I'm not going to do that. If I told you, you would be compelled to do things and make notifications to other units that you don't really want to deal with. I will tell you this, though. If that scumbag doesn't stay out of my way, you're going to have to lock me up for murder. And I'm not coming easy."

"So, you feel strongly about it," the lieutenant laughed.

"It is not negotiable at this time. Is he making a formal complaint?"

"No. I get the feeling he's afraid of you."

"Well, at least he has a grasp on the situation."

What Paddy declined to share with the lieutenant was that he had a previous history of issues with Police Officer Ralph Marten. When Paddy first got to the 83rd Squad, he responded to a DOA job on Wyckoff Avenue. A retired long shore-man who lived alone since his wife passed away, expired at home from a heart attack. When the chest pains first presented themselves, the long shore-man managed to call 911. He was sitting in his easy chair waiting for EMS to arrive when the fatal heart attack struck. All deaths in the City of New York, except those in the hospital or a nursing home, require a detective response.

Paddy was entering the apartment when he saw Ralph Marten furiously rifling through a dresser drawer. He watched Marten pull back some shelving paper from the bottom of the drawer and extract a fat stack of hundred dollar bills. It was at least four inches thick and had to contain a hundred-thousand dollars.

"Jack-pot!" Marten exclaimed as he turned around to see Paddy glaring at him.

"What do you think you're doing, Officer?"

"Splitting this with you *now*, I guess," Marten said.

Paddy took two steps to close the distance between them and backhanded Marten across the face. The stunned cop dropped the money back into the drawer and stared at Durr with confusion. Paddy grabbed him by the ear and led him out into the hallway.

"If I catch you back in that apartment, you thieving fuck, I will lock your fat ass up for burglary. I will put you through the system in that uniform you don't deserve to wear, and a gauze turban to hold your broken fucking head together. Are we understood?"

Marten nodded bitterly, but he stayed in the hall as directed. He was out there pouting when the DOA's son arrived. Paddy directed him to the money in the drawer. The son was grateful, relating how his father had never trusted banks. Paddy elected to sit on the information that banks were more trustworthy than some cops he knew. But Paddy's first night in the 83rd Squad began an uninterrupted period of despising and shunning Ralph Marten.

Paddy left the precinct into the cool October night, dreading the trip out to Long Island. He was unable to think of it as going home. The only real home he had ever known was the house in Plainedge, where he was no longer welcome.

CHAPTER NINETEEN

October 11, 2013
Long Island

As Paddy made the ride out to Nassau County he considered how he had let his life spin so out of control. He knew he was in this predicament because he had put himself there. He had let himself turn insular. It was just a matter of time before Mairead found it easier to just concentrate on raising their three children, than to keep trying to drag out whatever monstrous thing was eating at him. He didn't really want to talk about it anyway. So their conversations took on a rote pattern of disconnect. Mairead would ask Paddy about his day. Paddy would tell her about his cases and he would watch her eyes frost over. Mentally she had already checked out. She was just waiting for him to stop talking. He would recognize this and wrap it up quickly, tired already of the sound of his own voice. Mairead would run down what was going on with the kids, with school, with sports and socially. She would update Paddy with what nursing shifts she would be taking at the hospital this week, as well as what classes she would be teaching at the gym on the weekend. She would remind him of upcoming events, parties, meetings and fundraisers that one or both of them had to attend. Mairead knew he didn't hear a word of it. He never did. So she put a calendar on the side of the refrigerator. Every event, meeting, game and their respective work schedules went on it. It was there for easy reference, and it obviated the need for Paddy to remember that which he hadn't been paying attention to in the first place.

That they had gotten to such a state, sleepwalking through their lives together, was a surprise to Paddy. He thought no two people were ever more suited to be together. They grew up only three miles apart. She was in Glendale, Queens. He was in Bushwick, Brooklyn. They both went to parochial schools, receiving the thorough, if stern education only Catholic nuns could provide. They were both athletes. She played soccer and ran cross country at the Mary Louis Academy, and then Mount Saint Mary's in the Bronx, where she studied nursing. Paddy had played football, first at Brooklyn Tech, and then at Columbia in upper Manhattan. He had earned a bachelor's degree in English and Comparative Literature. So they were both smart. They shared a continuing obsession with fitness. The two of them looked fifteen years younger than their ages. And they looked good together. They were regarded in equal parts with admiration and jealousy by their peers. Either way, they appeared to have the marriage everyone else wanted. From the outside, they looked for all the world like the "*it*" couple. But there were differences, too. Paddy had come to understand just how formidable these were. He feared they might in the end, prove insurmountable.

Mairead had grown up in a big, loving house. She had three brothers and two sisters and her mom was forever talking about adopting or fostering more. Her father, Big Bill Dunleavy was the owner and operator of the eponymously named roofing company. He adored her mother, Sinead, and could deny her nothing. If she wanted to take in an entire orphanage, it would be okay with Big Bill. He was not content just to tell his wife he loved her. Every day he would make a point of reminding her he would do anything to make her happy, and he made her deliriously happy. The two of them were devoted and involved with each other and their children's lives. They were wholly supportive and affectionate. They expected great things from their children, but they weren't overbearing or demanding. They treated their kids like the exceptional people they were, encouraging their abilities and creativity, rather than insisting upon it. In this easy, supportive environment, the results were predictable. Four of the six Dunleavy children had become doctors. Mairead and her sister had gone into nursing. They had never given their parents one minute of concern. Except for Mairead. Big Bill had misgivings about the man, boy really, his daughter had fallen in love with. Bill loved the kid. He wanted to accept and embrace Paddy, but there was something dark and hidden about him. He was afraid that when this darkness went metastatic, it would consume the both of them. But he kept his concern to himself. Until two years ago, when he was dying of cancer at Memorial Sloan Kettering. Paddy had been in Manhattan on a case. He dropped in to see his father-in-law, whom he had grown to love and respect, and in many ways envy.

Even emaciated as he was, Bill was a tower of strength. He refused to bemoan his situation. He would not allow himself to wallow in self-pity. He wasn't just maintaining a brave face. He was truly thankful for the life he had lived, and overwhelmingly grateful for all the love and joy God had seen fit to give him. He was ready to die, content he would be loved and remembered in his absence. He ordered his adoring family not to grieve for him, knowing full well they would not obey him.

Big Bill had kept this indomitable spirit throughout the three-year ordeal of pancreatic cancer. In spite of the sickness, the excruciating pain, and the wasting away of his once tremendous frame, he never let that beaming smile fade. He joked that he wasn't dying. He was escaping one pound at a time. When Paddy came in to the hospital that day, Big Bill wasn't smiling anymore.

"How are you feeling, Pop?"

"I'm troubled, boy."

"Are you in pain, can I get you anything?"

"It's not me I'm troubled about. It's you, Paddy. I've always loved you like a son. I couldn't quite get a handle on you, but I loved you just the same."

"I know that. I love you, too."

"But there is something wrong with you, some kind of emotional disconnect. It's like you start to feel something, and then you just don't anymore. You're like an empty shell. I've noticed it since you were young. For some reason, you won't let yourself be yourself. You're afraid of something. So you hide from it. It's been getting worse."

Bill had hit a nerve. He realized his father-in-law had discovered the void that was at the very center of him, and he was right. Paddy was afraid of it. So he shut it down, like he had been doing all of his life. He denied the thing, and refused to feel it. It didn't make it go away.

"There it is again," Bill observed.

"Don't waste your strength worrying about me."

"It's not you I'm worried about."

"Then what is it, Pop? What can I do?"

"Promise me, Paddy," Bill said urgently, grabbing his son-in-law's arm. "When this thing tormenting you finally erupts, don't let it touch my Mairead. Please, don't hurt my little girl."

Paddy lied to his dying father-in-law. He promised never to hurt Mairead, even as he was hurting her. The thing had already erupted. He just hadn't identified what it was yet, or why it had always been there, lurking in the shadows. Paddy hugged his father-in-law. He kissed him on his forehead. He felt sick inside. They both knew he was lying. When he finally left Big Bill, the man was silently weeping. As he was walking down the hall to the elevators, Paddy felt the overwhelming need to take a shower. He had never felt so dirty in all his life.

When he got down to the street, Armando was waiting in the squad car. As Paddy got into the passenger seat he had a crestfallen look on his face that was a mix of disgust and guilt. Armando misread this for concern over Big Bill.

"How is he doing?"

"It won't be long now," was all Paddy said. He didn't want to talk about anything, with anyone. So he sat silently on the ride back to Brooklyn, wallowing in his sense of self-revulsion. He found himself repugnant.

Unlike Mairead, Paddy had not grown up in a big loving house. He had lived in a railroad apartment in a four-story walk-up on Hart Street in Brooklyn. He was the third of four boys belonging to Walter and Colleen Durr. Belonging to, but not necessarily wanted by his parents, Paddy had been conceived in the middle of a two-year sentence his father had been serving for Union corruption on the waterfront docks. This made his paternity a mathematical impossibility. When his father was finally paroled, Paddy was despised by the man. They lived as strangers in the same house. If there was conversation at all between the two, it was his father trying to communicate how utterly worthless Paddy was, and would always be. He would bitterly inform him that he was not his son, as if it was somehow Paddy's own fault. According to Walter, Paddy was destined for a short life of failure and misery. He predicted drug abuse, and long stretches of incarceration for the boy he called *imbecile*.

His mother was no better. She was a passive-aggressive, self-absorbed nightmare. She lived in denial of her own faults, but never tired of pointing them out in others, particularly in her sons. As a result, Paddy's brothers grew up stupid and mean. Whomever Paddy's real father might have been, he must have at least been intelligent, because his mother didn't have the sense she was born with. She refused to discuss the matter of his birth father, declining to even acknowledge his existence, let alone identifying him.

Unlike his brothers, Paddy loved school. He was very bright, and showed a natural curiosity, as well as an innate ability for learning. School exposed Paddy for the first time to positive reinforcement. It was his first experience with someone voicing an opinion about his abilities and future that wasn't predictive of doom. School also introduced him to sports. Sports allowed Paddy to form friendships with boys his own age, who appreciated Paddy's athleticism and prowess at whatever game they were playing. As opposed to his brothers, who just wanted to beat the snot out of him. While Paddy found school and sports a vehicle for escape from the misery of home, his brothers found heroin. It wasn't long before the three of them were dead. The oldest, Walter Junior, got shot down in the commission of a liquor store robbery. The other two, Malachy and Kevin died in a puddle of their own vomit and feces. Both of them overdosing on heroin a year apart. By the time his brothers had already achieved the maximum level of their potential, Paddy had moved out. He was living in the dorms at Columbia and hadn't even been informed of their passing. So to Paddy they were just gone, and not at all missed. He hadn't spoken to his parents since he was eighteen, and could think of no good reason to do so.

The other significant event of his young life occurred when Paddy was thirteen. He had hit that point when puberty was in full throttle. Paddy had grown to his full height of five foot eleven inches, and started to thicken through the chest and shoulders, all in the previous three months. He had also sprouted body hair and sporadic acne from all the testosterone coursing through his body. This concerned him, but it was no match for the worry he was experiencing from his seemingly perpetual erection. He had no understanding why it was happening, or any idea what to do with it.

Inez Vasconcellos lived in apartment 1R with her husband Hector. Hector was the superintendent for this and several other buildings owned by their landlord. He was frequently at one of the other buildings which were all on DeKalb Avenue. At sixty-three-years-old, and in failing health, Hector was not making the walk between Hart Street and DeKalb Avenue more than once a day. So he was seldom home. Inez was just thirty. She was lonely, horny, and frustrated. She was also hot in a sexy Puerto Rican sort of way. She was practically dripping with sexual energy. She was in the hallway getting the mail in her cutoffs and tube top when Paddy came down the stairs. She had a perfect understanding of what was going on with that bulge in Paddy's pants, and a good idea about what to do with it.

"Why are you always in such a hurry, *Papi?*" Inez asked him, halting Paddy on the stairs by gently placing her hand on his chest. Paddy looked up the stairs behind him.

"I'm trying to get out of here before one of those assholes I live with try to talk to me."

"Slow down. I need help with something in my apartment. You look big and strong. Will you help me, *Papi?*"

Paddy followed Inez into her apartment. When they got inside, she closed and locked the front door. She pushed Paddy back against the wall. She pressed herself against him, stuck her tongue down his throat, and grabbed a hold of his bulging crotch. In that instant, Paddy's world turned upside down. Inez began a sexual awakening and education for him that would last four years. Apart from the pure physical gratification, Inez introduced him to a whole new way of looking at himself. Paddy found the feeling of validation from being wanted sexually intoxicating. The exhilaration, coupled with the first real intimacy he had ever known, took his once healthy sexual curiosity and propelled it into the realm of dangerous obsession. He needed to feel Inez give way beneath him. He needed to hear her moan and cry out. Her exaltations and tremulous shuddering were like a drug for him. *Aye, Papi!* became the soundtrack of his young life. Paddy told himself and Inez that he loved her. He just might have. But he had no previous experience with it, so he couldn't be sure. Inez on the other hand, didn't believe in love. She just wanted to fuck. For Paddy, it was a distinction without a difference.

The relationship came to an abrupt end. Paddy was already a senior at Brooklyn Tech. He knew he would be leaving for college come August, probably never to return. He had started seeing girls at school, but they were really just sexual encounters, all curiosity with none of the requisite emotion to call them relationships. While Paddy may have loved Inez, it wasn't timeless. It wasn't ageless, and it definitely had a shelf life that was fast approaching. But Paddy still couldn't get enough of her. So he dropped in on Inez whenever he was able.

Neither one of them heard the front door open. Inez was bent over the arm of the sofa and Paddy was behind her, pounding away. Inez' screams must have muffled the sound of Hector coming in to encounter his wife in the throes of ecstasy with his seventeen-year-old neighbor. Hector went into the kitchen and came back with a .38 caliber revolver. He kept repeating *"You beetch! You beetch!"* before shooting Inez in the chest three times, killing her instantly. Then he put the gun to Paddy's head.

"Give me one good reason why I shouldn't kill you, you *puto?*" Hector asked.

In spite of being terrified, Paddy's face was an expressionless mask. He just shrugged. Hector looked at his wife, slumped dead over the couch and bleeding out. He started weeping.

"Look at what she make me do. The *beetch*, I love her too much."

Hector took the gun away from Paddy's forehead. He put it in his own mouth and blew his brains out the back of his head.

Paddy was still standing there in shock with his pants around his ankles when uniform cops from the 83rd Precinct showed up with guns drawn. Paddy had the presence of mind to put his hands up. Police Officer Bucciogrosso surveyed the hot mess in front of him. It quickly started to make sense to the veteran cop. Still, he had to ask.

"What the fuck happened here?"

Paddy told him the whole story, and all with his hands in the air and his pecker swinging in the breeze. Bucciogrosso let out a long whistle and regarded Paddy with a newfound admiration.

"Why don't you put that Howitzer away, kid? I think it's done enough damage for one day."

Paddy spent the next several hours at the detective squad in the old 83rd Precinct. The detectives left him alone with his thoughts for a long while. He found he did not care for their company. The horror and loss of this day were wreaking havoc with his psyche. The realization that he had lost the only person who had ever really cared for him was forcing him to feel a level of emotion with which he was utterly unfamiliar. The crushing sorrow of it all frightened him. He had never experienced anything so intense. He wanted it to stop. So he willed it to. By the time Detective Cosgrove, the case detective brought him into the interview room, Paddy was as dead inside as Inez and Hector Vasconcellos.

Detective Cosgrove told Paddy the scene told the story, and there was nothing to suggest any wrongdoing on Paddy's part. Except for the adultery, but that wasn't a criminal matter. The only part of his story Cosgrove would have had a problem believing was the part where Paddy said Hector had put the gun to his head. When Paddy asked him what had changed his mind, Cosgrove led him over to the mirrored viewing glass in the room. Paddy could see a perfectly round and raised burn mark in the center of his forehead, where Hector had pressed the just fired, and red hot gun. He could even discern the ridges at the edge from the rifling in the barrel. Cosgrove told Paddy a burn like that could be made no other way. He also assured Paddy the wound would probably heal and wouldn't leave any permanent scarring. Before Paddy could go, Cosgrove wanted to clarify one more thing.

"Is it true you've been having sex with that woman for the last four years?" Cosgrove asked. Paddy just nodded.

"Jesus Christ! You were only thirteen."

"I was big for my age," Paddy offered.

"According to Officer Bucciogrosso, you're big for any age."

When Paddy got to his Farmingdale apartment, he took a shower to try and wash off the grime and the vagrant awfulness of the day. He was only moderately successful. The stalled murder case, coupled with the latent anxiety over his crumbling marriage, left Paddy with an uneasy and slightly dirty feeling. Twenty minutes of hot water can only wash away so much. He went to bed knowing sleep wouldn't come. If he drank, now would be a good time to get piss-faced drunk and pass out for twelve hours. But that was not an option. Paddy had given up alcohol twenty years earlier. Alcohol made him morose, and that made Mairead unhappy.

A cigarette might have helped to calm his nerves. But he had given that vice up about the same time as drinking. Mairead quit smoking when she became pregnant with Patrick Jr. Paddy had quit as well, out of deference to her. They both agreed it was ridiculous for two former athletes to be smoking anyway. Neither of them took up the habit again. So Paddy was left to stare at his bedroom ceiling, prevented by his racing mind and the sound of his breaking heart from slipping into needed oblivion. He endured two hours of this before getting up, putting on gym clothes, grabbing his gym bag and heading to Gold's Gym in Levittown. Paddy was a member of this gym specifically because it was the only one in Nassau County open twenty-four hours-a-day. He ran on the treadmill for an hour, and lifted weights for another. The great thing about being in a gym this early in the morning, you could work quickly. All the weights and equipment are just waiting for you to use. You could get a three-hour workout done in a third of the time. Paddy was able to get in the arm workout he had to forgo on Friday and Saturday because of the homicide. Exercise usually exhilarated him. But he was so bone deep weary, when he crashed in his bed back in his apartment, he didn't even have the energy to undress or take off his running shoes. He stayed there until ten o'clock that morning, getting up only because of his full bladder. Once up, he made coffee, showered and put on work clothes to go to the house in Plainedge that didn't feel like his anymore.

CHAPTER TWENTY

October 12, 2013
Plainedge

When Paddy got to 16 Reading Lane, the place he had called home for the past twenty years, he let himself directly into the backyard, not wishing to impose upon Mairead. He got right to work, collecting all the winterizing chemicals from the pool shed. He introduced them into the pool. While he let the filter run for the requisite hour to circulate the chemicals, Paddy got to work putting away the cushions for the deck furniture and covering it for the winter. That done, Paddy pulled out the cover for the pool and the inflatable cushions. The mindless, repetitive nature of pool maintenance was the aspect of the work that appealed to Paddy. He could just shut off his brain and do the simple work with the sun shining on his face. It was not so much like thought as photosynthesis.

Once Paddy had the pillows in place, and the cover ratcheted down over the pool, it was time to lower the water level. So he attached a long vinyl hose to the backwash valve of the filter and ran it out around the side of the house and into the street. Once he threw the switch on the valve, it would be just a half hour or so until the water level was correct. Paddy estimated he could be done and out of there without actually having to speak to anyone in a little under an hour. Given the dread he was experiencing over his next encounter with Mairead, escaping in this fashion appealed to him. He knew he was only postponing the inevitable.

So he had decided to ring the front bell to tell Mairead he had finished. She removed the need.

Mairead came out to the deck in faded jeans and Paddy's powder blue Columbia Football sweatshirt. That hoodie never looked as good as it did when Mairead was wearing it. Her shoulder-length brown hair kept blowing across her face. As she brushed it away from her eyes, Paddy noticed she wasn't wearing her wedding ring anymore.

"I need to talk to you about something when you're done here," Mairead said.

"I have about another hour of work. I'll lock everything down and come in."

"I'll make a pot of coffee."

"That would be fine," Paddy said, not feeling fine about anything at the moment.

When he had finished with the backyard, Paddy let himself in through the sliding door from the deck. Mairead was already in the kitchen. She told Paddy to sit down while she fixed his coffee. Paddy saw a manila legal envelope on the kitchen table. It had an address label from Scarborrough, Dunne, and Mayweather, Attorneys at Law. Mairead's hand shook as she placed Paddy's coffee in front of him. He felt bad for her, and then chuckled at himself for doing so. It was a bit like a condemned man feeling empathy for his executioner.

Mairead was clearly uncomfortable. Paddy reached out and gently placed his hand over hers.

"I know what that is," Paddy said, nodding in the direction of the envelope. "You might as well just give it to me."

She handed over the envelope. Paddy smiled at her, trying unsuccessfully to ease her anxiety. He removed the sheaf of legal papers and put on his glasses to read them. He noticed she had listed *irreconcilable differences* as the grounds for the divorce. For that he was grateful. She wanted to be rid of him, but she wasn't trying needlessly to inflict pain. Paddy read each page carefully. Her terms were generous. She was looking for half of the equity in the house and not much else. They would share the outstanding debt they had accumulated. She wasn't looking for any of his future pension, or any of the deferred compensation investments he had made over the years. Of the savings or common investments they had made, she wanted only half.

The magnanimity of the demands didn't make them sting any less. When Paddy was done reading, He looked at Mairead over his glasses.

"Is this really what you want?" he asked her, while every fiber and cell in his body was screaming, begging her silently not to do this. With that, her composure gave way. As she started crying, she tried to explain through her sobs.

"I can't do this anymore. It's too much. I just can't get past it. I stood by you through everything, Paddy. Through the shootings, the indictment, even 911. I put up with your moodiness, your silences, and all the nightmares from your PTSD. I never minded, not any of it. But now, all I can feel is your betrayal. I can never trust you again. You lied to my face, and made me feel like something worthless. I loved you, and you ruined me. I get so angry at you, I want to hurt you. I want you to feel what I feel. And then I get mad at myself for wanting that. But I'll never have a life again as long as I'm with you. I need this to recover some semblance of myself. I need to repair my self-esteem. You did this to me, Paddy. You did this to us."

"You don't have to explain, Mairead. I'm not looking to share any blame. It's all mine. I told you if you got to this point, I'd give you whatever you wanted. That still goes."

Paddy signed and dated the Notice of Service form and handed it to Mairead. He put the rest of the papers back in the envelope and stood up to go.

"I'll show these to a lawyer and get back to you with any possible changes."

"I was hoping to avoid lawyers as much as possible."

"This is New York, honey," Paddy said. "You can't get divorced in New York without lawyers."

"I guess that's okay, but call before you come over," she said as she got up to walk him to the door.

"Before I go, I want you to understand something. I know what a number I did on you. I know I killed your trust. I hate myself for it. If I live a hundred years, I'll never forgive myself. But know this; my affair was not because of anything you did. You were the best thing that ever was going to happen to me, and I trashed it. I love you, but you're right. I'm no good for you. This happened because of what's wrong with me. You had nothing to do with it. I just made you suffer. I've never let myself be happy, because I was afraid, because I didn't trust it. So I would sabotage it. The truth is, I have never felt deserving of anything. You knew all of this, and you loved me anyway. I always secretly believed you would come to your senses, and leave me in the gutter where I belong. So when you tell me you want me out of your life, I get it. I don't even want me in *my* life. The reality is, you were always too good for me. I always knew it. Now you do too."

Paddy paused to look at his wife. Her eyes, so green and tear-streaked, were as beautiful as they always were to him. He took in everything; the spray of freckles across her nose, the lines at the corners of her full mouth that would become a wry smile. He let her scent wash over him. *Sand and Sable* had been making him crazy since they first started dating. It was doing a number on his olfactory senses now. She was still the most beautiful thing he had ever laid eyes on. He wanted her so badly he ached. He reached out to touch her left hand gently, the one where her wedding ring used to be. Just like that, she moved in and pressed herself against him. Her hand went instinctively to the back of his neck as she pulled his mouth down to her own. Then they were on each other like starving animals. They tore at each other's clothes like they were on fire. Paddy picked her up and practically ran up the stairs carrying her with her legs wrapped around his waist to their old bedroom. They made love with a frenzy, like it was the first time, like it would be the last time. They devoured each other for what felt like hours, until they collapsed, exhausted, spent. They had wrung everything there was to get out of each other. Mairead laid entwined with him, her head on his chest. Paddy felt her tears before he heard her quiet sobs. Then he felt them mix wetly with his own. He pressed his mouth into her hair to quietly whisper.

"I'm sorry. I am so very sorry…"

Paddy kept going over what had just happened with Mairead as they recovered their clothing, avoiding each other. It wasn't so much an attempt to make sense of it. He understood what happened. They had been melting into each other like this since they first met. With just a glance, a gesture, an inadvertent touch, they would suddenly be consumed in the chemical inferno of their desire for each other. Where Paddy was having difficulty was trying to get his mind around the fact that it wasn't more significant.

Their love, which was never in question, coupled with their insatiable hunger for each other, was not going to be enough to save them. Paddy had squandered too much.

"This was a mistake," Mairead said, as they looked for their clothes, scattered about the house. Paddy realized she was right, as the gloom and hopelessness of it all descended upon him.

"This doesn't change anything. I think it only makes it worse, if that's even possible."

"I know," Paddy said. But he didn't.

"I don't think you should come here if I'm home. You can come over when I'm at work, or if Casey is around. I think I can control myself in front of our daughter."

"I'll just come by when you're at work. Casey would rather not see me anyway."

"Can you really blame her? You embarrassed her. You embarrassed us all. She's just sixteen. She wants to pretend it never happened. Seeing you makes that impossible."

"I'll continue to make myself scarce. I'll call you after my lawyer reviews the divorce papers."

"You've already hired a lawyer?"

"I'm a detective, Mairead. I've got lawyers dripping off me. One of them will know someone who handles divorces."

"Thank you for understanding," she said, as she followed Paddy to the door, her arms folded across her chest, careful not to touch him again. As Paddy was leaving, he stopped briefly to turn and look at her.

"I'm sorry," was all he said. She nodded, and let him turn before closing the door behind him.

As Paddy got into his truck, it occurred to him *I'm sorry* might have been the truest words he ever spoke. It encompassed all the sorrow, grief, bitterness, and disappointment he was feeling at this moment. In a phrase, it understood all the shame and misery he had wrought. Now, leaving the home that wasn't his anymore, with divorce papers freshly served, gripped bitterly in his guilty hands, Paddy thought *I'm sorry* might as well serve as his epitaph. Admittedly, Padraig Joseph Durr was one sorry excuse for a man.

CHAPTER TWENTY-ONE

October 12, 2013
Farmingdale

When Paddy got back to his apartment, he stripped off his work clothes for the second time that day. He dumped these in the hamper, and wrapped a fresh bath towel around his waist. He checked the phone for messages. There were two. The first was from his son Patrick, a senior at Sacred Heart University in Connecticut. He was in his final college football season. He had been converted from a linebacker into a punishing, blocking fullback. This position shift suited his personality. He got to crush people on every play. Like his father before him, brute force and ignorance were solutions number one and two. Patrick had called to inform his father Senior Day would be the second Saturday in November. This was the annual celebration for the Football program where the seniors and their families were recognized on the field for their hard work, sacrifice and determination. It was a big deal at the university, like a second homecoming game. The mothers were presented by their sons on the field at halftime with bouquets of flowers, while their fathers got to look on proudly. At least, that's how it was supposed to go down. Recent events in the Durr household had complicated things.

"I have no idea what's going on with you and Mom," Patrick said on the machine. "I'm not getting involved with this shit. It's your mess. If you can't clean it up, I expect you'll do the right thing. Call me and tell me what's going on. I have to make arrangements whether you're coming with Mom or not."

The second message was from his oldest daughter, Katelyn. She was in her freshman year at Fordham University in the Bronx. She had a choice between scholarships in soccer or cross country. She had chosen soccer. The choice was a not so subtle dig at her father. The affair that was killing his family had been with Katelyn's high school soccer coach. She opted for the soccer out of spite as much as anything else. She had her father's capacity for grudge holding, and she was holding this one firmly. She gave him an update on her season, which was winding down. She was doing well, starting as a freshman, scoring goals and accumulating assists. She told Paddy they had a game this week at Hofstra, on Long Island. Then she told him she didn't want him to come.

"I don't need you fucking anymore of my soccer coaches," she said. She paused briefly, perhaps regretting the comment. But then she could be heard to mutter "Asshole," before hanging up.

Being fully updated on how his family felt about him, Paddy decided to address something else. He called Sergio Mendez to get an update on the status of Beatriz' phone number. Sergio answered and apologized. The phone wouldn't take a charge. Sergio said he was going to bring it into Sprint to see if they would replace the battery. Paddy told him not to do that.

"Don't mess with the phone anymore. Just keep it with you. I come back to work at four tomorrow. I'll call you when I hit Bushwick. I'll come and get the phone from you and take it to my guy. Is she the only Beatriz in your contacts?"

"She's actually listed as *Beatriz Willoughby*. So, you can't miss her."

Paddy then called one of his many lawyer friends, Danny Kirk.

"I met your friend Robert Ruiz yesterday. He's a nice kid. I'm going to take care of that thing for him."

"You're a good man, Danny Kirk."

"It's nothing. That was an injustice, what they did to that kid. I should have it shit-canned for him in about a week."

"I appreciate it. But I'm not calling about that. I need a divorce lawyer."

"Mairead's throwing you out?" Danny asked, incredulous.

"She served me with papers this afternoon. I've gotta straighten a few things out with the terms."

"Is she going for your lungs?"

"It's not like that. She's asking for too little. I don't need to give her another reason to hate me."

"I could give you one of the guys I used, but they're all barracudas."

"No barracudas. How many divorces are you on now?"

"Four and counting," Danny said proudly. "It's my favorite mistake. So I keep making it."

"You're good at what you do."

"I may have a guy for you," Danny remembered. "Hiram Borstein, do you remember him? He worked for me when I had the Gray Zone in Brooklyn. He's out in Nassau County with a full practice. He does everything, wills, closings, divorces, you name it. He liked you. He thought you were Wyatt Earp. He'll probably do it gratis for you."

"I just need him to do what I want done. This is my family. I want to be as generous as possible."

"I'm sure he'll do whatever you want. But divorces are expensive, Paddy. It's gonna hurt."

"It already hurts," Paddy admitted.

Paddy took the number from Danny Kirk, and called the office of Hiram Borstein. He reached an answering machine. He explained who he was and what he needed. He asked if Borstein would call him back at his earliest convenience, leaving his numbers. Paddy shaved and jumped in the shower, in a vain attempt to somehow scrape off the misery eating at him. Failing that, he was at least clean as he went into the kitchen to prepare a bowl of oatmeal to eat with his cold, grilled chicken breast. This he washed down with a pre-workout drink consisting primarily of branched-chain-amino acids and caffeine. It was as awful as it sounds, but when the growing bitterness inside you starts to make all of your food taste like ashes in your mouth, it really doesn't make much of a difference. It was just a matter of taking in fuel for the body, not delighting in it. After choking down his meal, Paddy put on his gym gear to go to Gold's to burn off what little energy he had left. This was the only way to guarantee that sleep would come, and Paddy desperately needed sleep. He was as weary as he had ever been, right through his bones and down into his soul.

CHAPTER TWENTY-TWO

October 13, 2013
Long Island

The ringing phone brought Paddy Durr slowly to his senses. He knocked the receiver from the cradle and had to find it on the floor before answering it. When he did, all he could muster was a dry, throaty *"Yawp?"*

"Is this Detective Durr?" asked the voice of Hiram Borstein.

"Thanks for getting back to me, Mr. Borstein," Paddy said, wiping the sleep from his eyes and trying to shake off the fog in his head.

"Call me Hiram. Danny Kirk told me what was going on with you. I'm sorry to hear it. But I think I can help you. Could you drop by my office this morning with the divorce papers?"

"Yeah," Paddy said, looking for the clock. "What time is it?"

"It's 9:30. Did I wake you?"

"It's alright. I needed to get up eventually."

"I didn't think gunfighters needed sleep," Hiram joked.

"We don't. We get drunk and pass out. It makes for difficult mornings either way. You're in Roslyn, right?"

"Yes, 10-25 Glen Cove Road, right behind the Wheatley Shopping Plaza."

"How does 11:30 sound?" Paddy asked.

"I'll see you then."

10-25 Glen Cove Road was a four-story glass and metal office building with an open and inviting front entrance to the lobby and elevators. In the center of the lobby there was an elaborate water feature with tropical flora around the faux waterfall. Paddy made his way over to the tenant directory, on the left wall just inside the front doors. The building was owned and operated by H.I. Borstein Associates. They had full occupancy consisting of various medical practices on the first three floors. The fourth floor was exclusively occupied by their law office.

Once off the elevator, Paddy proceeded to the desk on his left. Behind it in large bold letters on the wall was yet another sign that told him he was at the Law Offices of Hiram I. Borstein. Behind the desk was the receptionist. She appeared to be in her late twenties and had her brown hair pulled up into a severe bun. She wore a demure navy blue business suit that was painfully professional. Paddy thought she would have been pretty except for the pinched and severe expression on her face. She regarded Paddy over her glasses with a look that seemed to suggest she found something amiss, but hadn't quite figured out what it was yet.

"May I help you?" she asked Paddy, inspiring no faith she would.

"I'm looking for the Law Offices of Hiram I. Borstein. Do you have any idea where that might be?" She stared at him for a brief moment, seemingly trying to suppress the urge to call him an asshole.

"Do you have an appointment?"

"I'm supposed to be meeting with Hiram, about now."

"Who may I say is here to see him?"

"Tell him it's Wyatt Earp and to hurry the hell up. My horse is double parked." At this she finally smiled. She dialed a four digit extension.

"Hiram, your smartass detective friend is here. He's better looking than I expected, but he still looks like trouble. You really should get a better class of friends." She hung up the phone, and smiled sweetly at Paddy.

"You can go in and see my brother now. But if you have to shoot him, avoid getting blood on the carpeting. I just had it installed."

Paddy winked at her as she buzzed him through the interior doors. Hiram was in the large corner office in an otherwise unoccupied floor of offices. He called to Paddy and waved him in, excited to see him. He came around his huge and ornate partner's desk to shake Paddy's hand. At five foot one, and all of one hundred twenty pounds, Hiram was one of the slightest men Paddy had ever met. But in spite of his diminutive size, he had demonstrated a great deal of physical courage in his time prosecuting felonies in Brooklyn. He insisted on visiting every crime scene, and loved taking videotaped confessions from suspects. Paddy had never once seen him intimidated in the presence of a suspect, and as far as he was concerned, that was recommendation enough. Hiram also had an outsized appreciation for tough guys. He was excitedly pumping away at Paddy's hand when Paddy gently, but firmly squeezed, causing the smaller man to wince, but bringing him back to the reason he was there. He invited Paddy to sit in front of his desk. Then, rather than ensconcing himself behind the enormous and forbidding piece of furniture, Hiram brought over another chair and sat beside Paddy.

"Excuse the desk. It was my father's. My sister, Sarah would kill me if I tried to get rid of it. So I work around it."

"It's beautiful. It reminds me of Teddy Roosevelt's desk in the police commissioner's office."

"Enough about my furniture. What do you have for me?"

Paddy handed over the manila envelope with the divorce papers. Hiram read them carefully, making notes on a separate legal pad. Finally, he looked up at Paddy.

"These are very generous terms. In light of the fact that you've been married for more than twenty years, she's not asking for much."

"That's what I want to correct. She wants this done quickly. I'm okay with that. But she's being short-sighted."

"What do you want changed?"

"I want to keep her and the kids in the house until they're out of school and established. I'll take care of the mortgage, the taxes and the life insurance. All she has to pay are the utilities. In addition, while the kids are there, I want to give her a thousand dollars a month for food and whatever else they need. I'm gonna need access. I'll take care of the maintenance. I practically built that house. So if anything breaks, I can fix it. Also, the credit card debt; I can take care of that, give her a fresh start. The last thing, stipulate that I'll pay for the kid's school until they're twenty-one. They're on scholarship, so it probably won't be an issue. Everything else is acceptable to me."

"What about visitation?" Hiram asked.

"My kids want no part of me. They're adults anyway. If they change their mind, they know how to get in touch with me. I'm not pressing the issue."

"I can make these changes and have them for you on Wednesday."

"What about your fee?"

"I'm not taking your money for this. If it gets contested and we have to go to court, then we can talk about a fee. I'm thinking you can take my sister off my hands for me."

"You mean the Ice Queen out there? Do you want me to kill her, or marry her? Keep in mind, marriage with me has a shelf life. What's her deal, anyway? She seems too competent to be just a receptionist."

"Sarah is an attorney, and a good one. She's also the business manager for the firm. We don't usually have visitors before noon. So our receptionist is a part-time position. Besides, after I got done talking you up, she wanted to meet you."

"You can't be doing that, Hiram. I'm not all you have me cracked up to be."

CHAPTER TWENTY-THREE

October 13, 2013
Brooklyn

When Paddy reached Saint Nicholas Avenue and Cooper Street, he called Sergio Mendez. Sergio was just dropping off a fare in Greenpoint when he got the call. He told Paddy he could meet him in twenty minutes at the precinct. Paddy parked in the lot behind the 83rd Precinct. Then he went up to the squad to sign in. Matty Price's team was in the office, finishing their day tour. Paddy went down to the front of the precinct to wait for Sergio Mendez.

When Sergio pulled up in front of the precinct, Paddy walked directly over to him, obviating the need for Sergio to even turn the car off. Sergio reached into his glove box and handed Paddy a black Nokia phone. It had a peculiar gritty feel to it, and looked ashy. Paddy told Sergio he would touch base with him later. Sergio volunteered that he had been cruising up and down Willoughby Avenue hoping to see Beatriz. There had been no sign of her. Paddy cautioned him not to alert the witness the police wanted to talk to her. Sergio said he understood and drove off down Bleecker Street.

Paddy went up to the squad. He poked his head into Sergeant Krauss office and knocked on the door. Steve waved Paddy in.

"What's going on?" the sergeant asked.

"I've gotta bring this phone to TARU to dump the sim card."

"Whose phone is it?"

"The cab driver, Sergio. He has a woman in his contacts who messed around with my shooter and victim. I need to talk to her to find out the nature of those relationships, and who the killer is."

"What do you have on her so far?"

"Just a first name and the possibility that she lives on Willoughby between Knickerbocker and Wilson. I've run the name and the whole block. Nothing pops. I need that phone number."

"I have no doubt you'll get it. How did you make out yesterday with the pool?"

"Yesterday was a surrealistic nightmare."

"What happened?"

"Mairead served me."

"Oh shit, Paddy, I'm sorry," Steve said.

"I was just kidding myself if I thought this was going any other way. It is what it is. I'll deal with it."

"You know if you need anything," Steve left the rest unsaid.

"What I need is to work on my homicide. Murder puts things in perspective. It reminds me that no matter how bad it gets, I'm still walking on the right side of the grass."

CHAPTER TWENTY-FOUR

October 13, 2013
TARU, Queens

When Paddy got to TARU, he called his friend Detective Ronnie Kingsbury. The Technical Assistance Response Unit of the NYPD was responsible for developing any audio, video, or digital evidence that came up in serious investigations. The Telephone Unit was created as a separate subdivision of TARU in response to the prevalence of cell phones in use by criminals these days. This office was located in the basement of a warehouse on Union Turnpike in Glendale. When TARU was created in the 1960's, in response to the need to perform surveillance on the doings of The Weather Underground, the Black Liberation Army, the FALN and a host of other revolutionary groups, it was thought to be important to keep TARU secret, as well as the department's ability to eavesdrop on society's enemies. This secrecy was an attractive aspect for the detectives working there. As the years passed, the need for secrecy became obsolete. The government's ability to monitor the communication of its citizens was detailed weekly on television programs like *Law and Order*. After 911, the myth of secret electronic communication was exploded forever. The government could listen in on anything, and frequently did. In spite of the curtain being pulled back for all the world to see, some TARU members still liked to think of themselves as spies. In fact, they were little more than glorified audio-visual geeks. The rest of the detective bureau thought of them as tech nerds. Even still, they weren't letting go of their self-perception as spooks. If you didn't have an appointment, or contact with someone in the unit, they weren't answering the door.

Shortly after 911, Paddy had developed information on an ongoing terrorism operation on Fourth Avenue in Brooklyn. An informant reluctantly provided the cell phone number of the leader and conduit of this particular terrorist cell. The information was time sensitive. Terrorists had seen enough of the police playbook to know that they needed to dump their phones on a regular basis. It was not uncommon for them to change phones every day. This was a rare opportunity to view the call details and contacts of an active, operational terror cell. If Paddy got this information quickly, he could identify and roll up the whole cell, preventing the subway bombing they had planned for the next day. When he got to TARU unannounced, no one would answer the door. As Paddy stood there looking up at the surveillance camera that was recording him, knowing the dozen and a half detectives inside could hear him through the intercom, he got furious. So he went down the block to the firehouse and borrowed a pry bar, a sledgehammer and a fire axe. He went back to TARU with these implements, and rang the bell again. As expected, he got no response. So he smiled up at the camera above the door and composed his thoughts.

"I know you can hear me, you assholes. So listen up. I have actionable intelligence on a terror cell that has gone hot. I need your assistance. You are going to give it to me right fucking now. If this door doesn't open in three seconds, I'm going to chop it down with my fire axe. Then I'm going to lock up every last one of you cowards for aiding and abetting terrorism. So think fast."

When three seconds passed, Paddy started smashing in the steel door with the axe. On his third swing, the door opened and Paddy nearly buried the axe in a frightened detective's head.

"Are you crazy?" the TARU detective asked.

"As a shithouse rat," Paddy said, as he pushed his way in the door and grabbed the detective by his collar. "Where is your desk, asswipe?" Paddy demanded as he forced him deeper into the office. The detective indicated the vacant one with several computer terminals in the center of what was a large cubicle farm. Paddy shoved the detective to his desk and forced him into his seat, still holding the fire axe. He reached into his inner jacket pocket and removed his notepad. He put the notepad on the desk in front of the detective.

"That number," Paddy pointed at the pad. "Run it. I want all recent calls as well as all contacts. The last three days should do it. Then you're going to give me the same info on every number the first number had contact with, and so on."

"I just can't give that information out. I need authorization."

"How does the Attorney General of the United States of America grab you? Now run my shit, or I'll hit you with my axe until I find one of you jerk-offs with enough sense to be compliant."

The TARU detectives ultimately gave Paddy what he wanted. The information provided allowed the Joint Terrorist Task Force to thwart the planned strike in the subways. As anticipated, the entire cell was identified and rolled up. A full dozen and a half beds became more or less permanently occupied at Guantanamo Prison.

CHAPTER TWENTY-FIVE

October 13, 2013
Queens

Paddy was careful to ensure TARU received their fair share of the credit for the terrorism operation. While this did not exactly exonerate him for his attack on their inner sanctum, it went a long way in returning him to good standing with the unit. In the future, TARU would gladly assist Paddy with his investigations, ready as he was to share the credit for any success. He just had to call for an appointment first.

Ronnie Kingsbury had gotten to TARU a year after Paddy's meltdown at the front door. Prior to that, Ronnie had been a terrific Anti-Crime cop in the 83rd Precinct. But, irrespective of his street smarts and fearless pursuit of bad guys, Ronnie was a tech dweeb. He had been passionate about electronics since he was a kid. When he got his interview for the Detective Bureau, Ronnie asked Paddy if he could get him into TARU. This would be a tough sell. TARU had become one of those details on the job where the chiefs all wanted to send their kids. The word was, you needed a two star chief or better to get in the door.

Fortunately, Paddy's old Commanding Officer in the 34th precinct, Nick Aspramonte had just made Chief of Patrol. That was three stars, and Nick had always expressed gratitude to Paddy for creating the opportunity for him to resurrect his career. Paddy and his Anti-Crime team had been the go-to guys for Aspramonte, when he was the CO of the precinct. Though an exceptional leader, Nick was considered dead in the water as a captain. The problem was, Aspramonte was a low key guy. A decorated combat Marine in Vietnam, he had little talent for self-promotion, and no taste for it at all. Because of this, other captains and inspectors in Manhattan North with more dynamic personalities continued to step over Aspramonte for promotions. His quiet competence was going to be his undoing. Until one July evening in 1992, when Paddy set the city on fire.

Paddy Durr had been a member of the most prolific Anti-Crime Unit in the history of the NYPD. Mostly of Irish descent, with an Italian and a Mexican thrown in for good measure, the seven cops and their sergeant were responsible for more than four hundred gun arrests in a calendar year. They were on a pace to surpass that number in 1992. The night of July 3rd, Paddy and his partners had spotted a guy with a large caliber revolver sticking out of his waistband. The three cops quickly concocted a plan to approach the suspect. Paddy, who looked nothing like a cop at this point in his career, what with the long hair, earrings and goatee, would approach from the corner, presumably unnoticed. His partners would circle the block in their unmarked car. Though the vehicle was a non-descript Chevy Caprice that looked like a livery cab, Paddy and his partners had been jumping out of it to lock up bad guys with guns for the past two years. Every criminal in Washington Heights knew this car intimately. The cops learned to use that notoriety to their advantage. They would flush the suspect toward Paddy on the corner. Like most brilliant plans conceived on the fly, this one went bad almost immediately.

When the unmarked Caprice hit the block, the alert call went up as expected. But, instead of causing the suspect to walk toward the corner, he instead turned and walked toward the lobby doors of the apartment house on the right. Paddy caught up to the suspect just as he was entering the building. He was big, six foot two and at least two hundred and forty pounds. It was also later discovered he was a cocaine addict, and was high at the time of the encounter. When Paddy grabbed the suspect by the lapel of his sport jacket and identified himself as a police officer, the perp elbowed Paddy in the throat and dragged him backwards into the hallway, a cavernous marble enclosure more reminiscent of a mausoleum than anything else. This was fitting, because when Paddy got dragged into that hallway, he was certain he would die in there. What began was a five minute fight to the death for the suspect's gun, which he kept trying to draw, to shoot Paddy. Durr stayed close with his adversary, never letting him clear the gun from his waist. Several times during the hand to hand battle, Paddy tried to radio for assistance. But he hadn't intended to be in a building, so he didn't know the address of the one he was in. So while everybody knew he was in trouble, no one knew where to look for him.

After five hectic minutes of pure mayhem, with Durr taking the worst beating of his life, the suspect managed to pull his weapon and hit Paddy in the mouth with the barrel. Durr was able to grab the perp's right wrist and jerk the gun away from his face, but only briefly. As he was losing his grip on the sweaty and blood-smeared arm of the suspect, he drew his own revolver. As the perp's gun swung up again into Paddy's face, he had the fleeting impression he was looking down a manhole, the business end of a gun never being as big as it is when pointed in your face. But in that instant Paddy punched his gun out in front of him until the barrel was pressed against the perp's chest, and quickly fired twice. The suspect, already dying, spun to the ground at Durr's feet.

By this time the radio, knocked out of Paddy's hand earlier, had erupted into pandemonium. Every cop in Manhattan North was trying to find him. They were screaming at central in a futile attempt to add something to the conversation. But they had nothing to add but confusion, and there was plenty enough of that. Finally, Paddy found his radio on the floor. He holstered his own gun and picked up the perp's weapon from the ground, just in case it decided to take a walk. Not likely in a closed hallway, but not worth taking a chance with either. Paddy had seen too many guns disappear from crime scenes to trust this one to providence. The gun was staying with him. Paddy walked out to the front lobby doors and looked up. There was the address, 555 W 162nd Street. Paddy put over his location, as well as reporting he *had a perp down*. Central repeated the address and tried to ascertain if Paddy was shot. As he walked back over to his fallen adversary, Durr was just too exhausted and disoriented to answer. So he waited.

Moments later, Police Officers John Di Santis and his partner Danny Neylan came running into the lobby. Paddy must have been a fright to behold because Di Santis kept asking him where he had been shot. Paddy had trouble comprehending the question. So Di Santis and Neylan started stripping off Paddy's top layer of clothing to try and find the bullet wounds they were sure had to be there. Paddy found his words and explained. The big .357 Magnum he was holding had been the perp's gun. Only half of the blood covering him was his own, and none of it was from a gunshot wound. As more and more uniform cops arrived in the hallway, Di Santis and Neylan grabbed Paddy and rushed him to the Emergency Room at Columbia Presbyterian.

Mairead was working in the ER that night. There is always a handful of cops and EMT's hanging around an inner-city emergency room, and they all have their radios on. When Paddy first broadcast his call for help, Mairead heard it and recognized his voice. She did not recognize the terrified panic underneath it. She didn't believe Paddy was afraid of anything. So when she heard the fear in his voice, she was horrified. She listened to every subsequent transmission from Paddy over the next two minutes, and then the awful silence. The only sound now coming from the radios were the cops beseeching Paddy for his location, so they could find him and help him. And then the terrible frustration and despair when no answer came. If Paddy thought he was going to die in that hallway, Mairead and every cop in the city thought he already had. Several minutes later, when Paddy broadcast his location, Mairead still recognized his voice, but it had an exhausted, beaten quality to it. The echoes from inside the marble hallway gave his breathless words a hollow and ethereal quality, as if he was sending his last message from beyond the grave. Mairead had no cause for optimism when she heard they were rushing Paddy to the hospital. She had worked on too many cops that were already gone when their partners carried them into the ER, not to realize a trip to the hospital didn't mean you weren't already dead.

When Mairead saw Paddy walking through the front doors of the ER with Di Santis and Neylan, still very much alive, she bounded down the hall and pounced on him. Through a veil of sobs and tears, Mairead tried to brush away the blood from Paddy's face and neck. But it had become encrusted by now, and the futility of Mairead's efforts made them both giggle. When their lips locked they stayed in that embrace. As they were moved into their own private examination room, cops and supervisors from all over Manhattan were dropping in. They were there to show support and express their relief Paddy hadn't been killed. It was a spontaneous gathering, all raw with emotion, much preferred to an Inspector's funereal.

Mairead was fascinated. There was almost a religious bearing to the cops that came in from all over the borough. It was as if they had to be there.

"Why do they come?" Mairead asked.

"Out of respect, mostly, but there's more to it than that."

"I don't understand."

"Active cops are a different breed," Paddy tried to explain. "We're the gunfighters, the alpha dogs of the police department. We're not special, just different. We all think we're Superman; bulletproof, avenging angels of the Lord. We pretend no harm can come to us because we walk in the light. But the light doesn't stop bullets, and doing God's work offers no additional protection. When the shit hits the fan and even the alpha dogs are fighting for their lives, as cops, we're forced to confront our own mortality. We have to admit that this shit is real. It's not a game of cowboys and Indians. People die at this, and it's usually the good guys. So this pilgrimage, because that's kind of what it is, is as much a way to say *I'm glad we're not meeting at your funereal* as it is to say *thank you for reminding me to get my head out of my ass.* An event like this forces everybody to get back on their A-game."

When they were alone, Paddy told Mairead she had saved his life tonight. He told her the only reason he hadn't died in that hallway was because he needed to see her face again.

"I was done, Mairead. I had nothing left. When the gun came up in my face the last time, I was just waiting for it to blow my head off. But I had a fleeting vision of my partners having to come in here to tell you I bought it in some filthy hallway. I couldn't leave you like that. Somehow, I found the resolve to shove the gun out of my face and do what I had to do to get the fuck out of Dodge. Now you're stuck with me, and it's no one's fault but your own."

"I don't mind being stuck with you, Paddy," Mairead said, as she pulled him closer and rested her head on his shoulder. "But it would be a big help if you could stop trying so hard to get yourself killed."

CHAPTER TWENTY-SIX

July 4, 1992
Glendale, Queens

By the time the two of them got back to Mairead's house, the sun was coming up. The investigation of the shooting gave no one much cause for concern. It looked like a straightforward, justified shooting. The perp turned out to be a known enforcer for the drug cartel. He was, at the time of his death, considered a suspect in several recent shootings, and was the prime suspect in a particularly grisly double homicide. The gun he tried to shoot Paddy with had been stolen in a burglary in New Jersey two years earlier. Later ballistic examinations would match the weapon to several other crimes. The Duty Chief's Unusual Occurrence Report ended with the comforting observation that *there is no community un-rest at this time.* The final imprimatur was bestowed when the detective initially assigned to the case declared it *a bunt.* So after taking a shower, and changing into Mairead's brother's tee shirt and shorts, Paddy crashed on his future in-law's couch, and quickly fell into the deep, dreamless sleep of the innocent.

When Mairead woke Paddy at four o'clock that afternoon, Washington Heights was already burning. Mairead turned the TV on. Paddy was treated to the image of himself being burned in effigy by a mob on 162nd Street. Cars were on fire. Stores were being looted. A female reporter from Channel 5 looked earnestly into the camera and told her audience in a polished tone, as if the material had been written for her, that the riots were in response to the controversial shooting of a bodega clerk by a corrupt and brutal plain-clothes police officer. Nowhere in her report did the word *alleged* appear. That was because the mayor's office was careful to leave it out when they wrote it. The mayor of New York had already promised justice for Reuben Amaro, the would-be-murderer who had died the night before trying to kill a cop. But his status as a killer was just an inconvenient truth to be overlooked in view of the more important political expediency. The City of New York was due to host the Democratic National Convention in a month. The drug cartel, seeing an opportunity to force the police to back off on their aggressive enforcement of the up-town drug trade, made it plain to the mayor's office they were prepared to riot all summer unless they got what they wanted. What they wanted right now was a scapegoat. The mayor of New York was determined to give them the head of Police Officer Padraig Joseph Durr on a stick. But this was all just beginning. Paddy didn't yet appreciate the scope of the forces that were aligning against him.

Paddy's first call was to his partner, Tommy McPhee. Paddy and Tommy had been working together since they partnered up on late tours. While they were well-suited to work together. In reality, they were thrust upon each other. The two of them had been burning out partners separately for the previous year. Finally, their platoon commander suggested they work together. From the beginning it was clear their partnership created a sector car without an off switch. They fed off each other's energy and generally made a nuisance of themselves to the criminals in Washington Heights. They had been slinging guns together since. So many in fact, when openings needed to be filled in the Anti-Crime Unit, there wasn't even a discussion. The two of them were their sergeant's first two picks, in whatever order you wanted to put them.

Tommy told Paddy the newspapers and TV reporters had camped out in front of his co-op in Astoria. Someone in the police department had leaked Paddy's address to the media. They were actually doing live reports from his front doorstep. Meanwhile up-town, the media was putting microphones in front of anyone who cared to spew something. The Anti-Crime Unit was being branded as abusers, murderers, thieves and drug criminals. These were uncited, unsubstantiated and preposterous allegations that were being reported as fact. Even as the mayor was calling for calm, the drug dealers were importing and paying rioters from other parts of the city to keep the pressure on the police. They were looking to create a law-free zone in Washington Heights, and they were counting on their friend the mayor to help them do it. He had already scheduled a press conference for the following day. Various community activists, politicians and religious leaders were scheduled to attend. The mayor was enlisting as many hands as he could to help him build this particular frame.

Paddy next spoke with the union reps and the attorneys. They agreed he should stay camped out at his future in-law's house. The media and the police department didn't know the address or telephone number yet, so it was thought Paddy might avoid their gauntlet for a while.

As anticipated, the mayor's circus was performed without a flaw. Everyone played their part. The mayor again promised justice for Reuben Amaro. He went another step and announced that the City would pay for Amaro's funeral and burial in the Dominican Republic, using taxpayer money. The politicians and community activists decried the culture of police abuse that allowed the young man to be murdered. Finally, the Cardinal, the head of the Archdiocese of New York, blathered on about how he would bring all of the power and prestige of his position to ensure there were no cover-ups. Paddy was watching the fiasco in the living room with Big Bill, before he was due to meet with his attorneys later that day.

"Isn't he our Cardinal?" Big Bill asked.

"Maybe not after today," Paddy said.

But the showstopper was saved for last. The local corrupt councilman trotted up two women who claimed to be eyewitnesses to Paddy executing Reuben Amaro in the hallway. They told a blood curdling tale of abuse and murder. They claimed to have watched Paddy mercilessly beat the victim into the ground for several minutes before standing over him and shooting him in the back.

"Were they there?" Big Bill asked.

"No, and the only one who got beaten mercilessly that night was me."

"If they weren't there, how can they be witnesses?"

"That's easy, Pop. They can be lying witnesses. That's not really a new phenomenon."

"Are they going to be a problem for you?"

"That depends on how well they can lie," Paddy admitted.

The media onslaught continued day after day. Paddy and his Anti-Crime Unit were slandered daily in the papers and on TV. They were painted in the reports like they were some kind of super-squad of rogue land pirates, beating people, and stealing everything they could get their hands on.

The coverage was horribly and exclusively slanted against Paddy and his partners. With no respite, each successive day brought more bad news. The newspapers seemingly were trying to outdo each other, and the more sensational and outlandish the next allegation was, the more play in the media it got. July of 1992 became the month when responsible journalism, really any journalism, took a hiatus in New York. However, one positive piece showed up in the *New York Post* a few days after the shooting. The First Deputy Police Commissioner, a career cop and well-respected by the rank and file, told a reporter all the evidence available at this time indicated there was nothing to suggest any wrongdoing by the cop. He characterized the shooting as a confrontation between a young and decorated police officer and an armed career criminal already wanted by the police for shooting people.

This was a powerful, thoughtful statement, and it might have gone a long way in changing the public discourse from reactionary scapegoating to a rational examination of the evidence, until the mayor's office ordered the first dep to shut his mouth. The conversation devolved back to sensational allegations, rumors and unchecked hysteria. It was unmitigated nonsense, but it sold a lot of newspapers.

The following day, Paddy's attorneys and union reps got a call from someone in the first deputy commissioner's office. The unnamed staffer, a friend of the cops, informed Paddy's counsel that the mayor's office had issued a moratorium on any statements from the police department regarding the shooting. The story was to be *managed* exclusively by the mayor's press office. In addition, the New York County District Attorney had empaneled a grand jury to investigate this case. All further work on the case going forward would be handled exclusively by the DA's Office. The man from the first dep's office said the official policy and stance of the NYPD in this matter was as follows: nothing. The department was washing their hands of Paddy Durr. So without so much as a wish for good luck, they closed ranks around themselves and threw Paddy to the wolves. This was less than encouraging. It meant that his fate was now in the hands of the District Attorney, himself an elected official. Paddy didn't need a law degree to understand which side of the political expediency he occupied. The easy thing for the DA to do was to just indict Paddy for murder, and punt it to a jury in State Supreme Court. Toward that end, Paddy's lawyers informed him, the DA was seeking to interview him with his attorney present, as a precursor to having him testify in the grand jury, without immunity.

Two nights later, Paddy and Mairead were celebrating Mairead's birthday. They had intended to have dinner at their favorite restaurant on City Island, but recent events made a night out in public inadvisable. Paddy's newfound and unwanted notoriety made leaving home a dicey proposition. At this point, Paddy was still being treated like Public Enemy Number One in the media. While they hadn't found Mairead's house yet, it was just a matter of time before they would. So with this in mind, the Dunleavy family had decamped for the week to their summer home in Vermont, leaving the young lovers the house to themselves. Paddy had tucked his hair under a ball cap, put on sunglasses and a long sleeve tee-shirt to hide his tattoos, and ventured out to buy the ingredients for the meal he would cook that night for Mairead. He was going to try and duplicate their dinner in the Bahamas in January, when they were engaged. So he put on this weak excuse for a disguise, and ventured out into Glendale to shop for dinner, and hide in plain sight.

His first stop was the Karl Ehmer butcher shop on Cooper and Myrtle. Paddy bought a three pound USDA prime chateaubriand and politely ignored the old German butcher's cooking instructions. The next stop was the Edward's Superstore on Myrtle and Freshpond. Paddy took his time traversing the aisles in the supermarket, enjoying his anonymity. He carefully selected the fresh vegetables, dairy and bread he would serve that night. He stopped at the card store before heading to Wolfie's Liquors on Myrtle. There he selected a couple of bottles of a good quality merlot and a fifth of Jameson's Whiskey. His shopping complete, Paddy would have liked to sneak into his apartment in Astoria. But the media were still camped out on his front step. So the emerald pendant with the matching ring he had bought for Mairead last month would have to stay hidden for a while longer.

When Paddy got back to the Dunleavy house, Mairead was just getting home from work. He told Mairead to relax while he prepared dinner. He poured her a glass of the merlot and sent her in to change and decompress for a while. She kept popping back into the kitchen to check on the outrageous aromas emanating from the stove. Paddy kept refilling her glass and sending her back out of the kitchen. But she couldn't stay away for long.

"What am I supposed to wear for this occasion, Chef Paddy?"

"It's your birthday, baby. You can just wear a smile as far as I'm concerned. All else is optional."

When Paddy finally called Mairead to the table, he had outdone himself. He had faithfully reproduced the dinner from January, the night Paddy identified at that point as the happiest day of his life. Everything was perfect. From the hand tossed Caesar's salad with fresh shaved parmesan, to the chateaubriand, tender as warm butter and perfectly done rare, the way Mairead liked it. The grilled vegetable medley with homemade béarnaise sauce was as beautiful on the plate as it was delicious. After the sumptuous meal, Paddy served warm berries in hand-whipped cream with Irish coffee. He apologized for not having Mairead's gift. He explained it was under lock-down at his apartment in Astoria. He tried to describe the jewelry when Mairead stopped him.

"I saw them. They're beautiful."

"How did you see them?"

"Last week when you were in the shower, I saw them in your underwear drawer. By the way, why do you keep everything of value with your underwear?"

"I don't do that."

"Sure you do. It's all right there, your gun, your shield, your handcuffs and your money, and everything you have ever bought for me can be found in that drawer with your underwear."

"I guess I'm going to have to find a new hiding spot."

"Come on, you can't keep anything from me, Paddy Durr. I see it all, and I love every little bit of it."

Paddy let that sink in. He knew it was true. Mairead never lied to him. He didn't think she had the capacity. That's what made what he had to say next that much more difficult. It was breaking his heart, and he was afraid it would break hers too. So he just came out with it.

"I love you, Mairead, but I won't lie to you. This thing uptown is going bad. At the very least, I expect to be indicted for murder."

"So we'll beat it at trial," Mairead said, not batting an eye.

"It's not that simple. And the fact I'm innocent has no bearing on the matter. This is a political hit job. I am the lamb being led to slaughter. The best case scenario has me getting acquitted at trial, but that's two years down the road. Even then, it's only even money that I'll walk. The prosecution may throw so much shit at the wall that the jury might sell out and decide to let some of it stick. That's the reality of it, Mairead. There's nothing but bad broken road ahead. You didn't sign on for this. I can't ask you to endure it. I need to carry this cross alone. With that in mind, if you had any ideas about bailing, now would be the time."

"Fuck that, Paddy Durr!" Mairead said, standing and poking him in the chest. "If I have to take a bus to Riker's Island to marry you in an orange jumpsuit, then that's what I'm going to do. We are bigger than this. You are who I'm supposed to be with. So I don't even have a choice. I thank God every day for sending you to me. No one and nothing is going to come between us. This is *our* cross to bear. You don't get to do it alone. We'll fight them, Paddy. We'll fight them and we'll beat them. So don't talk to me about bailing. It's not even in the realm of possibility. You are my man, my one and only forever, and don't you forget it."

When Paddy pulled Mairead into him and their mouths found each other, it was a forgone conclusion dinner was over, and nothing was getting cleaned up until the following day.

CHAPTER TWENTY-SEVEN

July, 1992
Harlem

Toward the middle of July, things started to happen. Not necessarily good things, but things. The police department had no idea what to do with Paddy. They couldn't suspend him. In spite of all the allegations, he hadn't actually been formally accused of any wrongdoing. They had to put him back to work, but they couldn't return him to the 34th Precinct, what with all the rioting, death threats and burning of him in effigy. So the department gave him a non-job. Paddy was assigned to the Patrol Boro of Manhattan North, which was located within the 24th Precinct in Harlem. His duties consisted of him showing up, and nothing more. He was told he wasn't even permitted to answer the phone at the *Wheel*, which is what the operations desk of the Boro was called. So with that in mind, Paddy came to work in board shorts, a tank top and flip flops. A shoulder holster holding his five shot off-duty revolver was also an essential element of his uniform of the day. Increasingly, the tank top became less essential.

So Paddy split his days between working out in the precinct gym in the basement, and laying on a lounge chair on the roof. If nothing else, he was determined to be tan and fit when they dragged him to jail. Only once did a supervisor question his attire. Sergeant Earnest Spires was the commander of the wheel. He interrupted Paddy as he was on his way up to the roof to tan. Paddy was wearing his board shorts, sunglasses and a smile when Sergeant Spires stopped him. The little man seemed perpetually nervous about something. He had a pinched, red, and constantly runny nose. His eyes darted around as if he was trying to ascertain the presence of a threat. In as much as he was rumored to have been afraid of everything as a cop, perhaps he perceived danger all around him, even in this austere and protected environment, where no police work was expected, and certainly none would get done. Paddy was unconcerned about Sergeant Spires' threat radar. He was just trying to catch the last of the afternoon sun when the annoying little man stopped him.

"Officer Durr," Sergeant Spires addressed him. But he couldn't bring himself to make eye contact with the shirtless and tattooed cop. "Can I speak with you for a minute?"

"Make it a fast minute, Sarge. That sun won't stay up there forever."

"Do you really think this outfit is appropriate for a New York City police officer? The chief works right in that office. Do you think he wants to see you dressed like that?"

"I wouldn't call what the chief does work. And I have it on good authority that he is a good friend and appointee of the mayor. So what he wants is what the mayor wants. Specifically, to see me framed, convicted and buried under the jail. Since that appears to be exactly what is going to happen, why would I give a shit what he or anyone else thinks of my wardrobe?"

The little supervisor was dumbfounded. He had never been spoken to by a cop like that before, but he had been working in the un-real and protective cocoon of the administrative offices of the Patrol Boro of Manhattan North for almost his entire career. So he seldom had contact with a real cop, as opposed to the mealy-mouthed pencil pushers who gravitated to administrative work. They would never dream of speaking to a boss in that fashion for fear they would be banished back to the street. For the kind of cop who worked in the Boro, the idea of having to do real police work was an un-endurable horror. Paddy slipped by the sergeant and headed up the stairs to the roof. There hopefully, he could cook off some of the bad Ju-Ju coursing through his veins like so much battery acid.

CHAPTER TWENTY-EIGHT

July 15, 1992
Manhattan

Later that week, Paddy and his PBA attorney Rich Kornreich sat down to be interviewed by the District Attorney. This was a formal Q and A that was a necessary prelude to Paddy testifying in the grand jury. Since the case had been taken over by the DA, the PBA had little information as to the intent of the District Attorney in this matter. They had no idea how confrontational the Q and A would be. They were going in blind. Without any indication to the contrary, Paddy and his defense team planned for the worst. They expected a full-on ambush. The first clue this might not be so, was when they found out who the Senior Bureau Chief was handling the case. Peter Bergdorf had been one of the DA's go-to crisis managers for many years. To Paddy and Riches' surprise, he was not one of the reviled head hunters in the DA's Office they expected to face. Bergdorf's reputation for honesty and fairness was well known. In fact, he was highly regarded by the police. In 1988 he had won a difficult conviction in the murder of a young patrolman in Midtown South. During a robbery, the young cop, who was looking for one of the perpetrators who had fled to the roof, got kicked six stories down an airshaft by the suspect. The case was difficult because there was only two witnesses to the event on the roof, and one of them was dead. The case was circumstantial and regarded by everyone in the know as weak. While a conviction would be wonderful, no one was getting their hopes up.

Except for Peter Bergdorf. He fully expected to get a conviction. He spent the two weeks of the trial living out of his office. When he was not in court, he was preparing witnesses, reviewing evidence and shoring up any perceived weaknesses in the State's presentation of their case. His performance in court was masterful. He had the jury riveted to the testimony and evidence he introduced. Circumstantial though it was, Bergdorf made it all so compelling. By the end of the government's case, the defendant's lawyer was looking for a plea bargain. But the DA doesn't plea bargain cop murders. So, the defense was going to have to try and mount their case. Bergdorf had anticipated every tactic they might use, and refuted in cross examination every argument they made. But Bergdorf's best work on the case was saved for his closing statement. He dutifully enumerated and highlighted all of the evidence and testimony proving the defendant's guilt, but then he spent the next forty-five minutes lovingly painting a picture of the victim, Police Officer Anthony Boyle. Bergdorf, ordinarily reserved, allowed himself to get emotional. He never met the young cop, but he did his due diligence to get to know him intimately. Bergdorf interviewed everyone, from family members and co-workers, to his distraught young fiancé. He went so far as to interview Anthony's high school football coach, camp counselors and grade-school teachers. By the time Bergdorf had finished, every person in the courtroom felt they had lost someone extraordinary that meant the world to them. The jury returned the conviction in less than twenty minutes. The cops in Midtown South loved Peter Bergdorf like a brother because of it.

The interview started with Bergdorf's investigator, John Cantwell reading Miranda warnings to Paddy. This was expected, so it wasn't as ominous as it might have been. Cantwell, who was a retired Detective from Manhattan North Homicide, read the warnings with a professional detachment, but when he looked at Paddy for his responses, with his eyes alone the old detective conveyed his sympathy for the young cop, and his distaste for having to treat him like a suspect.

The questioning was straightforward enough. Bergdorf started by asking Paddy background questions, like where he was born, where he lived now, what schools he attended. Bergdorf wanted to know about the sports he played, the organizations and clubs he belonged to, the church he attended and any volunteering and community service he may have performed. He went over Paddy's entire employment history before he came on the department. When Bergdorf asked Paddy about family relationships, Paddy glossed over his non-relationship with his mother and father and three dead brothers and got right to his fiancée Mairead and her family, into which he had adopted himself. Two things stood out in Paddy's mind regarding this line of questioning. The first thing was that Bergdorf did not seem at all surprised Paddy was in a hurry to drop the subject of his birth family. This gave Paddy an inkling the DA had already done his homework. He wasn't asking any questions he didn't already know the answers to. The second thing Paddy noted was the DA's careful enumeration of the things which made him who he was as a person. The time and focus Bergdorf put on things like his coaching youth football and volunteering with the food and coat drives at the precinct every Christmas convinced Paddy Bergdorf wasn't going to try and present him to the grand jury as a thug with a badge.

The next subject examined was Paddy's short but eventful police career. They covered his assignments from the Police Academy, through field training and his work at the 34th Precinct. Bergdorf went into detail regarding Paddy's time in Washington Heights. They went over his arrest record, which was prodigious. They went over his Civilian Complaint and disciplinary record which was minuscule. They went over his previous shootings and the dispositions of them by both the DA and the Firearms Discharge Review Board of the NYPD. Bergdorf particularly wanted to know how Paddy had felt after his previous shooting where several of the perps had been killed. Paddy told Bergdorf the act of shooting another person, irrespective of the fact they were shooting at him, was a difficult thing. But he much preferred the emotional discomfort to the alternative, an inspector's funeral. Paddy assured the DA he had reconciled himself to the fact that he did what had to be done. Bergdorf then asked him how he felt about the time he had been shot. Paddy swallowed hard, and answered woodenly that he was fine. The wound was minor and it healed fast. He didn't think about it much anymore. He said he understood when you exchange fire with bad people, the likelihood is that somebody might get shot, maybe you. He was okay with it.

What he didn't tell Bergdorf was that he had been shot by one of his partners, and he was decidedly not okay with it. This partner, and he really fulfilled none of the requisites of the word, should not have been in Anti-Crime at all. In fact, if Paddy and his partner Tommy hadn't intervened and told the sergeant they would take Gus Demario under their wings, put a leash on him, and mold him into a useful member of the team, then he would have already been launched back to uniform patrol. They felt bad for Gus, so they didn't let it happen. But Gus Demario was an energetic screw-up. So he was difficult to leash. He would jump out of the car without warning and go running off to who knows where, after who knows what, without ever bothering to inform his partners. He was impulsive, obnoxious and as dumb as a box of hammers. He also had the disconcerting habit of firing his gun at inopportune times, like when his partners were in the line of fire.

At this particular time, Paddy and Tommy's chief concern was trying to figure out how to keep the idiot in the car. No amount of reasoning with Gus had any effect. He would yes you to death with a look in his eyes that made it clear he either didn't hear the conversation, or didn't understand it was about him. Having no other alternative, Paddy and Tommy rigged the rear doors of the unmarked so they could only be opened from the outside. Now when Gus got the uncontrollable urge to flee the car and chase phantoms, all he could do was pathetically pull at the disabled door handle and demand to be let out. Paddy or Tommy or both of them together would end the conversation by telling him in no uncertain terms to *sit down and shut the fuck up!*

While Demario could no longer escape and do random unpredictable damage, he still had to be let out of the car when it was appropriate to take police action. Unfortunately, even under these controlled circumstances, he was still a menace to himself and everyone else, particularly everyone else.

The night Gus Demario shot Paddy in the back was one of those times. Two other team members, Sean Moran and Peter O'Malley had an informant who always seemed to be around when things were jumping off. The informant ran in peculiar circles, being friends with drug dealers, gun runners and stick-up crews. He would provide the Anti-Crime Team with a heads up that something was about to go down. In this case, it was a gun sale. A crew from 173rd Street and Audubon Avenue were going to deliver five guns to a stick-up team in front of the McDonalds on Broadway and

170th Street. The stick-up guys were in turn going to use these guns to knock over a drug spot in the Bronx.

When Sean and Pete got the tip that night, they called a conference with the entire Anti-Crime team, meeting in front of Columbia Presbyterian's emergency room. Paddy, Tommy and Gus were in one car. Sean and Pete were in another. Sergeant Kevin Touhey and Armando Gigante were in the last. A quick tactical plan was formulated. Paddy, Tommy and Gus would set up at 169th Street on Broadway, facing north. Sean and Pete would set up on 170th and Broadway, opposite the scheduled delivery spot. Sergeant Touhey and Armando set up on 171St Street and Broadway. When the deal was about to go down, and everybody and the guns were on the set, the informant was to take his hat off and wipe his forehead. Then the Anti-Crime team would converge on the gathering and take everybody down. It was a simple, straight forward plan. What could go wrong?

A short time into the surveillance, the team noted the arrival of the informant in the company of three other males. One of them had a large manila envelope which was believed to have the money for the guns inside. The informant had told Sean and Pete the guns were to cost $2,000, four hundred a gun.

The team kept each other up-dated on their point to point radios. Sergeant Touhey told the team that he and Armando would take the guy with the envelope. In order for a gun sale arrest to stick, you had to have the money. Otherwise you merely had a criminal possession of a weapon collar. Good work to be sure, but pale in comparison to a gun sale beef.

A minute later Paddy spotted four males crossing Broadway at 170th Street. The shortest of the four was holding a backpack that appeared to be heavy. He also had a big black pistol sticking out of his waistband. As Paddy let everyone know what he was seeing, the informant made a demonstrative display of removing his Oakland Athletics ball cap, and wiping his head so vigorously you might have thought he was trying to wipe away his long and resplendent jherri curls. Sergeant Touhey ordered Paddy to get the backpack guy. Everyone else would take down whomever was left. When the sergeant gave the execute order, the Anti-Crime team leapt from their cars and engaged the perps.

Paddy descended on the perp with the backpack. He was a step away from tackling him to the sidewalk when the perp abruptly stopped and pulled the gun from his waistband, and in one motion dropped it on the ground. As the perp threw his hands in the air, Paddy heard two pistol cracks. Everything after seemed to happen in slow motion, even as it all occurred in an instant. Sometimes, in moments of pure chaos, your mind slows down. It separates and orders the important facts, giving you the ability to understand it and process the information with a clarity that had no business being there amidst all the bedlam and confusion. So Paddy understood the object that snapped through his long hair, just to the right of his ear was a bullet, fired from somewhere behind him. A second after, he knew with certainty the exploding pain in his back, which felt like he had been hit with a nine pound sledge was the second shot. As he was falling upon the perp, or falling from the incredible impact from being shot, Paddy considered the following; both shots had come from behind him. There were no suspects back there. He had heard no other shots. As he tried to wrestle the perp weakly into handcuffs and draw a breath which just wouldn't come, Paddy looked back in that direction. His partners, Gus Demario and Tommy McPhee were the only ones who had been behind him. Gus was the only one with his weapon out. Paddy could see a faint wisp of smoke still emanating from the barrel of Gus' recently fired gun. So there was no mystery to solve. Gus Demario had tried to kill him, and he just might have succeeded.

All the perps were taken into custody. Sergeant Touhey came running up to Paddy. The sergeant had his perp in one hand, and the envelope of money in the other. Touhey ordered the perp to lie face down on the ground next to Paddy's handcuffed suspect. Paddy had the backpack and it was full of guns, but Touhey didn't care about that at the moment.

"Who shot?" the sergeant demanded.

"Nobody's shot," Paddy told him, answering a different question than the one asked.

"No," the sergeant tried to clarify. "Who shot?"

"Nobody's shot," Paddy repeated. The exchange was starting to sound like Abbot and Costello's *who's on first* skit. But then a look of grave concern came over Kevin Touhey's face. He grabbed Paddy by the right elbow and turned him around. The back of Paddy's flannel shirt had become a curtain of blood. It was drenching his jeans and pooling at his feet. Touhey showed Paddy his hand, soaked with blood from where he touched him.

"Who shot, Paddy?" Kevin asked him again.

"I'm shot, Sarge," Paddy admitted as his eyes rolled up in his head. He would have hit the floor if Kevin and Tommy McPhee hadn't been there to catch him. They immediately carried him over to the unmarked to rush him to the hospital. Touhey ordered everyone, Anti-Crime cops and perps, who were all injured in the fracas to one extent or another, to get to the hospital forthwith. Touhey informed central dispatch they were transporting a shot member of the service and six injured perps to Columbia Presbyterian. He informed the patrol supervisor the block had to be held as a crime scene. The last thing Kevin Touhey did before rushing Paddy the three blocks to the hospital was address Gus Demario.

"If he dies, I'm coming to your house and I'm killing you in your own kitchen, you reckless motherfucker." Then Kevin jumped in the unmarked, hit the lights and siren and rushed his bleeding cop to the hospital.

When they got to the emergency room, Tommy and Kevin carried Paddy into the hospital, despite Paddy protesting that he could walk. They were descended upon by the ER staff. Paddy was put on a gurney and rushed into the crash room. He was searching for Mairead, who was working that day. He started to panic when he couldn't find her. Mairead's friend and fellow nurse, Annie Hoffman calmed Paddy. She explained Mairead was filling in at the pediatric emergency room around the corner. She promised Paddy she would personally run over to tell Mairead, and to assure her he was alright. Paddy thanked her, but neither he nor Annie were sure that he was alright.

Once in the crash room, the trauma nurses began cutting away Paddy's clothing. He told them he had been struck just the one time in the back. They believed him, but cut everything anyway. When they got to his blood soaked vest, the trauma surgeon located the bullet, imbedded in the layers of Kevlar. The projectile had not defeated the vest, but when the surgeon removed it, he could see the impact and the expended energy of the bullet had done fearsome damage. Though the bullet hadn't penetrated his torso, there was a jagged hole where the expanding energy of the round had torn his skin open. Paddy's right latissimus dorsi muscle, red, blue and enflamed, looked like it had been hammered to paste. The surgeon winced to look at it. The round had broken ribs on impact, at least two. The deep-red oxygenated blood leaking from Paddy's back made the surgeon fear that the lung had been punctured and collapsed. The fact that Paddy couldn't breathe, and the presence of a faint whistling sound coming from the wound confirmed it. The doctor applied a pressure bandage and ordered Paddy to x-ray.

Annie had run to inform Mairead of what had happened. She evidently told her more than was necessary, because Mairead knew the perps were also in the hospital. After she was sure Paddy was okay, after a fashion, she got right down to business.

"Which one of those scumbags shot you? I'm going to inject his heart with adrenalin and blow it up."

Paddy laughed at her fury, which was a mistake, because he started coughing up blood. Thankfully, this subsided quickly.

"Relax, baby. Gus shot me."

"Again?"

"Not again, last time he missed."

"Somebody has to stop that maniac before he kills one of you."

"Baby, I'm not worried about Gus Demario right now. I'm scared. I don't want the last face I see in this world to be some doctor. Just stay with me."

Mairead stayed with him. She held his hand through the x-rays. She was by his side in surgery when they put Paddy out to re-inflate his lung. She was there when he woke up. Though Paddy couldn't talk because the doctors had inserted an intubation tube down his throat, Mairead stayed with him and talked to him soothingly. She told Paddy about all the visitors and well-wishers he had. She got a little hot when she told him the mayor and police commissioner were too busy to visit. They sent a flunky over with a proclamation of some sort. Paddy wasn't surprised when Mairead said she tore it up and threw it at the guy's feet before chasing him off the ward. She brightened a little when she told Paddy Kevin Touhey had promised her he would make sure Gus was never again in a position where he could be a danger to anyone.

A couple of days later, when the tube came out of his throat, Paddy was visited by the detectives from the 34 Squad. Paddy told them the sanitized version of what happened, that he and his teammates had agreed upon. He left out the part about being shot by Gus. Because Paddy couldn't, or wouldn't say who shot him, and because the other Anti-Crime members wouldn't either, no one could be charged with attempted murder. The perps still went down for the gun sale and assault, but that was small potatoes. The detective's knew Paddy and his partners were covering for one of their guys, but they also knew they would never change their story. So they let it go.

Demario was on the list to make sergeant. Until he could be promoted, Sergeant Touhey gave him the option of a clerical spot in the Anti-Crime office, or going back to late tours. Demario elected to do the clerical job. Paddy never admitted to anyone but Mairead that Gus had been the one who shot him. He knew his other partners knew, but he wouldn't discuss it with them, and he wouldn't let them discuss it in front of him. He was determined to take this one to the grave.

Peter Bergdorf might have suspected there was more to the incident than was being discussed, but it was in the past and not germane to his present investigation. So he let whatever doubts he might have had pass.

The DA next got into the nuts and bolts of the shooting. He asked all the questions pertaining to what Paddy observed, thought, and reacted to. He went second by second through the confrontation until finally it was done. The perp was down. The weapon recovered. Everyone accounted for. The last thing Peter Bergdorf wanted to know this day was whether Paddy had seen anybody else in the hallway or on the steps. Paddy assured Bergdorf that he and Amaro were the only ones in the lobby that night, and he was the only one to leave alive. Satisfied for now, Bergdorf thanked Paddy and Rich Kornreich for coming in. They agreed to meet again the following Thursday for any follow-up questions, prior to Paddy's testimony in the grand jury on Friday.

When paddy and Rich left the DA's office, they headed over to the *Pig and Thistle* on Lafayette Street to get a bite to eat and discuss today's meeting. They sat in a booth and ordered soup and burgers, and waited until the waitress left them alone to talk.

"I don't get the impression they're looking to harpoon you," Rich said.

"No, no real curveballs today."

"We'll know better after Thursday."

CHAPTER TWENTY-NINE

July 22, 1992
Manhattan

The ensuing Thursday arrived. Paddy and Rich Kornreich were at the DA's Office at 1 Hogan Place as requested. The DA's investigator, John Cantwell came out to the lobby. Cantwell asked Paddy if he would be willing to temporarily surrender his service revolver to the DA, so it could be independently tested by the FBI's ballistic lab in Washington D.C. Cantwell promised he would personally have custody of the gun throughout the process, and would return it to Paddy the same evening when he returned from the Capitol. Paddy didn't have a problem with it, but he deferred to Rich Kornreich.

"What's the purpose of the re-test, didn't the NYPD Ballistics Section test it?"

"Yes, of course. And there were no surprises with the results. But we're duplicating everything independently."

"Again," Rich asked. "Why?"

"When this thing goes the way we expect it to, we don't want to give anyone the opportunity to suggest there was any collusion. Hence, the FBI. They're elitist numbskulls, but nobody questions them."

That was the first hard indication from the DA's office that the case was going to be fairly presented to the grand jury. The next indication was the title of the case as reflected on Paddy's grand jury subpoena. The first one, issued a week previously to cover Paddy's first Q and A session, was titled *The People of the State of New York Vs. Police Officer Padraig Joseph Durr*. The crime under investigation was listed as Penal Law Code 125.25, murder in the second degree. The subpoena for today's appearance had been amended. The title now read *The Investigation into the Shooting Death of Reuben Amaro*. The section for the Penal Law Code had been left blank. The last indication that Paddy was going to get a fair deal was delivered by Cantwell with a conspiratorial wink.

"You're going to start to see some things in the paper after today," Cantwell predicted. "The story should be turning around somewhat."

"How is that supposed to happen? I thought I was public enemy number one."

"Various unnamed sources from the DA's Office will probably be leaking certain items of evidence and testimony to the media we expect to be presented in the grand jury. You might see a fair amount of your background in there as well. It's a good story. When people find out who you are and the things you've done, they're going to like you."

"That would be some turnaround," Paddy observed.

"It would be, but it's justified. The only one not likely to be happy about it is the mayor. We told him the real deal on this, but he still wants you to swing for it. He said something about the greater good and *the needs of the city*. He practically demanded you be indicted. The big Boss had to remind him the DA was an elected official as well, operating independently of the mayor's office. Nowhere in his job description did the words *greater good* or *needs of the city* appear. Words like *truth, justice and fair and equal protection for all under the law* kept showing up prominently. So the DA told him he was going to stick with those things."

"How did the mayor take that?" Rich Kornreich asked.

"Not well. He called it an outrage."

Peter Bergdorf's second round of questioning was much briefer than his first. He took the time to narrowly and specifically establish and or reiterate several important points. Namely, the presence, or rather absence of any alleged witnesses in the lobby of the building, or on the stairway up to the first landing. He also wanted to establish which way Amaro was facing when Paddy shot him. This told Paddy the DA had found the rounds that went through Amaro, killing him.

When Bergdorf was done with all of that, he asked John Cantwell if there was anything else they needed to address. Cantwell thrust his chin in the direction of a three-by-four foot poster board leaning against the wall. Bergdorf nodded in agreement and picked up the poster board and turned it around for Paddy to see. Finally, a curve ball, the board was filled with the face-forward and profile views of suspects in the classic NYPD booking photo. But these *wets*, as they were called, were all just a little different than the usual mug shots. Some of the suspects were bandaged with gauze turbans and dried blood on their heads and faces. Some others were severely bruised and swollen about the eyes and lips in an almost cartoonish caricature of the human face. Paddy immediately recognized every one of them. They were all people who he had arrested for serious felonies, dating back to his first collar. They also shared the poor decision making skills which allowed them to opt to try and violently resist their lawful arrests. Paddy anticipated Bergdorf's next question, so he did some quick math. The poster board had six rows of five photos, thirty all together. Paddy knew from his last Detective Bureau interview that he had over 340 felony arrests. So when Bergdorf asked his question, Paddy was ready for it.

"Do you recognize these photos?"

"Every one of those guys were arrested by me for a violent felony, and resisting arrest."

"This seems a little excessive for just resisting arrest."

"That depends on what you consider resisting. I'm not talking about some weak-ass, run of the mill refusing to put your hands behind your back. You can't get charged for resisting arrest by me for that. These guys resisted arrest by trying to take my head off, or shoot me. Some of them tried to stab me. Two of them came at me with tire irons. One of them had an axe handle. That's the kind of resisting arrest I'm talking about."

"Some of these guys are hideous. How do you account for that?" the DA asked.

"That," Paddy said, pointing at the photos, "is an extraordinary example of personal restraint."

"How does one derive restraint from this?"

"Those photos were all taken a day after I arrested them. They were alive to pose for them, as opposed to being photographed on a slab at the morgue. I could have shot and killed every last one of them and been justified. Instead I elected to fight them into handcuffs, causing injury to myself more often than not. They also represent less than nine percent of the people I ever arrested. So yeah, I'm going with restraint."

"Even still, these guys are pretty well beaten to shit."

"I don't like using violence. It's never my choice to do so. But I'm not going to apologize for being better at it than the people trying to kill me. If you force me to hit you, you should understand that I'm going to start breaking things you don't want broken."

Bergdorf was impressed with Paddy's quick thinking and explanation for his actions. He remarked that Paddy had not wasted his Columbia education. He asked him if he ever thought of going to law school.

"I considered it. But then I remembered the only time a lawyer gets to help someone is when he's trying to undo the fucking another lawyer is trying to give them."

"That hurt," Bergdorf said.

"I'm just kidding. I didn't have any money for law school. So I chose to do this. Who knew I would like it so much?"

"Last question," Bergdorf promised. "With all that has transpired since the shooting, how do you feel about it right now?"

Paddy thought about that for a moment. What he kept coming back to was what the enormous stress was doing to Mairead. So he shared that with Peter Bergdorf.

"My fiancée, Mairead, is the sweetest, kindest person you could ever hope to meet. She's way too good for me," Paddy admitted. "A month ago she was planning our wedding and our *happy ever after*. She didn't have a care in the world beyond picking out her wedding dress and considering the infinite possibilities life seemed to promise her. Now her whole world is upside down. She hasn't had a full night's sleep since she thought I died in that hallway. I lay awake all night next to her, listening to her cry. She's guilty of nothing but loving a man who seems to be a lightning rod for trouble. She doesn't deserve this, and there isn't a damned thing I can do for her. When I see what this is doing to Mairead, I wish I had taken off that day. I wish I had been hit by a car on my way to work. Anything to spare her this. This is the first time since I took this job that I wish I had decided to do something else for a living. Worse than that, when I see

Mairead suffering, I secretly wish she had never met me. I think she might have been better off."

Bergdorf processed all of that. He felt bad for the struggling cop in front of him, but he liked what he heard.

"That's the last question I'm going to ask you in front of the grand jury tomorrow. You should answer it the same way. And if it's possible, you might want to muster a tear or two."

"I'm not really a crier."

The following day Paddy was sworn in as a witness in front of the grand jury. He answered questions for three hours. There were no surprises. During the questioning Paddy noted certain points in his testimony where the jurors seemed to nod, as if what they were hearing from him somehow cleared up or explained something they had heard previously. Paddy took this as a good sign.

As promised, Peter Bergdorf ended the questioning with the open ended inquiry regarding Paddy's emotional state. He answered much as he did the day before. To Paddy's surprise, he managed to squeak out one tear. A moment later, he wished he hadn't. One of the Grand Jurors, a small, officious, and energetic man, asked for permission to approach the witness. He came directly to the witness stand and leaned in to look at Paddy. He turned around and verified for the other jurors he observed a tear on the witnesses' face. Then he asked the DA for permission to physically verify the tear was real. Paddy answered for Peter Bergdorf.

"Touching me doesn't come with the price of admission," Paddy informed the little man. "You've gotten all you're gonna get out of me today. Go sit down."

Bergdorf thanked Paddy for his time and testimony, dismissing him.

CHAPTER THIRTY

August, 1992
Manhattan

As John Cantwell had predicted, the story in the media turned around. Information was leaked by unnamed law enforcement sources. The alleged witnesses against Paddy were now being referred to as the drug cartel employees they were. The lab reports by the FBI, which all supported Paddy's testimony, and totally refuted the allegations against him, were dutifully reported. The victim, Reuben Amaro, previously referred to in the media as a bodega clerk and clothing merchant, was acknowledged as a drug enforcer, wanted for murder. The best item by far though, was an editorial piece by the raconteur reporter Matt Mulvey. Mulvey liked to write about cops. But, it was seldom anything positive. He was fond of inserting himself into corruption stories. He would run them into the ground. Then months later, when everyone had almost forgotten about the story, Mulvey would release a book sensationalizing the bad cops all over again. This was a lucrative pursuit, but it served little purpose other than to turn people against the police.

In this particular article, Mulvey highlighted the key facts refuting the allegations against Paddy. Graphically written, the information was too precise and accurate to come from anywhere other than the grand jury minutes. After exposing the witnesses against Paddy as liars, Mulvey spent the second half of the article going over the gunfight, and the forensic evidence that verified Paddy's testimony. By the time Mulvey finished the article, he had declared Paddy a hero, with just enough vulnerability and sensitivity to remain likeable. Paddy read the article and wanted to throw up. He was uncomfortable with the idea of being a hero. He knew how close he came to being killed, and he blamed his own stupidity and bad tactics for it.

The article was accompanied by a second one detailing Paddy's background, with an emphasis on his life with Mairead. Someone had given the Daily News a photo of them. They were at the restaurant in the Bahamas the night they got engaged. They were tan and attractive. They were looking at each other so adoringly, there was no doubt they were deeply in love. Even with the grainy newsprint quality, you wanted to climb into the photo to be with them. Everyone wanted to be that happy just once in their lives. Paddy knew the photo could have only come from one place.

"Who did you give that picture to?" he asked Mairead that night.

"What picture?" Mairead said, playing dumb.

"The one at the Courtyard Terrace, when I was whispering in your ear. I told you I was going to bring you back to the hotel room and knock the bottom right out of you."

"You're a pig, Paddy Durr!" she said slapping his chest. "And you did not say that to me."

"Who did you give the picture to, Mairead?" Paddy asked again, laughing.

"Your friend, Eamon Mulroney from the PBA," she finally admitted.

"That's my favorite picture of us, and if you remember correctly, when we got back to the room, I did knock the bottom right out of you."

"Yes, I remember, but if you had said that, I never would have let you."

CHAPTER THIRTY-ONE

August, 1992
Washington Heights

After the story turned around, and the rioting continued unabated, the mayor finally figured out that the drug cartel bosses were not his friends, even if they did help him steal the election three years earlier by delivering illegal-alien voters in droves, and hiring surrogates to impersonate dead people. They had their own agenda. Their sole motivation in all of this was to loosen the police enforcement of their very lucrative interests. They didn't care one little bit if the mayor was going to lose his beloved Democratic National Convention. When the chairman of the DNC suggested they might move the convention to Philadelphia, the mayor was apoplectic. He finally ordered the police department to crush the rioting by any means necessary, and keep a lid on it until after the convention.

Thousands of cops had been detailed to quell the riots for weeks now, but they weren't authorized by their bosses to actually deploy. So they stayed in their vans at the staging-point at 125th Street and the Westside Highway. No one in charge had a plan, or the intestinal fortitude to execute one. Finally, the report that the mob was marching on the 34th Precinct was sent to the temporary headquarters at the station house. As their progress was reported on their way up Broadway from 162nd Street, the big bosses of the NYPD were unenthusiastic about making a decision. They argued with each other why someone else should take charge. Finally,

140

Nick Aspramonte, who had been living at the precinct since the rioting started, stepped forward.

"This is my command," he informed the Chief of Operations. "Can I be in charge for a while?"

The bosses were delighted. This was a no-lose situation for them. If, as they expected, it turned into a disaster, they not only had a scapegoat, but the very guy they would have chosen to throw under the bus. If he somehow succeeded, they could steal the credit.

"What makes you think you can do this?" the Chief of Patrol asked.

"I faced longer odds in Hue City in 1968. Besides, I have no career to protect, as you so frequently remind me. So I figure, what the Hell?"

Having assumed command, Nick brought all the captains and lieutenants on the detail into his office. He had a blown up map of the precinct covering an entire wall. He started drawing arrows and vectors on the map indicating avenues of dispersal for the crowd once their progress had been halted. His plan was simple enough, and relied on the basic impulse most people have not to be clubbed over the head and arrested.

The plan worked like a charm. As Nick had predicted, the vast majority of the mob melted away when they discovered the police were in earnest. Even still, over three hundred rioters were arrested. Subsequent questioning of the defendants revealed that most of them were from Brooklyn and the Bronx. They had been paid fifty dollars a day by the Washington Heights Drug Cartel to come and riot. Most importantly, the crowd was dispersed. For all intents and purposes, the riot was over.

Later that night, the police commissioner arrived at the 34th Precinct. The new PC was grateful for the excellent job done on his behalf. He inquired who conceived the plan. The Chief of Operations, the Chief of Patrol, and the Chief of Manhattan North were preparing to take the credit, when Captain Paul Carmody, the President of the Captains Endowment Association, piped up from the rear. Like Nick Aspramonte, Carmody had no career trajectory to protect, and he had no ambition other than to look out for the guys in his union.

"Those stuffed shirts you're glad handing were hiding in the precinct when Nick Aspramonte drew this thing up and led it on the ground," Carmody informed the commissioner. The chiefs were furious, but they weren't about to get into a pissing contest with the rambunctious union leader. Experience had taught them Carmody was a guy that just didn't give a shit. The axiom held, never get into fights with people who have nothing to lose. So they wisely kept their mouths shut.

The commissioner already was acquainted with his 34th Precinct Commanding Officer. They had met many times as members of the NYPD Marine Corps Association. Both of them had served with distinction in Vietnam. That was a bond which ran deeper than NYPD politics.

When Nick stepped forward at the commissioner's order, the PC lit up and warmly embraced him.

"My old friend from Hue City, when God looks out for a Marine, he sends another Marine. I'm gratified you were here. I won't forget what you've done for the city today."

True to his word, the PC did not forget. Within two years, *Captain Forever* Nick Aspramonte was promoted to Chief of Manhattan North. Two years after, he was elevated to the super-chief rank of three stars, and installed as Chief of Patrol, a rank and position he was content to retire at. Paddy went to see him on the day of his promotion to three-star-chief. Nick freely credited Paddy with creating the environment for him to salvage his career. Paddy offered to burn the city for him whenever he thought it was needed. They laughed, but Nick said in all seriousness, if ever Paddy needed anything on this job, he better not hear about it from someone else. Paddy thanked him and put that contract in his back pocket for future use.

When Ronnie Kingsbury asked if he could help him get into TARU, Paddy remembered Nick Aspramonte's promise. He told Ronnie he thought he could. Paddy called the Chief of Patrol's office. After the greetings and catching up, Nick got down to business.

"What can I do for you, Paddy?"

"I've got a friend who is being picked up by the detective bureau. He's a great street cop, but he's a tech-nerd. He wants to go to TARU. To be honest, I want him there too. It would be refreshing to have a real cop there to deal with for a change."

"TARU is a bit of a tough nut to crack. The PC is trying to make the details look more diversified and inclusive."

Paddy knew this would come up. Diversity and inclusion were big code words for the chief. He had been using them for years to justify taking care of his Latin-American teammates on the NYPD Softball team.

"You know I don't buy into that diversity crap. It should be the best applicant for the job, regardless of where your ancestors came from. If they were such hot shit in the first place, why did they have to leave? But on that score you can relax. Ronnie Kingsbury is African-American."

"Is he African-American like Armando Gigante was Mexican? Don't think I forgot how you snuck that big gringo past me in the *three four*."

"Ronnie was born, raised and still lives in Brooklyn with his family. He graduated from Brooklyn Tech ten years after I did. This is a guy you can get behind."

"I'll see what I can do," Nick told Paddy.

A month later, Ronnie Kingsbury was permanently assigned to TARU, and Paddy had a contact within the unit to deal with exclusively. Which was just as well, given the turbulent nature of his relationship with them in the past.

CHAPTER THIRTY-TWO

October 13, 2013
Queens

When Paddy got to TARU with Sergio Mendez' old cell phone, he called Ronnie Kingsbury from the front of the building. Ronnie came out to escort Paddy to his desk. Paddy gave Ronnie the phone. He expertly disassembled it and extracted the sim card. He gave the small plastic chip a cursory examination before inserting it into the sim card reader attached to his computer terminal. Then the detectives waited and watched the hourglass icon on the computer screen over the word *loading*. After a few minutes of watching the unchanging screen, Ronnie voiced some concern.

"It shouldn't be taking this long."

"I didn't think so, but this is your bailiwick. If it were left up to me, we would still be using call boxes and carrier pigeons."

As Paddy was saying as much, the screen changed abruptly. A dialogue box with a surfeit of exclamation points informed the detectives *the device was not recognized,* and *no data was detected.*

"I'm no expert," Paddy said. "But that can't be good."

"That's what we call an epic failure."

"That's just terrific. What do we do now, Ron?"

"Let me take a better look at that sim card. Maybe I can clean it up and salvage something."

Ronnie took a felt pad out of his desk drawer. He removed the sim card from the reader and placed it on the pad. Then he brought over a self-standing combination spot lamp and magnifying glass. This he used to further illuminate the sim card. Also from his desk drawer, Ronnie pulled out a zippered case. Inside was a pair of jewelers' glasses and a tool kit. He put on the glasses and used a set of rubber tipped forceps to closely examine the phone chip. The noises he made as he looked at the sim card did not inspire much confidence.

"There is nothing here," Ronnie finally said.

"You mean it's a blank sim card?"

"No. It isn't a sim card at all. I mean there is *nothing* here."

"I'm not following you."

"Take a look. A sim card is supposed to have magnetized gold plating on the edges of it. That's where the data is stored. It's what makes it a computer chip. You can see what I mean on this one," Ronnie said, producing another sim card from out of his desk drawer. Paddy looked at the two cards side by side. The difference was obvious.

"So someone scraped the data off the sim card?" Paddy asked.

"More like dissolved it."

"Could he have dropped it in a puddle, or maybe in the toilet?" Paddy asked.

"Water would warp the card. It wouldn't completely evaporate the data. It would have had to be acid, or some other corrosive substance."

Paddy called Sergio Mendez from his cell phone. He had to get to the bottom of what happened to the sim card. Paddy put the call on speaker so Ronnie could hear it as well. Sergio answered the phone and asked Paddy expectantly how he made out with the sim card. Sergio was confused when Paddy told him the sim card was blank.

"What was the reason you decided to get a new phone?" Paddy asked.

"I accidentally dropped it in liquid and fried the screen."

"Please explain."

"My brother is a photography buff. I was in his dark room with him. He was developing a picture of my girlfriend. I was bending over, looking at the picture materialize in the stop-bath-tub when my phone fell out of my shirt pocket and into the liquid."

"Did your brother happen to say what the liquid in the tub was?"

"He said it was a mixture of acetic acid, citric acid and silver nitrate," Sergio said.

"That would dissolve anything," Ronnie said.

"Including this lead. Back to square one."

CHAPTER THIRTY-THREE

October13, 2013
Brooklyn

When Paddy got back to the 83 Squad with the worthless sim card and cellphone, he had a host of other issues to deal with before planning his next investigative step on the homicide. Squad detectives only get four consecutive working days to run with a fresh homicide. After that, they are still responsible for the case, but they go back on the catching chart and have to work on everything with equal vigor. At least that was the theory. No detective worth a grain of salt would prioritize the myriad of domestic dispute allegations and misdemeanor assaults that were really just arguments among spouses or neighbors, over a homicide or shooting case. In reality, the everyday paper that usually crossed a detective's desk were just balls to juggle. The idea was to keep them in the air until they could be properly dispensed with. In spite of their lack of importance, these garbage cases were still time consuming and sucked away hours which were already scarce.

Paddy accessed his open case file in the computer on his desk. He saw that he caught two aggravated harassment cases, one of them domestic, and two grand larceny cases that were either lost property or false reports. Paddy knocked out fives on three of the cases indicating he had caught them and that they were being actively investigated. The other aggravated harassment case required immediate attention because of the domestic violence aspect. Paddy did a DV check on the alleged victim and her address.

He found twelve domestic incident reports filed by the complainant, all against her ex-husband. A background check on the alleged perpetrator revealed he had no contact with the police other than as a subject of the growing bunch of complaints by his ex-wife. He had three previous arrests for things like aggravated harassment, harassment, and violating the court order of protection.

Orders of protection had become a particularly infuriating tic under Paddy's skin. They were issued automatically and without the requirement of a scintilla of evidence beyond the complainant's statement of facts. That they might be motivated to lie was never considered. Aggravating as that was, what burned Paddy more was the fact that an order of protection was a piece of paper. It protected *no one*. What it did was turn every innocuous act into a crime, aided by the often subjective and flawed testimony of the alleged victims themselves. So now, things like rolling your eyes or sucking your teeth at your baby's mother could get you arrested.

Paddy ran the listed perpetrator's name through the photo system. He recognized him immediately. The guy was the owner and head mechanic of Pepe's Auto Repair on Wilson Avenue. Paddy knew him to be a decent guy who was well-respected by the neighborhood. A general picture began to develop. Paddy was not looking forward to the next phone call.

It was 0900 hours when Evelyn Rodriguez picked up the phone, and she was already drunk. When she found out it was the police calling, she went into a raving damnation of her ex-husband Pepe, whom she demanded be arrested and beaten for his many transgressions and shortcomings. Paddy had to hold the phone away from his ear, such was the shouting. He thought he could detect the smell of rum coming through the phone. Paddy called across the office to Matty Price, who was typing into his computer.

"I got a live one. Right up your alley, want to listen in?"

"Yeah, hit it," Matty said, smiling.

Paddy hit the speaker button on his desk phone. Evelyn was winding down on her diatribe. She was to the point of stacking curses and insults on her ex-husband. Paddy thought she was done when she paused for a second, but then the distinct sound of her swallowing whatever she was drinking could be heard through the phone. She began excoriating Pepe again by calling him a *maricon*, when Paddy stopped her.

"Evelyn, why do I have a police report from you in front of me?"

"That *cabron* Pepe didn't drop off the child support on Thursday."

"But he has until Friday. Did he pay you on Friday?"

"Yes," she said.

"Then, what's the problem?"

"When he came over Friday to pay me, I made him dinner. But he wouldn't stay. He just gave me the money and left. I told him I was going to call the police on him. He gave me the finger."

"We know you didn't call the police then. Or I would have had a completely different bullshit complaint in front of me. The report says he threatened you on the phone later that day. How did that happen?"

"I called him later to apologize. I asked him to come over again, but he wouldn't."

"I still haven't heard a threat, Evelyn."

"He called me a cunt," she finally admitted.

Paddy looked over at Matty Price, who was struggling to contain his laughter.

"I'm closing this case as unfounded for the following reasons; You called him, not the other way around. That's sort of a pre-requisite for aggravated harassment. Also, calling you a cunt is not a threat. It's just good commentary. Pepe nailed it. You are a world-class cunt. You keep telling the cops you have an order of protection, but you know that's not true. You yourself requested the court rescind the order. So you lied to the police. That's a crime. I'm going to give you a pass on that, just this once. But I'm red-flagging your name in the system."

"What does that mean?"

"It means from now on, whenever you make a police report, I'm going to be informed and assigned the case. I am your new personal detective. If I catch you lying again, trying to get the police to do your dirty work, I'm going to lock you up. Then I'm gonna take your kids away and put them in foster care. ACS will be notified. I'm going to tell them that you're an unfit mother, that you're drunk all day, every day."

"Please Detective, don't do that to me."

"I'm not doing it to you, Evelyn. You are."

"I don't know what to do," she cried.

"To begin with, stop calling the police with your problems. We don't fix problems, we arrest them. And your kind of problems only get worse with an arrest. Next, stay away from the rum. It's not helping you make good decisions."

"I just want Pepe to come home," she said pathetically.

"That's never going to happen. All you've done for the last three years is tell lies about Pepe and have him arrested. He's never going to trust you again." Evelyn could be heard weeping in the background. Matty Price was no longer laughing. He nodded at Paddy. Both of them understood what had to happen next.

"Evelyn," Paddy got her attention. "I've met you. Do you remember? You were here at the Domestic Violence office talking to Detective Boodle. Do you remember what I told you then?"

"You told me she was giving me bad advice. You said that knowing how to fuck someone over doesn't make it right, even if the police are telling you how to do it."

"You didn't listen to me. How did that work out for you?"

"Not good."

"Will you listen now?" Paddy asked. She said she would.

"Let's start with what you've got going for you. You're only twenty-nine. That's still young. When you're sober, you are a beautiful, intelligent, and capable woman. Your kids are in school. Fix yourself up and get a part-time job. Pepe is a lost cause, but he's never going to abandon his kids. Take the money and get on with your life. Good looking as you are, it won't be long before you find someone else. Do you think you can do that?"

"I think so."

"I think so, too. But I want you to call me in a week to tell me how you're doing. For right now, you need to take a nap. Make sure the stove is off, and lay down for four hours. If you should get the urge to use the phone before you're sober, resist it. You shouldn't be this unhappy. You've got too much going for you."

"I will, Detective. Thank you so much."

When Paddy hung up with Evelyn, Matty Price regarded him from across the room with esteem.

"That was masterful. But I have a few questions."

"Shoot," Paddy said.

"Is Evelyn at all beautiful, intelligent, or capable?"

"Working backwards, she can cook a meal without blowing up the house. That's capable for Bushwick. As far as her intelligence goes, she can read and write and use a telephone. On the beauty question, it's kind of subjective, and everybody is beautiful on the inside. But I personally wouldn't waste good rocks throwing them at her."

"Then, how is she supposed to find someone else?"

"Have you seen the dented up women the guys in this neighborhood chase after? Trust me, there is someone out there for Evelyn Rodriguez."

CHAPTER THIRTY-FOUR

October 14, 2013
Brooklyn

When Paddy Durr got to work the following day, Police Officer Tommy Crowe was at his desk, waiting for him. The kid looked uncomfortable and jumped out of the chair when Paddy arrived. Paddy motioned for Tommy to sit back down as he signed into the command blotter.

"What's up, Tommy?"

"The guys gave me coffee and told me to wait for you. They said I should sit here," Tommy explained nervously.

"You can sit in my chair whenever you want. But that's not what I meant. What can I do for you, son?"

"I told my mom what you did for me the other day. She said I had to come up and thank you for her personally. She wants to have you and your wife over to the house for dinner."

"I'll give your mom a call. Anything else?"

"I was kinda curious about the homicide. It was my first one. I wanted to follow-up on it, see if I could do anything for you."

Paddy regarded the young cop for a minute. In his jeans, work boots and flannel shirt he looked a lot like his father at the same age. He considered the kid's curiosity and desire to contribute to the case and decided they were genuine. He had something for him. But first he had to mess with him.

"What's with the soft clothes? You make Anti-Crime already?"

"No. I got a collar downstairs. The lou told me to break down."

"You dress like a *FLID,*" Paddy told him.

"What's that?"

"A Fucking Long Island Dickhead."

Tommy realized he was getting screwed with by the smiling detective. So he laughed along, liking the expression and planning to use it himself in the future. Paddy brought him back to the conversation.

"Is your arrest from Willoughby?"

"No, it's a domestic violence Assault from Troutman and Irving."

"Bring him up anyway. I'll debrief him for you."

"I'll go get him," Tommy said.

"Before you do, here's what you can do for me. I need arrests from Willoughby. Anybody arrested there, anybody arrested that lives there, I need to talk to them. Tell your squad. If anybody like that gets grabbed, you call me so I can question them."

"Okay, but what gives with Willoughby?"

"My case has dead-ended there. There is a female, mid-to-late-twenties, possible name of Beatriz who knew my victim and shooter intimately. She is supposed to live on that block."

"I'll get on that first thing tomorrow."

"Thanks kid. Now leave me your mother's phone number so I can thank her for the good job she did with you."

After Tommy brought his prisoner up to be debriefed, Paddy sent him downstairs to finish his arrest. With nothing else to do, Paddy was confronted with having to make a phone call he really didn't want to make. Paddy loved Katelyn Crowe like a big sister. He was in awe of her personal courage and resilience. He was touched by the steadfast loyalty she showed to the cops her slain husband had worked with. That she held that loyalty so deeply after twenty-five years, was as astonishing as it was moving. She had more understanding of honor and sacrifice than a whole platoon of cops. That she could give her blessing for her only son to follow in his father's footsteps and come on the job, a job which ultimately killed her husband, spoke of a resolute fearlessness Paddy did not think he could emulate if the circumstances were reversed. His son Patrick had said he might consider the NYPD after he graduated from college. He was already on the list to be hired, having taken the test when he was eighteen. He was presently on an educational hold, which could be lifted at his discretion whenever he was ready. Paddy told his son he didn't wish to discourage him from taking the job, but then he went on a twenty minute diatribe on how the job sucked, and was beneath the ability of an intelligent, capable young man like his son. Patrick grinned at his father's transparent attempt to guide him to safer pursuits.

"Are you going to work today, Pop?"

"Yeah. I go in for a *four to one* this afternoon."

"And how long have you been doing that now?"

"About twenty-eight years."

"Wow! That job must really suck."

They both had to laugh. Paddy knew Patrick was too smart and independent to be manipulated one way or the other. He was willful like his father. So if Paddy hoped to influence Patrick's decision, he would be best served by keeping his mouth shut on the subject.

But Paddy most dreaded calling Katelyn Crowe because he would have to admit to her how he had sabotaged his own life. He didn't really concern himself with taking the blame or accepting responsibility for his actions. He had long ago resolved himself to that. What he was dreading was the disappointment he would hear in her voice. She had always seen through Paddy. She saw right past the charm, the glowing, inviting smile designed to make you feel like you needed to be his friend. She saw through Paddy's tough-guy façade as well. She knew the tattoos and muscles were little more than paint to hide the broken and frightened child which still hid inside of him, informing, or more accurately misinforming his every thought and action when the child held sway. She saw it more than twenty-five years ago when she first met him at the 34th Precinct Christmas party. He came over to introduce himself, and say hello to his friend and mentor, Jimmy Crowe. Paddy couldn't help noticing the critical way Katelyn kept regarding him. She seemed to sense something was amiss with him. Paddy found her unwavering gaze unsettling, so he tried to charm it away.

"Jimmy talks about you all the time. I had no idea you'd be so beautiful."

"Oh bullshit," Katelyn said, laughing at him. "You were right, Jim. This one is as slick as owl shit."

"You're in for it now, Boyo," Jimmy grinned at Paddy.

"That little chippy you brought," Katelyn said to Paddy. "She's a neighborhood girl, cute as a button. Do you even remember her name?"

"Of course I do," Paddy said. But he didn't. Katelyn had him wracking his brain for it right now. He thought it was Marissa, or Marisol, or Maria, or something. When he looked back at Katelyn she was shaking her head at him.

"That poor girl. She's looking at you like you're Prince Charming. She's a deer caught in the headlights. I'm going to warn her to run before you break her heart."

Paddy stood there mutely as he watched Katelyn walk over and introduce herself to his date. They talked and laughed for what seemed like an eternity, but it was probably just twenty minutes. That's all Katelyn needed. By the time she was done, Marisol, (that was her name), had been Paddy-proofed. The next day at roll call, Paddy approached his friend for an explanation. Jimmy was already laughing at him.

"What the fuck, Jim! Why did your wife cock block me like that?"

"She said you reminded her of the asshole I used to be before she fixed me. I think that means she likes you. But that's no bargain, Boyo. Katelyn holds her friends to a high standard. You're gonna have to up your game."

"What I need to do is to keep far the fuck away from your wife, if I ever hope to get laid again."

But Paddy didn't stay away from her. At functions and parties he sought her out. He made a point of introducing his dates to her, by their correct names. It was as if Paddy needed validation from Katelyn. He sought her approval, and was bitterly disappointed each time it didn't come. Katelyn clearly liked him. She knew he was a loyal friend to her husband and zealously watched his back. She enjoyed his company and joked freely with him. But she never lost that bemused look when she spoke with him. It was as if Katelyn Crowe knew Paddy's secret, and Paddy didn't even know he had one. By now she had stopped sabotaging his dates. But she made her continuing disapproval known to him.

"These girls you bring around are so beautiful. How come I never see you with any of them twice?"

"I like being single," Paddy told her.

"What you're doing isn't called being single. It's called chasing your dick. And men who chase their dicks are usually running away from something else. What are you so afraid of, Paddy?"

"I'm not afraid of anything," Paddy lied.

In truth, even then Paddy vaguely understood he was consumed by fear. The problem was he couldn't identify what he was afraid of. It's difficult to slay a dragon when you can't see him. So he ran and hid from it. He built constructs to keep it at bay. Drinking, fighting, and womanizing were Paddy's armor against having to confront himself. At that very moment, Paddy was scared to death of the conversation he was having with Katelyn, afraid of what it might reveal, what it might force him to deal with, when he was so unprepared to do so. So he just kept his mouth shut. Katelyn sensed his fear. So she took pity on him as she tried to encourage him to get his act together.

"You've got to fix what's broke inside, Paddy. You want to be a good man. You want to help people. But that shit festering inside of you won't let you get there. Somebody fucked you up but good. You have to realize, what they did to you; they didn't love you. So they shouldn't matter. It's the past. Put it in your rearview mirror and move on. You'll never be who you want to be until you do."

Paddy felt like he had been punched in the gut. Katelyn had deconstructed him to his rotten core. Still, he wouldn't confront it. When he looked at Katelyn again, it was as if the punch in the gut had been replaced by a nine pound sledge. He never anticipated seeing tears in her eyes. The fact that she hurt for him was crushing. Paddy wanted to do anything to make it go away. He leaned over and kissed her cheek. He would fix this, he promised her. But he didn't know where to begin.

CHAPTER THIRTY-FIVE

October 14, 2013
Massapequa

When Katelyn answered the phone at home in Massapequa, she was delighted to hear Paddy's voice. She thanked him for helping Tommy get into the 83rd Precinct, and looking after him. Paddy assured her Tommy was doing well enough on his own. He told Katelyn how impressed he was with her son, what a fine young man he had grown into, and how much he looked like his father at that age. She got a little misty at that, but you could tell how proud she was of Tommy just by the sound of her voice. Paddy changed the subject, asking how work was going. Katelyn had been the head of guidance at Massapequa High School for several years now. She had become as respected by the community for her work in that position as she was revered by the police department for her sacrifice and work on their behalf. She told Paddy she still liked going to work every day. Kids haven't really changed that much. The challenges they have today aren't much different from what they were twenty-five years ago. She noted that the problems teens battled in Massapequa were different from East Harlem where her career began. Long Island problems were decidedly of a first world nature. No one in Massapequa was being materially deprived of anything. But there was still drug abuse, violence and emotional abandonment even in God's green acre. So there was work.

Katelyn had been brought up to speed on Paddy's recent career doings by her son, who was clearly fascinated with him. Paddy cautioned her to nip that in the bud quickly. He reminded her the last thing she wanted was the boy emulating him. Katelyn laughed, but she knew to what Paddy was referring. She let it go for a while. Paddy obligatorily asked how her "new" husband Ed was doing. Katelyn had met Ed at a grief counseling group in Massapequa. He had lost his first wife to cancer. He thought he was destined to be alone, until he met Katelyn. They had been good for each other ever since. She reminded Paddy they were married fifteen years ago, and Paddy had given her away.

"Ed thinks you don't like him."

"He's a fireman. It's not that I don't like him. I don't understand him."

"He retired from the FD ten years ago. What's to understand?"

"What did Ed say when Tommy wanted to come on the job?"

"He was scared to death for him. He wants Tommy to roll over to the fire department."

"That's my point exactly, Katelyn. These firemen go running blind into burning buildings, wearing nothing but a raincoat and a penis-shaped hat. Yet, they're scared shitless of the neighborhoods they work in and the people who live there. I don't get it. How can you be so crazy brave in the face of a formless, uncontrollable, and destructive force like fire, then be suspicious and scared of a seventeen-year-old on a street corner because he might have a box cutter in his pocket?"

"Speaking of formless, uncontrollable, and destructive forces, how are you doing with yours?"

And just like that, Paddy found himself smack dab in the heart of the conversation he most didn't want to be in. He thought of a dozen ways to begin to answer.

"I think I finally got a handle on them, just in time to be too late. Mairead is divorcing me."

"Oh Paddy, I'm so sorry. I know how you love her. Was it the thing on the internet?"

Paddy thought that was the perfect description for the impetus of what he regarded as the destruction of his life. *The thing on the internet*; small, insignificant, dirty and cheap, it required no further embellishment. It was awful, and it was everywhere. Reminders of Paddy's selfish treachery just wouldn't stop surfacing. The worst of it were the snide comments and the obsequious expressions of sympathy, poorly disguising the sense of superiority of the alleged well-wisher. And just when it looked like the hysteria was dying down, there came another round of emails with the accursed videos attached. But Paddy had to confront the fact that the thing was just the trigger of a chain reaction of secondary implosions which had always been there, waiting for a spark, waiting to consume him. Paddy was destined to wreck his and his family's happiness. Now he knew why, but it would do him little good at this point. The damage this time looked total.

"I didn't know you knew about that," Paddy said.

"Massapequa is one town away. We have the internet here. The thing went viral."

"I guess I knew that," Paddy admitted, thoroughly and freshly ashamed.

"The soccer coach? What could you have been thinking?"

In the next breath, Katelyn caught herself.

"That was unfair. I know you were punishing yourself as much as anything else. What you have to figure out, is why."

"I got that covered. I'm seeing someone about it. He knows you. He says he's not surprised I hold you in such high esteem. He suggested I talk to you about it. But this seems like a story that's determined to tell itself, to everyone. So I guess that's done."

"Who are you talking to?" Katelyn asked.

"James Cregan, in Wantagh."

"He's an excellent choice. He's been through the wringer himself a time or two."

"That's why Mairead picked him. This stuff is too bitter. I need somebody down in the abyss with me who's been there before."

"He can definitely help you."

"He's already helping me. But like I said, it's too little, too late."

"I don't believe that, Paddy. You have to fix yourself. Then you have to fix this. There is something not right in the world without you and Mairead together. Make this work."

"Yes ma'am," Paddy said. But his assent was without hope or conviction.

CHAPTER THIRTY-SIX

October 21, 2013
Brooklyn

A week later Tommy Crowe was waiting for Paddy at his desk when he got into work for his first *four to one*. The young cop was starting to look comfortable with his surroundings in the squad-room. This should have come as no surprise to anyone who remembered Tommy's father. Jimmy Crowe exuded such an aura of confidence and capability that he owned every room he walked into. His son was starting to develop those kind of chops. Paddy made a note to himself to bring in a coffee mug for Tommy so he could stop using Paddy's. He was getting tired of drinking out of Styrofoam whenever Tommy came around.

"What's up, Tommy?"

"I got something for you."

"I'm all ears."

"The super from 1112 Willoughby knows Beatriz. That's not her name. It's actually Gladys Beatriz Ordonez. She moved out about a week before the homicide. He doesn't know where she went, but he has her mail. He gave me this."

Tommy handed Paddy an official looking letter from the New York City Department of Probation, addressed to Gladys Beatriz Ordonez. The letter had been opened already. Paddy pulled out the contents. It was a request for Ms. Ordonez to contact her probation officer immediately, cautioning her that it was a violation of her probation to fail to fill out and return the enclosed questionnaire. The letter informed Paddy Ms. Ordonez had been convicted of misdemeanor larceny and criminal impersonation. She was an identity thief. Even though Paddy didn't know where she had moved, he had her criminal identity. Before doing another thing, he put out a Wanted Card for Ms. Ordonez, listing her as a material witness to a homicide. In order to cast the widest possible net for Beatriz, Paddy sent the Wanted Card out to other agencies as a *Be On the Look Out for*, or *BOLO* order. If Gladys Beatriz Ordonez was stopped, arrested, questioned or had any contact with law enforcement, Paddy would be notified. But in the meantime, he needed to find out what other possible information this superintendent had about Ordonez.

"What are you doing right now?" Paddy asked Tommy.

"I'm processing an arrest."

"Who is the boss on the desk?"

"Lieutenant Dailey."

"Good, *Handsome Dan* likes me. Let's you and I go talk to this super. I'll square it with the lou."

Handsome Dan Dailey was the most ironically nick-named cop in the NYPD. His face was an acne-scarred lump of featureless dough. His hair was thin and mousey brown. He wore it tight to his head and slicked back, revealing an uneven and misshapen skull. His teeth were a discolored collection of free agents who appeared to be trying to go into business for themselves. His eyes were an unmemorable brown and looked like two piss-holes in the snow. They were alert though, and gave a hint to the intelligent and capable man behind them. In stark contrast to his unfortunate face, Dan Dailey was otherwise as immaculate and squared away as anyone on the job. His uniforms were expertly tailored to reveal the physically imposing man who wore them. The rack of medals above his lieutenant's shield, which cascaded over his left shoulder, gave testament to the thirty years of hard police work he had been doing all his adult life. Regarded as a hard ass, he really wasn't. He was protective of his cops. Demanding the very best out of them. As such, while no one would have volunteered to work for Dan Dailey, everyone who did was a better cop for having done so, and had the added benefit of collecting *Handsome Dan* stories they never tired of telling.

The best part of Dan Dailey's nick-name was how he got it. He related it to Paddy one night at the desk. Dailey was covering the late tour for another lieutenant who needed the night off. Paddy was working through the turnaround. He had an extra Spanish coffee and was craving some human contact. He knew Dan liked his café con leche from his years working in Brooklyn North. So Paddy went downstairs to bring the lou a coffee, and to hang out. It was just the two of them behind the big desk. So after talking about the job for a while, Paddy broached the subject of Dan's nick-name.

"I gotta know, Lou, where did *Handsome Dan* come from?"

"I gave it to myself," the big lieutenant said behind a grin that was both delightfully mischievous and yet, somehow still horrible.

"I gotta hear this story."

When Patrolman Dan Dailey first got to his command out of the Police Academy, he was standing in his first roll call in the old 77 Precinct. He didn't know another soul in the room. The veteran cops were already snickering at him behind his back. When the sergeant finished the roll call and handed out all the sector and foot post assignments, he took the time to introduce the newest squad members. When he got to Dan he asked him his name. Dan introduced himself as Patrolman Dan Dailey, but most folks just called him *Handsome Dan.* Then he beamed that awful cubist nightmare of a smile at the sergeant. The whole squad lost it right there. From that day forward he was *Handsome Dan.*

"I figured, with a mug like this, I better own it on my own terms. You can't run from ugly."

So when Paddy approached the lou with Officer Crowe in tow, he had no doubt the lieutenant would accommodate him. He knew it would take some convincing, though. *Handsome Dan* ran a tight ship and he was nobody's pushover. When Paddy told the lou the kid had found a witness on his homicide and he needed Tommy to introduce him, the lieutenant was naturally dubious.

"You really need the kid, or is this bring your son to work day?"

"He found someone who can tell me who my killer is. Tommy has a rapport with him. I need the intro. We won't be more than an hour."

"Okay. I'll cover for the kid with the DA till you get back."

"Thanks, Lou."

"One other thing Paddy, I appreciate what you're doing for my cop. I know your connection, but most guys wouldn't honor the commitment like you do."

"I'm not going out of my way. He's the real deal. Like his father, he was born to do this shit."

"I know. That's why I put him in for plain-clothes conditions. I've gotta get him away from that moron, Julian Feigling."

1112 Willoughby Avenue was a four-story wood frame apartment house, with nine total apartments, including Jesus Corporan's basement dwelling. The superintendent had been living with his family in that apartment for fifty years. He had seen the neighborhood transform itself from the German-Italian enclave it had once been, to the largely Hispanic drug infested mess it had become. It was never a good neighborhood, but it was less seedy and violent before the drugs arrived in the early sixties. Jesus Corporan would lament the fact to anyone within earshot, including the drug dealers, who he warned fearlessly that they would never get a foothold in his building. He was a frequent caller to 911 when anything went down on the block, and he remained outside to direct the police when they came. The drug dealers tried over the years to intimidate him. He would not be intimidated. Even though he was now eighty-years-old, he was as ornery and unbroken as he was when he was a younger man. The drug dealers had wisely decided to avoid him. His grown children tried to convince him and his wife Maria to leave the neighborhood as they had done, but he wouldn't hear of it.

"Mr. Joe Fiordelino hired me to take care of his building in 1959," Jesus said firmly. "Now his son owns the building. He expects no less." So the Corporans weren't going anywhere.

When Tommy introduced Paddy to Mr. Corporan, the old man's face registered recognition. Paddy was sure they had never met, but Jesus was insistent that he knew him.

"When you come on the block, the scumbags leave in handcuffs. They're afraid of you. So I trust you."

Jesus brought them into his basement apartment. Maria insisted on making coffee for their guests. They were seated at the table in the kitchen when Mr. Corporan brought out a brown paper bag full of mail delivered to the occupant of apartment 1R since Beatriz Ordonez had moved out.

Most of them were credit card bills and new credit cards for a variety of names, allegedly living in that apartment. Paddy looked at a few of the bills. They were all maxed out to the five thousand dollar limit, and had long since gone dead. Ms. Ordonez had apparently been maintaining a lucrative business as an identity thief. He asked Mr. Corporan if these were still coming to the apartment. Corporan said they were. He went on to tell Paddy that he checked at the post office on DeKalb to see if Beatriz had left a forwarding address when she skipped out on six months back rent. Beatriz evidently wasn't concerned about her mail.

Paddy recorded all the names from the credit card statements and new cards. He would add them as aliases to the BOLO later. He asked Mr. Corporan if he knew anything about the murder he was investigating. Jesus told Paddy he only knew what he had overheard.

"Everybody talks in front of old men. Nobody thinks we're listening," Jesus told him.

He had heard that Beatriz' boyfriend, *Negro,* who Jesus did not like at all, got shot down by her old boyfriend, *Casper,* who Jesus liked even less. He heard their dispute had something to do with money *Casper* owed Beatriz for a cell phone, but he doubted that. Jesus figured Beatriz got her cell phones the same way she got everything else, she stole them. Jesus surmised the dispute had more to do with *Negro* trying to encroach on *Casper's* drug territory.

Mr. Corporan had no further information on *Casper's* given name. All he knew was *Casper* lived on Willoughby Avenue, on the other side of the park. But he hadn't seen him around the neighborhood since the shooting. Paddy thanked Mr. Corporan and asked him to hold onto the mail a while longer, in the event someone had an ID theft case going against Beatriz. Paddy told him he would look into it and get back to him. Then he gave Mr. Corporan his business card with his cell phone number added to it. He gave Tommy one as well and told him to write his name and cell number on the back. He gave Jesus both cards.

"Now you have direct contact with two friends. If you need anything from the police, unless it's an emergency, call us first."

When they left Willoughby Avenue, Paddy started heading up Flushing Avenue toward Queens.

"Where are we going?" Tommy asked.

"To get business cards for you."

In the car on the way back to the 83rd Precinct from Paddy's printer, Tommy asked Paddy why he needed business cards. Paddy explained that as cops, their greatest resource was information. If the people who had it didn't have a way to get in touch with you, they might forget they want to tell you about it. The business card is a tactile reminder.

"Why the two different cards?"

"The one with your cell phone number is for friends and informants. The other one is for everyone else. Make sure you know the difference. The wrong person gets a hold of your cellphone number and the torment won't end until you change it. Then you have to reconnect with your informants, one at a time. Do that once, and I guarantee you won't want to do it again."

"Can I ask you something else? Something personal?"

"Sure," Paddy said.

"What happened between you and your wife?"

"Whoa! Where the fuck did that come from?"

"After you talked to my mom, I asked her when you and Mairead were coming over to dinner. I wanted to make sure I could be there."

"What did she say?"

"Not much, but she got this very concerned look. She said it couldn't happen for a while. She also told me you were beating yourself up about it. She asked me to look after you. I don't know what she meant."

"Do you even know my wife?" Paddy asked, perplexed.

"No, but mom has pictures of you both. She's beautiful, and the two of you look good together, like you were meant to be. You don't see that much. I'm just wondering how something like that gets fucked up."

"Your mom is worried I'm distracted out here by my personal problems. She's right to a point. But the job is my only escape from having to think about the mayhem I've done to myself. So out here in the street, my focus is laser-like. Tell her not to worry."

Tommy said he accepted that, but Paddy could see his young friend was still concerned.

"Look, Kid, I'm here to show you how to do this job. I'll teach you how to be safe, keep the initiative, stay tactical, and get your ass home at the end of your tour. I can do that. But if you're looking for someone to show you how to live your life, do not follow my example. I can make a *meant to be* a *never should have happened.* I am a one man misery machine. So with that in mind, let's keep your questions related to the job. You can tell me anything about yourself you want. I just wouldn't recommend asking me for any advice in that regard. I'm seriously underqualified. I've demonstrated no ability to manage a personal life. I should have never been issued one."

CHAPTER THIRTY-SEVEN

October 21, 2013
Brooklyn

After running down the aliases for Gladys Beatriz Ordonez, and all the known previous addresses, Paddy was no closer to figuring out where she might have gone after leaving Bushwick. So he updated the BOLO, and typed the *five* on the witness information from Mr. Corporan. There was nothing more for him to do on the case. Progress was dependent upon finding Beatriz. Failing that, Paddy needed to debrief a prisoner, or have someone's informant tell him who *Casper* was. It was sit and wait time. So Paddy busied himself with his other open cases. They were the typical garbage most of the cases were. He could only focus so much on them. He kept getting distracted by Tommy's most poignant question, *how does something like that get fucked up?* Paddy knew what he had done. He just couldn't figure out how he let it get to that. Agonizing over it was driving him mad. So instead, he thought about how he and Mairead began. It didn't help much, but at least they were good memories.

Paddy remembered the first time he saw Mairead. She had just been hired at Columbia Presbyterian Hospital. All the nurses from *Columbia Pres* hung out at Coogan's Pub on Broadway, around the corner from the hospital. Paddy and his Anti-Crime teammates liked the young nurses. So they hung out there, too.

Paddy remembered that night vividly. He came into the bar and ran into Dave Hunt, one of the owners. While chatting with his friend, he saw

Mairead at the bar with a gaggle of the other nurses. They were drinking shots. Paddy was able to decipher this was some sort of welcome initiation for the new nurses. As soon as he saw her, he stopped hearing Dave. In fact, he stopped hearing everything. It was as if all the air went out of the room. All he could focus on was the pretty little nurse with the killer green eyes. He woke from his reverie to realize Dave had asked him a question, and was waiting for an answer. Paddy laughed.

"Dave, I have no idea what we were talking about. I only know that I have to talk to that girl right there."

"Jesus Paddy, she just got hired. Do you have to bang every nurse who drinks here?"

"It's not like that. There's something special about her."

"I never heard you say anything like that before."

"That's funny. I never thought I'd ever say anything like that."

So Paddy tied his long hair back away from his face into a ponytail. He smoothed out the front of his canvas duster and climbed the three steps up to the bar level. He walked right over to Mairead, who was talking to another nurse named Tabitha. Paddy had a one-nighter with Tabitha a few months previously. As he got nearer he thought he heard Tabitha tell Mairead, *that's him.*

"Hi," Paddy said smiling. "I'm Paddy Durr. I work over at the precinct."

"I know who you are," Mairead said. "I was warned about you."

"Warned? What's wrong with me?"

"Just that you've slept with half of the nurses in the emergency room. They think you're keeping a scorecard."

Paddy thought quickly and did the math. While he wasn't keeping score, he thought he had slept with a little more than half. He needed to make this girl understand he wasn't just looking for a one-shot deal.

"I'm not trying to hit on you. I just want to talk to you. Can I know your name?"

"My name is Mairead Dunleavy. But that's all you're getting, Casanova. I'm not a notch on anybody's bedpost."

"It's very nice to meet you, Mairead, and I don't have bedposts. I have a brass rail bed. But I'm not trying to get you into it. I just want to get to know you. Have a drink with me."

Mairead relented on the drink, but not much else. She parried every attempt by Paddy to gain a foothold with her. She let slip a lot of personal information, but only because Paddy was asking her direct questions. She would divulge something about herself, but would quickly remind Paddy he had no shot at all. Mairead seemed to enjoy the wounded look Paddy feigned each time she did it. So she kept it up.

As far as Paddy was concerned, he thought he was doing quite well. He had gotten a treasure trove of information from this impossibly beautiful girl, and he found her fascinating. She told him about her great big happy family in the house in Glendale. She told him about going to an all-girls high school. She told him about her college soccer career, and her college life in general. He managed to wheedle out of Mairead that she did not have a steady boyfriend at the moment. She told Paddy she chose nursing over being a doctor because she felt like she could help the most people in the shortest amount of time. She admitted she hated to see anyone in pain. She would alleviate it all, if she could. By the time Mairead finished filling in her background, Paddy thought he was already in love with her. Having never been in love, he couldn't be sure. But he was feeling things about Mairead he had never felt with anyone else. His every instinct told him this girl was special, unique even. He felt like every cell in his body was humming in contentment just being in her presence. He was determined to have more of that, maybe all of it, if he could.

Mairead realized the two of them had been talking exclusively about her for the last two hours. She wasn't sure how he did it, but Mairead conceded the young policeman was a gifted interrogator. She was having no more of that.

"We've been talking about me for hours. What about you? Tell me about you."

"There isn't much to tell. You already know I'm a cop. I imagine you could surmise I was in plain-clothes, given my hair and whatnot. What else do you want to know?"

"Everything. Start spilling."

Paddy realized she wouldn't be put off. So he gave her the highlights. Born and raised in Bushwick, he went to Brooklyn Tech, then Columbia, where he played football and earned an English degree that was of absolutely no use whatsoever in his chosen profession. He confessed he never had a substantive relationship with anyone before, so no steady girlfriend at the moment. He told her about his condo in Astoria. He jokingly described the décor as Spartan, but clean.

Before they knew it, it was two A.M. Mairead said she had to go home. She was due back in work at noon. Paddy offered to drive her. She told him firmly, no. She was sharing a car service with Tabitha. Paddy asked if he could see her again. Mairead told him she was confident he could find her if he wanted to. He assured her he did. Then Paddy did something he never had before. He reached into his pocket and pulled out a business card. He wrote his home phone number on the face of the card and gave it to her. From his awkwardness, Mairead guessed he was entering uncharted waters.

"That's my home phone. If you should get the urge between now and when I see you again, you can call me. If you wanted me to meet you somewhere, or you just wanted to talk, I would like that very much. I don't get many messages, but I'll start checking them if I think it might be you."

"I'll hold onto this, but if you want to talk to me again you better be prepared to share something about yourself. That background you rattled off sounded like a resume. I want to know something about Paddy Durr. If you can't do that, don't bother looking for me."

Paddy promised Mairead he would be an open book for her next time. He escorted Mairead and Tabitha to the car service in front of the bar. As he said goodbye, Mairead gave him a wave that buoyed his hopes. Tabitha shot him a death stare.

When Paddy came back in the bar, he went around to the side where his teammates were congregated. Tommy McPhee was getting ready to leave with one of the nurses. Kevin Touhey was working hard on convincing another one to take him home. Sean Moran and Pete O'Malley were watching the sports highlights on the TV and having a pint. So Paddy came over to join them.

"What happened, Paddy?" Sean asked. "Did you strike out?"

"I'm not even up to bat yet."

"Is she going to be a tough nut to crack?"

"I'm not even thinking about her in those terms. There is something about this girl. She could be a game changer for me."

"You're serious?"

"Yeah, man. She's not gone five minutes, and I already miss her."

"Oh, you're done now," Sean observed.

"Yeah, probably so. But I think I like it. I just have to find a way not to screw this up."

Of course, he would. It took him twenty-three years to do it, but the totality of the destruction he would wreak would be breathtaking.

CHAPTER THIRTY-EIGHT

October, 1990
Washington Heights

For the next week Paddy checked his messages almost hourly. He figured Mairead wouldn't call, but he wasn't taking any chances in case she did. His new obsession wasn't lost on his partners either. In fact, they had grown concerned. If Paddy, ordinarily as focused and tactical a cop as ever there was, didn't get his head back in the game, he was going to get hurt, or worse. Even if he wasn't paying attention, he was still a magnet for trouble. They all knew that in this business, the trouble you didn't see coming was the trouble that could kill you. Sean Moran was particularly worried about his friend. So in an effort to keep Paddy focused, Sean talked incessantly about the job in the Anti-Crime car. Paddy went along with it as far as he could.

"Will you just shut the fuck up already? You are wearing me out!"

Sean laughed, but it had the intended effect. A moment later when Sean turned onto 164th Street from Broadway, Paddy saw a guy on the sidewalk he recognized. He had locked him up for gun possession two years earlier. Evidently, he was out of jail and up to his old tricks. He spotted the Anti-Crime car and grabbed at the large bulge at his waist and abruptly changed direction.

"*Hot lunch* on the right, black hoodie," was all Paddy needed to say.

Sean jammed the car into reverse and backed up to cut the perp off. Meanwhile, Paddy and Tommy McPhee were bailing out of the car and drawing down on the perp. The suspect, showing incredibly good judgement, simply stopped and threw his hands over his head. Paddy rushed up and removed a black 9MM from the perp's waist. Tommy shoved the suspect against the car parked at the curb, and tossed him for more weapons or contraband. Sean came around and threw cuffs on him.

Sean and Tommy were greatly relieved. This was good, intuitive Anti-Crime work. They knew now, their friend was alright. This arrest showed that no matter how jerked up Paddy was over this girl Mairead, when the bell rang, he was still the police.

Because the Anti-Crime Team worked off a strict arrest rotation, Gus Demario took the collar. He was up. Paddy wrote a quick supporting deposition for Gus to give the DA, to ensure he didn't screw up the facts of the arrest, which was often his habit. Then he was off with the rest of the team to Coogan's.

Paddy had been stopping into Coogan's every night he didn't have an arrest, hoping to see Mairead again. When she wasn't there, he would have a quick beer with his partners and head home. He saw some of the other nurses at the bar. He would smile and say hello, but otherwise he would eschew further conversation. He was tempted to ask one of them to say hello to Mairead for him, but he had no faith they would accurately deliver his message. So he stayed patient.

Paddy's patience was rewarded this night. Being pay-day, Mairead was out for a drink with the other nurses. When Paddy entered the bar and spotted her, he was brought up short again. He had no idea how she did it, but with one look she could snatch the breath right out of him. Mairead sensed his presence and turned to smile at him. She was talking to Tabitha again. When he approached Mairead he made a point of saying hello to Tabitha as well. She just walked off in a huff. Paddy took the opportunity to catch up with Mairead. Her first week at the hospital had been busy, but she was already growing to love the work. Paddy asked her if she wanted to get a booth and talk. She said yes, but she had some conditions.

"Are you going to tell me about yourself? Or are you going to try and run that strawman bullshit on me again?"

"I'll tell you whatever you want to know. I'll tell you everything I can think of. If you want to know anything else, all you have to do is ask."

They got a pitcher of beer and sat down at the corner booth away from everyone else. Paddy poured her a beer and brushed her fingers as he passed it to her. She pulled her hand back in surprise, their touch almost electric. She laughed nervously.

"What the hell was that?" she asked.

"I don't honestly know, but it was cool. Do you want to try it again?"

She reached across the table and let him take her hand in his. Paddy thought he could feel her blood pulsing through her fingers, unless it was his heart, which was right now beating out of his chest. Either way, he was savoring the moment. He was staring into those maddeningly green eyes and counting the freckles, finely sprayed across her nose when she brought him back to reality.

"You're up, cowboy. What have you got for me?"

He told Mairead he didn't grow up in a happy home like her. He described it as a shithole of misery in Brooklyn. He told the story of his questionable parentage, and his father's animosity for him because of it. He described his father as a criminal. His mother was self-absorbed and ultimately killed herself with vodka and pills. His brothers were dead as well, one of them shot down during the commission of a robbery, the other two over-dosing on heroin. He confessed that he did not mourn them, and hoped his putative father would join them soon. He had been trying to escape them almost since birth. They were making it easy for him by dying. But he assured her, the physical and emotional abuse he suffered when he was young was now behind him. He could still get angry about it, but he didn't dwell on it. He viewed his escape from his family as a success story.

Mairead listened to all of this attentively, but other than squeezing Paddy's hand at some of the more painful revelations, she remained silent, letting him be out with it. Her eyes were moist when he finished, but they were the kindest most beneficent eyes he had ever looked into. So he didn't stop.

"I wasn't completely honest with you when I told you I was never in a long-term relationship. I was involved with somebody for four years. It's a fucked up story. So I don't tell it."

"But you're going to tell it to me," Mairead said.

Paddy told her the story of Inez Vasconcellos. He left nothing out. She showed brief traces of horror at the disclosure. Everyone understands that cruelty and exploitation exist. But you never anticipate talking to someone whose life was wholly comprised of it. It's even more difficult when it's someone you've started to care about. When Paddy got to the point of Inez' murder, Mairead was squeezing his hand so tightly she was crushing it. Paddy didn't even flinch. Instead he told her about the awful and suffocating sense of loss he experienced for the first time. He told her how Inez had been the only person who ever truly cared about him. He admitted for the first time, even to himself, losing her made him afraid to ever be that vulnerable again. Until now.

By now Mairead's eyes had become torrents. She wouldn't let go of his hand, but her face was a mask of pain and empathy. Paddy misinterpreted it as the door of possibility slamming in his face.

"I understand if I scare you. I know I'm damaged goods. I just thought I could be different with you. You do something to me. I'm still afraid. But I want to risk it with you. If I get hurt, then I get hurt. I have to take this chance. I think with you, I can be a whole person for once in my life. If this is too much, I would understand. Running is the smart move."

Mairead was shaking her head gently and wiping the tears from her face. She was still squeezing his hand, trying to regain her composure.

"I'm not afraid of you, Paddy Durr. You have a good heart. You just don't know how to use it yet. You can take me home now. There are some people there you need to meet."

CHAPTER THIRTY-NINE

October, 1990
Glendale

It was three o'clock in the morning when Paddy and Mairead got to her house in Glendale. Paddy was trying to be quiet, so as not to wake her family. He needn't have bothered. When Mairead opened the front door, she yelled up the stairs, announcing she was home, and had brought a friend. Her mother and father came down the stairs in their slippers and bathrobes and ushered them both into the big kitchen. Her father immediately put on a pot of coffee, while her mother heated up a big skillet on the stove and pulled a pound of bacon and a dozen eggs out of the refrigerator. Paddy was shoved into a chair by Mairead's father, who in the next motion stuck out his huge hand and introduced himself as *Big Bill Dunleavy*. Paddy grasped Bill's hand, stunned at the man's boundless energy this early in the morning.

"He doesn't talk, huh?" Bill said to Mairead.

"He talks. You just overwhelmed him. Let me introduce him properly. Daddy, Mimzy, this is my friend, Paddy Durr." Paddy looked questioningly at Mairead, and mouthed the word *Mimzy*.

"Oh, that's my special name for my mom. No one else is allowed to use it." Paddy smiled.

"It's a pleasure to meet you," Paddy recovered enough to tell Big Bill.

Bill took a long appraising look at Paddy. He wasn't quite sure what he was looking at, so he took a stab at it.

"What's with the hair and earrings? Are you a musician or something?"

"No, Mr. Dunleavy. I'm a cop. I work in the precinct near Mairead's hospital."

"They let you in uniform looking like that?"

"They actually encourage me to look like this. I'm in plain-clothes."

"That's still a lot of hair."

"Oh leave the boy alone, Bill," Mairead's mother Sinead told him. "I think his hair looks nice."

Mairead looked over at Paddy and winked at him, enjoying his discomfort at the unexpected grilling her father was giving him. Paddy pretended to be distressed, but really, he thought Mairead's parents were precious.

"How long have you been a cop?" Bill asked.

"Almost five years."

"I heard most cops go their whole career without ever having to pull out their guns. Is that true?"

"That hasn't been my experience."

"So how many times have you pulled out your gun?"

"Mr. Dunleavy, have you been to Washington Heights recently?"

"No. But it used to be a nice neighborhood."

"Well, it isn't anymore. A slow night is when I can go twenty minutes without pulling out my gun."

"Jesus," Bill whistled. And then it occurred to him to ask, "Did you ever have to shoot anybody?"

"Yeah," Paddy said.

"More than once?"

"Yeah."

"Did you ever kill anyone?"

"Uh huh."

"More than once?"

"Yes."

"Jesus! Are you okay, son?" Bill asked with genuine concern.

"Mostly, I guess," Paddy said grinning, taking the edge out of the conversation, but not the concern off Big Bill's face.

Mairead winced and looked over at Paddy, mouthing *I'm sorry*. She wasn't aware he had been through so much, and certainly never thought her father would pry so deeply. Paddy smiled at her and winked, letting her know he wasn't bothered by any of it. By this time, her mother had shoved a heaping plate of bacon and scrambled eggs in front of him along with a steaming mug of coffee. Paddy hadn't realized he was hungry, but he devoured it all. He thanked Sinead for the meal, which he said was delicious. She beamed when she told him he was always welcome. He shook Bill's hand again. Bill enclosed him in an embrace and thanked him for getting his little girl home safe. In a serious tone, he reminded Paddy to be careful.

Mairead walked Paddy to the front door. She grabbed him and apologized. She told him she had no Idea he had been in a shooting. He told her it was fine. He didn't mind talking about that. He told her he thought her parents were terrific.

"Sorry I didn't mention the shootings. That was work stuff. I would have told you about it if I thought you wanted to know. I just thought the other stuff was more important."

"It was. But you can tell me about work, too. I know you have a tough job. You need to talk to someone about it. I'd be more than happy to listen, any time you want to."

"I have to make a collar tomorrow, but I'm free Saturday night. Let me take you to dinner. I'll tell you all about my job."

"You mean, like a date?"

"Okay, if you insist."

"I don't know," she hedged.

"I know a local place. We can even walk there from your house. Just dinner and conversation, no strings attached. We can walk home like a couple of teenagers. Then you can send me on my way. What do you say, Mairead? Take a chance."

"Okay, sold. Pick me up at seven?"

"Absolutely."

Mairead reached up on her tiptoes and kissed Paddy on the cheek. Surprised, he lit up like a Christmas tree.

"Thank you for sharing that stuff with me. I know that was hard to talk about."

"As it turns out, not so much with you," Paddy told her as he was leaving. And on the ride home to Astoria, he couldn't stop touching his cheek where she had kissed him.

CHAPTER FORTY

October, 1990
Washington Heights

Paddy felt the bullets wiz over his head before he heard them. The fact that he had been looking in the wrong direction when it happened was deeply troubling to him. He had been scoping out the drug operation taking place on the corner of Saint Nicholas Avenue and 187th Street from his spot on the sidewalk across the avenue and a block away. There were a lot of people in the street and everyone's head seemed to be on a swivel, as if they all were expecting trouble. Experience had taught the Anti-Crime team that this made for a target-rich environment when it came to hunting guns. Because he looked the least like a cop, and would probably not be *made*, Paddy was usually chosen to man the OP, or observation post on foot. The bullets passing over his head from behind him quickly refocused his attention. What he saw when he turned around was in equal parts terrifying and ridiculous.

Richie Calderon, the present bull-goose of the Calderon family, was running down Saint Nicholas Avenue, being chased and shot at by a light-skinned Dominican guy who was half his size. The ridiculous part was Richie himself. He was wearing a knee-length houndstooth wool coat that was open and streaming behind him. He was also wearing mustard-colored genie pants whose color the cops had begun to identify as *Jose yellow*. He wore thin brown leather dock siders without socks, one of which he had already run out of. The other shoe was sure to follow. Richie was shirtless under this. His big, fat, hairy belly was thrust out in front of him as he ran. Complimenting this already outlandish get up was the fact that Richie was holding an enormous Cuban cigar in one hand, and a bottle of Barceló spiced rum in the other. In spite of the fact that he was being chased by someone intent on shooting him to death, the idea of discarding either item never occurred to him.

Paddy stepped in front of Richie and grabbed him by his collar, driving him to the ground behind the Anti-Crime car parked at the curb. Paddy told him to stay there, as he, Tommy McPhee, and Armando Gigante drew their guns and started running in the direction of the shooter, who by now realized they were the cops, and they would ventilate him properly if he didn't change course. So he turned around and headed back toward 190th Street, from where he came. But this perp was also wearing suspect footwear. So by the time he made it to 190th Street, the Anti-Crime team was on him. Unexpectedly, the perp raised the gun over his head and spiked it on the ground like a football. Then he put his hands up and turned around to be apprehended by the cops.

When the team got back to their car, Richie Calderon was gone. So, to make the attempted murder charge stick, they would have to find him. Finding him was not difficult. He was easy to find. Getting him to cooperate would be the hard part. The Calderon family had been running the drug business north of 190th Street since the early eighties. There were eleven brothers when they first got to Washington Heights from Santo Domingo. Within five years, they were down to eight. Presently in 1990, there were only five brothers left. The problem was not their business acumen. By all accounts, they were excellent drug dealers. Unfortunately, they were also assholes. Usually drunk, they were obnoxious, insulting, and randomly violent. Within a culture that viewed insults as breaches of honor, it wasn't long before their ungentlemanly behavior started to take a toll. Six dead Calderon brothers was the cost so far. In as much as the brothers had shown no desire or ability to evolve with their changing environment, the cops and the detectives in the 34th Precinct had every expectation that the butcher's bill would continue to rise.

When Paddy got his suspect into the 34th Precinct, he was able to ascertain that his quarry had been a recent arrival to New York from the Dominican Republic. A few things about his behavior started to get under Paddy's skin. The perp was exceedingly polite, directly answering questions pertaining to his identity and place of residence, but everything else was a mystery. He claimed to live alone. He had no employment, and no one to call to tell them he had been arrested. What irked Paddy was the fact that he claimed to speak no English, yet he followed the conversation of the cops intently. He had the unmistakable air of a professional criminal. When Paddy asked him in Spanish why he was trying to shoot Richie Calderon, the suspect smiled benignly at Paddy, and said in Spanish, "Yo quiero un abogado." That clinched it for Paddy. Definitely a pro. This was bad news for Richie Calderon. Someone had imported a professional to kill him. That contract was definitely going to get fulfilled, if not by this killer, then certainly by another.

With this in mind, Paddy decided to take a few additional steps with this suspect. He took an extra set of fingerprints from the perp that Paddy would keep with his paperwork for future reference if needed. Paddy took an entire pack of Polaroid photos of the suspect, including his scars and tattoos. Finally, he photocopied everything in the suspect's wallet and pockets. All of this in case the detectives might need it to find the perp later.

"We have a problem with the gun, Paddy," Tommy McPhee said.

"Let me guess, it's not operable?"

"He knocked it out of battery when he spiked it. I put it back together, but it looks like the impact sheared off the firing pin. You could pull the trigger all day and the fucker wouldn't fire."

"Well that sucks. So we have a .380 caliber piece of scrap metal?"

"That's about the size of it."

"Then I guess we better find that idiot, Richie Calderon."

When Paddy and Tommy McPhee got to Richie's apartment on 190th Street, Richie initially didn't want to open the door. Paddy convinced him if he did not open the door, Paddy would have to conclude Richie had been shot and was bleeding to death in his apartment. He would have no choice but to knock the door down. What he found when he was in there might result in an A-1 Felony narco rap for Richie. Richie was out in the hall a second later, ready to get the identification over with.

So paddy had his attempted murder collar, but he knew this was a temporary accomplishment. The lab was going to find the gun inoperable.

So the CPW charge was a wash. And under no circumstances, even under subpoena, would Richie Calderon testify in the grand jury. So in five days, the little man who Paddy was certain was a professional killer, would be back on the street with a fresh license to hunt Richie Calderon. Paddy kept his copies of the file in his drawer in the Anti-Crime office for the eventuality, now a certainty, it would be needed by the detectives.

Two months later Richie Calderon was shot to death inside of his *hoopdy* Cadillac, in front of his apartment building on 190th Street. When the call went over the air, Paddy and Sean Moran responded to the scene, after picking up the arrest folder from the previous shooting from the office. When they got there, Paddy went to speak with the lead detective, Bobby Smart.

"Is that Richie Calderon?" Paddy asked him.

"Yeah," Bobby said. "You know something about this?"

"Here is the arrest folder for the guy I locked up two months ago for trying to kill him."

"Why did the case go south?"

"The bad guy broke the gun, and shithead over there refused to testify."

"This is the scrip on the doer," Bobby said when he looked at the photos.

"You might want to cover the airports," Paddy suggested. "I got the distinct impression the guy was an imported pro from the D.R."

"We already alerted the Port Authority detectives. Let's see if we can get this guy id'd."

The witnesses did identify the suspect. Four hours later, Alonzo Carbajal was pulled off of the flight to Santo Domingo from Kennedy Airport, and subsequently charged and convicted in the murder of Richie Calderon. And then there were four.

CHAPTER FORTY-ONE

October, 1990
Glendale, Queens

Paddy arrived at the Dunleavy house promptly at 1900 hours. He was as conservatively dressed as he could manage from his somewhat limited wardrobe. He had two good suits that he wore for court, weddings, and police functions, but they were a little too formal for dinner out. So when he was down in Manhattan court this morning, drawing up the complaint from his arrest with the DA's office, during a break, he took a walk over to Worth Street under the World Trade Center. Brooks Brothers Haberdashers were located there. He got fitted and subsequently overpaid for a pair of charcoal grey slacks, a cobalt blue fitted shirt, and the nicest navy blue sport jacket he had ever seen. He was already set for belts, socks and shoes, planning to couple his new ensemble with his gleaming black penny loafers. He was counting on being the epitome of 1990 casual chic later that night. The clerk at Brooks Brothers was dubious about his ability to pay for the clothes. Until he took out his American Express Gold Card, leaving his wallet open long enough for the clerk to see his NYPD credentials. Then suddenly the clerk wanted to give him a credit card, and enroll him in a frequent shopper rewards program. Paddy, not so politely, declined the offers and instructed *Chauncey* (according to his name tag), to wrap it up, as he was in a hurry.

This is what he was wearing when he showed up in Glendale with flowers for Mairead's Mimzy, and a bottle of Glenfiddich single-malt scotch for her father. Paddy had tied his long hair back in a relatively neat ponytail and had removed all but the one diamond stud earring from his left ear. This was as presentable as he could make himself without a haircut, and that was just out of the question.

Big Bill answered the door and pulled up short, looking quizzically at Paddy in the doorway. He could not have imagined the transformation from this look to Paddy's plain clothes, crime fighter get-up.

"Are you the same kid I had breakfast with the other day?" Bill asked.

"I clean up pretty well," Paddy smiled.

Bill ushered him into the living room where his wife Sinead was sitting. Paddy said hello and gave the bouquet of flowers to her. She was surprised and pleased with the unexpected gift and got up to take them into the kitchen to put them in a vase. He gave Bill the scotch. Just as Big Bill was asking Paddy how he knew he was a scotch drinker, Mairead appeared on the stairs.

"Holy shit!" Paddy uttered under his breath, but still audible enough for Big Bill to hear. He couldn't take his eyes off the adorable creature descending the stairs, smiling at him. She wore a little black silk dress. Paddy later found out that she called it her *LBD* when he complimented her on it. She told him every woman had one. Paddy never saw one worn this well. She had a short navy blue bolero jacket, and her hair was a radiant mass of dark brown shimmering curls cascading down around her shoulders. She wore black pumps just high enough to accentuate the sublime muscle tone of her tan, athletic legs. As if this were not enough, there were those green eyes, capturing him and holding him hostage. Big Bill understood Paddy's discomfort. Mairead was the very picture of her mother thirty years before, and Sinead still had Bill spellbound.

"Breathe, son, before you pass out," Bill said, patting him on the back. When Paddy refocused on the here and now, he realized he was light headed.

Mairead came down the stairs and kissed Paddy on the cheek again. His legs felt like rubber, but he managed to stay upright.

"Do I look alright?" she asked Paddy, already seeing the answer on his face.

"I don't even know how to answer that. You are impossibly beautiful."

Mairead liked that assessment. She took Paddy's appearance in, admiring his outfit and conservative grooming. She joked that she wasn't aware there had been a refined gentleman under his wild man exterior. She said goodbye to her parents, and the two of them left for the restaurant.

It was a warm October evening, but Paddy kept eyeing Mairead's shoes with trepidation. Paddy asked Mairead if she was sure she wanted to make the seven block walk to the restaurant in her heels. She assured him the shoes were no problem.

"I played college soccer. I got this."

On the walk to Zum Stammtisch, the German restaurant on the corner of Cooper and Myrtle Avenues, Mairead wanted to play twenty questions. She asked Paddy what his favorite thing in the world was. She wanted to know what he liked to do more than anything else.

"You mean, with my clothes on?"

"Yes", Mairead giggled. "Exempting sex, what is your favorite thing?"

Paddy thought about it for a minute or so. He told Mairead he had three great loves in his life so far. They were in ascending order, literature, police work and football. Mairead was perplexed. She knew he played football in college, but he had been out of college for six years. Paddy related how he had played for the NYPD Football team his first three years as a cop. His last year with the team, he had become a player-coach, in charge of the linebackers and secondary. He had to give it up when he went into Anti-Crime. His new schedule would not permit the enormous commitment of time required to play and coach. So he resigned from the team to focus on his police career. It was the hardest decision he ever had to make. He said he hoped to get involved in coaching again later in his career.

Then it was Paddy's turn to ask some questions. He was well aware of her college soccer career. Her amazing legs were a testament to that. He observed that she was still in incredible shape, more so than should have been possible, even for a former athlete. Mairead admitted that when her playing career ended, she was looking for something to do to stay fit. She tried running, but after playing soccer all her life, she couldn't stay motivated to do it outside the context of a game. It was just time-consuming tedium to her. She ended up attending an aerobics class on a lark with one of her girlfriends. She was quickly hooked. The combination of strenuous effort, the yoga for flexibility, and all of it while moving to the pulsating dance music was intoxicating.

"You mean that Jane Fonda, Richard Simmons thing?" Paddy asked.

"More like Jane Fonda, but without those baggy knit leggings. They make me look like a munchkin."

When they got to the restaurant and were seated, Paddy ordered drinks for them both. He had the home-brewed Oktoberfest beer that was the house specialty. For Mairead, he ordered a Wiessbier with a slice of lemon on top. Mairead was fascinated with the rustic Bavarian décor of the restaurant. She particularly liked it when the waitress, in authentic country dress, kept calling them *Schatzi*. Paddy explained it was a German term of endearment, like calling someone sweetheart. Mairead liked it so well, she vowed to use it from now on.

They had a sumptuous dinner of goulash soup, steak tartare, and Yeager schnitzel. In spite of Mairead claiming to be full to bursting, Paddy was able to convince her to share a slice of the homemade strudel with him over coffee. The waitress brought two shots of Jagermeister on the house as an after dinner drink for the young couple. Mairead found the German liquor so bitter, she was grateful to have the strudel and coffee to chase the taste out of her mouth. After Paddy paid, leaving a generous tip for their waitress, Paddy and Mairead began the slow walk back to her house.

Paddy reached for Mairead's hand as they were crossing Cooper Avenue and she let him take it. Mairead raved about the food and ambience at Zum Stammtisch. She went on and on as if Paddy had not been there, relating every little thing, obviously delighted by it all. Paddy was content to just listen to her, and watch her animated facial expressions change as she would laugh at one thing or another. He was so happy just to be walking with her and listening to her voice that he started to feel disappointed about getting nearer her house. He didn't want this walk to end.

When they got to Mairead's door, she let him into the vestibule, and she stopped there. She told Paddy she would have to say goodnight. She had work in the morning. As disappointed as he was, Paddy didn't let on. He had no real expectation of anything more. He knew Mairead wasn't going to let him rush her into anything. But he was so enchanted with this girl, he didn't ever want to say goodnight to her.

"When can I see you again?"

"Are you working Tuesday afternoon?" Mairead asked.

"Yeah, I'm doing a 1430 by 2300."

"What the hell does that mean?" she asked, laughing.

"Oh, sorry. Sometimes I forget not everyone talks like a cop. That means 2:30 to 11:00 P.M."

"In that case, you can pick me up at noon. I will let you take me to lunch before we both have to go to work."

"I will be here promptly."

Mairead then let Paddy agonize through the next awkward moment, while she watched him puzzle over what to do next. She knew he was torn over whether to kiss her, or ask her permission to kiss her, or do neither. She laughed again as his indecision paralyzed him.

"For an alleged womanizer, you're not very smooth," Mairead observed. Then she mercifully made the decision for him. She reached up and clasped him behind his thick neck, through all of that hair, and pulled his face down to her own. When she locked her mouth on his, Paddy kissed her back hungrily. He would have stayed there for an eternity. Mairead broke the spell when she had to break contact. She sighed as she touched his face.

"You're a good kisser, Paddy Durr. I'll see you Tuesday."

"Fuck yeah," he whispered breathlessly.

CHAPTER FORTY-TWO

October 25, 2013
Washington Heights

October 25th, 2013 would have been a Friday of no particular distinction if it were not the 25th anniversary of the murder of Police Officer James Crowe. It was also the day Paddy Durr finally relented, and took off his wedding ring. It killed him to do it, but Mairead had made her intentions perfectly clear with respect to the dissolution of their marriage. Paddy was headed up to the memorial mass held yearly at Saint Elizabeth's Roman Catholic Church on 185th Street and Wadsworth Avenue. He was going to see many old friends of his and Mairead's. They knew enough that Paddy and Mairead were in jeopardy as a couple. Thanks to the internet, everyone knew that much. But with the exception of his present partners, and a very small handful of other people, Paddy had been reticent to announce what he viewed as the self-destruction of his whole life. He had no desire to answer questions about it either. But to mislead old friends into thinking they were still together somehow seemed disrespectful to Mairead. So he would leave the ring in a drawer, in his bedroom, in his apartment in Farmingdale. The ring had never been anywhere but on his left hand since the day he married Mairead. Anyone who cared to could figure it out for themselves.

Paddy arrived at the church and found Katelyn and Ed in front. He came over to say hello and was warmly greeted by them both. Katelyn hugged Paddy and kissed him on the cheek. She had a look of grave concern until Paddy smiled at her and assured her he was okay. She still eyed Paddy with care, but she seemed relieved he looked as well as he did. They were joined by Tommy and his girlfriend, Claire. Tommy made a point to formally introduce her to Paddy.

"Paddy, this is my girlfriend, Claire Muldoon," Tommy said.

"It's very nice to meet you, Claire," Paddy said.

Claire stared at Paddy with a wide-eyed curiosity that had him wondering what the hell Tommy had told her about him. She was adorable in that typically Irish way, with big green eyes and strawberry blonde hair leaning toward ginger. She had a milky white, freckled complexion that could look like white marble when the light hit it just right. So her attentive gaze wasn't as uncomfortable as it might have been. But it was still uncomfortable. Paddy decided to be proactive and ask her some things about herself.

"Where did you two kids meet?"

"At the NYPD Honor Legion scholarship dinner seven years ago. We were both getting awards. We had to make a speech, and I was so nervous. Tommy calmed me down and helped me with my speech. We've been together ever since."

"Where are you from, Claire?" Paddy asked. He thought he already knew.

"East Meadow," she said.

Paddy did some fast figuring, putting the NYPD Honor Legion, the red hair and freckles and East Meadow together. Now that he thought about it, she looked like her father. Much prettier of course, but she was unmistakably Gerry Muldoon's daughter.

"I worked with your dad in the Terrorist Task Force," Paddy told her. "He is a good man, and an excellent detective."

"I know. He told me all about it. I told him you were taking care of Tommy. He said there was no one on the job better to learn from."

"I think he overstated the case a bit."

"I don't think so," Claire argued. "He was telling Tommy and I some of the things you've done in your career. He said you've killed more people than cancer. So that's what they called you."

Paddy never understood how that nick-name got started. He had shot a total of four people in three different shootings, only three of them fatally.

If cancer had a body count of three, it wouldn't be worth mentioning. But somehow in the NYPD, three bodies made Paddy a hard bitten killer. It was pointless to argue. No matter how hard he tried to downplay it, his efforts were regarded as modesty, cementing the reputation even further. Unable to discard the albatross, Paddy finally elected to just wear it. A bad reputation has its uses. The criminals hear it too, and there is nothing scarier to a criminal than a gunfighter who is down by law.

"Not quite so many as cancer. You make sure you give your dad my warmest regards."

"I promise I will," she said.

Katelyn insisted Paddy sit with them in the front pews. When the procession went into the church, Paddy found himself seated behind and to the left of Tommy and Claire. The second row was fine with him. It provided just the slightest measure of anonymity, giving Paddy the opportunity to get lost in his thoughts. Except Claire wouldn't let him.

As the mass progressed, and the bishop addressed the assembled cops and students from Saint Elizabeth's elementary school, Paddy watched Claire's reactions. She was holding onto Tommy so hard it looked like she was afraid he'd be taken away. As the bishop spoke of the commitment and sacrifice of Police Officer James Crowe, as well as the faithful service over the years since of all the cops in the 34th Precinct, Claire began to weep softly. This forced Paddy to pay attention to what was being said. Now he couldn't hide in his own head. He had to face the reality of his sense of loss, and it was palpable. Jimmy Crowe had been the greatest positive influence of Paddy's life. He was his mentor, and his best friend, and he was taken from him suddenly and violently. He loved Jimmy more than he ever loved any of his miserable brothers. He knew his loss compared to Katelyn's was meager at best. So he felt selfish for hurting like this, still fresh twenty-five years later. Somehow Katelyn had salvaged her life. She raised a beautiful and devoted son. She found someone else to love, and it only took a glance to see how much Ed Morrissey adored her. Paddy realized then that though he liked Ed, subconsciously he resented him. Not for anything he did. He was wonderful to Katelyn and Tommy. He was as fine a man as Paddy could ever wish for the two of them. But he still resented him. For the simple fact that he was not Jimmy Crowe. Ashamed of feeling that way, Paddy vowed to himself to end that today. He would make a point of telling Ed how much he liked and admired him, and appreciated all he had done for Katelyn and Tommy.

When Katelyn addressed the congregation, she focused on the love and loyalty of the men and women who worked with her slain husband. She related the loyalty and brotherhood that Jimmy spoke of before he had been killed. She thanked everyone for sustaining her and her family through the dark times that followed. By now there wasn't a dry eye in the church, so Paddy didn't feel embarrassed about tearing up. He had started when Claire began weeping.

The final speaker was Deputy Inspector Andrew Casese, the present commanding officer of the 34th Precinct. The inspector admitted he came on the job in 1990, a full two years after Jimmy Crowe had been slain. But he had done his homework. Having spoken with Jimmy's friends and peers, he was able to share some anecdotes about Jimmy that gave a brief glimpse into the greatness of the man. He ended with a vow to uphold the high standards and traditions of the *old three four* that Jimmy would have insisted upon. He promised, on behalf of himself and his entire command, to never discredit or disgrace his memory, or the service of those great cops that followed. It didn't lessen the hurt, but it made Paddy feel like Jimmy's death still meant something important. Paddy felt like he belonged to something special, steeped in honor, greater than himself. For that he was grateful.

As the mass was ending, Paddy observed Claire one more time. She was looking at Tommy with a trance-like devotion, but there was something else there. Paddy struggled to identify it. She was almost enraptured with a kindness enveloped in a layer of desperation. She knew she loved Tommy, and she realized with horror that she could lose him as suddenly as his mother lost his father. Paddy wished he could comfort her, but he would have to lie to do it, and he wasn't about to do that.

After the procession filed out into the street to be saluted by the Honor Guard, Paddy pulled Ed Morrissey to the side.

"Katelyn says you think I don't like you," Paddy said.

"I didn't say it like that," Ed stammered, flustered by Paddy's directness.

"That's alright, Ed. I know I can be difficult. You were never a cop. So you're not gonna get me. For the record, I like you a lot. I respect you for everything you've done for Katelyn and Tommy. I'm glad you found each other. She deserves to be happy, and you've made her very happy. I'm proud to be your friend. I just wish I was better at it. I'm sorry I didn't tell you this sooner, but like I said, I can be difficult."

Ed was speechless. He stood for a moment trying to decide what to do. Finally he threw his big arms around Paddy in a bear hug. As he embraced him, Ed thanked Paddy for watching out for Tommy, who Ed said he loved like a son. Paddy told him he already knew he did, and he assured Ed that while he still had breath in his lungs, he would look out for Tommy, no thanks necessary.

Katelyn asked Paddy if he was going to join them for the luncheon at Coogan's. Paddy had to decline. He had to be in for the *four by*. Before he left, he beckoned Tommy over. Paddy thrust his chin in the direction of Claire, who was standing close by.

"She's a keeper," was all Paddy said.

CHAPTER FORTY-THREE

October 25, 2013
Brooklyn

When Paddy got to the 83 Squad, Matty Price had a telephone message waiting for him. His BOLO had popped in Manhattan. Gladys Beatriz Ordonez had been arrested for grand larceny and forgery in the Canal Street subway station by a Police Officer Devry from Transit District 2.

"She got pinched under the name Gladys Cornejo. Her prints came back about twenty minutes ago," Matty informed him.

"District 2, that's down by the Holland Tunnel, right?"

"I believe so. I got a number here for Officer Devry."

Paddy took the number from Matty. A Lieutenant Barnes answered what was apparently the phone at the desk. Paddy identified himself and requested to speak with Police Officer Devry. The lou told him Devry had a perp in the back cells awaiting the arrival of the Special Frauds Squad. He transferred Paddy's call.

Paddy was surprised when a pleasant female voice answered and identified herself as Police Officer Devry. Paddy told her who he was, and asked if the perp was in a talkative mood.

"She won't shut up," Devry told him. "She's been trying to talk her way out of here all morning. She keeps digging the hole deeper and deeper."

"I need to question her on a homicide. I can be there in less than an hour. Is that alright?"

"That's fine, Special Frauds won't be here till 1800, and they have a lot of work with this one."

"Great, tell me all about it when I get there."

The first one of Paddy's teammates to get in was Joe Furio. Paddy knew it wouldn't take much to get Joe excited about running out the door and into Manhattan. Furio had a desperate need to remain in constant motion. Like a shark, he had to keep swimming or drown in the stillness. Paddy baited the hook.

"Hey Joe, want to solve a homicide?"

Forty-five minutes later Paddy and Joe were parking their squad-car in a police lot at the mouth of the Holland Tunnel on Canal Street and West Broadway. There wasn't a police facility in sight. Joe was perplexed, wondering where they hid the precinct. Paddy had been here before. His terrorism case in 2002 centered on a threat to the subways. The lines under their feet all had direct access to Wall Street and the downtown financial institutions. So for Paddy's bombing case, District 2 was considered the temporary headquarters for the takedown, as well as ground zero for the terrorists.

"We're dealing with the mole people now, Joe. They have a whole alternate world of their own underground. So be mindful that these creatures might be skittish. They don't get out in the light much."

"Oh, cut the shit," Joe said. "I'm used to Brooklyn. The Transit districts are above ground there."

Paddy led them down into the Canal Street station. From there they followed the signs to two big oak doors bracketed by the classic big green lanterns found outside every police facility in the city. The sign on the door read *NYPD Transit District 2*. Paddy pulled the doors open. The detectives found themselves thrust into a scene that would be immediately recognizable to every cop in the world. They were in a busy, fully functional, subterranean police station. Paddy clipped his shield to his jacket lapel, walked up to the desk, and spoke with Lieutenant Barnes.

"I'm Paddy Durr from the 83 Squad. This is my partner, Joe Furio. I spoke to you on the phone about an hour ago."

"Oh right," the lou said, remembering the conversation. "Anita has her perp in the back cells. Take a right around the desk. Then walk till you can't anymore. You can't miss the cells."

The detectives followed the lieutenant's directions. They came to a door with a window in it. Above the window was a black sign with the word *CELLS* painted in white. That was easy. Paddy knocked twice, and the same pleasant voice he had spoken to on the phone earlier told him she would be right out.

When the door opened Paddy encountered what he thought was the most extraordinarily attractive female police officer he had ever seen. He drank in the sight of her, as he watched her step out into the hall. She looked to be in her early thirties. She had long thick hair the color of honey, pulled back into a high ponytail. Her skin was so smooth and flawless, it could only be described as creamy, and it was the color of café au lait. She was all of five foot four, and even in the notoriously unflattering police uniform, Paddy could see she was all sinewy muscle and curves. He surmised that she was an athlete. Her graceful movements, and the way she seemed to walk up on her toes, almost bouncing, had Paddy thinking she was probably a dancer. What captured his attention most however, were her eyes. Paddy had never thought hazel eyes were anything special, but Officer Devry's were different. They seemed to glimmer and capture the light. They complimented her brilliant smile, and seemed to suggest a spark of mischief. What he noticed last were the medals over her shield. They were the old time Transit medals, before the merge of the two departments. So Paddy had no idea what they were for, but he could see she had a lot of them.

Police Officer Anita Devry was momentarily as enthralled as Paddy. She liked the look of this detective in front of her. Tall, fit, with short brown hair just turning gray at the temples, and piercing blue eyes, she thought he was black Irish handsome, with an unmistakable rough edge. She observed the absence of a wedding ring, but noted with caution the indentation and untanned skin where one had recently been. She also didn't miss that tattoo sneaking out of his shirt collar and peeking out from the sleeve of the nicest fitting blue suit she had ever seen. But he wasn't saying anything. He was just staring at her, transfixed. So she broke the awkward silence.

"I think one of us is supposed to talk now," Anita said.

"Oh, I'm sorry," Paddy laughed. "I'm Paddy Durr. This is my partner, Joe Furio. I'm guessing you have your perp in the back."

"I figured you didn't want her to hear us."

"Good call. What do you have her for?"

"She was selling counterfeit Metro Cards."

"Why does Special Frauds want her?"

"She had eighteen different drivers' licenses, all with her picture on them. Plus, she had dozens of credit cards that all turned out to be bogus. Evidently, she is the biggest identity thief on the east coast. Special Frauds has had her on their radar for a while."

"Who are you dealing with over there?"

"Detective Shabunia."

"I know Carolyn," Paddy informed her. "She's the best detective in that unit. You're gonna get some work done with her."

"She seemed on point," Anita agreed.

"Is there somewhere in there we can sit your perp down and talk to her?" Paddy asked.

"I got a card table, four chairs and a railing on the wall to cuff her to. Will that suffice?"

"That should do nicely."

Anita lead Paddy and Joe back to the card table in the far corner of the cells area. Then she went and got her prisoner from the cell. Anita cuffed the prisoner to the rail and had her sit at the table. Gladys Beatriz Ordonez looked suspiciously at Paddy and Joe. She thought she recognized them, but she couldn't remember from where. Her curiosity got the better of her.

"Who are they?" Beatriz asked Anita.

"These detectives are from the 83rd Precinct. They want to ask you a few questions."

"That's where I know you from," Beatriz said. "You want to know about *Casper* and *Negro*."

"I know about *Negro*," Paddy said. "He's as dead as Julius Caesar. I need to know why, and I need to know who *Casper* is. Can you help me with that?"

"What's in it for me?"

"You will get the very best that I can do for you," Paddy told her seriously. "That's no little thing. I've been around a long time. I carry a lot of influence." Joe Furio had to work to hide his smirk. He had heard this many times, and appreciated it for the masterful load of bullshit it was.

Mistakenly believing they had a deal, Beatriz was effusive with information. She began by saying she used to be with *Casper*, but he was cheap. She started seeing *Negro* on the side. He was new in the neighborhood, and liked to spread a lot of money around. When Beatriz broke up with *Casper*, she said he flipped out and broke her phone to pieces.

Beatriz said *Negro* used that as an excuse to confront *Casper*. He actually got *Casper* to give him three hundred bucks for the broken phone. He didn't really care about the phone. *Negro* just wanted to see how far he could push him. After he got the money from him, *Negro* figured *Casper* was a punk. He decided that he was going to take both of *Casper's* drug spots.

"Those spots belong to the Latin Kings," Paddy informed her. "Did *Negro* know that?"

"*Negro* said he didn't care. He said if *Casper* wouldn't step up, neither would the rest of them."

She identified *Casper* as Oscar Nieto. She said he was twenty-two years old. He was locked up once for selling drugs, and once for beating up his baby's mother. Both arrests went down in the house on Willoughby, on the Queens side, between Saint Nicholas and Onderdonk. This explained to Paddy why they hadn't gotten anything on *Casper* to this point. They were only running the nickname for arrests in Brooklyn. It was an easy mistake to make, but a stupid one. It made Paddy wonder if he wasn't more distracted by his personal troubles than he thought.

Joe asked Anita where the detectives' offices were. He excused himself to do some follow-up on Beatriz' information. Paddy pumped Beatriz for any further information she might have for *Casper*. She gave him a cell phone number, but she couldn't vouch for how current it might be. She said *Casper* tended to go through phones frequently. The only thing more she knew was that he had family in Connecticut. She had no idea where. While they waited for Joe Furio to return, presumably with a photo of *Casper*, Paddy and Anita chatted each other up.

"You look like an athlete. Do you train?" Paddy asked.

"I study dance, for twenty years now. I was thinking of opening a studio and teaching, but this job doesn't leave a lot of free time, and it certainly doesn't leave you much money."

"I don't know if you can make a living at dancing, but it's definitely working for you."

"What about you Mr. Muscles. What's your deal?"

"I used to play football back before electricity was invented. Now I'm just a gym rat."

"Well, it's definitely working for you, too," she said smiling, with the spark of mischief that kept popping up.

Paddy asked Anita if she was married. She said never, but she just ended a disastrous, five year relationship.

"Why disastrous?" Paddy inquired.

"In the end, I figured out he just wanted me to be his mommy. I need a man. Not a child."

"Sucks to be him," Paddy observed.

"What about you? Are you married?"

"I'm in the process of getting divorced."

"Where in the process?"

"She served me. This week I give her back the amended papers. It's just a matter of her filing them with the court."

"Was it her fault or yours?" Anita asked directly.

"All mine," Paddy admitted.

"Wow, you didn't even flinch."

"I figure come the end of the day, you have to be who you are, and you've gotta own the things you've done. You can run from yourself for a while, but it's gonna catch up with you. Why not dispense with the denial and just get it over with?"

"Does this approach work with all the girls?" Anita joked.

When Paddy leaned in to laugh, he smelled Anita's perfume, *Sand and Sable*. Abruptly, he was transported back to January of 1992, Paradise Island. That was the scent Mairead was wearing when they had gotten engaged. Paddy's face became a tableau of clouded memory and crushing pain, with just a hint of defeat. Anita noticed immediately.

"When did that ring come off?" she asked.

"This morning."

"It's not really gone, is it?"

"At this point, it's probably imprinted in my DNA."

"I'm sorry I brought it up," Anita said.

"It's just as well," Paddy shrugged. "I was going to ask you if you'd have dinner with me some time, but I think I better not."

"How much trouble could we get in over dinner?" Anita wondered.

"You said yourself you need a man. I am somewhat less than that right now. What I am is a broken fucking toy. I got nothing for you but trouble and heartache."

"You're very hard on yourself," Anita observed. "You know you're allowed to have a life, Paddy."

"Theoretically, yeah. But no matter how much I enjoy your company, how much I like talking to you, how easy you are look at, the overriding and controlling impulse effecting everything in my life is the simple fact that I still love my wife, and I don't want to be with anyone else."

Anita considered this. She saw the disappointed, beaten look in Paddy's eyes. She could see he was hurting and the wound was still fresh. She wished she could offer him comfort, but sensed he wouldn't have it. So she tried to lighten the mood just a little.

"Too bad, Paddy. It might have been fun." That, at least got him smiling again.

"You have no idea how big a bullet you just dodged," he told her.

"Oh, I think I have an idea," she smiled.

At this point Joe Furio came back with a folder full of papers. He handed Paddy an arrest photo of Oscar Nieto. Paddy showed it to Beatriz.

"Who is that?" Paddy asked her.

"That's *Casper.*"

Then Beatriz decided to play a gambit. She had listened carefully to the conversation between Paddy and Anita, and she thought she sensed weakness. She also completely overestimated the strength of the cards she was holding. She wasn't holding any cards at all.

"Good luck getting me to testify," Beatriz said. "I won't say shit unless this forgery thing gets squashed."

"Testify?" Paddy scoffed. "I wouldn't let you near a courtroom, unless it was in handcuffs. I'm done with you. You've served your purpose as far as I'm concerned. *Vaya con Dios,* Beatriz."

"Wait!" Beatriz said, sensing her brilliant gambit falling to pieces. "You said you would do your best for me."

"And so, here it is. When my friend Detective Shabunia gets here, throw yourself at her feet and beg for mercy. Tell her everything she wants to know. Give till it hurts. Otherwise she will nail you to the wall and carve you out, like a canoe. You will measure your time in decades. They will bury you under the jail. My professional recommendation is that you avoid that outcome, if at all possible."

"You suck!" Beatriz spat at him.

"No one appreciates good advice anymore," Paddy said, winking at Anita.

After Anita put Beatriz back in her cell, she came out into the hallway to talk to Paddy. Anita said she thoroughly enjoyed the interrogation. She thought Paddy played Beatriz to perfection.

"That's nothing," Paddy told her. "Wait till Carolyn gets here. She's gonna deconstruct that woman until there's nothing left but a puddle of piss, and that she'll send to jail."

"I can't wait."

"You did a great job on this case, Anita," Paddy said, handing her his business card. "That wasn't *all* bullshit. I really do have some influence. I've collected a lot of people over the years who want to do me favors, and I don't need anything anymore. So, I end up using those favors to help friends. You qualify. So if there's anything you want to do on this job, anywhere you want to go, chances are I can help you. All you've gotta do is call."

"But no dinner?" Anita joked.

"No dinner," Paddy smiled.

"What are you guys going to do now?" she asked, curious about the murder case.

"This thing is going to break wide open now that we know who *Casper* is. We're gonna go back to Brooklyn and chase the momentum."

CHAPTER FORTY-FOUR

October 25, 2013
Brooklyn

When Paddy and Joe got back to the 83 Squad, Paddy constructed photo arrays for Oscar Nieto AKA *Casper*. Satisfied the arrays were fair, Paddy printed a dozen of them. The computer placed *Casper* in position number four in the bottom left corner. His first call was to Detective Romeo Amodeo. When he told Romeo he had a possible perp ready to be identified, Romeo said he would be right over.

Paddy's next call was to the taxi driver Sergio Mendez. As was usually the case, Sergio was working. When the call came, Sergio rightly assumed Paddy had found Beatriz.

"How are you?" Sergio asked.

"My day is improving. I need a favor, Sergio."

"Anything, my friend."

"Come to my office as soon as you can get here. I have a few pictures for you to look at."

"You know who the shooter is," Sergio concluded.

"I don't know how you did it in the Dominican Republic, but here, I can't tell you more until you view my photo array. It would be considered suggestive."

"In the Dominican Republic, this guy would have already been dumped in the sugar cane fields," Sergio informed him. "I think I like your way better. It just seems fairer."

Paddy next called Bobby Ruiz. When Paddy asked him to come to the Squad, Bobby didn't hesitate. He didn't ask why. He said he would be right there.

Romeo Amodeo arrived with Sergeant Jimmy Boland, the favored C Team supervisor from the Homicide Squad. Jimmy Boland was everything his cohort Sergeant Robert McPherson was not. He had been a respected detective and a supervisor in the detective squads of Brooklyn North for fifteen of his twenty-two years on the job. He was smart, reasonable and courteous. Best of all, he was not afraid to get his hands dirty with the dangerous side of police work. There was nothing quite so comforting when you were going through a door for a murderer, than being with a guy you knew would stay behind his gun when the bullets started flying. For those reasons, Jimmy was popular among the squad detectives.

"Young Detective Amodeo, and one of my very favorite sergeants, this day just keeps getting better."

"I'm glad to hear that, Paddy. I'm not looking to get launched to Missing Persons," Boland joked.

"I had nothing to do with that. That jerk-off torpedoed himself."

"I know all about it. Truthfully, I needed that imbecile gone. He was like a cheap pair of underwear. You knew he was gonna be up your ass all day, and all you were gonna get for your trouble was irritated. So, bon voyage."

"Glad to have your help, Sarge. Grab some coffee and I'll bring you up to speed."

After they had gotten their coffee, Paddy updated Romeo and Jimmy on the case. He told them he was waiting for his two best witnesses to look at the photo array. Paddy said he was confident of an id, and he had five addresses in Brooklyn and Queens to look for *Casper*.

Sergio Mendez was the first to arrive. Paddy introduced him to Sergeant Boland and explained Sergio's role in the case, as well as his previous law enforcement experience. The minute Paddy laid the photo array on the desk, Sergio put his finger on photo number four.

"That's *Casper*, the guy I saw shoot the other guy on Wilson Avenue. He's the one that dropped the gun on the hood of my cab," Sergio said instantly.

Sergio offered his opinion that he didn't think *Casper* was around anymore. He hadn't seen him in the neighborhood since the murder. Paddy agreed with Sergio, but he assured him there was nowhere in the world *Casper* could hide from him for long.

A few minutes later, Bobby Ruiz came to the Squad. He was beaming as he vigorously shook Paddy's hand. He seemed unsatisfied with the gesture, because when they stopped shaking hands, Bobby spontaneously embraced Paddy in a bear hug.

"I guess Danny Kirk straightened out what he was supposed to straighten out," Paddy surmised.

"He did everything you and Joe said he would. The case is off my record, like it never existed. I can't thank you guys enough."

"You can thank me by looking at my pictures," Paddy told him.

When Paddy laid a fresh array on the desk in front of Bobby, what happened with Sergio was duplicated. He picked out number four immediately. Bobby said he was the guy that gunned down Luis. Paddy thanked Bobby and sent him home.

With the two ids, Paddy had enough to satisfy the DA's requirement to authorize an arrest. So before Paddy prepared the Wanted Card and BOLO for Oscar Nieto, AKA *Casper*, he conferred with the riding DA in the Homicide Bureau.

ADA Melissa Chen was a well-respected homicide prosecutor with several years' experience. Paddy had worked with her on another murder case, and she was impressive. He was glad she would be catching this one. The only possible down-side to Melissa Chen was of no fault of her own. She was exotically beautiful, with her half Puerto Rican half Chinese ethnicity. She was known with respect among the detectives as *China Rican*. She loved the name. She was also young, single, and flirtatious. Paddy never considered her flirting anything other than an innocent and clever decision on her part to play the very strong cards she had been dealt. Men tended to bend over backwards for beautiful, flirtatious women. Paddy's only concern in this direction was that given his present situation, he would allow himself to get distracted, more so than he feared he already had. Paddy resolved to keep a firm handle on that.

After he briefed Melissa on the case, and faxed her copies of the pertinent *fives*, she agreed with Paddy and authorized the arrest of *Casper*.

Paddy and Romeo just had to find him. She also gave Paddy her cell number in the event she was off when he made the grab.

Sergeant Boland suggested they go out six deep in three cars to start hitting addresses. That posed a numbers problem at the moment. His team had been running shorthanded for the last few months. They numbered three between Paddy, Joe and Armando. So Paddy got on the phone and called the desk. Lieutenant Dan Dailey answered. Paddy told the lou his dilemma and asked if he could borrow one of his plain clothes conditions teams for an hour or so. Dan Dailey said he didn't have to guess which team he had in mind. He could be heard on the phone going over the radio on the desk to central, ordering 83 conditions II to 10-02 the Squad. Tommy Crowe responded over the air to acknowledge. Paddy thanked the lou, and waited until his help arrived.

When Tommy and his partner Andy Summers got to the Squad, Paddy introduced them to Jimmy Boland. Then he briefed them on what was happening. He told the young cops he would be riding with them, and by riding he meant driving as well. Sergeant Boland and Romeo Amodeo would be in the Homicide car. Joe Furio and Armando Gigante would be in the Squad auto. Photos of the wanted perp were dispersed and the cops saddled up for the manhunt.

The first address they hit was 24 Arion Place, between Broadway and Bushwick Avenue. This was Oscar Nieto's last known address. He was supposed to reside in the basement apartment of the two family house. Paddy didn't believe he was there anymore, but the address had to be eliminated. When they got to the front of the house, Joe and Armando went around to the back, in the unlikely event *Casper* was home, and tried to beat a hasty retreat out the rear. Tommy and Andy Summers would maintain front security.

"I think we got everything covered," Jimmy Boland said.

Paddy advanced onto the porch and knocked on the door for the first floor. An elderly Spanish woman answered. She was relieved when the men on her porch with guns turned out to be the police. She identified herself as Esmerelda Villalobos, the owner of the house. She recognized *Casper's* picture as the young man who had been renting her basement apartment. She said he moved out abruptly on October 12th. She knew because she had been asking him for the rent. On the 11th Esmerelda finally caught up with him. He promised to pay her the next day. He moved out sometime that night when she was sleeping. He didn't leave the rent behind. She said she had no idea where he went, or for that matter, where he had come from. She had a cell phone number for him, but it was out of service. It was the same number Beatriz had given for *Casper*. So the detectives were back to square one with phone numbers for their suspect.

Esmerelda invited the detectives to come in and look around. She led them down the stairs into the basement apartment. It was clean and bright, and other than a ratty couch and plush chair, and a stripped bed in the back room, it was empty. *Casper* had left in a hurry, but he was thorough. There were no papers, mail, old phone bills or anything else that might have given a clue as to where he had gone. Paddy left Esmerelda a business card if she should hear from *Casper*. He told her if she needed anything else, she could call him as well.

"Can I get rid of that awful furniture he left behind? I didn't want to throw it out, in case he came back."

"You most certainly can. He won't need those things. I'm going to take care of his housing and furniture needs for the next twenty-five years or so."

"Oh, that's nice," Esmerelda said, oblivious to the fact that her former tenant was a stone cold murderer.

The next location they hit was the home of Oscar Nieto's mother. Juana Nieto lived in apartment 2E of 235 Willoughby Avenue, between Emerson Place and Classon Avenue. When Paddy arrived at the apartment, Juana Nieto didn't seem at all surprised to see him. She offered without being asked that Oscar wasn't in the apartment, hadn't been there in two years, and the detectives were welcome to come in and look for themselves. Paddy's experience had taught him that only two types of people invited the police in for a search for a wanted person. The first type were those people who knew for a fact the wanted individual was not there. The other was the type of person who thought the wanted perp had such a clever hiding spot, the cops would never find him.

With that in mind, Paddy would never pass up an opportunity to look around. He would just confine his search to the most unusual spaces. He would look for things like captains beds. Perps loved hiding in the negative spaces behind the drawers. Dumbwaiters were another favored hiding spot.

False walls in closets and behind furniture were also prime spots to look. The bathtub was another common hide. Then there was the oldest trick in the book. Look for feet protruding from under draperies. For some reason, bad guys loved to hide in the curtains. None of these locations were particularly clever. But bad men and their enabling families seemed to think they were. After Paddy eliminated everywhere a five foot, six inch, one hundred and thirty-five pound male could hide, he settled down to speak with Juana Nieto.

"Where is Oscar?"

"I don't know," Juana lied.

"Yes, you do. In fact, you've been in contact with him probably every day since he shot *Negro*. I know you're not going to tell me where he is. But you need to convince him to come in and see me. If he keeps running, no one is going to give him a chance to tell his side of the story. The guy he shot was so bad, I'm tempted to give him a medal for shooting him. The guy would have probably killed Oscar if he didn't beat him to it. He has a good shot at a self-defense case, but not if he doesn't come in. So when you talk to him, give him my numbers."

Paddy gave her his business card with his office and cell numbers. He assured Juana they were going to be in touch.

"You haven't gotten rid of me with this visit. I'm going to be back, at least every other day until he comes in, or I find him. It would be better for Oscar if I didn't have to find him."

"I'll give him your number if I hear from him," she said.

"Okay, see you tomorrow."

The last address in New York on the list was the home of *Casper's baby-mother*. Lisbeth Altamorano lived in the basement apartment at 17-06 Willoughby Avenue, between Saint Nicholas and Onderdonk Avenues in Ridgewood Queens. Paddy didn't believe *Casper* would be here either. Lisbeth had once had *Casper* arrested for assault. He left her with a three-year-old son and no means of support. Perhaps she had something interesting to say about her former love.

There was no rear means of escape at Lisbeth's apartment. So all the detectives came to the front door. The basement door was under the stone steps leading up to the parlor floor. When Lisbeth opened the door, she also was not surprised to see the detectives.

"*Casper* doesn't live here anymore," Lisbeth said without being asked.

"When did he leave?" Paddy inquired.

"When I had that son of a bitch arrested for beating me up."

Paddy asked if they could come in and ask her some questions. She readily agreed, but not because she wanted to help. She was looking past Paddy and eyeing Romeo Amodeo hungrily, like he was a piece of meat. That's who she was talking to when she told the detectives to come right in.

Lisbeth Altamorano was a twenty-two-year-old single mother on welfare and food stamps. She was attractive in a ghetto fabulous hoodrat sort of way. When she spied the young handsome detective in the nice suit eyeing her up and down, she started working her assets for all they were worth. With her Sophie shorts and tight tee shirt, braless underneath, her curvy hips and ample breasts were being perfectly showcased. Romeo looked smitten. That was a problem for later. Now Paddy needed to interview her.

She was more than happy to provide whatever information she could, while smiling coyly at Detective Amodeo. She told Paddy about the address on Arion Place. She told him about *Casper's* mother on Willoughby. When Lisbeth was informed he was not at either location, she said he must be at his grandmother's in Connecticut. She gave Paddy the address, 2068 Main Street, in Bridgeport.

"It's the first apartment on the right. His brother Freddie lives there, too. But I think he might be in jail for something."

"Do you know his grandmother's name?" Paddy asked.

"Everyone always just called her *Abuelita*."

"Do you know the phone number there?"

"No, but a couple of days after the murder, *Casper* called me and warned me not to talk to the police about him. I took the number he called from my caller ID. Here it is," she said, giving the slip of paper to Romeo, who promptly handed it to Paddy.

"What did you tell him?" Paddy asked.

"I told him to go fuck himself."

"And he said?"

"He said that he killed *Negro*. I could be next."

"What did you say to that?"

"I told him he had a little dick, and hung up on him."

Paddy thanked Lisbeth for her candor. He left his business card, knowing he was not the detective she would call if she needed something. Still, it was the proper thing to do. Romeo lingered behind to talk for a bit more with Ms. Altamorano. He joined the other detectives on the street a minute later.

Paddy had one more address to hit, but it was in Bridgeport, Connecticut. He wanted to do some background work on the address and the new phone numbers he had first. So he decided that Connecticut would wait for tomorrow night. He rode back to the precinct with Tommy and his partner. The young cops thoroughly enjoyed their adventure working a homicide. Paddy commended them for their professionalism and promised to keep them up-dated with the case, particularly if their services were needed again.

Sergeant Boland and Romeo Amodeo agreed to be back the next night for the trip to Bridgeport. They left for the night, back to the homicide squad.

Paddy called Ronnie Kingsbury in TARU to run the numbers Paddy discovered during this day's investigation. He told Ronnie he needed all the numbers dumped from October 10th until the present, incoming and outgoing calls. He also told Ronnie he needed to know where the tower was that the perp's cell phone was originating from. Ronnie told Paddy he'd have the information in the A.M.

Paddy called the Detective Bureau of the Bridgeport Police Department. He got a Detective Colleridge on the line who was helpful. He informed Paddy that 2068 Main Street was a known drug location. Freddie Nieto was also known to his department. He verified Freddie was doing a three year bit for selling crack to an undercover. Colleridge was unfamiliar with Oscar Nieto. He also knew nothing about a grandmother. When Paddy informed Detective Colleridge he would be coming up the next night to look for his perp, Colleridge hesitated.

"What's wrong," Paddy asked.

"The detectives in this town aren't the real crime fighters in the department. In truth, we're a bunch of old guys who take care of the city's political contracts. We smooth things out and shuffle paper around. We're fixers, not gunfighters."

"So, I'm on my own?" Paddy asked.

"The guy you want to talk to is my nephew," Colleridge said. "Sergeant Sean Gilmartin runs the Street Crime Unit up here. They do the guns and narcotics cases and they know every shithead in Bridgeport. These are the guys you want to bang doors down with, not old guys in bad suits."

"I appreciate your candor, Detective," Paddy told Colleridge, as he took his nephew's cell phone number.

Paddy called Sergeant Gilmartin's cell and left a detailed voicemail for him, including the fact that he came highly recommended by his uncle. He expected to touch base with him early the next morning. After typing the *fives* on this night's progress, Paddy forwarded the case to Sergeant Krauss' computer for review. Then he went home, such as it was.

CHAPTER FORTY-FIVE

October 26, 2013
Farmingdale

Paddy was up at dawn. In spite of the lack of sleep, he was oddly refreshed. He attributed that to his homicide breaking open. Nothing energized him like a manhunt. Having nothing else to do for a while, he went to the gym for a couple of hours. This allowed Paddy to put his thoughts together and weigh his options regarding his next move. He decided one way or another, he was going up to Bridgeport tonight. It would be nice to have more than one address to visit, but the worst case scenario was raising up the drug area in Bridgeport by showing *Casper's* picture around. A possible benefit, if he was up there, was the heat might chase him back to Brooklyn. Then catching him would be like shooting fish in a barrel.

Paddy planned to visit Juana Nieto again before heading north. This was to reinforce to her that he wasn't going away until her son was in custody. But first, he wanted a look at those phone records. The results might limit the scope of his search.

By the time Paddy got home from the gym, it was 0900 hours. He called Ronnie Kingsbury to check on the phone work. Ronnie told him the dumps were ready to pick up. With respect to the cell tower information for *Casper's* phone, Ronnie told Paddy he had good news and bad news. The good news was the phone was active and pinging off of the one tower on the north side of Bridgeport. The bad news was the phone hadn't been used since October 12th, and it hadn't moved.

"He dumped it where he's hiding and forgot to turn it off," Paddy surmised.

"That sounds right. He probably picked up a burner phone when he got up there."

"I'm going to have to review the dumps to see if his mother is getting any calls from Connecticut," Paddy said. "I'll be in in an hour or so to pick up the records."

After ironing a shirt and shining his black oxfords, Paddy put on his *lucky* black suit. Fresh out of the dry cleaners, Paddy had worn this suit to close more than a dozen homicides. He hadn't intended to be wearing it when those cases broke, it just happened that way. Today he was wearing it because he wanted to force the issue. He needed a break. The pink shirt was also chosen to send a message. Only a badass could pull off a pink shirt on a manhunt. The black and red striped power tie, gold Detectives Endowment Association watch and diamond pinky ring were for the benefit of the Bridgeport Police Department. It maintained the aura of the NYPD Detectives as the *greatest detectives in the world*. It said to the agency he was visiting, "In New York, we go out to catch murderers and look like we rolled off Saville Row to do it." When travelling, it was incumbent on the detectives to bring the requisite style and flash to go with the very large substance the NYPD was famous for. A charcoal gray London Fog top coat completed the image.

Paddy called Sean Gilmartin's cell phone. The Sergeant told Paddy he would have a team to assist him when he got up there. Paddy called the office and spoke to Sergeant Krauss. It was just a formality, but Paddy needed a supervisor's permission to start his tour early. He told Steve what he needed to do and the Sarge put Paddy in the book, starting his tour from an outside wire at 0930 hours. Paddy left for the drive to TARU on his way to the Squad.

When Paddy got there, Ronnie Kingsbury came out to meet him with the documents in a manila folder. He told Paddy he had copies of everything he ran. So, if in the course of his investigation, he needed anything else checked, Ronnie was only a phone call away.

"You're getting bored in there, aren't you, Ronnie?"

"I love the tech stuff, but sometimes I miss catching bad guys. I don't want to forget what that feels like."

"You never forget. It's in your blood."

Being in Glendale already, Paddy decided to drop in on his mother-in-law---while she still was his mother-in-law. Paddy had tried to stop by and check on Sinead at least once a week, especially since Big Bill had died. He always brought her staples; like bread, milk, eggs, and whatever else she might need. In actuality, she needed nothing. Her six children were diligent in seeing she had what she needed, and the girls, Mairead, Allison and Kate were a constant doting presence. The truth was, Paddy missed Sinead and craved her company. In spite of all he had done, even as badly as he had hurt Mairead, Paddy knew Sinead still loved him. That for whatever reason, she still believed in him. Not to the point that she gave him false hope that he could rescue his faltering personal life. She told him he was a good man, and he would continue to do good things. Right now he needed to believe that. So he went to see Sinead for reinforcement, and to ask her advice.

Paddy got to the big house in Glendale after picking up the groceries from Stop and Shop on Cooper Avenue. As he suspected, Sinead didn't need them. She let him bring the food as much for Paddy's benefit as for her own. She instinctively knew that Paddy needed to do something decent for her. So she let him perform this simple kindness. Sinead brought her son-in-law into the kitchen. She fixed him a coffee before putting the groceries away. Sinead grabbed her own coffee and sat down at the kitchen table. She asked Paddy how he was holding up, concerned if he was eating enough, or getting enough sleep. He assured Sinead that physically he was fine. She told Paddy she was worried about the other parts.

Paddy looked at his mother-in-law from across the table. She always had the most compassionate and kind eyes. She was regarding Paddy with those eyes now. She knew every dark secret he once had, every awful, selfish thing he had ever done to her daughter. Yet she still cared for him and worried about his well-being. Paddy marveled at her ability to forgive, or at least look past his weakness to see something of value where Paddy did not. He knew if someone had hurt one of his daughter's the way he hurt Sinead's, it would take the hand of God to prevent Paddy from murdering them. He did not have Sinead's capacity for forgiveness. Which is probably why, he knew, he couldn't forgive himself.

He looked at Sinead. Paddy had to wonder at her remarkable beauty. At 78 years old, she still had those brilliant green eyes and the smattering of freckles across her nose, probably no different from when she was a young girl. Her skin was still smooth and perfect. The only give-away to her age were the small crow's feet at the corners of her eyes and the tiny smile lines at her mouth. When Sinead's hair had started going gray, she let it. It was now a lustrous platinum that she kept pulled back in a ponytail, revealing her still delicate neck and shoulders. She was a stunning woman and Paddy could see Mairead in her. In fact, Paddy knew that in thirty years, Mairead would probably be the very picture of her mother. The thought depressed him. Given the trajectory of their relationship, Paddy had no reason to believe he would be part of Mairead's life anymore, and he lamented that he wouldn't have the chance to see it.

"What's troubling you, Paddy?" Sinead asked.

"What isn't?" he said. "But in particular, I wanted to see what you thought I should do about Patrick's Senior Day at Sacred Heart."

"What do you think you should do?" she asked.

"Of course, I want to be there, but I think my presence would ruin the day for everyone. Patrick just wants me to do the right thing. He won't say what that is, but I think he wants me to stay away for his mom's sake. He's just being protective of her. So you've gotta respect that. Then, there's everyone else to consider. Katelyn hates me. Casey pretends I don't exist. And when I'm around Mairead, she just hurts all the time. So I don't think I'll be missed if I stay away."

"It sounds like you know what you should do," Sinead observed.

"Yeah. I just wanted your opinion. I also wanted to encourage you to go in my place."

"Oh, I don't want to intrude," Sinead said.

"Don't be ridiculous. Patrick will love to have you there. Don't you remember how he would get so excited when you came to his games when he was little? He played his best when you were there. Then after the game, all he would do was ask, 'Did Grandma see me do this?' and 'Did Grandma see me do that?' I told him you saw everything, and you were his biggest fan. He would swell up like a tic. You deserve to be there."

"What am I supposed to tell Mairead, that I'm just inviting myself?"

"No. Tell her I spoke to you and told you I couldn't make it because of work. Tell her I suggested you go in my place. Mairead will be happy to have you along."

"I don't know what to say."

"Say you'll go, and take a lot of pictures."

"I'll do that," Sinead promised. Then she paused for a second. She took Paddy's hand in hers. "What else is bothering you?" She asked.

"I don't think we're going to be seeing much of each other anymore. Mairead wants a divorce. I'm going to give it to her."

"I know. But a divorce is just a piece of paper. You still have children together. You don't stop being a family because a judge says so."

"She doesn't want to see me anymore."

"She doesn't want to see you *now*," Sinead corrected him. "She doesn't want to see you because it still hurts. It only hurts because she loves you. I know my daughter. She's never going to stop loving you. She wouldn't know where to begin. Right now, she can't get past the hurt because it's still fresh. And every time she starts to put it behind her, that damned video pops up again, ripping open the scars, setting her back to square one. Emotionally, she can't get any traction. Give her time. You're already giving her space. She might come around."

"I doubt it. Otherwise, why divorce me?"

"Mairead is one of those people who have to do *something* in a crisis. She has a need to be proactive. That's just who she is. A few months down the road, she could just as easily decide to be *undivorced*. I don't want to give you false hope, Paddy, but this story isn't written yet."

Paddy smiled for Sinead's benefit, but he didn't share her faith. He was still happy he came to see her. Her advice was sound. She was also the only family he had at the moment who didn't want to stick a fork in his eye. He hugged Sinead and kissed her cheek, thanking her for agreeing to attend Senior Day on his behalf. Then he left to go to the 83rd Precinct.

CHAPTER FORTY-SIX

October, 1990
Glendale, Queens

Two days after their first date, Paddy was at Mairead's house in Glendale, promptly at noon. Dressed casually, he wore jeans, a three button Henley pullover, a canvas thigh-length car coat, and Doc Martens leather boots. His outfit was stylish enough, and easily convertible for Anti-Crime work. He wanted to dress better, but it was lunch and a ride to work. So practicality won out. Mairead, thankfully was dressed casually as well. Her jeans, cotton sweater and denim jacket were the perfect complement to Paddy's own get-up. Her only concession to style, other than the impeccable and flattering fit of her clothes, were her shoes. She wore a distressed brown leather lace up ankle boot with a two inch heel. They looked almost antique and were so delicate, he couldn't help but finding them sexy as Hell. Mairead had an extra gym bag with her. Paddy asked her what that was for. Mairead told him it was her white Reeboks for work, her scrubs and extra clean underwear and socks.

"Are you running away?" Paddy asked.

"My mother taught me to be prepared."

"What are you preparing for?"

"You'll just have to wait and see, Paddy Durr," Mairead said playfully.

They got in Paddy's car and went uptown. Mairead told Paddy about a lunch special at Coogan's. He had something else in mind. They continued north on Broadway. He made the left onto 177th Street and found parking at the curb. They walked up to Broadway and came to the front of *El Tropical*. The authentic Spanish restaurant in Washington Heights. At least, that was what the owner Arturo Venegas had told Paddy. As far as Arturo was concerned, he was first. All others were pretenders. Paddy had no cause to disagree. The food was amazing. Mairead had never eaten Spanish food, so she was a little apprehensive. Paddy promised she would love it.

When they entered the restaurant, Arturo saw Paddy and came bounding out from behind the counter.

"Patricio! Mi amigo, como esta?" Arturo said, hugging Paddy, and kissing his cheek.

"Bien," Paddy said.

"And who is this lovely young woman?" Arturo asked, switching to English.

"Arturo, this is my dear friend, Mairead Dunleavy. Arturo is the owner and Head Chef of El Tropical," Paddy said.

Arturo kissed Mairead's hand and welcomed her to "The finest Cuban restaurant in the world." He seated them in a booth at the window and took their drink orders. Mairead told Paddy she didn't know there was a Cuban community in New York. Paddy told her the story of how Arturo came to New York via the Mariel Boat lift. In 1980 Fidel Castro decided to jettison his prisoners, his mentally ill and anyone else who was found undesirable. Arturo had a cousin who owned a jewelry store on 185th Street and Saint Nicholas Avenue. There was a very small contingent of Cuban exiles living there at the time. When Arturo cleared the containment camp in Miami, he made his way to his cousin's home in New York. There he met his wife, and learned the jewelry business. But his love was cooking. He saw the vacuum of Spanish cuisine available in the Washington Heights area. Other than the Puerto Rican Cuchifrito shop on 181st Street, there was nothing. So he and his wife saved their money and secured a bank loan to open El Tropical in 1985.

Arturo brought them coconut and mango *batidos*, a kind of smoothie, along with the cokes they ordered. He also brought them a fresh seafood ceviche, aromatic from the lemon, lime and cilantro. Arturo took Paddy's order for the both of them. He ordered in Spanish, intentionally keeping Mairead in the dark. When Arturo left, Mairead leaned in to whisper.

"What am I eating?"

"You'll have to wait and see," Paddy winked.

"Was Arturo a criminal?" she asked more cryptically.

"No," Paddy clarified. "If you were to pull Arturo's lower lip down, you would find a Star of David tattooed there. The Cuban Government did that. It was a way for them to keep track of their *enemies of the state*."

"Arturo's Jewish?"

"Most of the Cubans from this area are. Like many corners of the world, Cuba is a shitty place to be Jewish. Arturo's only crime was not being a good *Communista*. The only thing he did to get that designation was to be born Jewish. The Castros don't trust Jews."

"That's horrible," Mairead said.

"I'm sure it was, but Arturo will be the first to tell you that getting kicked out of Cuba was the best thing that ever happened to him."

Arturo brought their lunch over. Paddy had ordered *chicharones de puerco,* a type of fatty pork, fried crisp, delicious with lime juice. After this appetizer, they dug into *pernil* with *arroz con habicheulos*, roast Cuban pork with yellow rice and black beans. After lunch, they had flan with caramel sauce and *café con leche*. By design, Paddy asked Arturo to keep the portions small, and he complied, but the food was so rich, Paddy and Mairead felt swollen like tics when they were done. Mairead said she had no idea how she was going to work, as full as she was. Paddy told her to stop complaining, at least she didn't have to chase criminals.

"Try that on a belly full of rice and beans."

Arturo came over to bid them goodbye and thank them for coming in. He didn't bring a bill. He never did. Paddy left twenty dollars on the table. He knew Arturo would dutifully give it to his wait staff. But he wouldn't take any money from Paddy for himself. Paddy had argued with Arturo over the years that his generosity was too much. This argument got nowhere. Paddy tried staying away for a while. Arturo realized he wasn't coming in. He started bombarding the precinct with indignant messages until he returned. Paddy just had to resign himself to the fact that Arturo regarded him as his friend, and as far as Arturo was concerned, friends don't pay. So, to assuage his guilt, Paddy tipped generously.

"What did you do for Arturo that he treats you so well?" Mairead asked on their way to the hospital. Paddy thought about it for a minute before answering.

"Nothing. He just really likes cops. But you can be sure, if he ever asks me for anything, I'll move heaven and hell to see that he gets it."

"Isn't that against the rules?" Mairead asked.

"Absolutely. But this is one of those times when what's allowed by the police department and the right thing have nothing in common with each other. Given that choice, I'm gonna do the right thing every time, and the department can get fucked."

When Paddy dropped Mairead off at the hospital, they agreed that if he didn't get stuck with a collar, he would take her home after work. She kissed him and said she hoped to see him later. He was determined to do just that as he headed uptown to the *Three Four*.

CHAPTER FORTY-SEVEN

October, 1990
Washington Heights

When Paddy got to the Anti-Crime office, he checked the arrest sheet. He was gratified to see he was not up for a collar. That meant he could take Mairead home tonight.

At about 2030 hours, Sean Moran spotted a guy coming out of a building on the corner of 158th Street and Amsterdam Avenue. He was carrying an Intratech 9 millimeter machine pistol. When Sean bailed out of the car, the guy turned around and fled back into the building. With Sean and Pete O'Malley behind him, the perp ran up to the fourth floor and into an apartment with a door that was more vault than anything. Pete called the other Anti-Crime units over on the point to point radio. Sean went to work on the door, trying to mule kick it. It didn't even vibrate. Pete updated the team, telling Sergeant Touhey to bring the ram and sledge. They had a barricaded perp.

When the rest of the team got there, Touhey sent Paddy and Tommy up to the roof to come down and cover the fire escape, so the perp couldn't flee that way. Gus stayed behind to lend his considerable size and brute force to the project of bashing down the door.

When Paddy and Tommy were in position outside the windows of the apartment, they informed their teammates. A few minutes later, the door went down and the rest of the team began a security sweep of the darkened apartment. When Gus Demario entered the living room, he already had his gun out. When he looked up at the windows, backlit by the moon, he saw the shadow of two figures on the fire escape. Gus wordlessly brought his gun up and fired four times in rapid succession at the shadows. He would have emptied his revolver if Sean Moran hadn't tackled him.

Outside on the fire escape, Paddy could see the team enter the apartment. As he was looking through the diaphanous haze of the sheer curtains in front of the window, he thought it was a trick of the light when it looked like Gus was pointing a gun at him. Until the window exploded in his face. He felt the broken glass before he heard the shots. The bullets were travelling faster than the speed of sound, so when Paddy considered it later, it made sense. Why Gus would shoot at him never did.

By the time Tommy yanked Paddy to the floor of the fire escape and out of the line of fire, the shooting was over. Tommy took out his penlight and started to look for bullet wounds. Paddy's face was a mask of blood from the shards of glass sticking out of it. Amazingly, the only thing Gus managed to shoot was Paddy's car coat, in three places. Two bullets had perforated the pocket at his left hip but somehow missed him. The hole in the popped leather collar was more troubling. A centimeter to the left, and Paddy would have been a dead man.

The perp had heard the gunfire and ensuing pandemonium. He realized if these cops were going to shoot each other, his survivability had dropped to zero. He came out of the back room with his hands high over his head.

"Don't shoot! I give up!" the suspect yelled, throwing himself face down on the floor.

They found the Intratech in the room he had come out of. After verifying Paddy was just cut by the flying glass, Touhey had Sean and Pete take the perp and the firearm to the station house. He told Gus and Armando to meet him at the hospital. He jumped in with Tommy and Paddy and drove the three of them to the Emergency Room. Paddy convinced the Sergeant not to make the incident a firearms discharge. It would be less aggravation if they just wrote it up as Paddy injuring himself falling through the window. It would also mean Gus wouldn't receive Charges and Specifications for an unauthorized discharge. That wasn't Paddy's motivation for wanting to shortcut the process. In spite of looking like he had taken a walk through an abattoir, he still hoped to take Mairead home tonight. A firearms discharge investigation would have made that impossible.

When Tommy and Kevin led Paddy into the hospital, Mairead saw him and almost fainted. The cops calmed her and assured her it was just cuts from flying glass. His eyes were fine, other than the blood that kept running into them.

"How did this happen?" Mairead demanded. She hadn't heard anything on the police radios in the emergency room. The whole operation had gone down over the point to point radios.

"I fell through a window," Paddy said sheepishly.

That sounded like a lie to Mairead, but she whisked Paddy into a room and ran to get the surgeon on duty. He came in and examined Paddy under a bright light. He determined the wounds were superficial and not deep enough to compromise any muscle, tendon or nerve function. He authorized Mairead to remove the glass and disinfect the wounds.

So Mairead got a fresh surgical kit with latex tipped forceps, and spent the next half hour carefully removing glass shards from Paddy's face. Paddy thought the act felt incredibly intimate. He was actually enjoying the gentle attention and care Mairead was administering. At one point Paddy saw her start to tear up. He didn't want that.

"And for our third date," Paddy said softly. "Your mother picked broken glass out of my face."

"Shut up!" Mairead laughed. "You're going to make me screw up."

Paddy knew he was jumping the gun, talking about having children with her. But she didn't call him on it. He decided to take that as a good sign. She was curious about something else.

"You're not at all clumsy. So how does someone like you fall through a window?"

"You're not buying it, huh?"

"No. Apart from the fact that it would be out of character for you to just fall, this glass imbedded in your face came from a window that shattered out at you, not you falling into it. The pieces are too small. Also, when you took your coat off, a piece of copper fell on the floor. It must have been stuck in your collar. I know what that is. It's copper jacketing from a bullet. You also didn't have those three holes in your coat when we were at lunch. So what gives?"

"Swear you'll keep a secret?" Paddy asked, knowing she would.

"I swear," she said, hooking pinkies with him.

"I was on a fire escape covering a window. One of my partners inside the apartment mistook me for a bad guy and shot at me," Paddy admitted.

"Which partner, the big stupid looking one?"

"Don't be too hard on Gus. With that mug and his tiny dinosaur brain, life has been hard enough."

"I worry about you being around him."

"Me too," said Paddy.

After Mairead finished cleaning up Paddy's wounds and disinfecting them, he left to go *end of tour* at the precinct. Fortunately, he had a spare shirt in his locker to replace the blood-soaked Henley. So he took a shower and changed before heading back to the hospital to pick up Mairead.

She was waiting for him. She was back in her outfit from lunch and Paddy thought she looked adorable. The low light under the ambulance bay gave her an air of mystery. Until she saw him and lit up with that amazing smile. She ran over to him and kissed him, raking her fingers through his wet hair.

"Do you want to get a drink before I take you home?" Paddy asked.

"Oh, I'm not going home tonight. I think it's time you showed me your apartment, Paddy Durr."

CHAPTER FORTY-EIGHT

October, 1990
Astoria, Queens

When Paddy got the door opened to his apartment, Mairead walked in and dropped her purse and gym bag on the floor. She pulled Paddy in behind her by his coat lapels, and pushed the front door closed behind him. Mairead shoved him against the door, grabbed his hair behind his head, raised up on her toes to pull Paddy's mouth to her own. In the next instant, they were tearing at each other's clothes, pausing only to explore and caress the freshly exposed skin. When enough clothing was removed to allow it, they had each other there with Mairead pressed back against the wall, and Paddy thrust deeply into her. The frenzied animal desperation of their need for each other overwhelmed them both. They were left shaking in the aftermath of it. But only for a moment. Paddy hoisted the half-dressed Mairead up, and carried her into his bedroom.

They took care to remove what was left of their clothing. For the next couple of hours, they patiently explored each other, leaving no square inch of flesh unvisited. Paddy took all of her in, learning every curve, sinew, and bend of her body. He tried to memorize each freckle and crease, promising himself to soon return. They had each other again and again. Exhaustion should have taken them over, but it could find no purchase. They burned too hot, the fuel of their desire seemingly endless. They fully devoured each other.

It was finally hunger that was able to pry them apart. Neither of them had eaten since their lunch at Tropical, and the calories they expended getting after each other had to be replenished. Paddy grabbed the phone by his bedside and ordered forty dollars of Chinese food from Lee Ho Fook's on Ditmars Boulevard. They were famous for their big dishes of beef chow mein. Best of all, they were open all night and delivered.

They lay there in bed waiting for their food to come. Paddy was idly running his fingers down along Mairead's lower back, and over the curve of her perfect derriere, pausing there to caress the smooth skin and firm muscle beneath it. Mairead looked over her shoulder, watching him.

"With this job, I haven't had the time to work out as often as I should. My ass is getting so fat," she said critically. Paddy laughed out loud.

"What's so funny?"

"Mairead," Paddy said patiently. "The only way you could ever call your ass fat is if that word suddenly became a synonym for perfect."

"It's not perfect."

"Oh, it's perfect. As in, without flaw, and if the food gets here before you sit up, I'm eating my Lo Mein off of it."

"You're an animal," she smiled.

"Wild as hell," Paddy agreed, as the buzzer at his front door sounded.

Paddy jumped up and put on a pair of gym shorts. He found his wallet in his pants, in a pile by the front door. He opened the door and startled the man in the bicycle helmet with his Chinese food. Paddy smiled to try to put him at ease. Failing that, he handed the man a fifty dollar bill and took the shopping bag of food from him.

Mairead went into Paddy's closet and put on one of his best dress shirts. She rolled the sleeves up and asked him what he thought. Paddy told her it looked better on her than it ever did on him. It was a simple powder blue cotton oxford, but with the buttons open in front just enough to let the tops of her amazing freckled breasts peek out, it was hotter than any piece of lingerie Paddy had ever seen. He warned Mairead if she didn't stay outside of his arm's length, they were never going to eat their food.

They did eat it though. And once their carbohydrate stores were replenished, they were back in bed to burn some of that fuel off. And so the night went into the morning. They finally slept, exhaustion ultimately taking its toll. They collapsed, tangled up in each other. Paddy would later recall those few hours rest as some of the best sleep he ever had.

Paddy woke to find Mairead sleeping with her head on his chest, cooing softly. He gently lifted her head off of him, and laid it softly on the pillow. It was already 1100 hours. Paddy used the bathroom and made a pot of coffee. While it brewed, he watched Mairead sleep. He thought she was unbearably beautiful. He wanted to stay in this moment forever. But to even prolong it, he needed to make a phone call.

Paddy called Kevin Touhey at home. He was fortunate to catch the boss in. Young for a supervisor, Kevin had the same boundless energy as his cops. So he was seldom home.

"Hey Sarge, its Paddy. I'm gonna need an E-Day," Paddy said, using the police vernacular for an emergency excusal. Paddy spied Mairead pretending to be asleep and not listening.

"Is everything alright?" Kevin asked. Paddy looked over at Mairead, making eye contact with her. He wanted her to hear the next part.

"Better than alright, Kev. I just had the greatest night of my life, and I can't let it end."

Touhey knew instinctively what he meant. He also sensed his friend was experiencing a profound life-changing event. Before he met Mairead, Kevin had never heard Paddy talk like that. He also had never seen him so confident and happy. Touhey would have to break it to his Anti-Crime team that an era had ended. Paddy Durr was through chasing tail.

"Okay Paddy. Between today and the swing, you've got three days. Don't run off and get married without telling us. The team could use a party. We'll see you Tuesday."

"10-04," Paddy said, hanging up.

Mairead was sitting up now, looking at Paddy with benign wonder. Even with the little pink cuts in his face from the glass she had to remove the night before, she thought he looked vaguely angelic. His long hair was tangled, mussed, wild and flowing down his back. His muscular chest and shoulders were relaxed, and even the tattoos on his big arms no longer looked threatening. He reminded her of a painting of the Archangel Michael. In this light, he would not have looked out of place if he had six foot wings protruding from his back. But even with all of that, it was the look of pure adoration he beheld Mairead with that put her over the edge.

"The best night of your life?" she asked.

"And it's not even close. It was positively transformative."

"I'm not sure I know what you mean."

"Yes you do. You know exactly what you've done to me. I never said this to anyone before, but I am hopelessly in love with you. I can't bear the thought of living another day without you. It just wouldn't make sense anymore. And I've felt this way since the first time I saw you in Coogan's. I just thought you should know. I'm not running a short con here, Mairead. I'm in it for the long haul. I want it all with you."

"I know you do, Paddy Durr. I love you, too. Now come over here and be my boyfriend, and do boyfriend stuff to me."

"Oh, I'll do plenty," he said as he stalked her like a jungle cat from across the bed.

Later on, after they showered together, and made a mess of each other in there as well, Mairead surveyed Paddy's apartment. She agreed the décor was Spartan. So they reluctantly put on clothes and went to Macy's so Mairead could properly decorate the space in which she told Paddy she planned to be spending more time.

After arranging the throw pillows, curtains and picture frames around the apartment, it took on a more homey and comfortable feel. They started to make plans for dinner, but got distracted and ended up in bed again. Paddy didn't know how long he could keep this up, but he was determined to try until he was at least desiccated and blind. Then he thought he might reconsider the issue.

CHAPTER FORTY-NINE

October 26, 2013
Glendale, Queens

On Paddy's way to the precinct from Sinead's house, he got a call on his cell phone from Hiram Borstein. He put the phone on speaker and told Hiram to go ahead. Hiram told Paddy he was going over the financial statements for him and Mairead. He told Paddy he was not only being overly generous, he was waiving the right to an enormous sum of money. Big Bill had liquidated his business before he died. Bill and Sinead agreed the money should be split amongst their children. Mairead's share was a little more than eight-hundred-thousand dollars. The money was sitting in a tax deferred account, jointly held by them both. Ira informed Paddy that since the money was a gift before Bill died, it didn't qualify as an inheritance and was in fact marital property. Paddy was entitled to half of it.

"I don't want a penny of it."

"As your attorney, I can't in good conscience let you walk away from that kind of money."

"You're fired," Paddy said.

"What?" Hiram asked, perplexed.

"I asked you to do one thing, Hiram. I gave you explicit instructions about what I wanted. I didn't ask you to review the financials and look for money for me. That's not my money. Bill never intended for me to have it. If he knew what a shit I was to his daughter, he probably would have used it to have me killed. Mairead's just going to end up giving it to our kids, which is what I wanted anyway. In any event, I wouldn't sleep if I took money from her. Can you do what I asked you to?"

"Of course, Paddy. I knew you would say that. I didn't think you'd fire me, but I knew you wouldn't want that money. I had a responsibility to bring it to your attention."

"You're hired again. Are the papers ready?"

"You both just have to sign them and then her attorney can file them with the court. Do you want me to send them to her lawyer?" Hiram asked.

"I'll try and pick them up tomorrow. Think of a fee. I need to pay you something."

"I really didn't do much. How does a hundred bucks sound?"

"Like a bargain. I'll see you tomorrow."

CHAPTER FIFTY

October 26, 2013
Brooklyn

Paddy got to the 83 Squad and right to work looking at the phone records from Ronnie Kingsbury. First he looked at the activity on *Casper's* cell phone. The last three calls on it were made on the evening of October 12th. One was to his mother's home phone. The call lasted twenty-two minutes. The next call, lasting only three minutes, was to Lisbeth Altamorano. The last call was to a number Paddy did not recognize. It was a 917 area code, so it was a cell phone. The conversation was just short of ten minutes. Paddy circled that number in red felt pen. He would have Ronnie Kingsbury run it for the owner and call detail. It would be nice to know that stuff now, but barring a life-threatening emergency, the phone company wouldn't return the subpoena for at least a day.

Paddy looked at the cell tower report for *Casper's* cell phone. Just as Ronnie had reported, the phone was active and consistently hitting the same tower in north Bridgeport. The probability was *Casper* dumped the phone, leaving it on. He likely got a burner phone to replace it. But something about that idea was sticking in Paddy's craw. There was a flaw in the reasoning, but he couldn't put his finger on it. He laid the report to the side, intending to get back to it.

Finally, Paddy looked at the dumps for Juana Nieto's home phone. What he noticed immediately seemed to jump off the page and hit him in the face. No less than three times a day since October 12th, calls came into Juana's phone from the same number bearing the 203 area code of Bridgeport. That meant the number was probably a landline. This Paddy circled three times in red felt pen. As he did so, he realized what was bothering him about the cell phone *Casper* presumably dumped. The battery should have died weeks ago. The phone was being charged somewhere near that cell tower. If they could narrow down its location within a couple of hundred yards, the Fugitive Task Force had the ability to pinpoint its location. Paddy made some notes on that and planned to call Detective Ron Johnston later.

Paddy called Ronnie Kingsbury to get the new subpoenas rolling. Paddy bounced his theory about the cell phone off the expert. Ronnie agreed.

"I should have thought of that," Ronnie admitted. "That phone should have gone dead within forty-eight hours. He's definitely charging it somewhere. The problem is, if he doesn't call anyone on it, there's no way we can triangulate on the signal."

"Fugitives has a new tool. If we can get close, as long as the phone is on, we can find it. We'll see what I can discover up there tonight."

"I probably won't get these new dumps until tomorrow. But if I can shake out a favor and get them tonight, I'll hit you on your cell,"

Paddy was about to call Brooklyn North Homicide to find out when Romeo Amodeo was coming in when his cell phone rang. The caller ID said it was Carmela Del La Fuente. Paddy couldn't imagine what she was calling for, her work on this particular homicide was complete. Unless it was personal. They were friends. He thought perhaps she needed a favor.

"How are you doing, Carm?"

"I'm fine." But she didn't sound fine.

"What's the problem? You don't have to soften bad news for me. Just tell me."

"I would rather you came down to see me."

"So it's morgue business, and it's personal. Tell me right now, does it involve my family?"

"It's your father," she told him reluctantly.

"I didn't know I still had one of those. The fucker finally died, huh?"

Carmela stammered something unintelligible. She wasn't prepared for this type of reaction. Paddy realized her confusion and discomfort.

"I can be there in twenty minutes," he told her.

Twenty-one-and-a-half minutes later, Paddy was in Carmela's office. She hugged him and said how sorry she was to be the one to have to tell him about his father's death. Paddy thought it was time to dispel any misunderstanding she was harboring about the nature of his relationship with the man.

"While I would never turn down a hug from you, I feel compelled to tell you that my father's death in no way represents a loss to me. This is good news. I'm glad to hear it from a friend. Now what do you need me to do for you?"

"I need you to make an identification."

"Then let's do that."

Carmela brought Paddy back to the refrigerated lockers. She pulled out a numbered locker drawer. The gurney was positioned so the first thing that slid out was the body's feet. These feet were nasty. They were grimy and fetid and had twisted toe nails that looked like infected corn chips, and the smell was nauseating. The only clean thing on them was the ME's toe tag identifying the stiff by number. As the body further emerged, Paddy noted the blotchiness, the bruising, the emaciation, and ground-in filth that seemed to be the general condition of the deceased. Then there was his face. It looked like someone had stretched latex over a pointy and misshapen caricature of a not quite human head. The eyes were sunken so deep, it seemed like the sockets were empty, as opposed to the void of empathy which characterized them in life. His cheeks were sallow, and sunken as well. The nose was crooked from being broken so many times, and bulbous and veiny from the many years of alcohol abuse. His father's mouth was instantly recognizable. Paddy had never heard it utter a kind word, and the perpetual sneer it was bent into had not abandoned him in death. Finally, his hair was a mangy and matted confluence of white twisted wire, mixed with vomit, urine, and filth. All in all, his appearance was a self-inflicted atrocity.

"That is Walter Durr, in all of his glory," Paddy said.

"Isn't he your father?"

"That's what my birth certificate says. But he was in the middle of a three-year bit upstate when I was conceived and born. I am happy to report that he and I share no genetic material whatsoever. What I'm curious about is how you managed to link him to me."

"He had this in his pocket," Carmela said, showing Paddy a wrinkled, dirty piece of paper. In a faded and palsy scrawl were the words, *my son is Detective Padraig Durr, NYPD.*

"I see the white foam dried around his nose and mouth. I'm assuming it was an overdose. Where did the wretch meet his end?"

"They found him in a shooting gallery in the Bronx, East 194th Street and Bainbridge Avenue."

"How fucking fitting."

"Paddy, I don't know you to be callous. What's going on here?" Carmela asked.

"I could tell you what a shit this man was to me, but you wouldn't be able to get your mind around the cruelty of it. I will share my earliest memory of my father with you, though. I remember my mother was giving me a bath. I was about four. She walked away to answer the phone or something. My father came into the bathroom to piss. He was drunk again. He was always drunk. Between him teetering around and having a tiny dick, he was pissing all over himself. I laughed. Because when you're three, that kind of shit is funny. He didn't agree. He came over to the tub and forced my head under the water and held it there. I know I was thrashing and kicking, trying to get him off me. But I was a little kid. What chance did I have? I know I blacked out. My mother must have intervened before I drowned. I came to in the ambulance on the way to the hospital, puking soapy water all over myself. When the doctors and nurses wanted to know what happened, I wouldn't talk about it. I wouldn't answer anybody's questions. The doctors thought I might have brain damage from the oxygen deprivation. Then they wanted to know where all the scars, burns and bruises came from. My mother convinced them I was just clumsy. I don't know if they bought it, or they just didn't want to get invested in someone else's misery. Now, that wasn't the first awful thing he had ever done to me. But it's the first thing I remember. For most of my childhood, if we had any interaction at all, it involved him either punching me in the head or putting cigarettes out on my back. It continued like that until I got big enough and mean enough to make it stop. Now, if all that served to make me callous, did I really have a choice in the matter?"

"Paddy, I'm so sorry. I had no idea."

"How could you? Mairead and my *shrink* are the only people I ever told that story to. And now you."

"What do you want to do with the body?"

"I would like to defile it, but that's just beneath me. You should have left him in the Bronx. It's a shorter trip to Hart Island from there."

"Do you really want him buried in Potter's Field?"

"To have him buried under a numbered brick, on a remote island, that nobody ever visits appeals to me. Hopefully, in a year or two no one will remember he ever lived at all. That would be fitting, and altogether proper."

On the way back to the 83 Squad, Paddy thought of the last time he had seen Walter Durr alive. It was late in 1993. Paddy was a *white shield detective* assigned to the 108th Precinct Detective Squad. That's where the department elected to bury him after the Washington Heights riots. He got a call from a detective in Brooklyn North Narcotics. His father had been arrested on Troutman Street for possessing two bundles of heroin. A *bundle*, or *deck* consists of ten glassine envelopes of the narcotic. Twenty glassines, considering they were all for Walter's personal use, is an enormous amount of dope. It also constitutes a felony. Detective Collasanto asked Paddy if he would come down to the "Old" 94 Precinct on Driggs Avenue in Greenpoint. This was the headquarters of Brooklyn North Narcotics. Paddy told him he would be right over.

When he got there, Collasanto was clearly agitated. Paddy apologized for his father being an asshole. Collasanto was curious how Paddy knew his father had been acting like a prick.

"He's been one his whole life. He's not about to change today."

"I called you out of respect. After what they did to you up-town, I thought I owed you as much. But this guy is a real hard guy to want to do a favor for."

"Thanks. Let's go see him so we can both be rid of him," Paddy told the detective.

When they got into the cell area, Paddy could already hear his father ranting and threatening everyone within earshot. When they got to the front of his cell, Walter stopped talking for a second, but only for a second.

"You see," Walter challenged Collasanto. "I told you he was a big shot. You're in deep shit now."

"Could you open the cell for me?" Paddy asked. Collasanto wordlessly complied. When Paddy walked into the cell, Walter spread out his arms as if to receive an embrace from Paddy. Paddy delivered a vicious right fist into Walter's unprotected diaphragm, knocking all the air out of his lungs and driving him to his knees. Then Paddy backhanded him in the face. Except for Walter struggling to breath, there was a momentary blessed silence. Paddy stepped back out of the cell and Collasanto locked it. The detective looked concerned.

"Is he hurt?"

"I've seen him take worse beatings and not even remember them the next day."

"I can knock his charges down to misdemeanors, but that's the best I can do. He was already in front of the desk in the *eight three* when he started dropping your name."

"I don't want you to do that. Keep the felony. Add on a resisting arrest charge. Did he talk to anyone else on the set before you pinched him?"

"Yeah, he spoke to a few mutts out there."

"Then hit him with a drug sale charge, too," Paddy suggested.

"Are you sure?"

"Uh-huh."

Paddy reached into the cell and grabbed Walter by the hair on the back of his head. He pulled his face into the bars, ensuring the crossbar was pressed against his windpipe, rendering Walter temporarily speechless. Paddy wanted to be certain he understood what was said next, and he didn't want it confused by anything the old junky had to offer.

"Listen carefully, you shitbird. Stop telling people you are my father. You are not. I am the son of some guy your wife fucked while you were in prison. I get another phone call like this one, I'm coming to choke you out. Now take your pinch like a man, and shut your rotten fucking face!"

Paddy let go of Walter's head and dropped him in a heap on the floor of the cell. That was the last time he saw Walter Durr alive.

CHAPTER FIFTY-ONE

October 26, 2013
Brooklyn

When Paddy got upstairs to the squad, Matty price had a message for him. Detective Dave Molinari from Brooklyn North Gangs was looking for him. Paddy took the message and sat down at his desk to return Dave's call. Molinari was the Latin King specialist in Gangs. He was rumored to have a highly-placed confidential informant in the gang. Paddy knew Molinari was a good detective, but he was manic. In constant motion, he was in possession of too much information. No human being could possibly process everything he put on his own plate. So to work with him took some patience, and not a little concentration. But, if you could work around his lunacy, the results were often spectacular.

"Do you know anything about a guy named *Negro* who got smoked outside Angela's diner, maybe in early October?" Molinari asked Paddy, in all seriousness.

"You mean the homicide I've been discussing with you at least once a week since it happened?" Paddy asked sarcastically. "Yeah. I know a little about it."

"Oh shit! I didn't realize that was your case."

"No matter. What do you have for me now?"

"My CI was on Starr Street the morning *Casper* got the gun and went over there to smoke him."

"Where is your CI right now?"

"He's in my office,"

"I'll be right there."

Brooklyn North Gangs was located in the deep rear of the second floor of the 81st Precinct on Ralph Avenue. When Paddy got to Dave's office, he immediately recognized Molinari's CI from Starr Street. Heriberto Clemente was known in the streets as *Clambake,* due to his propensity to wear shorts, tank tops, and sandals, long after the weather had gone too cold for any reasonable person to want to do so. Today, a week short of November, Clambake was wearing khaki shorts, a Tommy Bahama shirt and a pair of Ocean Pacific flip flops. Clemente was known to be the second in command of the Latin Kings' set from Starr Street. He had emerged from prison as fifth in the pecking order two years ago. But murder and incarceration had worked to his advantage, and he had been promoted several times. He had now risen to the esteemed rank of *Enforcer.* That he had managed such a feat while snitching out every drug deal and crime the Latin Kings had committed over the last two years was a testament to his extraordinary skill, as a gang banger and an informant.

For the purpose of this debriefing, Paddy would operate under the fiction that he didn't already know Clambake, and would refer to him only by his CI number, BNG 2354. He told the following story:

In early October he was hanging out at Starr Street and Knickerbocker Avenue. He had just dropped off two G-packs (two thousand glassines of heroin) to the Latin King drug spot upstairs. It was sometime around 5:30 to 6:00 A.M. when Elephant Boy drove up in his white van. He got out and told Casper Negro was eating breakfast in Angela's on Wilson Avenue. He said Negro had his car parked on Noll Street. EB went to the side door of his van. He has a hinged trap under the carpet there that he uses to hide drugs and guns. He reached in and pulled out a .38 revolver and gave it to Casper. EB told Casper to go down there and "take care of our problem." Then he warned him not to come back until it was done.

Casper took the gun and headed down Knickerbocker. Clambake said he never thought Casper would go through with it. But, about a half hour later, he heard a shot, followed a few seconds later by five more. A few minutes after that, Casper came running back onto the block. He was shaking like a leaf when he told EB that Negro was dead. EB asked him where the gun was. Casper told him he dropped it when he got hit by a cab running away. EB gave him some cash and told him to disappear. Casper walked off the block toward Irving Avenue. Clambake didn't see or hear from Casper until two days later when Casper called from Bridgeport. He said he was hiding at his Abuelita's place. He was looking for some money to tide him over. Clambake told Casper he would bounce his funds request off of EB. He knew EB wouldn't send the kid a dime.

"That fat, greedy *maricon* looks out only for himself," Clemente observed bitterly.

"Why are you only telling us about this now? It's been a month."

"I was saving the information until I needed it."

"And what makes you need it now?"

"I got grabbed tonight selling two G-Packs to undercovers in Canarsie."

"The Latin Kings are branching out to Canarsie? I thought the Jamaicans and Haitians had that neighborhood on lockdown," Paddy asked. Clambake lit up in a smile.

"This wasn't an LK deal. I put this thing together for myself and my family. No Latin King involvement."

"Where did you get two G-Packs?"

"That was the beauty of this plan. I broke into *EB's* van and took the dope from his trap. Nobody knows I did it. *EB* is still on the hook for those G-Packs. The Kings from the Bronx who supply him on consignment are gonna want their money. *EB* can't hold onto money long enough to have any cushion. When the Bronx finds out he can't pay, they'll send somebody down to Starr Street to shoot that fat fuck in his dick."

"Which brings me to my second question," Paddy said. "You just gave me *EB* for accessory to murder on a silver platter. You robbed him of twenty-thousand dollars' worth of dope, and set him up to take the fall for it. You obviously have an enormous hard-on for him. I have my own reasons for hating him. What did he do to you?"

"I was selling drugs for him when I got pinched five years ago. *EB* made all kinds of promises to take care of my family while I was upstate. As soon as I got shipped north, *EB* went to see my wife. My son was just an infant. He figured she was desperate. So he kicked it to her. When she told him to go fuck himself, he turned his back on them and never gave them a penny. I vowed right then to get that motherfucker. So, that's what he did to me. I want him broke, and I want him dead. I'll settle for seeing him go to prison. The Kings will end up killing him in there anyway."

Paddy regarded Clemente for a moment. Clambake never broke eye contact. He sat there impassively waiting for Paddy to tell him what came next.

"The information is accurate, credible and of tremendous value," Paddy told Dave Molinari. "I assume you're having trouble with the Narco Bureau Chief. John Young doesn't understand the term *working well with others*. So I'll call Homicide and have them straighten him out. You need Clambake for your RICO case, yes?"

"He is my RICO case," Molinari admitted.

"What are the conditions of his cooperation?"

"That's the thing. We never had leverage on him. He came in cold, looking to fuck the Latin King Nation. I understand his motivation, and I trust it, but what do we do about this new drug case?"

"I got an idea. Is Eddy Feely still running the Gang Bureau?"

"Yeah, he's good. He'll play ball with whatever you have in mind."

"We have Feely request jurisdiction for this drug case as part of your on-going RICO," Paddy said. "Then we have Buscarello from Homicide lobby on Feely's behalf. When the DA hears what this guy can do for everybody, he's not gonna give a shit about two G-Packs of heroin. The only thing that changes for you, Clambake, is you're going to have to plead guilty to a sealed indictment for the dope. Your cooperation works that off before a sentencing hearing."

Paddy addressed Molinari.

"I assume, after the takedown he and his family go into witness protection?"

"That was the idea," Molinari confirmed.

"Okay, Clambake, here is your new deal. We now have leverage on you. Nobody is looking to beat you up over it, but if you don't hold up your end of the bargain, you and your family don't get into Witsec, and you get pounded for the dope. Are you okay with all of that?"

"I figured it would go something like that," Clemente said.

"One other thing. You don't get to save information for later anymore. You report to Dave when shit goes down, not a month later."

"I'm good with that," Clemente said.

"Let me call the Homicide Bureau. Dave, you tell Feely what we're up to. He needs to get on board now."

"Detective Durr," Clemente interrupted. "If I knew it was your murder case, I wouldn't have sat on the info."

"Why is that?"

"You were always respectful to me. You knew my business, but you never showed me up on the street. You did your job, but you at least let me keep my dignity. That goes a long way with me. I feel like I owe you one."

"Help me get *EB*, and we're square."

"Count on it," Clemente said.

CHAPTER FIFTY-TWO

October 26, 2013
Bridgeport, Connecticut

When Paddy got back to the 83 Squad, Romeo Amodeo was waiting for him at his desk. Paddy had Romeo come into Sergeant Krauss' office so he could update the two of them on the recent developments in the case. It was already 2200 hours. Steve suggested that if they were going up to Bridgeport, they should leave soon. He authorized Joe Furio and Armando Gigante to go with Paddy and Romeo. Steve said he would stay back in the squad and handle any flak from the Boro or the chief of detective's office when they got word they were hunting a killer in Connecticut.

Paddy called Sergeant Gilmartin to tell him they were delayed by the new developments, but they were still coming north. He told Paddy to call him when he got up there. He would rendezvous with Paddy's crew at the Police Headquarters parking lot on State Street.

Paddy drove up I-95 in one squad car with Romeo, while Joe and Armando followed in another. Romeo asked Paddy what time he thought they might be done. Paddy thought that was a curious question to ask in the middle of a manhunt.

"You got somewhere else you need to be?"

"I was hoping to hook up with Lisbeth tonight."

"Lisbeth, *Casper's* baby-mother?"

"She's hot."

"Yeah," Paddy said. "A hot mess. She's a hoodrat, Romeo. What the hell are you thinking?"

"I'm just looking for a little something on the side."

"Your tan isn't even faded from your honeymoon yet, and you're already looking to run around on your wife?"

"You cheated on yours," Romeo pointed out, defensively.

"And look how well that worked out for me. Look, I'm not going to moralize and try and tell you how to live your life. I hardly qualify. I just want to point a few things out, and maybe give you the benefit of my experience. I met your wife. She's adorable, and she thinks the sun rises out of your ass. You are perfect together. That is a rare and fragile thing. If you do this thing, this cheap, tawdry thing, you will never have the chance to be perfect again. Once it's gone, it's gone forever. Even if you get away with it, even if your wife never finds out, you'll know. And you'll punish yourself for it. I'm asking you as a friend to reconsider. I don't want to see you make the same mistake I did."

Romeo told Paddy he would think about it, but he wasn't happy having his conscience brought into the conversation. He brooded over the problem the rest of the way to Bridgeport.

After linking up with the Bridgeport Street Crime Unit, the cops and detectives came up with a quick Tac-plan. Going eight cars deep, it was easiest just to cover all the exits and bum rush what had become an abandoned crack house. 2068 Main Street was an attached red brick two-story apartment house with four units. The building had a front porch and another in the rear. With no roof access or entry to the adjoining residences, the possible suspects were trapped. If Oscar Nieto were here, he would soon be found. No one was slipping out of this noose.

When the cops hit the building, there was a brief moment of pandemonium among the crack heads squatting there. After the location was secured, Paddy walked among the handcuffed two dozen or so junkies and vagrants with a flashlight and Oscar and Freddie Nieto's pictures. Neither were present. Freddie being incarcerated, his picture was being shown only for information. Unfortunately, the dealers were uncooperative, and the squatting junkies were so beyond wrecked that they were unable to focus on a picture, let alone answer the simplest of questions. A search of the building recovered four loaded guns, a large amount of crack, and a fair total of US currency. The Bridgeport cops were ecstatic. Paddy on the other hand, had nothing to show yet for his field trip north. He and Joe Furio stood in the street in front of the building as more uniform police from the Bridgeport PD showed up to assist with the bust. Paddy was looking everywhere but the house they had just hit. Then he found what he was looking for.

"There you are," Paddy said.

"Did you find the *sentinel?*" Joe asked.

"Four houses down, across the street."

"Old black guy, yellowy tee-shirt, sneering at us from behind his screen door?" Joe asked for clarification.

"That's him."

"He looks ornery."

"I have faith in your ability to reach the better angels of his nature, Joe."

"I'd be more confident if I had my blackjack."

Every block, in every urban city in America had a sentinel. He or she was the one neighbor who saw everything. They knew everybody's business, because they made it their business to know. It was as if they never slept, observing and recording everything. The only problem was figuring out how to motivate them to share their information. Usually, they collected the info only as a way to fuel their bitter resentment and sense of superiority over their neighbors. You could find them ensconced in a window, or as this one was, with his face pressed against his screen door. He had been at this for so long the screen had stretched around his face leaving a mask-like impression. Now, if he walked away, it would appear that the aura of himself had been left behind in bas relief in the rusty screen. As the detectives moved nonchalantly toward their sentinel, his disdain for the police became more animated. He was definitely the neighbor they needed to speak with. Motivating him to share was the problem. Fortunately, Joe Furio was a master motivator. Which was good, because the detectives were on a short clock. They couldn't keep coming up to Bridgeport to sweet talk the information out of the man. So he would have to be forthcoming, or deeply regret his obstinance.

As the detectives approached the man's front porch, he started berating them loudly. "Motherfucking white cop motherfuckers" was the gist of it. "Get the fuck off my porch" was the other recurrent theme. Joe continued through the vitriol, pretending not to hear him. His hand cupped to his right ear in a comical pantomime of the hard of hearing. Until he had gotten to the front of the screen door. The man was by now almost apoplectic, his eyes bulging from his head as he screamed and spit. Joe was directly in front of the door when he took the right hand that had been cupped to his ear, and drove it up into the man's nose, right through the screen. The silence was instant, as he fell heavily back on the dirty carpeting behind him.

"Did you hear any of that?" Joe asked, innocently.

"Yeah, I think he told you to come right in. He would be happy to look at your photos. At least that's what I heard."

The detectives entered the house. Joe knelt down to grab the man by his salt and pepper and wildly disheveled afro. He had a rivulet of blood trickling from his left nostril. Joe shook him to get his attention. The man looked up into Furio's eyes, properly afraid.

"My partner here is going to show you pictures and ask you questions," Joe told him. "Answer his questions. Don't lie. If you do, I'm going to beat the shit out of you in your own house, on your own shitty rug. Got it?"

"You guys aren't from Bridgeport," the man observed.

"No." Paddy said. "We are dangerous men from a very bad place, and we don't have time for whatever your problems are with the Bridgeport Police Department. Do you want to help us? Or should I just let my partner knock those last four teeth down your throat?"

"I'll look at your pictures."

When Paddy showed the man the picture of Oscar Nieto, he responded immediately.

"That's *Casper*. His grandmother used to own the house the police hit tonight. She moved to the north side a year ago."

He didn't know where exactly, except that it was near the highway. He said he only knew her first name, Yvette. He hadn't seen *Casper* since the grandmother moved. Paddy showed him the picture of Freddie Nieto. The man angrily said that asshole had stayed behind at the house and turned it into a crack den. He claimed to be the one to dime Freddie out to the police. He was proud to have participated in having Freddie put in prison.

"If you called the police on Freddie, why give us shit for just coming over to talk to you?" Joe asked.

"I live here alone. If these animals figure out I'm talking to the police, they'll kill me. I'm an old man. I can't protect myself anymore. All I got is this house."

"Fair enough," Paddy said, helping him to his feet. "Feel free to motherfuck us when we leave. We'll play along." Then Paddy reached into his pocket and produced Sean Gilmartin's business card. He gave it to the man.

"If you want to clean up your neighborhood, you call that sergeant. He'll work with your information confidentially and protect you. You won't have to live scared anymore."

"Who are you guys?" the man asked.

"No one," Joe told him. "We were never here. Now don't forget, make a scene when we leave."

The man came back to his place at the screen to begin his barrage at the detectives as instructed. It was effective enough, but you could tell his heart wasn't in it anymore. He made all the noise, but the hate just wasn't there.

Sean was waiting in the street for them up the block. He saw where they had come from and heard the old man continuing to yell at them as they walked away.

"I see you met our mayor," Sean joked.

"Is that who that was? You get a lot of 911 calls around here?"

"Yeah, but they're all anonymous."

"I'm willing to bet they're all from him."

"Really?"

"He told me he was the one who gave up Freddie. I gave him your card. When he calls, help him. He's old, alone and scared. But he wants to help. I won't go so far as to say that he's a nice old man. He's as mean as a snake. But he sees everything, and he'll tell you all about it if you ask him right."

"I'll look forward to his call," Sean said. "Was he helpful to you?"

"Grandma that used to own this house is named Yvette," Paddy said. "She moved to the north side about a year ago. He didn't know the address, but said it was near the highway. I assume he meant I-95."

"There are new low-income townhouses over there. It's right under the cell tower your suspect's phone keeps hitting."

"Is there a way to get a tenant's list?" Paddy asked.

"I don't know. It's a HUD project. That's federal. They don't usually share information. But I'll try tomorrow."

"Thanks, Sean. If we get a jump from the phone records, or you can find out who Yvette is, we'll come right back up."

The detectives from Brooklyn got back in their unmarked cars and began the long journey south on I-95. Paddy took the opportunity to notice the new two-story townhouses next to the highway and under the shadow of the enormous cell tower. When they came back, this was where they were going to find *Casper*, Paddy was sure of it.

Back at the 83 Squad, Paddy put a call into Ronnie Kingsbury. He told Paddy he couldn't get the phone dumps until the A.M. So after briefing Steve Krauss, and doing the fives to update the case, there wasn't anything left to do. He told Romeo he was coming in for the *four by* tomorrow. He asked him what he was going to do.

"I'm gonna go home to my wife," Romeo said.

"You're not hooking up with Lisbeth?"

"No. That would have been a mistake. A good friend talked me out of it."

"I just showed you the downside. You made the right decision by yourself. Go be with your wife. I'll see you tomorrow afternoon."

CHAPTER FIFTY-THREE

November, 1990
Astoria, Queens

At twenty-two-years old, Mairead had never been in a relationship with anyone where she was so intent on spending every free minute with them. That she had fallen so hard for Paddy not only surprised her, but scared her a little. She was spending most nights at his condo in Astoria. As their schedules didn't mesh perfectly, sometimes Paddy would have to drop by the hospital to give Mairead the keys when he got stuck at work with an arrest. She jokingly suggested it would be easier if he just gave her a key. The next day, Paddy had a set made for her. When she took the car service to the condo to wait for Paddy to finish his shift, she discovered that rather than clean out a drawer in his dresser for her, like he said he would, he bought a chest of drawers for her that matched his bedroom set. She saw that he also cleared off the top of his own dresser for her perfumes, jewelry and whatever else she wanted to keep handy. But her biggest surprise was the closet in his bedroom. He had completely cleaned it out and moved his clothes into the hall closet. So if Paddy had shared her fears, he was venturing boldly forward in the face of them.

Paddy was scared. But not about anything to do with spending time with Mairead. He already knew without a shred of doubt that he wanted to spend the rest of his life with her. He didn't say as much. But he spent an inordinate amount of time trying to figure out things to do for her, or give her before she could even ask. The thing he dreaded was what would happen when Mairead was there, and he experienced one of what he called his *night terrors*.

They had a recurrent theme based upon real events. In the summer of 1988, two months before Jimmy Crowe had been killed, Paddy and Tommy McPhee were working a late tour. At about two thirty in the morning, during a blisteringly hot August, they had just returned from Central Booking after dropping off a prisoner from an arrest they made earlier in the tour. Parched, they decided to stop by the beer distributor on 207th Street and 10th Avenue. The owner, Mickey O'Driscoll was a retired cop. Presently, he owned the biggest beer distributorship in Manhattan. He didn't do any retail business, but he always kept a case or two of frosty Heinekens in the refrigerator behind the counter to share with his workers and the cops he liked enough to invite. For some reason, he really seemed to like Paddy and Tommy. The beer would be so cold that when you removed it from the freezer, and the condensation would hit it, the bottle would frost over with a fine white icy coat. Mickey called this effect *the wedding dress*. On this hot morning, Tommy and Paddy were looking to get their hands around one of those.

When they got to the distributorship, something just seemed wrong. The lights were on inside and out on the loading docks. Ordinarily, Mickey's guys would be loading and unloading trucks all night and into the morning. But there was no one out there. Paddy went over the radio to Central to check if she was holding a 10-11 (a notice of alarm) for the location. Central told Paddy she had nothing like that on her screen. The cops decided to investigate anyway. They asked Central to send two sectors, no lights or sirens, for back-up. When the other two sector cars got there, Tommy and Paddy explained their concern. They decided to enter the warehouse spread out from the loading dock. They would perform a security sweep working up toward the counter and office, where hopefully they would all meet, and discover nothing wrong. But there was much wrong on this morning.

Unbeknownst to the cops in upper Manhattan, there was a particularly ruthless and violent commercial-robbery team terrorizing much of the city. They liked to beat and shoot victims. They sometimes engaged in rapes if women were present. They were already responsible for two murders. Several more victims were in hospitals in critical condition. But thus far, the crew had only struck in Queens, the Bronx and a diner in Baldwin, on Long Island. The diner was a particularly nasty piece of business. Fourteen female patrons had been subjected to forcible rape or sodomy during the commission of the robbery. One male patron was forcibly sodomized as well, when he protested the treatment of the women. This was a sick and violent bunch. But the cops in the *three four* knew nothing about their existence. Since they hadn't hit in Manhattan, no one thought to brief the cops there about the pattern.

It was only their own good instincts that informed these six cops from the *three four* that they might be walking into a catastrophe. As the cops cleared the aisles of the enormous pallets of bottled and canned beer, and approached the front counter, Paddy heard an unfamiliar voice cursing and demanding the safe be opened. Then he heard the unmistakable sound of a shotgun stock smashing against a skull. Paddy heard Mickey O'Driscoll growl back in his distinctive Irish brogue.

"How the fook am I supposed to open the safe when ye got me fookin' hands cuffed behind me back, ye ijit?"

This elicited another butt stroke. Paddy peeked out around the corner of the skid of beer he was using as cover. He observed four males in dark clothing. Two had pump action shotguns, typically called street sweepers. The other two had Mac 11 machine pistols. All four were wearing blue or red bandanas over their faces, like bandits in an old Sergio Leone spaghetti western. Paddy used hand signals to inform his partners of the tactical situation. He signaled to Officer George Perry to come to him. When Perry came over, Paddy whispered for him to go outside and call a full blown 10-13, Officers in Distress. Paddy wanted everyone coming lights and sirens. He intended to use the ensuing distraction to confront the perps from what he thought was good cover.

This plan was thwarted when the little perp with the shotgun ordered one of his cohorts to start shooting the cuffed workers. The report of a shotgun blast, and the subsequent screaming ended all debate about what had to happen next. Paddy leaned out around the corner, and drew down on the perp with the shotgun who had just killed Mickey's foreman, Jesus.

"Police! Don't move!" Paddy ordered at the top of his lungs. Then he fired twice, striking the killer both times in the chest, good grouping from twenty feet. The perp merely flinched. Then all four perps opened up on

Paddy at once. He ducked behind the pallet of beer. Paddy and Tommy scurried back out of the line of fire. Paddy's face was covered with beer foam and broken glass. The insanity of the moment caused him to laugh.

"Make a note. Bottled beer makes for shitty cover. We're gonna have to shoot and scoot. We got nothing to hide behind, and they're gonna kill everybody if we don't take them out."

"We'll leapfrog. Two aisles at a time. Then back. They got nothing to hide behind either," Tommy pointed out.

So they started to hop from aisle to aisle. They would pop out only long enough to shoot twice and move. The two of them were hitting their targets, they were sure of it. But these perps weren't going down. Their first thought was that the perps were high on Angel Dust. But even PCP can't stop a chest wound from bleeding out. They figured correctly that the perps were wearing body armor. They also had hand grenades and claymore anti-personnel mines. But they either hadn't figured out how to use them, or it hadn't yet occurred to them.

At the next corner, Tommy popped out low and shot one of the perps twice in the chest. Paddy went high and fired two at his head. They hit their target. Paddy saw the pink mist spray behind the perp's head before he fell straight to the floor. He almost spent too long admiring his work, because the other three perps opened up on him. He had to dive to the floor. He and Tommy scooted over two more aisles. This time they reversed roles. Paddy went low and Tommy delivered the head shots. But Paddy didn't shoot his target in the chest. He went lower, and struck him both times in the groin. This was the perp who had murdered Jesus. It was a slight justice that he was in excruciating agony in the seconds before Tommy McPhee blew his head off.

Then they were moving again. This time they both went high. The second perp with the machine pistol's head disappeared in an explosion of pink and gray. The two cops were preparing to engage the last perp when they heard the shotgun go off again. Assuming the perp was executing Mickey and his workers, Paddy and Tommy rushed the counter. But no one was there. Then they heard Mickey's voice.

"The coward cocksucker blew his own *fookin* head off. Now cut me out of these flex-cuffs, for *fook's* sake."

Paddy went over the radio to call off the 10-13, just as the cavalry were arriving. After verifying that the perps were dead, and establishing a crime scene for the shooting and the murder of Jesus, the Patrol Supervisor ordered a sector to take Paddy and Tommy to the hospital. Other than glass cuts from the exploding beer bottles, neither cop thought he was injured. But they followed orders. First though, Paddy snagged two six packs of Heineken from Mickey's freezer. This is what they were drinking after they were medically cleared at the hospital and the psychiatrist came in to brief them on the effects of Post-Traumatic Stress Disorder.

"What the hell is that?" Tommy asked.

"That is a psychological ailment that effects people like yourselves who are exposed to a violent, traumatic event," the doctor explained.

"Sounds like cry-baby pussy shit to me," Tommy scoffed.

"Still," the doctor persisted patiently. "You need to know the symptoms in case it isn't."

He went on to explain that if the cops were to experience PTSD, the symptoms would present themselves as an acute stress disorder for about a month after the event. They should look for increased irritability, sleeplessness and or hyper-arousal. If these should devolve into full-blown PTSD, they could expect recurring nightmares, flashbacks and a numbing of the memories of the event. He cautioned the young cops to take this seriously as the effects could be debilitating if not dealt with early and correctly. His warnings fell on deaf ears, as he knew they would.

"It doesn't sound like anything that can't be cured by a cold beer," Paddy said, offering the doctor a Heineken.

"About that," the doctor said. "You shouldn't drink for a while. Alcohol tends to exacerbate the effects of PTSD."

"Thank you for your concern and the good advice, Doc," Tommy said. Then he toasted him and took a satisfying swallow of ice cold beer. The young psychiatrist could only shake his head as he left the two cops to their beer and macho pretensions of invincibility.

The nightmares began for Paddy three days later. He found himself bounding out of bed in a soaking sweat, his heart thundering out of his chest. At first, the source of his terror was formless. But as time went on, the event in the beer distributorship was re-experienced in one of two ways. Both of them involved horrible feelings of fear and futility. In its first manifestation, Paddy was either unable to pull the trigger of his gun, or when he pulled it, the bullets would trickle out of the gun and fall pathetically to the floor. The other scenario involved the foreman Jesus. In it, Jesus is flex-cuffed. His face is bleeding, and he is quietly weeping. The look on his face, seeking a measure of mercy that will not come, is altogether pitiful and heart rending. And then Jesus' face disappears in a bloody shotgun blast. When that one first hit, Paddy found himself shaking on his knees at the foot of his bed, praying to a God he wasn't sure he believed in, begging him to remove the abomination from his consciousness.

The effects of Paddy's disturbance was taking a physical toll on him. Tommy wasn't faring much better. They talked to each other about it. They weren't sleeping. They weren't eating. Their nightmares were similar. They did not involve any fear of their own death or injury. They seemed to focus on the enraging helplessness they felt in being unable to affect anything. They were distraught, and felt responsible for not being able to save Jesus. They knew this was irrational. But they were powerless to stop it. But the big tip-off that something was wrong was the absence of the partners' confounding and limitless energy level. It was gone, replaced by a listless, dreamlike lethargy. Jimmy Crowe was the first to notice.

Jimmy had been in a shooting a few years earlier that still caused him psychological blow-back. So he knew what he was looking at when he saw Paddy and Tommy sleepwalking through their waking hours, like they were moving under water. Jimmy was forced to shoot a deranged man who was about to immolate his eleven-year-old son. If he hadn't taken the shot when he did, the perp, the innocent boy and the four cops present would have burned alive in the accelerant-soaked room. As justified as he was, Jimmy was still distraught over it. His wife Katelyn made him see someone outside the department to discuss the issues that were at the time, killing him. What he learned about PTSD and about himself was like an epiphany. He vowed he would never let another cop suffer the way he did. So when he cornered Tommy and Paddy in the locker room at the *three four*, they had no choice but to listen to him.

Jimmy related his own experience. Then he made them talk about theirs. He listened patiently. He didn't correct them. He didn't ask any questions. He just let them vent. When Paddy and Tommy were all talked out, Jimmy gave them the benefit of what he had learned, the hard way.

"What you're feeling, the hopelessness, the helplessness, has nothing to do with experiencing a near-death event. Psychologically that shit is meaningless to guys like us. What you are banged up over is having to kill four people and not being able to save the foreman, Jesus. It doesn't matter that those animals deserved every bullet. As evil and awful as they were, they were still human beings. The hard truth of the matter is there is nothing you can do that is more psychologically and emotionally repugnant than to kill another human being, and it doesn't matter the circumstances. Some people simply can't bring themselves to do it. They choose their own death rather than to take a life. Fortunately, your training and dedication allowed you to do the right thing. We have the misfortune of having a job where sometimes, we have to take a life to save others. It's a horrible responsibility. And the price to pay is a nutcrusher. But, I believe it's worth it."

Jimmy let that sink in. Paddy and Tommy seemed relieved to be talking to someone who knew about the awful place they were in. Instead of the back slapping and misplaced congratulations, when each of them felt more like perpetrators of an atrocity, they were finally relating to someone that knew they were hurting, and why. Then Tommy remembered Jesus.

"What about the foreman?" Tommy asked.

"I was getting to him," Jimmy said. "You think you're responsible for his death. I know you do. But right now, we're going to put that fallacy to bed once and for all. There wasn't a god-damned thing you could have done to save that man. You had to wait. You were outmanned, outgunned, and for all you knew, you could have precipitated those mutts into killing all the hostages. You acted correctly. You acted heroically. You disregarded your own lives and saved fifteen people who you know would have been murdered in cold blood if you hadn't. Can we agree on that?" The cops nodded, conceding the point.

"Now the bad news," Jimmy told them. "You're still going to go over this in your head. You're going to play *what ifs,* and run scenarios through your mind where things turn out differently. Don't do it. It's a fool's errand. We can't know what might have happened if we acted differently. And we couldn't change anything if we did. We're not water walkers. We're not mind readers. None of us has an *S* on his chest. We're just cops. If we were that smart, odds are we would have found a way to make a living that didn't involve carrying a gun. In the final analysis, we are just the rough men willing to do violence on behalf of those who can't. We protect people who can't protect themselves. It's ugly, and I won't tell you to embrace it. But you're going to have to accept it. Otherwise, you'll need to find another line of work. In your case, I don't think that'll be necessary. I don't know any two guys more suited to this. You have the perfect balance of ruthlessness and humanity. You just need to talk this shit out with a professional."

Then he gave them the business card of his psychologist. He told them that this guy was outside the department, and they should keep it that way. The NYPD didn't yet understand PTSD, and if you told them you had it, their only solution was to take your guns away. Good luck getting those back.

"One last thing," Jimmy remembered. "Talking to someone will help, but it's not going away any time soon. You're going to have to deal with this recurring for a few years. But it gets easier when you know why you feel the way you do, and it does lessen over time. So give yourselves a break, and be patient."

Jimmy was right. It did get better over time. Talking to the psychologist and reading up on PTSD also went a long way toward understanding the stress and anxiety Paddy and Tommy were going through. The symptoms didn't disappear, but they did abate. At least enough for the young cops to function. Until late October, when Jimmy Crowe was murdered.

Paddy and Tommy were two blocks away on Saint Nicholas Avenue and 162nd Street. They were watching the enforcer of the drug spot there. They were trying to figure out where he had the gun hidden, when they heard Jimmy and his partner pick up the aided case on 161st Street and Broadway. The next thing Paddy and Tommy heard was Dennis Barbuck screaming over the radio that his partner had been shot. Paddy and Tommy were the first unit to respond, having been so close. Barbuck was a distraught mess, standing over Jimmy Crowe, who was struggling to breathe through the viscous blood he was coughing up. Paddy scooped him up and carried him into the backseat of their radio car. Tommy grabbed Barbuck and threw him into the passenger seat. Then he jumped into the driver's seat, and radioed central they were transporting a shot MOS (member of the service) and his partner to the hospital. Tommy tried to put out a description of the perps as best he could, but Dennis Barbuck had already shut down, and nobody was getting anything out of him at that point.

Paddy was holding Jimmy up in the backseat in an effort to allow the blood to clear his lungs and throat. Paddy was worried he would choke to death before they got him to the trauma room. What Paddy couldn't know was that choking was the least of Jimmy's problems. He had been shot once, under the armpit. His heart had been perforated. The desperate gulps of air he was taking in Paddy's arms would be his last. Paddy would later tell Jimmy's widow Katelyn that he fought bravely. He told her when Paddy asked him to hold on, Jimmy nodded and looked at him with a determined, resolute expression.

What really occurred in that backseat was altogether different. Jimmy grabbed Paddy with what little strength he had left. When Paddy looked into his face all he saw there was a fear that seemed to consume him. Jimmy's eyes had gone wide. Like he knew he was dying, and it scared him. The realization terrified Paddy. Until his well-practiced denial impulse took over. He told himself Jimmy hadn't just shuddered and stopped breathing. Paddy was saving his friend, so he couldn't be dead. All of this transpired simultaneously as Tommy careened under the ambulance portal at Columbia Presbyterian. Paddy was out of the car in an instant, sprinting into the emergency room with Jimmy in his arms.

Paddy stood mutely by in the trauma room. He watched the surgeons and the nurses remove Jimmy's uniform and search for the wound. It wasn't apparent at first. The armpit didn't effuse much blood. The damage and bleeding, which was catastrophic, all occurred internally. When the trauma surgeon discovered the entrance wound under Jimmy's arm, his shoulders visibly slumped. He understood before anyone else that this battle was already lost. Paddy read the doctor's body language and understood as well. He stood there and wept over his friend, as the surgeon called for a scalpel and a rib spreader. They opened Jimmy up and manually tried to massage his heart back to life. The resultant arterial spurting told the story of the futility of it all. That nine millimeter bullet had torn through two valves and the aorta of Police Officer James Crowe, who was pronounced dead by the surgeon at 0230 hours.

Paddy's PTSD took on a whole new dimension with the murder of his friend. Along with the guilt and sense of responsibility he felt for the death of Jesus from the beer distributorship, he now had the death of his friend for which to blame himself. The resultant survivor's guilt hit Paddy like a building had fallen on him. If he felt bad about the death of Jesus, he carried the murder of Jimmy Crowe like a cross. The fact that Paddy wasn't even there in no way ameliorated his sense of guilt. He was inconsolable and refused to listen to reason. The scenarios were innumerable as they ran through Paddy's mind like a poison. He blamed himself for not backing up Jimmy and his partner on their job, which was ridiculous. They were on an ambulance case for a difficulty breather when they ran into the robbery team who killed Jimmy. Nobody backs up ambulance cases. And the sector concerned would think there was something wrong with you if you did. But Paddy refused to accept that.

He blamed himself for not finding the wound under Jimmy's arm. The theory being, if he had applied pressure to the wound soon enough, he could have prevented Jimmy from bleeding out. This ignored the fact that the bullet had destroyed Jimmy's heart beyond repair, and he bled out internally. But mostly, and it was the source of all of Paddy's frustration and sense of impotence, he was angry at himself for not being there to kill the motherfuckers who murdered his friend. He never even got a look at them, but his sense of failure was absolute. No amount of reasoning and talking it out could convince Paddy otherwise.

This was the perfect storm of sub-conscious guilt and self-recrimination residing in Paddy's head. Buried for the most part, but still present, it would emerge without warning. The flashbacks had stopped. But he couldn't stop his mind from dwelling on one or both events. In waking hours, it would manifest itself as a brooding, seething anger. He was angry at himself, feeling responsible for the deaths of Jesus and Jimmy in equal measure. Paddy had learned to tamp down the feelings of rage and futility. So he was at least functional. But at night, in that dreamscape where reason could command no purchase, Paddy would find himself on his knees, whimpering, weeping, and shaking with fear. He was anything but functional. The anxiety was crushing. At times it felt like a piano was sitting on his chest, so difficult was it to breathe. Most times, when he was so afflicted, Paddy would get up and turn on every light in his apartment. He would shower, eat, read, anything really, just to avoid going back to sleep. Paddy would lie to himself that he was just too wired to sleep. In truth, he was afraid to be cast back into whichever nightmare was tormenting him presently. These episodes were infrequent enough that Paddy could cope with them. He was told by the psychologist they would one day end. But Paddy was beginning to fear they never would.

He was encouraged by the fact that he had not experienced an episode while sleeping with Mairead. Paddy had begun to allow himself to believe she was the talisman that would finally allow him to rid himself of these night terrors forever. He should have known better.

Paddy woke with a sharp pain in his inner thigh. He realized quickly that he had Mairead in a choke-hold, and was searching the front of her body for a gun that wasn't there. She had pinched him to wake him up. When she did, he released the grip on her neck. He let out an audible moan, as if he were in pain. But it wasn't pain. It was despair. Mairead spun around in his arms and clutched Paddy's head to her chest. He was soaked with sweat and shaking. When he realized he had almost hurt her, Paddy folded in on himself and sobbed pathetically. She held him tighter and rocked him softly, gently consoling him. She assured Paddy that she was okay. He hadn't hurt her. She held him like that until he could come fully awake and compose himself. When he did, Mairead reached over and put on the night light. She sat up and stroked the tear and sweat soaked hair away from his face.

"What happened, baby?" Mairead asked gently.

"Bad dream," was all he said.

"No. You were in a death fight with someone. I want to know what scared you so badly."

Paddy thought about it for a while. He wasn't stalling. He was struggling for the words to explain to Mairead what he only understood incrementally himself. She sensed he was working on it. So she remained patient.

"Do you know anything about PTSD?" he asked finally.

"I though that's what it might be. Do you have it?"

"Yeah. I got it pretty bad, it turns out."

"How did this happen to you?"

"Do you remember when I told you about Inez?" She nodded.

"I never properly dealt with that. I never thought much on it. Occasionally, I would have a nightmare. But nothing like this. I always felt a sense of guilt over that whole thing. She didn't deserve to die. I don't know why I was allowed to live. Those were tough questions, so I suppressed them. Until a couple of years ago. Bad shit started happening all at once. Now I carry guilt for Inez along with the fallout from those other things. It's been getting better, less frequent. But when it hits, it's bad."

"I know about Inez. Tell me about the other things."

Paddy went on to tell Mairead about the gun fight in the beer distributorship. He told her about the murder of the foreman Jesus, and how he felt responsible. He told her that realistically, he shouldn't feel bad about killing those perps. No one ever needed killing more. But somehow, he still felt shitty about having to do it. He had gone to talk to someone about it, and it was getting better. Then he told her about the night Jimmy Crowe had been killed, when all of Paddy's hard won progress and developing coping skills had gone right out the window. He explained to Mairead that in spite of all evidence to the contrary, he felt responsible for Jimmy's death. He knew it wasn't rational, and in rational moments he could pretend to understand that none of it was his fault. But he still had to sleep. That's when his subconscious got to stretch it's legs and shove all rationality away. Sleep is where the doubt, and recrimination, and guilt lived. They were relentless, attacking him in his dream state, when he was powerless to fend them off. He had learned to just ride the nightmares out. But Paddy had never had one with anyone else in his bed before. The fact that he had almost hurt Mairead was freaking him out.

Mairead assured Paddy she was fine. She wasn't as scared by the event as he was. She told Paddy that before he grabbed her, he started breathing heavily and rocking from side to side in his sleep. When he let out a moan, Mairead thought he was having a sex dream. But then he started yelling the word *No* repeatedly. So, she knew it couldn't be sex. The next thing she knew, he had her in a choke-hold, demanding to know where the gun was.

"When I pinched you, how fast did you come out of it?"

"Immediately," he said.

"Then we might be able to head these things off before they start."

"I'll try anything. But I don't see how this can work."

"When you start breathing heavily and shaking, I'll slide over and gently wake you up. We won't let it get past that point."

"What if you're asleep and don't realize it's happening?"

"You're not a little man, Paddy. When you start shaking, so does the bed, the floor, the furniture and me. Nobody is sleeping through that."

They gave it a try and it seemed to work. The few times when an episode would start, Mairead would intervene. She would calm Paddy down and they would hold each other until they fell asleep. Sometimes they would make love before drifting off together. Under these circumstances, the nightmares never recurred the same night. It was one and done. They would talk about it in the morning to try and understand what if anything triggered the event. Mairead started keeping a dream journal for Paddy. It was effective. The nightmares were coming less frequently. And when they did, Mairead would interrupt them before they could do much damage. So they thought they had a handle on it. If Paddy would have just cooperated by not wandering into gunfights, they might have.

CHAPTER FIFTY-FOUR

September 4, 1992
Astoria, Queens

Friday, September 4, 1992 was a warm Indian summer morning in Astoria. As Paddy reached over Mairead to answer the phone on his night stand he noted the time on the digital clock. It was 8:42 A.M. The caller id indicated the call was coming from the Manhattan DA's Office. He thought perhaps the call was to tell him where and when to surrender for the indictment he had begun to discount as a possibility, but hadn't completely ruled out.

"Durr," Paddy said answering the phone.

"Good morning, Paddy. It's John Cantwell."

"Is it a good morning, John?"

"I think so. Meet me for breakfast so we can talk."

"Can I bring Mairead?"

"That's not a good idea. That would make her a witness when I divulge secret grand jury material to you. I don't think you want her involved in that."

"Fair enough. Where and when do you want me?"

"Do you know the Neptune Diner on Astoria Boulevard and 31st Street?"

"I've been thrown out of there a few times," Paddy joked.

"Meet me there in a half hour."

As Paddy hung up the phone, Mairead waited for him to explain the phone call. She could see he was still puzzling it out for himself. So she waited for him to compose his thoughts. She could tell he had pieced it together by the resigned look that came over his face.

"So what was that all about?" she asked.

"John Cantwell, the lead investigator for the DA has news."

"Good news, or bad news?"

"He wouldn't say. But he wants to buy me breakfast. So presumably, it's nothing that would kill my appetite."

"He doesn't want you to bring me?"

"No. Whatever he's going to tell me, he's not supposed to tell me. He says it's for your protection, but his also."

"What do you think he's going to say?"

"He's either going to tell me we're totally fucked, or we're shopping for your wedding dress this afternoon. I will call you from the diner when I know."

"Oh goody!" Mairead said as she mussed his hair and kissed him. "I love shopping."

CHAPTER FIFTY-FIVE

September 4, 1992
Astoria, Queens

When Paddy got to the Neptune Diner, the place was almost empty. Cantwell was in a booth in the back. He waved Paddy over. When the waitress came, John ordered a western omelet with bacon. Paddy stuck with coffee.

"So what is the big news, John?" Paddy asked when the waitress had left.

"The grand jury voted yesterday. It was unanimous. The shooting was justified. But you're going to have to sit on that information for a few days. As a courtesy to the mayor and the police commissioner, the DA is going to delay the announcement for a week."

"Why is that?" Paddy wondered.

"The police department wants time to prepare if there is any backlash. The mayor has his own agenda."

"He's wanted my head on a stick since this thing jumped off. I'm not surprised."

"I don't think you appreciate his treachery. I had to brief him yesterday after the *No True Bill* was voted. He did not take it well. He called it an outrage."

"Well, fuck him if he can't take a joke."

"I wish it were that simple. He's not done coming after you. He's already lobbying the Justice Department to try you for Civil Rights offenses. He won't get anywhere with that. The law is specific that your actions had to be racially motivated to constitute a crime. There is no evidence of that. And the Civil Rights Division won't touch anything that isn't a slam dunk."

"So what am I worrying about?" Paddy asked.

"He's going to be mayor for at least two more years," Cantwell informed him. "He is good friends and political allies with the US Attorney for the Southern District. He thinks you made him look bad. Don't be surprised if he looks to back door you with the US Attorney by going after your Anti-Crime team."

"He can go after us all he wants. There's nothing there," Paddy told him.

"You don't understand the shark infested waters you're swimming in with these people. The truth means nothing to them. It's all politics and agenda. I spoke with the mayor yesterday. I presented all the evidence and testimony, and explained the impossibility of your guilt in this case. He wouldn't even listen. He didn't care that you were innocent. What he said was that the city wouldn't stand for such a verdict. He screamed at me like I was a six-year old. I had to get out of there before I punched him in the face. Make no mistake, Paddy. He's coming after you. And the fact you're innocent might not be any protection."

Paddy considered this information. He wasn't really surprised, not about the grand jury or the mayor's vendetta. Paddy had begun to suspect things were becoming too easy the last few weeks. The story had turned around in the media. No one was burning him in effigy anymore. The riots had burned themselves out, and wouldn't reignite at this point regardless of the grand jury's finding. So while his lawyers and union representatives had become confident, Paddy was still looking for the scorpion under the next rock. Now, he was sure he had found it.

"Thank you for the information about the grand jury, and the heads up on the mayor. I'll make sure my guys are aware of the danger."

"You do that," Cantwell said, as Paddy stood to leave.

"One other thing, before you go. What the hell is up with Gus Demario?"

"I warned you and Bergdorf not to put him on the stand," Paddy reminded him.

"He was one of your partners that night. We had no choice."

"What did Gus do now?"

"After the vote, the jury foreman told me they weren't going to indict you. But he wanted to know if they could do anything to Demario. They hated him."

"That happens with Gus. His stupidity has a certain militant quality. Most people despise him instantly. He's not so unlike the guy in Gracie Mansion, in that regard."

CHAPTER FIFTY-SIX

September 12, 1992
Manhattan

A week later, Paddy was in Manhattan court to testify on a gun arrest from the previous year. In light of the tenuous nature of Paddy's freedom, the individual assistant district attorneys were reticent to go forward with any of his felony cases. It would be difficult to present a police officer to the court as a credible witness, when your own office might be indicting him for murder. So the DAs were in somewhat of a quandary. They had to answer *ready*, or incur a penalty assigned to their *speedy trial time*. Many a case had been lost over the years to the technicality incurred by simply not watching the calendar. This particular ADA, Pamela Grunswag, was not especially heroic or aggressive. But she gambled the defense was bluffing when they answered ready for trial. So she did too. The hearing was scheduled for 1000 hours, in front of Judge Ruben Matos. Matos was a stickler for courtroom proceeding. So he wasn't having anybody's nonsense with this case. He obviously knew who the Government's star witness was. It made little difference to him. He personally reached out to both side's counsel. He warned them if they appeared in his courtroom and answered ready, the hearings were going to occur today and proceed to picking a jury Monday.

Pamela Grunswag hesitated when the question was asked. She swallowed hard and told the Judge the Government was ready. Matos told the DA he would be back in touch. Fifteen minutes later the Judge's clerk called Grunswag and told her the defense blinked. The case was being put over for a month. That meant Paddy had a free day to wander around downtown, or he could return to the Boro. But how much weightlifting and sunbathing could one man endure?

Paddy's decision was made for him when a breathless young paralegal stuck her head into the office and announced that the DA was having a press conference this afternoon to release the findings of the *Washington Heights Grand Jury*, as it had come to be known. So Paddy called Mairead at the hospital to give her the heads up. She asked him to come and get her. She wanted to be with Paddy when they heard the news. He took the subway to get Mairead, and the two of them rode the train nervously back downtown. In spite of having been forewarned of the results, Paddy knew enough not to trust anything promised until it was delivered. So the slightest bit of doubt remained to fester.

Paddy and Mairead got down to Canal Street an hour or so later. It was a little after noon. The DA's televised press conference was scheduled for 1300 hours, the universal lunch hour observed by Criminal and Supreme Court. Paddy led Mairead down Baxter Street to Foglios' Restaurant and bar, a popular watering hole for the DA's and cops at court. Paddy and Mairead snuck in quietly and Paddy spoke to the bartender, Dempsey. He ushered the young couple into a booth in the rear of the restaurant that had a clear view of one of the several TVs dotted around the room. Paddy ordered coffee, not wanting to be seen drinking during what should be a somber occasion. Mairead, having not killed anyone recently, and having no personal enemies present, was fine with a glass of wine.

Paddy on the other hand, had several enemies nearby. He had scanned the bar and took stock of his standing among those present. Mostly the room consisted of DAs who had finished their morning court business. The cops would be filing in shortly at the lunch break. Paddy had observed over time that the District Attorney's Office was a peculiar conglomeration of two distinct types of people. The first group were the alpha personalities who wanted to punish criminals. They viewed themselves less as lawyers and more like cops. These were the DAs who ran out and had shields made for themselves as soon as they were hired. They weren't official, and they were frowned upon by the DA. There wasn't even anywhere for them to wear them. But they had to have them. It made them feel like John Law.

These DAs were decidedly friends of the police. They appreciated the cops. They were even protective of them. They understood that cops were human and made mistakes, but they were inclined to view them as being of the good faith variety, and tended to give the cop the benefit of the doubt. Paddy estimated these DAs comprised about half of the room.

The other group was the sneering, vicious cop haters. They viewed all law enforcement as lying, brutal thugs with badges. These DAs were usually elitist educated snobs. They came out of law school with the misunderstanding that they were going to *fix* or take down the system they were convinced by their professors was irreparably broken. They thought they were going to redress every perceived injustice perpetrated by people they viewed as underclass gorillas with guns. They were awful prosecutors because they inherently mistrusted their own best witnesses, and the police work which made the prosecution possible in the first place. As a result, most of them either elevated to a deputy bureau chief position, mostly removed from direct contact with the police, or they remained in place as cop-hunters. For them, Paddy knew every case was merely another opportunity to burn a cop. He avoided these DAs like syphilis.

Even in their protected bunker-like position, Paddy and Mairead could only stay hidden for so long. The path to the restrooms meandered through the dining room. Several patrons registered recognition when they saw him. Most of it involved respectful nods, but there were a few disparaging sneers as well. In any event, Paddy and Mairead's privacy was mostly respected. Other than the waitress taking their orders, they were left alone.

The television cut away to a conference room in the DA's Office. The reporters were speculating as to what the decision of the grand jury might be. They were all over the spectrum and spinning possible repercussions for each scenario. As Paddy had come to discover, the media didn't know anything. Evidently, that was no reason to stop talking. Finally, the District Attorney came to the podium. He had in his hand a volume of paper that turned out to be a forty-five page report detailing every aspect of the grand jury's investigation. This was unprecedented. He read the report in front of the cameras.

The DA began by detailing the thoroughness of the investigation, citing hundreds of items of physical evidence as well as hundreds of witnesses interviewed. He commended the assistance of the Medical Examiner's

Office, the private pathologists and crime scene experts hired by the family of the decedent. He thanked the FBI for their cooperation, duplicating the testing already done by the NYPD. He described the case as *the most comprehensive grand jury investigation in the history of New York County.*

He got to the meat of the evidence and testimony. He detailed the background of the alleged victim, Reuben Amaro. Originally portrayed as a hardworking father of two, the DA detailed the evidence to the contrary. Amaro, he said, was a convicted drug dealer and enforcer for the drug gang who ran 555 West 162nd Street. The DA's investigators had found numerous witnesses to corroborate that Amaro *always* carried a gun. He was wanted for two separate felony warrants at the time of his death. In addition, he was considered a possible suspect in two unsolved homicides in upper Manhattan. The Medical Examiner found Amaro to have enormous quantities of cocaine in his blood stream, and he was high at the time of his death. He prefaced what came next with this explosive piece of evidence. The DA said Amaro was found to be the cousin of one of the two females who claimed to be witnesses, and all three were members of the same drug organization.

The DA spoke at length about those witnesses. He detailed their allegations and testimony as to what they saw, and then he took those allegations apart, piece by piece. Using independent witness accounts and the physical evidence, he disproved every element of their testimony. He used the independent pathologist hired by Amaro's family to prove that where the witnesses claimed to be, had no view of the hallway where the confrontation took place. Paddy would later find out the DA had incontrovertible evidence that one of the female witnesses was actually at a birthday party in Brooklyn at the time she claimed to see Paddy murder Reuben Amaro. The DA would have prosecuted her, but it would have involved burning a confidential informant. The DA summarized that *their testimony was not corroborated by the physical evidence in the case. It is actually contradicted by that evidence.*

The DA went on to detail Paddy's testimony in minutia, and how it was corroborated by the physical evidence, and supported by independent witness testimony. Almost as a sop, the DA spoke about Paddy's background and career to this point. He called Paddy an aggressive, exemplary police officer with an unblemished reputation, held in high regard by the DA's

Office and Court as an honest and credible witness. In short, he was turning Paddy into a bullet-proof witness and supercop. By now heads had started peeking into the dining room. Paddy and Mairead's presence was now a matter of fact. As the outcome of the grand jury became a forgone conclusion, the dynamic of the bar changed. The cop-hater DAs started to melt away, disappointed they wouldn't get to see a cop go down on this day. The bar was now filled with cops, and DA's who wanted to be cops. So what happened when the DA announced the grand jury had found Paddy justified wasn't as surprising as it might have been.

Everyone from the bar filed into the dining room to face Paddy and Mairead and gave them both a prolonged standing ovation. Paddy embarrassedly acknowledged them with a wave, mouthing the words *thank you*. After they had gone back to the bar, the waitress came over to their table.

"About fifty different people in there want to buy you two drinks. What should I do?"

"Thank them for me," Paddy told her. "But we're just going to need the check."

"There is no check. Dempsey wouldn't hear of it."

Paddy thanked her and left a ten dollar bill on the table for a tip. Then he and Mairead tried to sneak out the door. Paddy was immediately shanghaied by the cops and DAs in the bar. They swarmed him with backslaps and congratulations, insisting he drink a shot with them. Mairead smiled and shrugged at him. She told him to relax and have a few drinks. She needed to make some phone calls.

Mairead spoke to Dempsey who had the waitress bring her back to the office to use the phone there. By now Paddy's partners had figured out where to find him. They formed a protective cocoon around him at the bar, while Paddy was forced to drink round after round of Jägermeister.

Meanwhile Mairead was on the phone with Fritz, the owner and banquet manager of Zum Stammtisch. When she said her name, Fritz immediately recognized that he was speaking with the pretty little Irish girl who called everybody *Schatzi*. Not unaware, Fritz congratulated Mairead on the outcome of the grand jury. He asked her how he could help her.

"I need the backroom for tonight, for between thirty-five and fifty people. Can you do that for me?" Mairead asked.

"Do you want a full menu?"

"I think it's going to mostly involve drinking, but I want the menu available. Is seven o'clock okay?"

"The room is yours, Mairead. We'll figure everything out when you get here."

"Thank you, Schatzi. We'll see you at seven."

When Mairead came out to the bar, Paddy was decidedly glassy eyed and his ordinarily erect posture seemed to be succumbing to the effects of gravity. But she could see he was being well protected by his boys from the Anti-Crime team. Mairead knew they would see no harm came to their partner, here or anywhere else. She gave Tommy McPhee and Sean Moran the nod and gestured toward the door. They promptly grabbed Paddy under the arms and led him out the door onto Baxter Street. Mairead followed them out onto the street. She informed the team about Zum Stammtisch tonight. She trusted them with whom to invite. Paddy said unsteadily that he had to sign out. Kevin Touhey told him he would take care of it, and call the assholes at the Boro to let them know Paddy was *end of tour*.

"I had like nine Jägermeisters. There's no way I can drive," Paddy informed everybody.

"I got you, baby," Mairead said. "Where are we parked?"

They wobbled together down Baxter Street until they got to his car. Mairead was fine driving, in spite of this being her first time navigating the streets of Manhattan. The only incident worth noting was while they were going over the Williamsburg Bridge. Paddy had to lean out the door to void the pickled contents of his stomach. Having done so, he put his head back and went to sleep, not waking until they were in front of Mairead's house in Glendale. Once there, after being mobbed and embraced by her family, Mairead took Paddy's suit and spruced it up for him while he showered and shaved and prepared himself for what would prove to be a legendary night of celebratory drinking.

CHAPTER FIFTY-SEVEN

October, 2013
Farmingdale

The morning was cold, wet and dark. An early nor'easter had blown in overnight. Paddy thought the depressing and tumultuous weather created the perfect setting to pick up and deliver divorce papers to a wife he had no desire to divorce. As he drove to Hiram Borstein's office, he tried to think about his homicide case. But no amount of distraction could shield Paddy from the bitter disappointment he was experiencing. So he just gave into it, and allowed his countenance to match the awful weather.

When Paddy got to the parking lot of Hiram's office, he took a moment to recompose himself. He used the dropdown mirror over the visor to approximate a face that didn't look like it wanted to hurt someone. He saw he was only partly successful, but it would have to be enough.

When Paddy got upstairs to the reception area, he was greeted by Sarah Borstein. This time, she was in a white blouse, and a simple black skirt. Paddy could see the jacket from the suit hanging on the coat rack behind the desk. So her outfit could be completed and court ready at a moment's notice. But Paddy didn't think Sarah was going to court. Her hair was loose and flowing behind her, around her delicate neck and shoulders. The tresses thick and curly, they framed her face. She wasn't wearing glasses. Paddy realized her brown eyes were larger than they appeared the first time he met her. It occurred to him that Sarah was actually stunning. She had to work to hide her beauty.

Sarah looked up when Paddy came in. She could see from the tension in his face that he was suffering. That was not always the case with their divorce clients. More often than not, the client looked like they were casting off a burdensome yolk. Sarah saw none of that in Paddy. Her softer exterior allowed her to express an empathy that wouldn't have been possible with her more severe professional appearance.

"Hello, Paddy. Hiram is in court. But I have everything you need right here," she said, indicating a legal envelope on the desk in front of her. Sarah removed the papers and started going over the contents. She indicated the changes made at his request.

"All you have to do is sign them, have them notarized, which I can do for you. Then give them to Mairead's lawyer to review. Once they sign them and file them with the court, you are officially divorced."

"Let's get this over with," Paddy said, taking out his pen. Sarah indicated where he was to sign. Paddy did so, and Sarah pulled her notary stamp from the desk. She notarized and dated the document, and put it back in the envelope before handing it to Paddy.

"We can Fed Ex it to Mairead's attorney if you want."

"I'm going to personally deliver them today."

"What are you, a glutton for punishment?"

"No," Paddy laughed. "She's going to be at work this morning. I'm going to leave them with a note on the kitchen table."

"As your attorney, can I know what the note will say?"

"As my attorney, you may not. But don't worry. I'm not threatening anybody. I will break no laws today."

"I guess I can trust your judgement. Hiram says you insist on paying us."

Paddy handed her the hundred dollar check. Sarah wrote out a receipt for him.

"Is there anything else we can do for you?" Sarah asked, handing Paddy the receipt.

"Your brother wants me to take you out," Paddy told her.

"Did he mean kill me, or date me?"

"He wasn't specific. But I think he meant the latter."

"So, what are you going to do, Detective?"

"The right thing. I count you and your brother as friends. If you and I were to get involved, that might not be so. In fact, I'm sure of it."

"That's just as well," Sarah said, seeming almost relieved. "I'm dealing with some issues of my own."

"Do tell," Paddy inquired.

"My last relationship was with another woman. Hiram knows, but I think he's in denial. I don't know what my deal is right now. I'm definitely attracted to you, but frankly, I'm confused. You're dealing with enough right now without having to sort through my drama."

"I gotta tell you, Sarah," Paddy said smiling. "You just get more interesting by the minute."

When Paddy got down to the car, he took his reporter's notebook from the glove box. He thought about it for a moment, and then started writing.

Mairead,

Please have your lawyer review the changes I made. I think you both will agree my terms are not only more generous, but fairer, too. The papers are ready to be filed. Just sign them. Please understand that none of this is what I want. But if you do, then it has to happen. I have no words to express how sorry I am that I brought us to this. Know that I would give anything to undo it if I could. Living with how badly I hurt you is the most difficult thing I've ever had to do, and wounds me deeper than anything ever has.

Paddy

Paddy tore the page from the steno pad and clipped it under the paperclip holding the divorce papers together. He then drove to the house in Plainedge. Seeing Mairead's car not in the driveway was a relief. He let himself in the front door and placed the legal envelope on the kitchen table where Mairead couldn't miss it. Paddy knew it wasn't much of a homecoming, but at least there was no one there to hate him but himself. Then he was back in the car and on his way to the 83rd Precinct

CHAPTER FIFTY-EIGHT

November, 2005
Plainedge

Paddy's career as a high school football coach, and the genesis of his eventual fall from grace came about accidentally. He was at Plainedge High School assisting the coaches of his son Patrick's twelve-year-old youth football team. Paddy had no intention of coaching. His schedule, unpredictable as it was, wouldn't allow him to make the commitment he felt necessary for such an endeavor. But his experience and knowledge were still sought after. So when he could make it, he attended practice.

There were several positive aspects to that arrangement as far as Paddy was concerned. The first benefit was that Paddy could correct the stupid, dangerous fundamentals that commonly crept out of the minds of youth football coaches. Most of them weren't coaches at all. They were symptomatic of a disease known as *Daddy Ball*. That's where Dad, usually a frustrated football player of limited accomplishment, volunteers to coach his son's team. The usual outcome involved the coaches' son becoming the team's quarterback or "star" running back, in spite of having no talent whatsoever. All coaching was then centered on trying to showcase a kid who often had no desire to be on the field at all. This put every other player on the team at risk. The other danger was the winning-obsessed fathers who thought they were the Bill Belichicks of youth football. The bizarre and dangerous ideas that flowed from these people were scary. Paddy made sure he was around enough to veto the wilder of these schemes and plans. Since Patrick was by far the best player on the team, Paddy had the understanding of the coaches that his wishes would be respected, or he would pull his son off the field.

An example of such a scenario was when the head coach got the brilliant idea to try and make a quarterback out of Patrick. Patrick admittedly was an excellent football player. But he was not the deft and agile athlete who should be playing quarterback. What he was, was a twelve-year old man-child who would rather run through and over a tackler than around him. Furthermore, Paddy knew he couldn't catch or throw. So when Bob Reilly, the head coach suggested he was going to make Patrick the quarterback, Paddy was incredulous. He took the football from Bob's hands and called out to his son ten yards away. "Catch," Paddy said as he soft tossed the ball directly at Patrick's hands. As Paddy expected, Patrick swatted at the ball with his club-like hands, knocking it to the ground. "Throw it back," Paddy told him. Patrick picked the ball up and returned a helicopter of a throw that flew fifteen yards over Paddy and Bob's heads.

"He's a fullback and a linebacker, not a quarterback. Don't try and re-invent the wheel, Bob. Come the end of the day, it's still round."

He had been with the team since Patrick had started playing at nine-years-old. The coaches and players had matured together and had become an excellent and well coached team. As a result, there wasn't much for Paddy to do. So he was watching the high school's varsity practice on the adjacent field. They were finishing their defensive practice and were going over deep quarter's pass coverage. The left cornerback kept getting burned on the deep fade route. Paddy could see the kid kept opening his hips to the inside and losing contact with his man. The defensive coaches were yelling at him, but they weren't addressing what Paddy regarded as the fundamental flaw in his technique. The player was athletic. He ran every bit as well as the receiver who kept burning him. So fixing his footwork should have been an easy remedy.

Paddy was loath to insinuate himself into another coaches' dominion, but the mistake was so simple, and the effect so egregious, he couldn't leave it unaddressed. He had followed the high school team since he and Mairead had moved out to Plainedge, when they were first married. Coincidentally, that was also the year Buster Melnick was named the head coach. He enjoyed rooting for Buster's teams. Offensively, they were exciting and innovative. They put up a lot of points. Defensively however, they left much to be desired. They weren't bad as much as poorly prepared and coached. As a result, they were always competitive, but they weren't going to get by the powerhouse programs in Conference III, like perennial champion Lawrence. Lawrence could score every time they had the ball. If you didn't have a defensive plan, you were dead. Clearly, Buster's focus and expertise was on the offensive side of the ball. Unfortunately, his defensive coaches couldn't match his excellence. So Paddy excused himself from his son's practice and meandered over to the gate leading to the main field.

As Paddy got there, Buster Melnick was just leaving. Paddy approached him and introduced himself. He informed Buster he was working with the Bobcats youth program on the next field. Then Paddy qualified himself by pointing out he had played and coached for the NYPD against Buster's teams when he was the offensive coordinator for the Fire Department. Buster thought he had recognized Paddy. Now he knew from where.

"I remember you. You were a linebacker, number forty-five. You and Georgie Dobrisette ended up coaching that defense from the field. You guys used to kick my ass," Buster remembered.

"Don't sweat it, Buster. We had a bigger student body than the FD, a much deeper talent pool."

"You didn't beat me with talent. You took away whatever I wanted to do. Then, when I made adjustments, you took them away, too. How come you're not coaching anymore?"

"I got busy with my career. Between that and raising a family, there wasn't time anymore. George is still coaching though. He's the defensive coordinator at Seaford."

"I know. He's got one of the best defenses in the county, year after year. Thank God they're in conference IV. I could use a guy like that."

"On another matter, I was watching your corner get burned on the deep fade tonight. He doesn't suck, but his feet are bad. He keeps opening his hips to the inside. He loses the receiver just long enough to get out of position. Your coaches must have been isolating on something else, because they never mentioned the mistake to the kid."

"Would you be willing to try and fix it right now, before they hit the shower?" Buster asked.

"Sure," Paddy agreed.

Buster sent one of his players to run and get the necessary ballplayers. Once on the field, Buster introduced Paddy and told his cornerback to listen to him carefully. Paddy took the kid, who looked totally flummoxed after the disastrous practice he had just endured, and told him to shake it off. He explained his repeated mistake. Then he showed him how to open his hips to the outside. He explained by opening to the inside, he was losing contact with the receiver just long enough to be hopelessly out of position to defend anything thrown outside the numbers. The kid looked like he had an epiphany. When they ran some reps, the player used his new-found proper technique, and defended every one, picking off a couple for interceptions. When they broke practice, the cornerback practically floated off the field and into the locker room.

Buster tried to hire Paddy on the spot. Paddy tried to demure, but Buster wouldn't relent. Paddy finally agreed to serve as a kind of defensive consultant. He would attend Thursday's defensive practice every week. He agreed to take film on Monday of Plainedge's upcoming opponent. He would break the film down and make suggestions for a defensive game plan. Paddy promised to attend the Friday night games, work permitting. He would sit up in the coaches' box and radio defensive adjustments as needed. All of this was predicated on whether or not a homicide went down in the 83rd Precinct. Buster was made to understand that if a body dropped, all bets were off. He consented to every condition.

Paddy's influence was immediate and profound. Plainedge's defense went from competitive to dominant. Moving the players into the correct position and providing them with an idea of what their opponent was trying to do to them allowed the players to maximize their considerable athleticism and truly excel. The focus of the defense changed from just trying to keep pace with the other teams, to wanting to shut them out. They became such ball-hawks that they regarded a game without a defensive score as a failure. Paddy knew they had arrived as a unit when he heard his *mike* linebacker tell the quarterback, "If you guys just don't give up a safety, I guarantee you at least a tie. No one is scoring on this defense."

As promised, Plainedge advanced through the Conference III playoffs unscored upon. They met a loaded Lawrence team who was averaging forty points a game for the County Championship. The game was played at Hofstra University's Shuart Stadium on a cool Thursday night in late

November. Paddy had looked at film of every game Lawrence had played for the last two seasons. He had crafted a game plan designed to force Lawrence to run the ball into the strength of the Plainedge defense. Lawrence was a great throwing team, but they could not run on Paddy's linebackers and safeties. It was a big deal the next day when Newsday reported that Plainedge's defense had shut out one of the most prolific offenses in Nassau County history. Unfortunately, the fact that Plainedge had failed to score, and that they lost the county championship on a safety, when their long snapper launched the ball over the punter's head and through the end zone, also had to be reported.

In any event, Paddy had found his reintroduction to football exhilarating. When Buster asked him to sign on for the next season as the defensive coordinator, same conditions applying, Paddy immediately accepted. It was after this meeting in Buster's office that Paddy first had the misfortune of meeting Roxanne Barcellos. As Paddy and Buster were leaving his office, they ran into her while she was on her way into the gym. She got right in their way.

"Who is the new meat, Buster?" Roxanne asked, staring at Paddy appraisingly.

Buster introduced them. He explained to Paddy that Roxanne was the girls' varsity soccer coach. He informed Roxanne that Paddy was the new defensive coordinator for the football team. Roxanne seemed to pay Buster no mind as she looked Paddy up and down. Paddy noticed she was tall, maybe five foot ten, and all of a hundred and twenty pounds. She was wearing a Plainedge soccer warmup jacket, open in the front just enough to let her ample cleavage peek out. In spite of it being a week before Thanksgiving, Roxanne was still wearing high and tight cross country shorts. They were on the questionable side of decency, and left nothing to the imagination. Paddy could see her legs were impressively long and well-toned, ending in pink trimmed white anklets in little red Nike track shoes. Her hair was a wild mess of brown curls with blonde highlights that looked like she had just finished having sex. Paddy would come to understand that this was her look perpetually. Her eyes were a dark smoky brown and shined like they were looking for trouble and thought they had found some. Her bone structure had Paddy trying to guess at her obviously mixed ethnicity. Her skin was smooth and coffee brown, and suggested something Latin. But Paddy was sure there was more going on there. Roxanne shook Paddy's hand and held it longer than was necessary. Then she smiled at him.

"I'm looking forward to seeing more of you, Paddy," she said before turning and walking away, working her toned, shapely ass with a purpose.

"Roxanne is our resident cock teaser," Buster said.

"No she's not," Paddy corrected him. "That right there is a man eater, looking to leave nothing in her wake but heartache and destruction."

"You sound like you have experience."

"Before I met my wife, those were the only kind of women I dated."

CHAPTER FIFTY-NINE

Spring, 2001
Plainedge

Roxanne Barcellos had been a second team All-American in soccer at Hofstra University. She was considered the greatest female soccer player ever to emerge from Plainedge High School. When she had been cut three straight years from the women's national team during the selection process, she realized her future in soccer might lie in coaching. She had a degree in physical education, and the rapt attention of the Plainedge superintendent of schools, who had a penis and delusions of grandeur. She played her sex appeal for all it was worth during her job interview. That's how she became the women's varsity soccer coach of Plainedge High School at twenty-four-years old. She also relished the fact that she got to settle what she thought was an old score with her former coach. She had never liked him, since he rebuffed her sexually when Roxanne was in her junior year. She threw him under the bus during her interview when she suggested that not only wasn't he a very good coach, but he seemed distracted from soccer when he was around so many teenage girls. She created a vacancy and filled it with one sentence.

In spite of the fact that Roxanne got her job by using sex, lies and innuendo, she turned out to be a terrific soccer coach and gym teacher. Her unbridled and dripping sexuality ensured that almost immediately, she became known to the students, faculty and parents as *Foxy Roxy*. Within three years she was the chairperson of the physical education department.

Her rapid ascension only had a little to do with the art of sexual blackmail. Only twice did she sleep with male counterparts vying for her position. They suddenly didn't wish to be promoted when Roxanne threatened to expose them to their wives. She had elevated the soccer program until they were perennial championship contenders, winning several County and State titles. Roxanne insured her future success by getting involved with the youth soccer program in Plainedge. She ran clinics for the young players to teach them proper fundamentals and skills, but also to identify and nurture any of the girls with outsized potential. She ran coaches' seminars for the youth coaches to learn to implement the Brazilian soccer style she favored. The girls' soccer team became the winningest team at the school. Meanwhile, the youth soccer program in Plainedge grew and flourished, providing Roxanne with a sort of minor league to develop talent for her. She had built a little empire for herself.

But it galled her to know that in the ultimate scheme of things, none of that success mattered. Plainedge was football country. Compared to that, no one cared about girls' soccer. So Roxanne got even in her preferred way. She slept with the entire varsity football coaching staff, one at a time. Roxanne would seduce every coach but Buster Melnick, who cared only about football, and was immune to her charms. Not being able to ensnare Buster, she did the next best thing. She went after his assistants and fostered dissension among them. She let each believe he was *the one*, until she had moved onto the next one. Before long, Roxanne had the coaches meetings for the football team resembling "The Night of the Long Knives." But football coaching staffs were notorious for their turnover rate. So the damage Roxanne could do was only temporary.

When Roxanne met Paddy, she was sure she could make short work of him. She saw the way he looked at her. She recognized the hungry way he undressed her with his eyes. This one was a predator. She recognized the look because she was one, too. She knew he liked the bait. But she would discover there was a big difference between liking the bait and taking it. Paddy firmly deflected her advances, even challenging and taunting her.

"Come down to my office," Roxanne said. "I have something to show you."

"I've seen one before. Nice, but not as unique or special as you might imagine."

"What's the matter, are you afraid?" she challenged him.

"Roxanne, if I come down to your office, you'll be sleeping under my window like a cat. I'll never be rid of you."

"We'll see about that," Roxanne said. Paddy watched her walk away, swinging that ass for all it was worth.

Paddy had little trouble keeping Roxanne at arm's length. Mostly he avoided her. When their paths had to cross, Paddy was ready to parry Roxanne's enticements. Her clever attempts to get Paddy downstairs into her office were really quite clumsy and transparent. As they had no business in common, Paddy saw no reason to even contemplate descending the stairs down into what was known by almost everyone as Roxanne's *sex cave*. But to make sure, Paddy broke it down for her.

"You've got a better shot at hitting the lottery."

"So, I have a shot?"

"No, you don't. I am married, with children who look just like my wife. I'm nuts about her, and if that weren't enough incentive, she's way hotter than you. Now, why would I risk all that just to tag some skank ass on the side?"

Roxanne didn't care for the characterization, but she didn't have a response either. Unfortunately, like all truly committed obsessives, *No* just means *not yet*. So she wasn't done with Paddy by a long shot.

CHAPTER SIXTY

February, 1973
Rio de Janeiro

Roxanne Barcellos' evolution as a suburban man-eater began in the most unlikely of ways. Her father was world-renowned Brazilian soccer star, Paulo Barcellos. Her mother was the darling of the Israeli Olympic team from the 1972 Munich Games. Marnie Katz was the lone bright spot for the Israelis after the Black September massacre at the Olympic Village, where eleven of Marnie's teammates were murdered by Palestinian terrorists. Two days later Marnie, who was unheralded and unexpected to finish anywhere near the leaders, won the Gold medal in the two hundred meter hurdles. Her victory was so unexpected, it was met with a sense of wonder. That Marnie Katz was devastatingly beautiful, with the lithe, athletic body of a supermodel, only made the story more compelling. She emotionally dedicated her victory to her slain teammates, displaying profound humility. She became the most beloved Israeli athlete of all time.

The world opened up for Marnie like it was her own private oyster. She graced the cover of every news and fashion magazine in the world. She had no choice but to become a model. Everybody wanted a piece of her. It wasn't long before the little girl from Tel Aviv started hanging out in the most exclusive social circles around the globe. Her world became one of movie stars, race car drivers, elite athletes and billionaires. This was the setting where Marnie met Paulo Barcellos. Paulo was the celebrated mid-fielder on Brazil's 1970 World Cup Championship soccer team.

Marnie was in Rio de Janeiro for Carnival. She was the featured guest of Glamour magazine, gracing their cover for the fourth time since winning her medal. Paulo was an invited guest, as well as one of the most revered Brazilian athletes of all time, second only to his teammate Pele. They were at Glamour's reception party when they discovered each other. They were the two most beautiful people in the room, so it was an inevitability. They began a love story that Marnie thought would span the ages. Sadly, she would discover, *once upon a time* was a false promise, and *happily ever after* was a lie. But for a while, it was very good. Paulo and Marnie were soon married and became the international couple everyone wanted to be near. They had it all, money, style, beauty, and an endless line of people who wanted to give them more.

In 1975, the owner of the New York Cosmos of the North American Soccer League decided the United States was ready to embrace world class soccer. So he went about compiling the greatest international soccer stars ever to play on one team. He began by signing Giorgio Chinaglia from Italy. Next came Franz Beckenbauer from Germany. But the coup was Pele. Regarded as the greatest soccer player the world had ever seen, he was a must have for the Cosmos. Pele was willing, but only on the condition that his favorite mid-fielder, Paulo Barcellos be offered a contract as well. That was how Paulo and Marnie became the toast of New York society.

Until Roxanne was born. Then Marnie became a doting mother in a Manhattan penthouse. Paulo remained a fixture in New York's vaunted nightlife. There were rumors and insinuations about Paulo taking up with various actresses and models. Marnie let it fester until Roxanne was three and could be left with a nanny. She tried to reinsert herself into her former position, but things had changed since she left. For one, Marnie's body had altered after childbirth. Her chest and hips had thickened. She was still a strikingly beautiful woman, but she no longer fit the mold of emaciated heroin chic that dominated the fashion scene at the time. No one wanted her to model their clothes.

Marnie also discovered her Olympic glory had a shelf life. The drama and heroism of the 1972 Olympics were an almost forgotten footnote of history, at least as far as the fashionistas of the New York social scene were concerned. Adding to all this, was the fact that Paulo no longer showed much interest in spending time with Marnie or their young daughter. It wasn't long before their marriage was an irretrievable mess, with Paulo stepping out on Marnie in the most shameful and public way. For now he was still paying the bills, but that would end soon enough.

The owner of the Cosmos had overreached. The American sporting consumer was not ready to embrace professional soccer. By 1979, Pele had retired. Chinaglia and Beckenbauer soon followed suit. Without their stars and the lack of a signature franchise, the league folded. Paulo Barcellos still had some soccer left in him. So, he signed with Arsenal F.C. in the Premier league, and left for London. He took the money with him, and didn't even bother to say goodbye to his wife and daughter. They would never hear from him again.

Marnie had some of her own money, but not enough to sustain the Manhattan lifestyle she had grown accustomed to. Luckily, her sister Alyah had married a prominent surgeon and was living comfortably in East Hills, on Long Island. Marnie couldn't quite afford East Hills either, but she had enough to buy a small house in Plainedge. Once there, she continued her education by taking night classes at C.W. Post. She earned a Master's in Education to go along with her Bachelor's from Tel Aviv University. Within a year, Marnie was teaching history and coaching women's track and field at Plainedge Middle School. Once employed, Alyah watched Roxanne while Marnie went to work. It was a convenient arrangement, but Marnie never forgave Paulo for his betrayal and abandonment. She stoked a smoldering flame of resentment for not only him, but all men. She had many prospective suitors. But she was determined to never let anyone get close enough to hurt her or her daughter again.

It turned out Alyah had no better luck with men than her sister. Her surgeon husband moved out of the mansion in East Hills, and in with his young assistant. Divorce followed, and the Katz sisters and their daughters moved into a large mother-daughter in Plainedge. It should have been a happy and healthy living arrangement. The girls, all within a year of each other, were natural athletes. They played soccer together and flourished in school. They had inherited their mothers' stunning good looks. They were funny, smart, and had pleasant dispositions. There should have been no limits to their popularity. But, the simmering bitterness borne by Marnie and Alyah was transferred to their daughters. The girls were taught that men were selfish, vane, destructive animals who cared for no one but themselves, and could never be trusted. The message, so stridently imparted to all three girls, took root most deeply in Roxanne. Harboring her own fierce resentment for her father, Roxanne elevated her mistrust for men into a holy quest to make them pay.

As Roxanne grew and developed into a young woman, she saw how easily she could turn men's heads. She discovered how she could get most anything from them with little more than a coy smile and a flip of her curly hair. She understood early on the power of her sexuality, and she honed it into a weapon. She started breaking boy's hearts in middle school, and hadn't had her fill yet when she met Paddy Durr.

CHAPTER SIXTY-ONE

January, 1993
Long Island City

After the grand jury finding, Paddy and Mairead thought they had put the drama of Washington Heights behind them. It had been made clear to Paddy by the department that he would never work in upper Manhattan again. He did not anticipate being dumped into the 108th Precinct, though. That just felt like punishment. He was assigned to the Detective Squad, and would be promoted to detective in 18 months, but he was dubious as to how much detective work could be done in Long Island City. When Paddy inquired from the Chief of Queens Detectives why he was being assigned there, he was told it was the deepest they could bury him in the Detective Bureau without a shovel. The chief told Paddy to relax, learn his craft, and in time he could work his way back to a busier precinct. But for now his primary mission was to stay out of trouble.

"And for God's sake, don't shoot anybody else for a while," the chief implored him.

"I'll do my best. But if somebody needs to get shot, they're getting shot. My ass is going home at the end of tour."

"Fair enough," the chief allowed, before sending Paddy back to his command.

Meanwhile, Mairead had managed to find a position in the trauma center at Elmhurst Medical Center. The pay was better, and the commute was practically non-existent. Most importantly, she now had the flexibility to coordinate her schedule with Paddy's.

They were married that spring. Once it became hers, Mairead totally changed the décor and dynamic of Paddy's apartment in Astoria. She made the spacious one bedroom a homey and pleasant place to live. But it was still a one bedroom dwelling. If they didn't learn to keep their hands off each other, or at least come up for air once in a while, they were going to need a bigger place.

Their belief they had escaped Washington Heights was as premature as it was naïve. PTSD is a stowaway. It will come with you even if you leave the island. Paddy's followed him to Queens. So too did his legendary black cloud. Even in the sleepy bedroom communities of Long Island City, Sunnyside and Woodside, Paddy had the uncanny ability to find violent criminals with guns. Fortunately for him and the chief, he was able to disarm these miscreants without having to air them out. Paddy had thought he had missed the adrenaline rush from such encounters. So at first he relished them when they occurred. To wind down, Paddy and Mairead applied copious amounts of alcohol. Which, as it turns out, was exactly the wrong thing to do.

Mairead's favorite furniture addition to the apartment was the king size, rise post bed with a canopy. She had always wanted one since she was a little girl. When Paddy gave her the green light to do whatever she wanted, the first thing she bought was the bedroom set.

Mairead awoke with a start when she felt something solid whistle past her face. She heard Paddy wheezing and growling somewhere beyond the foot of the bed. He kept repeating in a panic, "Get the fuck away from me!" When Mairead flipped the light on the night stand on, she saw her husband, naked of course. He was shiny with sweat, his chest heaving from his raspy breathing. His eyes were somewhere else altogether, full of fear and panic. Paddy had ripped the corner post from the bed, splintering it at the base. He was wielding this enormous piece of wood over his head like a five foot long war club. He looked like he was getting ready to swing it again when Mairead threw a pillow at him and shrieked his name. Paddy calmed down and drifted back to reality in slow stages. He looked at the bedpost in his hands as if he didn't know how it got there. The realization came over him in a wave. He understood if he had hit Mairead with that post, he would have killed her. With that, he collapsed at the foot of the bed, a moaning, sweating mass of desolation.

Mairead jumped up and managed to drag Paddy back into bed. She held him until he calmed down and his breathing became less erratic. Mairead went into the bathroom and got a towel and a damp, cool washcloth. She spoke to him softly while she wiped his sweaty body down.

"Everything is okay, baby," Mairead assured him. Paddy looked up at her, embarrassed.

"I don't know why this keeps happening. I'm afraid one day I'm going to kill you."

"I'm not that easy to kill, even for a hard guy like you. Now tell me what the nightmare was all about," Mairead said, getting out the dream journal she had been keeping for Paddy.

Paddy told her Reuben Amaro evidentially was not going gentle into that good night. Psychologically at least, he wasn't done tormenting them. He described for Mairead how he was back in the hallway on 162nd Street. In a common theme from previous nightmares, Paddy found his gun wouldn't fire. The hammer just kept dropping on dead rounds. What was actually the post from their bed, in the nightmare became a riser he ripped from the staircase in the rear of the hallway. Mairead listened patiently. She asked Paddy if he could think of anything that might have triggered it. Paddy was at a loss. He reminded Mairead they had a great night together. She met him at the bar on the corner across from the precinct. They ate. They drank a lot. They laughed all night, and went home and made love. Where was there a trigger in that?

Then Mairead made an observation. She posed it as a question. Had he ever had one of these nightmares on a night when he hadn't been drinking? Paddy thought hard on it. Then he referred to the dream journal. He conceded he could not remember having a nightmare where alcohol wasn't involved. Paddy promised Mairead he wouldn't drink for a while, and they would see what effect it had. But being a man of extremes, he knew he had taken his last drink. They went to sleep with Mairead lying on his chest.

The next morning Paddy was up and cutting the other three posts off the bed with his sawzall. He sanded off the cut edges and stained and varnished them until they looked somewhat civilized. He apologized to Mairead. He told her when he was sure he wouldn't hurt her with it, he would buy her a new canopy bed. Mairead said she didn't care. She was much more concerned with the well-being of her man than about any stupid princess bed.

As much as finally getting a handle on the PTSD was a comfort to them both, it would prove to be the least of their problems. A much more sinister and dangerous force was already at work and lurking unseen in their immediate future.

CHAPTER SIXTY-TWO

Early spring, 1994
Manhattan

Unbeknownst to Paddy and Mairead, or any of the Anti-Crime team members, the Official Corruption Unit of the US Attorney for the Southern District had been secretly investigating the Anti-Crime team. This investigation began uncoincidentally, the week the grand jury had acquitted Paddy for killing Reuben Amaro. As Paddy had been warned by John Cantwell, the Mayor of New York had walked this investigation over to Saint Andrew's Place and called in a political chit to have the Anti-Crime team probed for civil rights offenses. Several successive federal grand juries were empaneled and they listened to allegations of wrongdoing from alleged witnesses, really just defendant's the team had arrested. The US Attorney had been investigating since November. The case had ground to a halt. The feds had thrown as much shit at the wall as they could get their hands on, but they couldn't get anything to stick.

In a move reeking of desperation, someone in the US Attorney's Office leaked the story to the press. The next day's cover of the Daily News had a picture of the Anti-Crime team under the banner headline that read *Cops or Cowboys?* The gist of the story was a repeat of the unsupported allegations already dismissed by the grand jurors. The columnist presented both sides of the story in an attempt to appear fair. The team was either heroic defenders of the community, or scourges with no regard for the constitution. Thus far, the grand jury was of the opinion the former was true. The article was specific in stating that the investigation excluded Police Officer Padraig Durr. Paddy was still being widely celebrated as a hero in law enforcement circles. The feds no doubt, didn't want to further alienate local police agencies, who would already look unfavorably at an investigation that was clearly not focusing on dirty cops, but allegedly overzealous ones. Paddy had been around long enough, and had been in hot water frequently enough to know that when a newspaper article says specifically that you are not a subject of an investigation, it's because you are the target. He understood his name recognition made him the prize. He knew the point of the article was to try and shake something loose. It was a common enough tactic in Organized Crime cases. But these were cops, not rat gangsters. Cops accused of wrongdoing in the course and commission of their jobs don't plead guilty. They don't cut deals. They don't sell out their partners. They can, in good conscience justify their actions, even if excessive or extra-legal, as part of their sworn duty to serve and protect. So nothing was going to shake loose.

The Anti-Crime team from the 34th precinct was now the "old" Anti-Crime team. The members had been scattered to the four winds shortly after the summer of 1992. Each of them were in investigative assignments around the city. The only one left in the *three four*, now assigned to the detective squad, was Sean Moran. Sean was the first to start making calls when the paper came out. The team agreed to meet at The Pipers Kilt on 207th Street and Broadway that night, to discuss their new status as suspects in a federal investigation. They all knew they would be followed. They also realized their phones were probably tapped or at least being monitored. So they agreed they would conduct themselves as if the walls had eyes and ears.

That night the team commandeered a booth in the rear of the bar. A pitcher of beer was ordered. Paddy astonished his old partners by ordering club soda. He explained his stomach had been bothering him, leaving his nightmares a story for some other time. There were more pressing issues to discuss. The six of them, Paddy, Tommy, Sean, Armando and Pete, along with Sergeant Touhey considered what was in the article. More importantly, they discussed what was not there. Other than accusing them of being overly aggressive, there was no intimation of any other wrong-doing. There was no mention of theft. There was no suggestion of brutality. There was just the persistent allegation of the team not having proper cause to make the arrests they had made, by the hundreds. The source of allegations like that could only come from one place.

"This whole deal comes from the mutts we arrested, or their slimy shithead lawyers. Troubling to be sure, but not very daunting," Kevin Touhey observed.

The feds were on a fishing expedition.

"They're going to try and approach us, to see if the paper scared one of us enough to cut a deal," Paddy predicted.

"If we tell them to go fuck themselves and lawyer up, they got nothing," Tommy observed.

Kevin Touhey had another opinion. "If we listen to their sales pitch, we might get a better idea of what they're fishing for."

"I think we already know that, Kevin. It's right in the article," Paddy pointed out. "If they approach me, I won't talk to them. I won't listen to them. And if they come to my home, they've got three seconds to get lost or I'm shooting one of them, maybe all of them."

The team discussed it amongst themselves. They knew where Paddy stood. Kevin Touhey and Pete O'Malley were the only ones who advocated listening to anything. Tommy McPhee had sound advice if the two members were going to take that strategy.

"If you're going to do that, ask if you're under arrest. Don't get in a car with anyone. Don't agree to meet them anywhere. Let them make their pitch on the fucking sidewalk. You can listen to what they have to say, but the minute they ask a question, lawyer up and walk away."

Having a unified strategy and a plan of action, the team as a whole felt better. Enough so that they started catching up with each other since they last worked together. Tommy was in the 103 Squad. Sean was in the 34 Squad. Pete O'Malley had gone to Manhattan North Narcotics. Armando Gigante was in Narcotics in Brooklyn North. Kevin Touhey had ravaged his knee chasing a perp about a month after the riots. He was on the verge of being put out on disability.

When they got around to Paddy, he complained bitterly about being buried in Queens. Tommy was the first to tell him to stop crying. McPhee went on to relate how Paddy was still running into guns in one of the slowest precincts in the city. After getting tired of being made fun of,

Paddy announced Mairead was pregnant. The sonogram was last week. It was a big, healthy boy. The team was ecstatic, pounding him on the back and wishing they could buy him drinks.

"That's wonderful, Paddy," Sean Moran said for all of them.

"Yeah," Paddy agreed. "I just hope I'm not in the clink when he's born."

CHAPTER SIXTY-THREE

Early spring, 1994
Manhattan

The first member of the Anti-Crime team the US Attorney's office elected to contact was the unit's sergeant. Kevin Touhey agreed to come into their office to speak with them. When he showed up with an attorney, who refused to let him say anything, the feds were furious. Having no one to question, all they could do was make a sales pitch on why he should cooperate with their investigation. Unfortunately for them, their chief appointed salesperson in this case couldn't sell a glass of water to a burning man.

Bronwyn Fainberg had been appointed a US Attorney straight out of Harvard Law eight years ago. She had come from New England money, but it was new money. Washed by one generation of legitimacy, it was still dirty money. Nevertheless, the family had pretensions of belonging to a higher station. Her grandfather had been a Jewish émigré from Russia. He arrived in Boston in 1918 with a business acumen, and a certain moral ambiguity regarding the use of violence.

Grandpa went to work for Charles "King" Solomon, the earliest recognized leader of organized crime in Boston. The organization ran all of the illicit prostitution, gambling, narcotics and loan sharking racquets in the New England area. Then prohibition arrived, and so had the Fainberg family. Grandpa Mordecai took the Solomons into the quasi-legitimate businesses necessary to transport and distribute illegal liquor. It wasn't long before the group owned, or at least controlled every truck on the eastern seaboard.

Mordecai's next venture was to start buying every knitting mill in Boston. Originally, this was a scheme to place speakeasies in the spacious basements of the mills, hidden by the knitting operation above, but the garment trade became so lucrative Mordecai was almost relieved when prohibition was repealed. Bronwyn's father Melvin eventually inherited the family business. He expanded their financial concerns into banking, the legitimate kind. The family was still getting their cut of the illicit loan sharking operation. In fact, the Fainbergs never relinquished their concerns in the Boston underworld. They still got a cut or tribute for almost every illegal transaction that took place in the state of Massachusetts.

Crime and politics in the city of Boston are difficult to distinguish from each other. Where one ends and the other begins is blurred. The one rule of thumb that has always been true is money buys power and influence. Melvin had a lot of money. He craved the other two. He had spent the last forty years cultivating political alliances and relationships that not only benefitted the family business, but burnished their reputation as well. Melvin knew he could never seize the reigns of political power in New England. His connection to organized crime was one generation too recent. But his daughter was far enough removed. Melvin had carefully excluded Bronwyn from ever working for the Fainberg family business. He had his political cronies bestow a variety of blessings on his daughter, like the educational fellowships, scholarships and internships that came flowing her way. When Bronwyn graduated from Harvard Law, Melvin used one of his connections in the Justice Department to have her appointed as an Assistant United States Attorney in New York.

Bronwyn Fainberg distinguished herself as a tireless worker. She adopted the fed's motto *"For the greater good"*, but understood better than anyone what it really meant. The greater good meant what was best for Bronwyn, in her unquenchable thirst for prestige, influence and power. She suffered from the disease common to federal prosecutors. She was blind to anything that might suggest she was ever mistaken. She chose her targets based upon their ability to enhance her standing, irrespective of their innocence or guilt. Then she dedicated the unlimited resources of the Justice Department into "proving" the conclusions she began with in the first place. She had cemented her standing within her own office. Her co-workers had given to calling her the *Ice Queen,* for her cold, calculating precision in all things beneficial to herself. But she was never going to achieve the one thing she had set as her primary goal when she went to work for the government. While she had managed to get promoted in-house to Deputy United States Attorney, and placed second in command of the Official Corruption Unit, she would never be elected to anything.

When Paddy had the misfortune of meeting Bronwyn Fainberg, he thought she was unspeakably ugly. But it wasn't merely her hideous countenance that made her so. She was thoroughly awful from the inside out. Humorless, except when experiencing glee at the misery of others, to call her face dour did it no justice. She was incapable of a genuine smile. Her sneaky, beady eyes were positively reptilian. They were surrounded by the most awful, mottled, red, and inflamed face Paddy had ever seen. And the areas that weren't so afflicted were marred by acne scars. In the midst of this fiery, painful looking mess, was a thin-lipped sneering mouth. Incongruously, Paddy could see that her teeth were perfect. These he could tell, were the product of years and tens of thousands of dollars of cosmetic dentistry. Bronwyn's teeth were the only un-ugly thing about her. Her hair was a tangled wiry mess, trying to be brown, but surrendering to a wan grayish hue. Paddy started to believe she was so ugly, even the sun refused to shine on her. Her awful hair reflected no light whatsoever. This mess of a head was badly supported by a weak neck that tilted forward. Her shoulders were hunched and pinched inward, as if to protect her reedy chest. This posture suggested to Paddy either premature osteoporosis, or she was a buzzard. It was probably a bit of both. Durr had the leisure of making these observations over several second-hand encounters. AUSA Fainberg had first made a nuisance of herself with Kevin Touhey, Pete O'Malley and Sean Moran. By the time Paddy would have his chance to see her up close, his impression of her was already burned into his retinas.

On the subject of her investigators, Paddy had been given a heads up on them from the Manhattan DA's man, John Cantwell. John had known both of them from his days in the NYPD. He described the two former detectives as "ass sucking parasites" who would do anything to advance themselves.

"If they even try and say hello to you, don't respond, other than to tell them to go fuck themselves. But do it in front of witnesses, or they'll try to use it against you."

Paddy made sure his partners were aware of all of this. So when AUSA Fainberg and her two investigators put the hard sell on Kevin Touhey, he wasn't buying. He instructed his attorney to inform them he would have no further business with them without the benefit of either a subpoena or an arrest warrant.

Next up on the hit parade was Pete O'Malley. By now, Pete knew exactly what he was dealing with when the two former detectives approached him outside his home in the Bronx. For some reason, the unholy trinity of AUSA Fainberg and her investigators identified Pete O'Malley as the potential weak link in the Anti-Crime team. Pete was a few years older. He was married with two boys, and owned his home. He also had a growing side business as a contractor with his two younger brothers, who had emigrated with him from Donegal. Given all he had to lose, the government was sure he would throw his teammates under the bus to protect it.

This idea was emblematic of the misunderstanding these people had for everyone in law enforcement. They habitually ascribed their own weakness, fear, and utter lack of loyalty to everyone else. In spite of being rebuffed time and again, they could never understand why people refused to cave in like the craven cowards they assumed everyone was. It never occurred to them that their subjects might possess a surfeit of honor which would prevent them from selling out their compatriots. It never occurred to them because these were qualities they didn't possess. Pete O'Malley tried to help them understand.

"Am I under arrest?" Pete asked them when they stopped him outside his house.

"No, of course not," said the older, fatter investigator. The Team had taken to calling him Special Agent Foster. The other investigator, naturally, was Special Agent Grant.

"Oh, *dat's* a relief," Pete said in his sing song brogue.

"We just want to talk to you," Grant chimed in.

"Talk? Oh I love to talk. I could talk all day. It's my very favorite *ting*," Pete said pleasantly.

"Why don't you hop into the car then? We'll sit down somewhere and discuss how you can help yourself. These other guys are young. They're reckless. You've got a family, a business that's just getting going. You own your own house. You have a lot to protect," Foster pointed out.

"Protect myself from what, exactly?" Pete asked the fat investigator.

"These other guys are bad news. They've put you and your family in jeopardy, trampling people's civil rights, flaking them, and lying about it in court. You don't want to go down for their bullshit," Foster said, selling it hard.

"Oh *geeze*, sure I don't. *Dat* would be dreadful."

"Then hop in the car," Grant offered. "We can help you."

"Oh boy, and *tanks* so much. I dearly appreciate your concern for me. But this is the point of the conversation when I tell you to go shit in your hat. I have an attorney. You can find out his name by calling the PBA, if they'll take your call, which I doubt, you miserable rat bastards. And as far as selling out my partners; I would sooner tear the tongue from my head than say a bad word about them. They are my brothers. They are the kind of cops you wish you could have been for just one day of your wasted, miserable, horseshit careers. Now fuck off and trouble me no more," Pete told them.

"You're making a mistake, kid," said Foster.

"I've made them before. Everyone has. The key isn't in the making. It's whether or not you have the balls big enough to survive them. Mine are as big as church bells. Now scurry away. Your cheese is getting cold."

CHAPTER SIXTY-FOUR

Mid-Spring, 1994
Manhattan

Failing to persuade Pete O'Malley to serve as their snitch, the feds next approached Sean Moran. As he promised he would, Sean slammed the door in their faces after telling them to go fuck themselves. They next tried to get to Tommy McPhee. But he was seldom home, and had taken to coming and going by way of the fire escape of his building, for no other reason than to mess with and frustrate the investigators tasked with watching him. His federal tail never figured this out, and reported to AUSA Fainberg that McPhee never left the building.

They never approached Paddy. Either they heard his threat to shoot them, and took it seriously, or they weren't ready to tip their hand about the true target of their fishing expedition. Either way, the clock was ticking on their ability to find him. In a week, he and Mairead were moving into her parents' house temporarily, while their new home in Plainedge could be made ready to move into. Paddy had a few more rooms to paint, and the floors to sand and urethane before it would be their home. He intended to keep his living arrangements secret from the police department. Given the feds were looking to throw him in prison Paddy figured, what's a little Charges and Specifications for failing to update his address? As far as the job and anyone else in city government knew, Paddy lived in Astoria.

But unbeknownst to the former Anti-Crime cops, the feds had another tactic in play. Pete O'Malley's old informant had approached the US

Attorney's office and offered to set the team up in exchange for leniency for his brother, who had been caught by the DEA selling ten kilos of cocaine to a federal undercover. This was the same informant who had given the team the gun sale caper on Broadway, where Paddy had been shot. The informant had remained in touch with Pete O'Malley, who didn't have it in him to tell the guy to go away. He had been calling Pete over the last few months trying to give up an alleged drug and gun operation in the Heights. Pete tried to explain that the team was no more. He tried to put the informant in touch with Major Case Narcotics, but he kept blowing off the meetings. All in all, there were a total of five short phone conversations over the space of four months. To O'Malley, they were meandering, innocuous and utterly unmemorable. To AUSA Fainberg, they were the raw material she needed to construct a classic perjury trap. She thought Officer O'Malley might be more effusive under indictment.

A month after the informant's last phone call to Pete O'Malley at the Narcotics District, Pete was served with a subpoena to testify in the federal grand jury. The title of the grand jury was redacted. So Pete and his attorney had to conclude that he was the subject, but they couldn't figure out what federal contact he might have had to testify about. He was granted *Use Immunity*, meaning he was compelled to testify. According to this feature, Pete's testimony could not be used against him in a future prosecution. Unless he was found to be lying, in which case, he would be indicted for perjury. Pete would ultimately find out this was exactly the point. They didn't care what he had to say. It was immaterial to any crime under investigation. They just wanted to catch him being *untruthful*. The team would soon discover the word had a different meaning in federal court than it did in the real world.

That Friday Pete reported with his PBA counsel, Kieran Entwhistle, to the Federal Courthouse at Foley Square. He was sworn in as a witness in the grand jury. Unlike state court, there were two prosecutors present for the questioning. AUSA Fainberg and a decidedly nebbish, bespectacled and mousey colleague of hers. They positioned themselves on opposite ends of the jury box, forcing Pete to physically turn in the direction of the questioner. They alternated frequently. It wasn't a problem early on, when they were merely going over his personal and professional background.

This was standard grand jury boilerplate. But then, the questioning started to take on a more confrontational tone.

The AUSA's started asking him if he knew several names he was unfamiliar with. They all turned out to be aliases for the informant. Finally, AUSA Fainberg asked him if he knew an Oscar Nieves. This was the name Pete knew his informant under. It was the name he had registered him with the police department, and it was the name with which he paid him. Pete was confused when Fainberg kept driving home the point that he claimed not to know the other previously mentioned names. Until he heard the tapes of the phone calls between him and Nieves. Dispersed intermittently within the conversations, but at the time seemingly incongruous and ridiculous, Nieves could be heard announcing, "You know my name is also Jonny Cueblo?" These sudden and disjointed snippets could be found throughout the five phone calls. As they weren't important to Pete at the time, and certainly weren't germane to anything they were talking about, he had no reason to remember them.

The questioning continued for six hours, with the AUSA's alternating their queries more and more rapidly until the next question was fired before Pete had completed answering the one before it. He could have asked for a break. He could have asked to confer with his attorney out in the hall, but he didn't. Like the good cop he was, he tried to answer every question to the best of his ability. Pete would come to understand his memory wasn't as able as he thought it was. After several hours of this barrage, O'Malley became understandably defensive. He started failing to recall things a reasonable person should have. But his brain was on overload, and it was unfair to expect him to continue operating efficiently. But the point of this proceeding wasn't fairness. It was to trap him. AUSA Bronwyn Fainberg had done that.

After Pete was dismissed from the grand jury, the US Attorney asked Kieran Entwhistle to bring his client back to her office that evening at 6 PM. When they got there, Fainberg produced a sealed indictment warrant for Police Officer Peter O'Malley for thirty three counts of perjury. Every time Pete testified in error, or had a failure to recall something Fainberg told the grand jurors he should have recalled, he was hit with another count. It was absurd. It wasn't of any assistance or importance to any bona-fide investigation. And of course, it wasn't fair.

Armed with her sealed indictment, Fainberg again made her *Queen for a Day* cooperation pitch. She had gambled it would give her enough leverage to push Pete past the tipping point. She was flummoxed when her gamble fell flat on its ass.

Pete leaned over and whispered in his attorney's ear. The PBA attorney told Pete firmly, "I can't say that. I'll just tell her you're not interested." Pete nodded his assent. He was dismissed from the room while his lawyer worked out the terms for his surrender when Fainberg unsealed the indictment. He would surrender himself at federal court on the ensuing Monday.

Bronwyn Fainberg had a bewildered and troubled look. She knew she had just indicted a cop for very nearly nothing. She thought the mere fact of the indictment would scare him into cooperating. When it didn't happen, she was left with an investigation and subsequent prosecution that had already cost a fortune, had accomplished nothing, and was nowhere near ending. Worse, she knew the alleged crime was a fiction based upon the failed memory of an inarticulate witness. None of the questions or answers even had the potential to provide material assistance to anything legitimately under investigation. Fainberg had painted herself into a corner. She knew she had put her career in peril. She was going to have to get a pound of flesh from one of these cops if she was to save herself. If someone didn't go to jail in this case, her big dreams of electoral office were over. She determined that someone would swing for this. But first, she had to know what O'Malley had told his lawyer.

"Are you sure you want to know?" Entwhistle asked.

"I have to."

"He said to tell you to go fuck yourself, and fuck the Queen when you get there."

"He truly doesn't care," Fainberg marveled. "He'd rather do sixty months in a penitentiary on the other side of the country than talk to me."

"Yes, but he told you that already. He also said you should enjoy your cervical cancer, inasmuch as it's inevitable. He's a big believer in karma, and you have much to answer for. He said, when it comes, he hopes it hurts."

Fainberg silently fumed at this. She glared at Entwhistle as if he had been the author of the remarks, and she hadn't practically begged to hear them. The attorney shrugged at her to communicate his ambivalence. Like everyone else who met her, Entwhistle hated Fainberg, and cared little for her delicate sensibilities, inasmuch as they were every bit the fiction her indictment was. Her glaring got her nowhere, but she wanted the last word.

"O'Malley better be here at 0900 hours. Or I'll have the US Marshalls at his house in the Bronx."

"Good luck with that. When they hear how you railroaded this kid, they won't lift a finger for you. You'll be stuck relying on those soulless imbeciles you call investigators, and let's be honest, those two couldn't catch venereal disease in a ten-cent whorehouse with a sea-bag full of dimes."

Realizing she wasn't getting the last word, Fainberg turned on her knobby heels and marched awkwardly away. Entwhistle thought she moved like a penguin with a stick up its ass. He collected his client in the hallway, and the two of them went back to the PBA Office to make arrangements for his bail bond for Monday.

CHAPTER SIXTY-FIVE

Mid-Spring, 1994
Manhattan

Bronwyn Fainberg spent the better part of the weekend in her office preparing the charges and bail motions for Pete O'Malley's arraignment on Monday. When she was done, her motion sounded more suitable for a war criminal than an alleged fibber. But she was determined to make her application, and repay O'Malley for his insolence. She also had come to the conclusion it was time to roll the dice and subpoena her true target. She figured after just skirting a murder charge, Police Officer Durr might be more amenable to flipping than O'Malley was. If not, she could always snare him in the same kind of perjury trap she got O'Malley with. He was just another ignorant cop, after all. She justified her actions by reasoning that if Al Capone could be brought down for tax evasion, then why couldn't she hang some *dirty* cops for perjury?

Fainberg finally went home Sunday night to prepare her best and most expensive business suit for the arraignment. She should have saved her time and money. When Paddy saw her enter the courtroom the next day, he told Tommy McPhee and Sean Moran that her physique and overwhelming hideousness made the garment look like a dirty sack of radishes.

The courtroom was jammed with the cops and detectives from the 34th Precinct. They were all in their dress blues and standing in defiance of what they believed was a vendetta against their brother, Pete O'Malley. The presiding judge, Paris Brundage warned the cops that they could remain, but if they disturbed the decorum or disrespected his court he would have no problem remanding them into federal custody in their shiny uniforms. He invited anyone who thought they could not abide by this rule to leave now. Not a cop budged.

The court was brought to order. O'Malley's case was called. The clerk read the thirty-three count indictment. Then the defendant was instructed to rise. When Pete O'Malley stood, so did every other cop in the courtroom. The judge asked Pete if he understood the charges against him. He said he did. Then Judge Brundage asked him how he plead. "Absolutely Not Guilty!" Pete announced clearly. The clerk recorded the plea and the judge instructed everyone to sit.

"Before I get to the bail application, I have to do some house cleaning. This indictment is a mess," Brundage informed the court, but he was glaring at the government's table.

Fainberg rose to object, but the judge cut her off.

"Stow it, Ms. Fainberg. This is my courtroom, and I intend to run it. I'll invite your argument when I'm good and ready to hear it. Which will be never," he said, forcing the US Attorney to wither into her chair.

"The first thing I'm doing is dismissing thirty of the counts related to the defendant's failure to recall. It's all the same thing. You get one count. What the government has tried to do is what we in East New York used to call *piling on*. Well, it didn't get over on Pitkin Avenue, and it aint' getting over here. That leaves us with two counts of lying, and one count of forgetting. Make your bail applications accordingly."

Kieran Entwhistle rose from the Defenses' table and began what was going to be an impassioned plea for bail based upon Police Officer Pete O'Malley's extraordinary character and decorated career of police and community service. The judge smiled and halted the PBA counsel.

"Is the defendant a US citizen?" the judge asked.

"Yes, Your Honor," Kieran said.

"Does he have a family, and own his own home?"

"He does, Your Honor."

"Is he employed by the City of New York?"

"He is an eight year veteran of the NYPD."

"Then just ask me for an ROR, already," the judge instructed.

"The defense requests the defendant be released on his own recognizance," Kieran complied, a little confused.

"I will now hear the Government's argument," Brundage said sourly.

AUSA Bronwyn Fainberg rose to greet the court. She did her best to smooth what was the mess of her wardrobe, and proceeded to attack the character and deeds of *Rogue* Police Officer Peter O'Malley. Her allegations were nothing short of slanderous. But the judge let her continue for a while before interrupting her.

"Okay. I get it. The defendant is a bad guy. What does the government want?" the judge asked.

Fainberg went on to ask for, but really demanded a one-million-dollar cash bail, with no bond permitted. She wanted Pete's and his family's passports seized. She wanted his assets and bank accounts frozen. And if the defendant should somehow be able to make his bail, she wanted him confined to his home with an electronic bracelet. The judge smiled at AUSA Fainberg, fascinated with her audacity.

"Let me get this straight; You want to take all of this man's hard earned income and real property. You want to deny him the company of his family, his friends and his home. You want to deny him the ability to support himself. All for telling *porky pies?*"

Fainberg looked confused.

"Oh come now, Ms. Fainberg. You're from Boston. Surely you're familiar with the expression. *Porky pies*, rhymes with lies. Fibs, tall tales; all serious crimes to be sure. But if we are to bury a man such as this for these meager charges, how are we to blush when more capital crimes, like bootlegging, murder, extortion, prostitution and drug trafficking rear their ugly heads?"

In that moment, Fainberg understood the judge's enmity toward her and her case. She would not risk having her family's name and background dragged onto the record. Neither she nor her father could afford that kind of exposure. So she informed the court that the government was rescinding its request for bail.

"I thought it might," Judge Brundage said. "The defendant is released on his own recognizance."

Kieran Entwhistle didn't know why the Judge was making his life so easy, but he wasn't going to let the opportunity pass.

"Your Honor, the Defense would like to make a motion for dismissal based upon the utter lack of materiality of the alleged perjuries to any bona-fide investigation. The government's stated goal in the investigation was in no way thwarted, obstructed or otherwise affected, even if the perjuries were in fact perjuries. It is the defense's intention to prove they were not."

"I would tend to agree with counsel, but I'm not going to litigate that now. You can file that motion and any others for the hearings."

Judge Brundage dismissed the court and grinned at AUSA Fainberg as he retired to his chambers. Fainberg didn't yet know the source of the judge's antipathy for her, but she clearly understood it was acute. There was no way her flimsy indictment would survive this judge's circumspection. A feeling of hopelessness seemed to drop over her. She was unfamiliar with it. But if she had an iota of empathy for the people she randomly targeted in her prosecutorial career, she might begin to understand. But empathy was a quality Bronwyn Fainberg was without.

Judge Paris Brundage had empathy though. At the moment, he had much empathy for Pete O'Malley. He also had a score to settle. Bronwyn Fainberg was the granddaughter of the Boston gangster who had Judge Brundage run out of the FBI as a young agent. The judge would consider it an honor and a privilege to end this criminal family's incursion into the government.

This information about Judge Brundage, later uncovered by Kieran Entwhistle, was greatly encouraging to Pete O'Malley. Fainberg concurred. She began boxing up things in her office for the expected move out of government employ.

CHAPTER SIXTY-SIX

Late-Spring, 1994
Manhattan

In 1994 in Manhattan, the US Attorney's Office was preparing to bring to court the largest Mafia prosecution in history. With over two hundred defendants, the scope of the trial would be unprecedented. They had just finished empaneling the jury when the assigned judge, Cyrus Malkin, removed his glasses, clutched his chest, and face-planted on the bench. He was already dead when the clerk got to him. The aneurism that had been unseen in his brain for the last two years had finally given way to a fatal hemorrhage.

The protocol for replacing Federal District Judges on the eve of trial was employed. Every judge not already on trial in the district went into a quasi-lottery bin. The name that came out would be assigned to the Mafia trial. That judge's calendar would then be assigned to the judge with the least seniority in the district.

That's how rookie federal jurist Wellesley Kip got assigned the Peter O'Malley case. Once Judge Brundage's name came out in the lottery, Judge Kip assumed his entire case load. In theory, this was the only fair way to do the thing. In practice, it turned out to be the most patently unfair way for Pete O'Malley. It wasn't Judge Kip's intention to screw Pete over. But because of his inexperience, (this was Kip's first trial) and his naiveté, it became a forgone conclusion.

At that time, there was a popular axiom in place among the federal district judges. It went, *when in doubt, trust the Government.* Judge Kip never heard that uttered by Judge Brundage. Brundage believed the exact opposite to be true. If they were to have a conversation, Brundage would have counseled Kip to be very wary of the Government in general, and AUSA Fainberg in particular. But that conversation never occurred. Kip would learn the hard way that when in doubt, you should stay in doubt, until you can figure it out for yourself.

Fainberg was delighted with the new Judge. She knew she could manipulate him any way she saw fit. The end result might not be the career topper she had hoped for, but at the very least, she would have her pound of flesh in the form of Peter O'Malley. Her justice department career, once so perilously close to ruin, would at least be salvaged. She started to replace those things in her office which she had recently boxed up.

At the next court appearance, Kieran Entwhistle filed his motion to dismiss. Judge Kip listened politely before denying the motion. Then the newly energized AUSA Fainberg filed sixteen motions before the court. They were all related to the anticipated tactics that would be employed by the defense. It became clear the government's strategy in this case would be to try and prevent Pete O'Malley from making any type of defense. Fainberg was attempting to exclude witnesses and lines of inquiry before they could even be made. Judge Kip let her do it. At the end of the days' proceeding, Fainberg dropped all of her pretenses and had Paddy Durr served with a grand jury subpoena by a federal marshal present in the courtroom. She sneered at Durr as she watched him being served. Paddy smiled obsequiously at her, and flipped her the bird. Then he left the courtroom to call his lawyer.

After meeting with Rich Kornreich, Paddy decided he would honor the subpoena by showing up, but that was all. He would refuse to accept the proffered *Use Immunity.* Other than identifying himself and providing career background information, he would refuse to answer any questions whatsoever. As far as obeying the extraneous grand jury instructions, Paddy was having none of that. The government wanted him to testify in civilian clothes, with no police department insignia or identifiers. Paddy was marching into that grand jury in full battle regalia. He would wear his class A, dress blue uniform with all the ribbons and medals prominently displayed. If the Government's intent was to indict a cop, they were going to have to deal with the recruiting poster that this particular cop embodied. Rich Kornreich cautioned Paddy his actions bordered on obstruction. Paddy told him he didn't care.

The day before Paddy's grand jury appearance, he got called down to the office of the Chief of Queens Detectives. Assistant Chief Dominick Pasquale had been ordered to re-inforce the US Attorney's instructions. It seemed the government intended to sacrifice him on the altar of political expediency, and the police department would lead him to the slaughter. Chief Pasquale told Paddy not to appear in uniform. He ordered him to go un-armed and without NYPD insignia of any kind. This included his shield, a tie clip, or even a lapel pin. Lastly, and most importantly, the chief told him;

"Whatever you do, don't even think about taking the fifth."

"Are you my attorney now?" Paddy asked him.

"No. I'm your boss," the chief fumed. "And as such, I am compelled to inform you of certain things. The department sat on its hands and left you to dangle during your last shooting. They didn't do anything in particular to hurt you, but they didn't lift a finger to defend you either. This time, they've taken a side. It's not your side. Every big boss in the department is lined up against you. It's coming from on high. I know these men. They're my superiors. Given the choice between protecting you and advancing their careers even one iota, there is no choice at all. The mayor wants you thrown down the shitter. They are going to see that it's done. Believe me when I tell you Paddy, if you invoke the Fifth Amendment tomorrow, you'll be in big trouble."

Paddy smiled bitterly at the chief. There was so much he wanted to say, but he knew there was no point beyond the puerile satisfaction of ranting indignantly at a superior officer. Besides, Paddy knew Chief Pasquale was not the source of his troubles, just a symptom. Pasquale was disinclined to help him. The chief had been directly ordered by his superiors not to. So he wouldn't. Paddy decided to keep his sanctimony to himself. When the silence between them grew uncomfortable for the chief, Paddy reluctantly let him off the hook.

"Is there anything else, Boss?" Paddy asked.

Chief Pasquale smiled self-consciously at his young officer. He suddenly felt tired all over. He was embarrassed to be in the position of having to advise Paddy contrary to his own penal interests. He was embarrassed because he knew Paddy saw right through it. He also knew this cop would do whatever he thought was the right thing, regardless of what trouble it might buy him down the road. Which was another thing the chief felt shame for. While Dominick Pasquale was never the kind of cop Paddy Durr was, he at least had a modicum of integrity. Now he found himself in the position of having to order this young man to bare his neck for his own noose. Any illusion of integrity was now gone like so much smoke.

"There's nothing else," Pasquale said.

CHAPTER SIXTY-SEVEN

April 18, 1994
Manhattan

When Paddy got down to the Southern District Courthouse, he looked like he was dressed to be promoted to commissioner. His uniform was crisp and expertly tailored. His medals, not usually worn but permissible in the *dress blues,* were evenly arrayed, dangling from his right breast pocket. His shield had just enough tarnish and dents to look battle tested. The leather rack full of citations pinned above it cascaded up and over his shoulder. He looked like a recruitment poster. In light of the US Attorney's instructions about coming unarmed, Paddy had to wait at the security desk with the marshals while they vouchered and secured his three authorized firearms. This delay, reported to AUSA Fainberg, caused Paddy to be five minutes late. He had his receipt for his guns and made his way up to the grand jury on the 22nd floor. Fainberg and another US Attorney were waiting for him at the elevator bank.

"You were told not to be in uniform, and to come un-armed," Fainberg screeched at him, waving a bony finger in his face. Paddy did everything in his power to remain impassive. He spoke as evenly and calmly as he could.

"Not by anybody I am inclined to obey. I am not sworn. This hallway is not the grand jury. So you don't get to ask me anything. You don't get to tell me anything. You need to shut your fucking cake-hole, and get that knobby claw out of my face. Unless you want to lose it. Then by all means, leave it there. I'll bite it off at the shoulder."

Rich Kornreich was coming around the corner and saw the dead-eyed stare his client was regarding the US Attorney with. He jumped between them before any foolishness could occur.

"AUSA Fainberg, why are you speaking to my client without me being present?" Kornreich demanded.

"He threatened me!" Fainberg whined.

"I heard it. It was no threat. He gave you a reasonable choice, and some sound advice. You know you're not supposed to talk to him. What you're doing might well be construed as intimidating a witness. And who the hell are you?" Kornreich demanded of the other attorney present. The nebbishy, bespectacled man stammered and cleared his throat. He did not answer the question. So Rich tried again.

"Look at my face. Hear the words. Who are you?"

"This is AUSA Milton Myersohn. He's assisting me," Fainberg said.

"Good. He can be a witness for the complaint I'm filing against you with the Office of Professional Responsibility."

"Your client didn't comply with the grand jury instructions."

"He doesn't have to. He's not your witness. If he wanted to show up in a clown suit, it's his prerogative as a US citizen. Now, if you have anything else to ask him, you will do so in the grand jury."

Fainberg stormed away with her minion in tow. When they were out of earshot, Kornreich addressed his client.

"Damn, Paddy, you look good."

"Let's hope the jurors agree."

"I'm sure they will, but you're not off to a good start. Pissing off the prosecutor who is trying to indict you is generally not a good idea."

"I haven't even started getting off to a bad start. If she's pissed off now, she's really not going to like what happens next."

When Paddy was led into the grand jury by the marshal, he had his hat tucked smartly under his arm. He walked erect, with his chest out, as if at attention. He made a concerted effort to make eye contact with as many of the grand jurors as he could. It had the desired effect. The jurors seemed fascinated with him. So Paddy played to his audience. He smiled at the jurors and nodded as he took his seat.

AUSA Fainberg was set up at the podium to the far left of the jurors. Myersohn was on the opposite end. After explaining *Use immunity* and the witnesses' responsibilities pertaining to it, Fainberg began by asking Paddy to identify himself. She ran through his police career from his time in the Police Academy to his present assignment in the 108 Squad. He told the jurors he was recently married, and he and Mairead were expecting their first child in May. Between the police material and the endearing personal information, the jurors were transfixed. Then Fainberg thought it was time to get down to her intended business, before the grand jury collectively adopted the witness. Paddy had some business of his own he wanted to get down to.

"Officer Durr," Fainberg began. "Do you know an Elias Mosquano?"

Paddy knew Mosquano. He had arrested him several times for things like robbery, weapons possession and assault. Mosquano beat every case by either intimidating any witnesses before trial, or killing them. He also had a lawyer who made an automatic complaint against the police when his client was arrested. Paddy had dealt with the anticipated questions in the past when Internal Affairs had interviewed him. The allegations were unfounded, and Paddy knew nothing that came out of Mosquano's mouth could hurt him. But that's not what he said to AUSA Fainberg.

"On the advice of counsel, I decline to answer that question on the grounds that any answer I may give will be used by you, AUSA Fainberg to incriminate me. Just like you did to Police Officer Peter O'Malley."

The jury was abuzz. They had no idea who Pete O'Malley was. This was a different jury than the one that indicted O'Malley, but the implication was delicious. When the jury foreman asked Fainberg who that was, she practically bit his head off.

"That is not germane to this investigation!" she thundered. Then she narrowed her awful gaze at Paddy.

"You've been granted *Use Immunity*. You must answer the question."

"I didn't ask for immunity. Besides, *Use Immunity* offers me no protection whatsoever from an overzealous government shrew whose only goal is to entrap me in a perjury, just like Police Officer Peter O'Malley."

At the mention of Pete's name again, the jurors all perked up. They began looking curiously at AUSA Fainberg. As if to say; *Why can't we know about Officer O'Malley?* Fainberg was losing this jury. She had surrendered the initiative. Paddy snatched it away. The parade of scoundrels that had told tales out of school about Paddy and the Anti-Crime team had done little to engender any belief the jurors might have had. After two days of listening to the same whining complaints from people who were clearly criminals, they had grown to detest those witnesses, and regarded everything that came out of their mouths as lies.

Now they got to hear Police Officer Padraig Durr, a real cop, with all the ribbons and medals to prove it. He was engaging. He was eloquent. He was good looking. After being repulsed by AUSA Fainberg and her "witnesses" for the past two days, they leapt at the opportunity to be seduced by Paddy Durr. Fainberg realized Paddy was hijacking her grand jury right from under her. She signaled to Myersohn. They would now try and ratchet up the pressure on Paddy by questioning him from opposite directions. The tactic had worked to confuse Pete O'Malley. She figured it might work again.

Paddy on the other hand, was aware of the tactic. He knew his rights as a witness. He knew he didn't have to submit to being questioned in this way.

"Do you know…?" was all AUSA Myersohn got out before Paddy cut him off. While still looking impassively into the craven face of Bronwyn Fainberg, he held up his right hand, halting and silencing Myersohn.

"Stop right there," Paddy said. "I am not here to be interrogated. I will only be addressing questions from one of you. So, if you have anything of value to do today, *Specs*, I suggest you get to it. Because when I put the period on the end of this sentence, you will cease to exist as far as I'm concerned. Now, AUSA Fainberg, you may inquire."

With that, Fainberg lost her mind. She started screeching at Paddy that he would not give her directions in her own grand jury. Paddy took the opportunity to correct her again.

"This isn't your grand jury. It's theirs'," Paddy said, indicating the jurors with a sweep of his hand. "You probably haven't told them that, though. Did you tell them they could ask questions and direct the investigation where they wanted it to go? I bet you didn't."

Not wishing to have this discussion in front of the Jurors, Fainberg decided to advance her inquiry.

"Do you know an Omar Duiplaice?" she asked Paddy.

"On the advice of counsel, I decline to answer that question on the grounds that any answer I give will be used by you, AUSA Fainberg, to frame me for something. Just like you framed Police Officer Peter O'Malley."

The horses had gotten loose. The cart was on fire, and it was rolling down the hill. This was now a runaway jury. There was no way Fainberg was going to be able to stonewall the jurors on Pete O'Malley now. She realized she wasn't going to get Paddy to perjure himself. The best she could hope for would be to fashion a flimsy indictment for obstruction of justice. Her vindictiveness and poisonous fury dictated she must. So she continued to ask her questions. When the smoke had cleared, Paddy had invoked his constitutional right not to incriminate himself twenty-nine times. When she was done, Fainberg stated she was dismissing the witness, as he was obstructing the investigation. Paddy decided he wasn't done pissing up her leg yet.

"Aren't you going to give the grand jury an opportunity to ask questions of the witness directly? Isn't it their prerogative to do so?" Paddy asked benignly. Fainberg conspicuously slumped at her podium.

The grand jury foreman stood up and announced he had some questions.

"What happened to Police Officer Peter O'Malley?"

"Several weeks ago, AUSA Fainberg and another US Attorney, possibly *Captain Pipsqueak* over there, dragged Pete in here and interrogated him for six hours. They framed him for perjury when he failed to remember specific facts about five forgotten phone conversations. So, now he sits at home with his family, suspended from the NYPD. This hero cop, who has been wounded twice in the line of duty, has to wait to hear his fate in federal court for a perjury that was the vindictive invention of AUSA Fainberg."

The assistant foreman then stood up. He raised his hand unnecessarily. Paddy acknowledged him.

"Those two medals under your right breast pocket, the green ribbons with the Maltese Crosses, what are those?"

"Oh, you're a veteran," Paddy observed, noting the assistant foreman's familiarity with military decorations. "Those are Police Combat Crosses. They are the second highest decoration awarded for valor by the NYPD. I have two. So does Pete O'Malley."

"What do you have to do to get one of those?"

"Generally speaking, win a gunfight."

"What's the highest decoration?"

"The Medal of Honor."

"What do you have to do for one of those?"

"Lose the gunfight. The Medal of Honor is usually awarded posthumously. I want no part of that award. I've been to enough *inspector's funerals*. I don't want to bury one of my partners, and I don't want anyone to have to bury me."

With that, AUSA Fainberg stepped in and formally dismissed Paddy as a witness. Paddy thanked the grand jury for their time and attention. As he stood to leave the jury-room, the grand jurors spontaneously rose and began applauding him. Bronwyn Fainberg stormed out of the room. Paddy couldn't help but chuckle. He politely asked the jury to stop applauding him. They complied, and Paddy left the room.

Bronwyn Fainberg was waiting for him in the hall.

"I'll have you indicted by the end of the day," she sneered.

"Why don't you write a little music to go along with that, *Cuntessa*? I've heard it so many times lately, I think I might want to dance to it."

Fainberg stormed back into the grand jury, slamming the door in Paddy's face.

"How did it go?" Rich Kornreich asked.

"It was interesting. I hijacked the grand jury from her. They hate her as much as I do. I'm still probably going to be indicted, though."

"For perjury?" Rich asked, dumbfounded.

"No, obstruction. I took the fifth twenty-nine times."

"Wow! That might be a record. Sam Giancana only took it a dozen times in front of the Kefauver Commission."

"I guess they didn't ask Sam enough questions."

CHAPTER SIXTY-EIGHT

April 18, 1994
Long Island City

Paddy accepted a ride back to the 108 Squad from Rich. On the way, they discussed how he would act if the feds came for him tonight. Ordinarily, law enforcement officers were given the courtesy of surrendering with their attorneys after an indictment. But Paddy and Rich both knew Bronwyn Fainberg was through observing courtesy when it came to Paddy Durr. She would send the FBI to execute the indictment warrant as soon as she had it in hand.

Paddy and all the Anti-Crime members had been through this drill already. Lawyer up, and don't say jack. Who after all, wants to talk to the FBI? With respect to the indictment, Rich told Paddy he couldn't be sure until he reviewed it, but he didn't think it would hold up. He couldn't see how Fainberg could make a convincing argument for materiality. There was nothing there but smoke. How could you materially obstruct nothing?

"I hope you're right, Rich," Paddy said getting out of the car in front of the 108th Precinct. "If I didn't have to go to prison, that would be peachy."

When Paddy got upstairs to the Squad, he was met by Detective Marco Gemignani, the DEA Delegate for the 108 Squad. He told Paddy Chief Pasquale wanted him in his office *forthwith*. So the two of them jumped in a squad car and headed over to the headquarters of Queens Detectives, in the 112th Precinct.

Paddy was led into the chief's office by his adjutant, Detective Francesca Bender. She had been the chief's clerical officer since their days together in the 105 Squad. Their relationship was rumored to be more than professional. She was known throughout the Job by her apropos moniker of "Fran the Can." Paddy didn't care about any of that. He had developed a good working relationship with her in his short time in Queens. He found her smart, likeable, and helpful. About the speculation regarding Fran and the chief, Paddy wouldn't have given that sort of talk the time of day. But Paddy knew something no one else did. He once asked Fran how she dealt with all the gossip and rumors that abound with an attractive, young, female detective working for the chief.

"I pay it no mind. It's juvenile. Besides, I'm gay," she said.

"I never would have gotten that, Fran," Paddy said, surprised.

"You're not going to out me now, are you, Paddy?"

"Out who? Out what? I don't know what the fuck you're talking about."

"I knew I could trust you."

"It's immaterial anyway. You'll always be "Fran the Can" to me."

"You know, I never minded that nickname. And I do have a nice can."

That was something they both could agree on. Right now Fran had a concerned look as she led him into the chief's office. She let him in and closed the door.

Paddy strode to the front of the chief's desk and snapped to attention, offering and holding a crisp military salute. The chief looked like his eyes would pop out of his head.

"What the fuck are you wearing? Did you testify in that?" the chief thundered.

"Yes, sir."

"What part of our conversation was I unclear about yesterday?"

"I understood every word."

"But you decided to do whatever the fuck you wanted. Is that about right?"

"I protected my penal interests."

"You were ordered to appear at the grand jury and testify. Why in God's name did you take the fifth twenty-nine times?"

"Because they didn't ask a thirtieth fucking question," Paddy growled back at him.

Chief Pasquale realized this cop had hit the tipping point. He knew Paddy no longer cared what happened to him. He had the resolute look that told you he had already prepared for the worst. What came next was just lights and noise.

"I don't know what I'm going to do with you," the chief said in frustration.

"Chief, I know those orders came right from the mayor's desk. They were designed to hurt me. They were illegal. You had to know when you gave them they had a zero chance of being obeyed. I understand if you're looking to take me down for it. But it's what had to happen. If that's what you want, go for it. But don't think for a second I'll just lie down and let you do it."

"I know you don't believe me, Paddy. But I'm not looking to hurt you. A very small handful of bosses on this job are pulling for you. They like and respect you. After what you went through up in the Heights, you impressed the hell out of everybody. But this administration is impossible to maneuver around. No mayor has ever hated cops more. He'd disband the whole department if he could. We just have to be patient and play the game."

"It's not a game, Chief. And you can't protect me. Neither can anyone else in the department. But I suspect I won't be your problem for much longer."

"What are you talking about?"

"I'm going to be indicted for obstruction of justice sometime this afternoon. When it drops, I'll automatically be suspended. How long after that do you imagine it will take the mayor to order the police commissioner to fire me? My guess is nano-seconds."

That took the chief by surprise. He hadn't suspected the day held so much portent. He liked this cop. The chief knew he was going to make a great detective, if the system would just let him alone to do the job. Pasquale felt like a part of him was dying. He had dedicated the last forty years of his life to the job. He had always felt like the department made him a part of something unique and special, noble even. Now he felt like he had been living an illusion. His naiveté had been stripped away, leaving him with an unvarnished picture. He now felt like a cog in a sick, destructive machine that was intent on eating its own, and for no other reason than to heal the bruised ego of a selfish, morally bankrupt politician. Before today, he had never felt like a bureaucrat. As much as he hated the word, he hated the feeling more.

"I don't know what to say," Pasquale admitted.

"You don't have to say anything, but if my name should come up, let it be known, I went out like a cop. Tell whoever asks, they could fuck me over, but they couldn't keep me from coming to work and doing the job. Even when I knew they were out to get me, I brought my lunch pail and went to work. Make sure everybody knows that much. They might have taken me down, but they never touched what was pure."

"I'll tell them."

When Paddy left the office, Francesca was waiting for him at the door. Her eyes had welled up with tears, and her lower lip trembled as she reached out and embraced him. Of course she had heard every word. That was her job as the bosses' adjutant.

"It's not right, what they're doing to you. The injustice of it makes me sick. I'll be praying for you and Mairead."

Paddy kissed her on the forehead and thanked her. But he couldn't bear the crestfallen look on her face. When he pinched her on her ample bottom, Fran broke up laughing through her tears, in spite of herself.

"I like you better laughing, Fran. And Mairead and I will be fine."

CHAPTER SIXTY-NINE

April 18, 1994
Manhattan

When Paddy got back to the 108, three FBI Agents were in the squad waiting for him. When he walked in, the most senior looking one approached him.

"Are you Police Officer Padraig Durr?"

Paddy laughed at him and tapped the name plate under his shield.

"Did you acquire your awesome intuition and observation skills at Quantico?" Paddy asked. "Or were you born Hercule fucking Poirot?"

The Agent was holding a Federal Arrest Warrant. Paddy knew who that was for.

"Okay, Elliot Ness. Just let me lock my guns up in the squad safe, and I'll let you arrest me."

"Actually, we're supposed to seize those," the agent informed him.

"That's not going to happen without a search warrant and an I.O. 9 hearing. Unless you want to slap leather for them. Slow man dies?"

The agent swallowed hard and froze where he stood. In eleven years with the FBI, no one had ever questioned his authority. So he had no idea how to react to this hard-case cop who just challenged him to a gunfight. Having laid down the law with respect to his fire-arms, Paddy let the agent off the hook and declared victory.

"I guess you don't get invited to many shoot-outs in Official Corruption, huh? I'm going into my lieutenant's office to lock these up. You wait right here."

Paddy went into Lieutenant Patterson's office to give him his guns and apprise him of the situation. Paddy straightened his uniform one last time in front of the mirror in the bosses' office, and headed out to surrender to the feds.

"Don't you want to change into something else?" the agent asked Paddy.

"Fuck you, Boy Scout. You came to arrest a cop today. This is what you get. Later, when you're leading me into the *bookings* wearing your bullshit FBI raid jacket, people will see it on the news. They'll say, 'Ooh look, a cop,' they won't be referring to you."

"Suit yourself," the agent said. Then he reached into his pocket and pulled out a card. He didn't get far when he started reading from it.

"You have the right to remain silent and…"

"That's enough of that, dip-shit. Do you even know the law?"

"I am an attorney," the agent protested.

"Not a competent one. That warrant you're holding is an accusatory instrument. Absolute right to counsel attaches. You don't get to ask me shit. Now put that card away. You're embarrassing yourself. If you ass-clowns are done fucking around, could you take me to jail now?"

When Paddy got to the federal booking facility under the courthouse on Pearl Street, the media had already been alerted. Every local and network television station had a reporter and a cameraman there, as well as dozens of print reporters and photographers from the various metro newspapers. The feds parked at the top of the ramp to maximize what was known as the *perp walk*. Paddy was prepared for the throng of media he would have to walk through. The lead agent asked him if he was ready. Paddy told him to straighten his hat for him, so they could get this donkey show over with.

As Paddy was pulled from the backseat of the Fed car, klieg lights and flashbulbs went off in a blinding wall of light. Paddy didn't flinch. Even though he was handcuffed, he pulled his shoulders back, pushed out his barrel chest, and effected a determined, but untroubled countenance. He would not allow himself to be led, not by inferior people such as these. He marched through that gauntlet like Douglas MacArthur returning to the Philippines.

CHAPTER SEVENTY

April 18, 1994
Manhattan

When Paddy was finally allowed to make a phone call, after the feds had made a big production of photographing and fingerprinting him, Mairead was furious. Paddy had prepared her for this situation last night. It was the probable outcome. So she wasn't surprised. Her anger was solely focused on AUSA Bronwyn Fainberg. Paddy quickly reminded her that he was on a monitored phone. He didn't want her making any idle threats. These people were notorious for their lack of a sense of humor. Mairead was too savvy not to control herself. But there was no one presently walking the earth who hated Bronwyn Fainberg more. Mairead was the one that gave Fainberg the now exclusively used nickname of *The Cuntessa*.

"Mairead, I need you to do some things for me," Paddy told her, bringing her on point, and away from the very nasty things she wanted to do to Fainberg.

"I'm right here," Mairead assured him.

"Call Rich Kornreich. I'm sure he knows, but tell him I'm in the bookings under the federal court. They're going to arraign me at about 2300 hours tonight. So, he's got to get here."

"Rich is here, along with Eamon Mulroney from the PBA. We're going through our closing papers looking for the deed to the house in case the judge sets bail."

"Mairead, please put the house papers away. Under no circumstances will I allow the house to be put up for collateral."

"But we don't have any other money, Paddy. All our liquidity went into the house. How are we going to make bail?"

"We're not going to. This is a bullshit indictment. Tell Rich to stop dicking around and get it dismissed. Or they're going to have a uniform cop cooling his heels in the MDC for the weekend."

"I have to get you out of there. I can't leave you in jail. It's just a house," Mairead pleaded.

"It's not just a house, Mairead. It's everything. It's us, and all of our sweat and hard work. It's the sticks and stones of our foundation. We're going to raise our family there. It's where we'll play with our grandchildren one day. Right now it's pure and it's perfect. I'm not letting these parasites spoil it in any way. They don't even get to know about this house. I will burn it to the ground before I let them touch it. I can do three days in jail. Hell, I can do five years if I have to. But I am not letting them touch what's dear to us. Some things have to remain sacred. So honey, if you love me even a little, put the fucking deed away."

Paddy had to fight with Rich Kornreich and Eamon Mulroney on the phone. They explained the feds insisted on a nominal bail. The house was the only equity he had. Finally, they were forced to relent. To make sure they understood the gravity of the situation, Paddy explained the consequences.

"If either of you show up in court with the deed to my house, if anyone so much as mentions it, I will choke you the fuck out, right in the courtroom. Now, put my wife back on the phone."

Paddy did his best to calm Mairead, but he had upset her. She couldn't reconcile the value her husband was placing in something as unimportant as a house. Mairead was prepared to live in the street, if it meant being with Paddy. But Mairead had the benefit of growing up in a huge house full of people who loved her and were committed to her protection and happiness. Paddy on the other hand, had grown up in tenement apartments, unwanted, unloved, and untethered to anyone or anything. Mairead understood the house was incidental. It was the people in it who made a family. He was just learning this. But after buying the house in Plainedge with Mairead, Paddy finally felt grounded. He felt for the first time in his life that he was home. He loved the house not for what it was. Admittedly, it needed a lot of work. It was Paddy's dream to fix the flaws, and fill the house with the people he loved, starting with Mairead. It was his intention to fill it with Durr babies until she made him stop. Then he would love and protect them all inside those four walls. To Paddy the house was sacred ground, and he needed to keep it that way. If he had to do a couple of days in jail so it could remain unsullied, then so be it. He couldn't make Mairead agree with him, but he got her to at least understand where he was coming from. She agreed to put the deed away.

"I need you to bring me one other thing. It's on my nightstand. I think I'm going to have a long weekend, so I can use it." Paddy could hear Mairead giggling on the other end.

"How come every time life starts to get weird, you need that thing?" she asked.

"I never had a security blanket growing up. I had to settle for Joseph Heller."

When the arraignment started, Paddy was standing at the defense table with Rich Kornreich and another PBA attorney who was assisting him. The courtroom was a sea of uniform police and assembled media. Mairead and her parents were at the rail behind Paddy, along with Eamon Mulroney and the PBA Board Officers. Paddy was still in his dress uniform, somehow managing to keep it unwrinkled. As Federal District Judge Lawrence Mathers entered the courtroom, he couldn't stop looking at Paddy. Before he called the court to order, he satisfied his curiosity.

"Is that the defendant?" the judge asked, pointing at Paddy.

"This is Police Officer Durr, Your Honor," Rich Kornreich answered.

"What is he wearing?"

"That's his NYPD dress uniform."

"I can see that. It's very impressive. My question should have been, why is he wearing it?"

"This is what he was wearing when the FBI arrested him this afternoon. He has had no opportunity to change his clothes," Rich informed the judge.

"Is there a good reason the defendant had to be apprehended? It's customary to allow law enforcement officers to surrender at a later date with their attorneys. Why did that not happen here?"

"The defendant knew he was being indicted," AUSA Fainberg jumped up and said. "He was deemed a flight risk. That's also reflected in the probation report."

"Is that so?" the judge fulminated. Then he addressed Paddy directly, which gave Rich Kornreich no small amount of dyspepsia. "Are you likely to flee the United States over a one count obstruction of justice indictment, Officer Durr?"

"Your Honor," Paddy began. "I am a nine year veteran of the NYPD. I am presently still employed by the department. I was born, raised, and still live in New York. I have never been outside the country. I don't even own a passport. My wife is here. We are expecting our first child in May. Who would run from such a thing? I am as likely a flight risk as an emu. I read the probation report. It's fifteen pages of garbage. So is the indictment."

AUSA Fainberg jumped up to object. The judge gently gestured her back into her chair.

"This is an arraignment. I haven't even called the court to order. Let's do the arraignment. We'll listen to everybody's argument and decide accordingly," Judge Mathers decreed.

After the indictment was read and pumped up for all it was worth by AUSA Fainberg, Rich Kornreich spent a half hour tearing the whole thing to shreds. Then he spent another half hour detailing the incredible service and sacrifice to the community Police Officer Durr had accumulated in his short career. It was as full of hyperbole as Fainberg's tirade, but at least it was based on something genuine. Unlike her indictment, which was purely an exercise in vindictiveness.

The judge then inquired if there were any motions. Rich Kornreich presented a motion to dismiss the indictment based on a lack of materiality. It was twenty-two pages long. Paddy was impressed. He didn't realize Rich had anticipated this outcome. He began working on the motion the day Paddy got his subpoena for the grand jury. After Rich got a copy of the indictment this afternoon, he went back into his computer to tweak a few things. But all of the precedents and case law were already in place. The result was a brilliant piece of lawyering. Kornreich was justifiably proud of himself.

Of course, AUSA Fainberg would attempt to refute the motion. So, the decision would be put over until Monday morning.

The judge moved on to bail applications. AUSA Fainberg read the probation report, citing the same nonsense about risk of flight as before. Then she asked for a one-million-dollar cash bail. Mafia hitmen didn't have to fork over that kind of money. Fainberg was shooting for the moon. She wasn't about to leave her guns holstered. She would empty them all in her quest to get Paddy Durr.

Rich Kornreich then eviscerated the probation report. He cited in greater detail the points Paddy had made to the judge earlier. He snuck in a little argument about the speciousness of the government's investigation, just to give the judge something to chew on for the weekend. Then he asked that the defendant be released on his own recognizance.

The judge considered it, but then compromised. He set bail at one-hundred-thousand dollar bond. That meant Paddy could be released by putting up ten percent, or ten-thousand dollars to secure a bail bond. Rich argued this was unfair. He pointed out that Paddy and Mairead were expectant newlyweds, living from paycheck to paycheck. They didn't have a thousand dollars, let alone ten. The judge inquired if the defendant owned any real property that could be put up as collateral. Rich told him there was none the defendant was willing to expose to these proceedings. The judge then addressed Paddy directly again.

"You realize if you don't put up a bond or collateral, you will spend the weekend in the Metropolitan Detention Center?"

"If Your Honor thinks that's fair, then so be it," Paddy said, with the withering, dead-eyed look he was becoming famous for.

The judge felt slimy doing it, but he wasn't breaking precedent. He remanded Paddy to the MDC, to return Monday morning. The judge would hear arguments on the motions and make a decision. They could revisit the question of bail then.

Before the marshals could cuff him and lead him over to the MDC, Paddy reached over and hugged and kissed his wife. Mairead was trying to be brave, but the tears were streaming down her face. She looked so crushed Paddy had to do all he could not to cry with her. He asked her if she brought *the thing*. She reached into her bag and produced a battered, coffee stained, and copiously annotated soft covered edition of *Catch-22*, by Joseph Heller. Paddy had discovered the book in eighth grade. He had re-read it more than a dozen times. It was as much a talisman for him as it was a metaphor for the absurdity his life had once again become. It didn't explain the chaos, but at least it afforded him the understanding that he wasn't the only one cast adrift and swirling within it.

CHAPTER SEVENTY-ONE

April 18, 1994
Metropolitan Detention Center

After being processed by the federal correction officers, Paddy was relieved of his uniform and given a bright orange jumpsuit with the letters DOC stenciled on the front and back. He had a matching pair of orange Nike shower shoes. He was allowed to keep his underwear. Everything else was inventoried and safe guarded. The officers at the MDC were professional, but Paddy sensed they were going out of their way to be respectful to him. When they brought him onto the *Protected Wing*, he was sure of it. When Officer Corrigan put him in his cell, Paddy inquired.

"What's with the special treatment?"

"You're a cop. By all accounts, a good one. There's no way we're putting a fellow law enforcement officer in general population with those animals. You wouldn't last the three days."

"Oh, I'd last. Probably pick up a murder charge or two, but I'm walking out of this place."

"Somehow, I don't doubt it. But you've got enough on your plate already. The least we can do is see you get to court on Monday, unmolested."

"I appreciate it. I hope I can return the favor someday."

"There's a lot of buzz about this case. From what we're hearing, Fainberg finally overran her leash. Supposedly, the judge is already furious. It's about time she gets hers."

"So, you're acquainted?"

"That shrew is well known to us. She's gone after several of us on bullshit inmate allegations. For no other reason than to ingratiate herself with a potential witness or cooperator. She railroaded some good people in here for doing their jobs. She treats people like us as expendable. We're not even human to her. Well, it looks like the worm is finally going to turn. Word is, this case is shit. We're pulling for you."

Officer Corrigan left Paddy to his empty cell to read about the *Soldier in white*. According to Yossarian and Dunbar, the book's protagonists, the *Soldier in white* was never really there. Under all of that plaster, gauze, and tape, there was nothing. Paddy could relate.

CHAPTER SEVENTY-TWO

April 20, 1994
Metropolitan Detention Center

The remainder of Paddy's weekend passed slowly. He spent most of it reading *Catch-22*. When he finished on the second night, he immediately began reading it again. Mairead and Rich Kornreich visited for a couple of hours every afternoon. Rich was growing more and more confident the judge would dismiss the indictment. But he couldn't promise anything.

Paddy took advantage of the visits to hold Mairead and gently rub her baby bump, which was just starting to show. He spoke soothingly to her and their unborn child, telling them all about the plans he had for their home, and futures. Paddy promised no matter what happened Monday, they were not going to be denied their little piece of perfection. He swore he would make it so.

The food was institutional awful. His meals were brought to him in his cell. Paddy ate enough to sustain himself, but no more than that. Seeing the prisoner was leaving much of his meals un-eaten, Officer Corrigan snuck Paddy protein bars from the commissary. So, he was able to hold it together, at least until Sunday night. Then the strain of his confinement finally wore on his last nerve. He started pacing in his cell. When that did nothing to calm him, Paddy did push-ups and crunches in the small space next to his cot. He was a nerved up, sweaty mess when Corrigan showed up with another correction officer and his captain.

They wordlessly led Paddy out of his cell and down to the elevator bank. The captain had to use his master key to allow the elevator to descend into the basement, where they were taking him. Paddy didn't ask. He was just grateful to be out of that ten by seven foot box. He wasn't concerned these officers meant him any harm. They had already demonstrated nothing but courtesy toward him. So, he let them lead him.

When they got to two gray metal doors at the end of the hallway, the captain swung the doors open, and Paddy was led into a state of the art fitness center. There were rows and rows of treadmills, elypticals and Stairmasters. There was every manner of free weight and exercise machine available, and all of it brand new. Paddy thought he had gone to heaven. The captain informed him heaven was only open for the next two hours. He told Paddy this was their new employee fitness center. It wasn't due to open until Monday afternoon. He thought it might be a good idea for someone who knew what they were doing to field test the equipment.

Paddy quickly shrugged out of his orange jumpsuit and kicked off his shower thongs. He ran jog-sprints on the treadmill for the next hour, in his bare feet and underwear. When that was done, he ran over to the free weight section and began hurrying through as much of an upper body workout as he could accomplish in an hour. It was substantial.

When he was done, the officers brought Paddy back to the locker room, where he was permitted to take a shower. They gave him fresh clothes and shower thongs before leading him back to the elevators. By the time they got there, Paddy was as placid and docile as a Hindu cow, a far cry from the nervous wreck he had been only two hours before.

"I don't know how I can ever thank you guys. You might have just saved my sanity."

"Get some rest kid," the captain told him. "I got a good feeling you're going home tomorrow."

CHAPTER SEVENTY-THREE

April 21, 1994
Manhattan

Judge Lawrence Mathers entered the courtroom angry, and got hotter by the minute. He was glaring at AUSA Fainberg so hard, Paddy thought she would burst into flames. After calling the court to order, the judge got right down to the matter of the motion to dismiss.

"I have read the Defenses' application several times over this past weekend," the judge said to Rich Kornreich. "It is a brilliant piece of litigation. Your case law and cited precedents were spot on. You are to be commended. Is there anything else the Defense wishes to add at this time?"

"No, Your Honor," Rich said.

"Wise choice. Thank you for your brevity."

Then the judge turned his full attention to the government's table. He invited AUSA Fainberg to make her argument regarding the motion. For the full hour Bronwyn Fainberg went on, the judge grew more and more acerbic. But he let her continue without interruption, copiously making notes for himself. When she was done, Fainberg attempted to sit.

"Don't you dare sit down!" the judge thundered. "You stand there and listen to my decision."

Judge Mathers began by calling the indictment the most egregious injustice he had seen in twenty-five years on the federal bench. He ridiculed Fainberg's investigation as a specious witch hunt. He berated her for failing to even make a convincing argument. He ruled that the government failed to prove there was a pending federal judicial proceeding. He pointed out that an open ended and meandering grand jury investigation, which smelled suspiciously like a fishing expedition, did not qualify. Inasmuch as there was no proceeding, the defendant could not have known one existed. Finally, the judge said, the defendant could not have had any intent to interfere with a proceeding that did not in fact exist. Then the judge announced he was going off the record.

"AUSA Fainberg, you are easily the most reprehensible individual I have ever encountered. Because of your ego, your vanity, your vindictiveness and your downright meanness, I was allowed to wrongly incarcerate a young family man, a dedicated public servant, without a scintilla of evidence or justification. You willfully misrepresented the facts to perpetrate this farce. You intentionally mislead the grand jurors by misstating the law when you charged the jury. Having read the full breadth of the testimony and alleged evidence presented in this matter, it has become clear to me the only reason the defendant was subpoenaed in this case was for the express purpose of ensnaring him in an illegal perjury trap. When he proved too clever to fall prey to your vile tactics, you used this pathetic excuse of an indictment as your instrument of revenge. I should have dismissed this piece of garbage Friday night. As it is, I will be referring you to your own office for prosecution for Official Misconduct. Be sure, I will be communicating my grave concerns about your ethical fitness to the federal bar association. I believe your continued accreditation by that board should be called into question. Now I'm going back on the record. This indictment is dismissed without prejudice. Now, get the hell out of my courtroom!"

AUSA Fainberg, her second seat, and her investigators quickly collected their things and slinked out of the courtroom. The assembled cops in the court had to do all they could not to applaud the judge. They sat on their hands and waited for him to finish. The judge addressed Paddy directly.

"Officer Durr, I cannot adequately express my anger and dismay at the shabby treatment you have received from your own government. I will make every effort to see this injustice is exposed, and the culpable punished. I will be writing an excruciatingly detailed decision in this case. I will be very happy to provide your counsel with a copy of it, if you should decide to redress this matter civilly."

"Thank you, Your Honor," Paddy said.

"That uniform is still looking sharp," the judge observed. "You wear it well, and do your department much credit. As a city resident, I am personally gratified to know you will be back to work protecting and serving the people of New York. Your conduct and composure throughout this ordeal has been nothing short of awe inspiring. I can only hope the future treats you and your family better. You certainly deserve it. Godspeed to you, Officer Durr. You're free to go."

After the judge left the bench, the cops assembled finally let loose. Their hoots and shouted cheers reverberated around the courtroom. As court was no longer in session, the marshals made no effort to stop them. Paddy joined Mairead and his in-laws at the rail behind the defendant's table. Mairead had a deer caught in the headlights look about her. She was exhausted, and the surreal stress of the last three days made it difficult for her to process what had just happened. She was understandably unsure of herself and her instincts.

"Does this mean we're in the clear? Do you think they'll leave us alone now?"

"I think maybe it does. I think maybe they just might," Paddy said, fairly crushing her in an embrace he would relinquish only reluctantly.

CHAPTER SEVENTY-FOUR

April 22, 1994
Long Island City

Paddy returned to the 108th Squad for his regularly scheduled *four to one* on Tuesday. He was welcomed back by his co-workers as if he had been on a long swing, as opposed to being in jail for the weekend. It felt a little creepy. He went into the bosses' office and said hello to his lieutenant, Paul Patterson. Patterson seemed delighted to see him. He came around his desk and shook Paddy's hand.

"Damned glad to see you, boy!" he said.

Patterson went to the safe and gave Paddy his guns. He told Paddy if he wanted to chill out a little bit, to decompress after the weekend ordeal, it was alright with him. The police work could wait. It wasn't going anywhere. Besides, he knew Paddy was up to date on his open cases. The kid was good with his paper, a rare quality for a rookie investigator. But Paddy wasn't concerned with his caseload at the moment. The fact of the matter was, he felt the work load in Queens wasn't enough to even break a sweat over. There wasn't much to do. So there wasn't much to type.

What Paddy was concerned with was his duty status. No one had told him anything officially. Judge Mathers made reference to Paddy returning to work when he dismissed the indictment the day before. So Paddy came to work. What he was supposed to do now would have to be clarified for him.

"What's the deal with my duty status?" Paddy asked.

"According to the telephone message that came down yesterday at 1300 hours, you are full duty," Patterson said.

"Really?"

"No shit, Paddy. They even back dated the order to Friday. The telephone message was specific. There was no break in service. It's like the suspension never happened. I made the Boro send me a hard copy of the personnel order to be certain. I already put a copy in your personnel folder."

Though Paddy now appeared to be clear of the claws of Bronwyn Fainberg, Pete O'Malley would not be so fortunate. Fainberg's frame up indictment of Paddy had exposed her as overzealous and willing to break the law to further her own career. She was rebuked professionally by her own bar association. The US Attorney removed her from her position, relocating her to a civil litigation section that guaranteed she would never again see the inside of a courtroom while employed by the government. Though she was prevented from doing further harm, the havoc she had already wrought with the indictment of Pete O'Malley would not go away.

The government didn't mind doing some quiet house cleaning, but they still suffered from the common federal law enforcement malady of not being able to publicly admit they were ever wrong. So rather than dismiss Pete's faulty indictment, the US Attorney assigned one of his top-guns to make the indictment bulletproof. He did this by manipulating the rookie judge into granting all of his pre-trial motions. Judge Wellesley Kip followed the axiom to the letter. Being in doubt, he trusted the government.

Pete O'Malley was prevented from making a defense. As gifted as Kieran Entwhistle was, he couldn't accomplish much without being able to cross examine the government's witnesses, and confront their putative evidence. Judge Kip prevented that when he permitted the US Attorney to enter the informant's testimony second hand. A federal investigator read the grand jury testimony of Oscar Nieves into the record. Coupled with the phone taps, the governments' case started to look formidable. Had Kieran been able to cross examine the unpredictable and volatile Nieves, he would have broken him over his knee. That's why the government hid him. When Kieran was prevented from calling Bronwyn Fainberg as a hostile witness, the Judge allowed the government to paint Pete into a corner. Leaving the jury no other choice, they convicted Peter O'Malley of two of the three counts of perjury.

Judge Kip seemed to realize he had made a mistake, but he did not reverse the verdict as he could have. Instead, at sentencing, he granted Pete a three-step-downward-declination in the mandatory sentencing guidelines. Kip sentenced him to twelve months and a day in federal prison. Pete did his bullet at the FMC in Lexington Kentucky. He returned home to the Bronx, and continued to grow his business with his brothers. His acumen and work ethic allowed him to flourish in spite of the mistreatment of his adopted government. Though very successful in business, Pete was in his heart still a cop. But after the second circuit court of appeals shot down his request for a retrial, Pete resigned himself to a future as a carpenter. He would no longer try to reclaim his place in a system that treated him with such disdain.

Thus ended the career of one of the greatest, most heroic cops in NYPD history. It ended not with a bang, not with a whimper, but with a dirty, vengeful government cover-up. Peter O'Malley had become the government's pound of flesh.

Even though Lieutenant Patterson told Paddy the job was acting like his indictment and suspension never occurred, something was still fundamentally changed. Paddy noticed a certain trepidation on the part of the detectives and supervisors he dealt with. They all had that look, like they sensed trouble when Paddy came around. They seemed to be waiting for the other shoe to drop. Some of his co-workers started to make excuses not to go out in the field with him. So, Paddy started working cases on his own. This was expressly forbidden, as it was insanely dangerous. But leaving Paddy Durr with the choice between arresting a bad guy, and leaving the job undone, the job was going to get done. Paddy would call for a uniform sector team over the radio to assist him when he made an arrest.

This got back to Lieutenant Patterson pretty quickly. He called Paddy into his office and read him the riot act about it. Paddy yessed the lieutenant to death, and agreed to whatever he wanted, rather than intimate that his co-workers refused to work with him. When he went out in the future, Paddy would make his arrests without any back-up. This was not at all what the boss had in mind when he told Paddy to stop using patrol cops to work his cases with him. But, with no one to tell the boss about it, Patterson never found out. Paddy continued to rack up arrests and positive performance evaluations, but he noticed on his bi-annual evaluations, issued every six months, the bosses had stopped checking the box that recommended him being promoted to detective.

When Paddy brought the subject up to Lieutenant Patterson, he was less than astonished to learn the directive had come down through channels. He was not to be recommended for promotion, because he was never going to be promoted. The department, at the prodding no doubt of the mayor's office, was going to keep him in rank, and let him die on the vine in Queens. It appeared that someone might have thought he would become disheartened and quit. They were mistaken.

Paddy dropped in to the Chief of Queens Detectives office. Fran was happy to see him as always, but there was a glimmer of sadness behind her eyes. Paddy didn't want to burden her with his troubles any further. So they chatted about Mairead and their baby on the way. By this time, they had discovered from the sonograms they were having a boy. This delighted Francesca.

"Paddy, I'm so happy for you both," she said as she hugged him.

Fran had met Mairead at the Queens Detective's Christmas Party. They hit it off like they were long lost sisters. When Fran's mother had to have a medical procedure performed at Elmhurst Hospital, Mairead arranged to get assigned to be her nurse in recovery. In Fran's eyes, the Durr family were special people. After all they had been through, they deserved a break. She would do anything to help Paddy. But she was only the chief's clerical officer. She delivered the orders. She couldn't write them. Right now, she checked with Chief Pasquale to inquire if he would see Paddy. When she hung up with the chief she spoke quickly.

"He'll see you, but don't push too hard. And don't get discouraged," Fran advised, already knowing the outcome. Paddy winked at her and went into the chief's office.

"I can't help you, Paddy. You are stuck in the 108 Squad."

"What about my gold shield? I'm supposed to be promoted in June."

"I can't help you with that either. You are not going to make detective."

Paddy started looking around the room. He noted all the plaques on the chief's *hero wall* behind his desk. Most of them made reference to devotion to duty, honor, and valor. He looked at the dispassionate face of Chief Pasquale, telling him in no uncertain terms that he was personae non grata. To Paddy, the plaques on the wall started to seem ironic.

"What are you looking for, Paddy?" the chief finally asked.

"Someone with an eleven foot pole."

"Why is that?"

"Because, no one with a ten foot pole will touch me. You would think I had leprosy."

"For the purposes of this job, you do."

"So what should I do now, Chief?"

"What are you even doing on this job?" the chief asked. "You can get hired here with just a GED. You have a degree from Columbia University, for Christ's sake. Surely you could be making more money somewhere else. You're a young man. Go do that. Take care of your family."

"Is that what the job wants? I should just quit?"

"If you don't, they will make you wish you had," the chief said ominously.

Paddy regarded the chief with the dead-eyed, malignant stare he ordinarily reserved only for scumbags. In Paddy's opinion, the chief now qualified.

"That was exactly the wrong thing to say to me. I don't quit, ever. Washington Heights couldn't kill me. The mayor couldn't frame me for murder. The US Attorney's Office managed to indict me. But not for long. In the end, they got to suck a big fat one. And through all of that, all I did was come to work. Even now, every goddamned day, I come to work and chase the vermin back into their holes. I protect the weak. I punish the wicked. And all of this, with no regard whatsoever for my self. It's almost a fucking religious calling. So no one, and nothing is going to make me quit. I'm going to make not promoting me an embarrassment for you. You'll have to wear it like a scarlet letter. And you'll deserve it. Because you know what you're doing is wrong. It's unjust. It's dishonorable."

"I'm just following orders," the chief said.

"You know that argument didn't work at Nuremburg, right? Someday, you're going to have to answer for not having the balls you were born with. There's right and wrong, and somebody is keeping score."

"Go back to the 108, Officer Durr. Don't come down here again," the chief said finally.

"No worries," Paddy said over his shoulder as he was leaving. "I don't associate with cowards."

CHAPTER SEVENTY-FIVE

Late-Spring, 1994
Long Island City

Things continued as before in the 108th Precinct. Paddy came to work in the squad. He caught his cases. He worked them alone. He closed his cases. Along the way, he had started to rack up an impressive amount of pattern-robbery arrests. His supervisors may have been loath to praise him, but the same could not be said for the community council of Long Island City. The merchants and residents wanted to make him *Police Officer of the Year*. So they did. At the award ceremony at The Waterfront Crab House, not a single member of the Detective Bureau attended. Paddy didn't concern himself. This plaque, like the many others he had been awarded over the years, would go into a cardboard box and be tucked away up in the cock-loft of his garage. He didn't need a *hero wall*. He had a home and a growing family.

In May that year, Padraig Joseph Durr Junior came into the world. Named so at Mairead's insistence. Paddy thought the name had been stigmatized, but of course he relented. He had never figured out how to refuse her anything. He wasn't going to start now. Mairead's only proviso was that he would be known as Patrick. No one would be permitted to ever call him *Little Paddy*.

A month later, the orders came down for promotion to detective. The five other white shields who had been assigned to the 108 Squad on the same day as Paddy were all on the list. Paddy didn't even bother looking for his name. He took the opportunity to feign disappointment, and requested a few days off from the lieutenant, ostensibly to clear his head. Really, he just wanted a few days without interruption to finish the second bathroom he was installing in his family room.

And so it went through the balance of the year and into the next. Mairead was pregnant again. Paddy occupied his time making home improvements. The house was starting to take the shape he had envisioned for it. His career was seemingly in a rut. Actually, it was in an abyss. But, he had other things with which to concern himself. Then he didn't let it bother him. But occasionally, the injustice of it would rise up and smack him in the face.

One such time was at the memorial mass for the slain members of the 34th Precinct. Sean Moran was there. At the post mass reception across the street in the gymnasium of Saint Elizabeth's, Sean related a conversation he interrupted at a detective training seminar. Two new detectives from the 108 Squad were overheard by Sean bashing Paddy. Another detective who knew Paddy from Manhattan North had asked them how he was doing. They started going on about how he was one way, and out for himself. They questioned his abilities as a detective and suggested that he was somehow inadequate for the rank. Sean jumped right in.

"What the fuck did you just say?" Sean demanded of the now surprised *Queens Marines.*

"He's not fitting in," one of them offered meekly.

"That's not what you said. You said he was *one way.* You said he was out for himself. That's not the Paddy Durr I know. That man would take a bullet for me. He dove into the middle of a shooting to rescue a dying cop. Then he carried that cop into the emergency room, even though he was bleeding out all over him. He's been in more gunfights than you've got years on the job. He may be the most unselfish cop I've ever known. He would lay down in traffic for me if I asked. And as far as his abilities and fitness to be a detective, you two don't make a pimple on Paddy Durr's ass. If I hear you say another bad word about my friend, so help me God, I will send you home with your fucking teeth in your pocket."

The two Queens detectives spent the rest of the seminar trying to avoid Sean Moran. Sean wouldn't identify or even describe them to Paddy. He already had enough troubles. Sean didn't think a confrontation, which was the guaranteed outcome, would help him any. He only related the story because he wanted to remind Paddy that he had his back always, and that nobody in Queens did.

It was after this conversation that Paddy ran into his new friend, Inspector Giuseppe Possollipo. Inspector Possollipo, or *Joe Pos* as the cops lovingly called him, had recently been the CO of the *three four*. He had been brought in from Brooklyn to oversee the split of the command and the creation of the new 33rd Precinct, covering the southern end of the old *three four*. This was the city's solution to the Washington Heights riots. When the precinct opened early that spring, at the ribbon cutting ceremony, Joe Pos put his arm around Paddy's shoulders. He pointed him to the east, overlooking Edgecombe Avenue and into the Bronx, with Yankee Stadium visible in the distance.

"That right there is the House that Ruth built," he said pointing at the stadium. Then he turned Paddy around in the direction of the gleaming new police facility on the corner of Amsterdam Avenue and W 170th Street. "And that right there is the House that Paddy Durr built."

Paddy had met Joe Pos at social functions hosted by the 34th Precinct Club. Sean Moran had introduced them. Knowing Joe Pos' backstory, he thought they should meet. They bonded instantly. Joe Pos had so far had an illustrious police career. He started as an active cop in the 83rd Precinct. While in anti-crime there, he had to duck an indictment by an unscrupulous Brooklyn DA who wanted to charge him with murder after a particularly harrowing gunfight with a robbery crew. Joe Pos survived and went on to make detective in the 77 Squad, before he decided he wanted to be the boss. Then he took the promotion express up the ladder. He aced every promotion exam, and his otherworldly competence, in a talent pool almost bereft of it, made his ascendance a sure thing. There were only ten years and many parallels between them. They hung out whenever they could, which wasn't all that often. But when they were together, they felt like they were cut from the same cloth. Joe Pos had gone on to be promoted, and as a reward for doing such a fine job overseeing the split, he was given the choice of what precinct he wished to command. He chose the *eight three* without hesitation.

Paddy was on his way to the men's room after hearing Sean's story, when he bumped into Joe Pos. Paddy had a puss on his face.

"What the hell is the matter with you, Paddy?" Joe asked with genuine concern.

"What's the matter with me? I'll tell you what the matter with me is. If I don't get out of Queens soon, I'm going to march down to the Boro and take that empty suit they call a chief hostage. I'm done with these cowards, Joe."

"Relax," Joe Pos told him. "Do you want to come to the *eight three* and work in my Squad?"

"If you could get that done," Paddy said, having no confidence he could, "I'll come over to your house every day to walk your dog and wash your car."

"You don't have to do all that. Just make robbery and gun collars for me."

"If I can do it in the 108, you don't think I can manage it on Knickerbocker Avenue?"

"I know you can, Paddy. That's why I'm asking for you. Let me make a few phone calls. I'll call you at home in a couple of days."

Paddy thanked Joe Pos. He didn't know it yet, but Paddy had found his man with an eleven foot pole.

CHAPTER SEVENTY-SIX

June, 1995
Queens

Two days later, Joe Pos called Paddy at home. He gave him explicit instructions. He was to pick up a UF57, the NYPD request for transfer form, which Joe Pos had already filled out for him. Paddy was to bring this form to the Chief of Personnel, then the Chief of Detectives. Then they would deal with Chief Pasquale. Paddy was further directed if anyone along the way were to give him any static whatsoever about the transfer, he was to tell them emphatically that this was *a Joe Pos contract.*

The next day Paddy started making his visits. He got static every step of the way. But when he said the magic words, "This is *a Joe Pos contract,*" everybody suddenly became compliant. Paddy was given what he asked for, and sent on his way. After clearing the first two hurdles, Paddy called Joe Pos. Pos knew Paddy had the signatures. So he didn't even ask. Joe told Paddy to go see Chief Pasquale. He was to point out that all of the chief's superiors had already signed off on the transfer. Then he was to tell the chief Joe Pos wanted it done, now.

Paddy got down to the Boro a little while later. Detective Francesca Bender was at her desk. She got up to say hello, and kiss him on his cheek, but Fran was unquestionably pissed off about something. Paddy hoped it wasn't him.

"Can I see the chief?" Paddy asked.

"Go ahead. He's hiding in his office. I'm done keeping the barbarians at the gate one more minute for that phony blow-bag."

"I'm sorry you had a falling out with him, but if it's any consolation, I'm about to ruin his day."

"Excellent! Leave the door open so I can hear it."

Paddy walked unannounced into the chief's inner office. He surprised the boss when he said hello without preamble.

"What the hell are you doing here? I thought I told you not to come back."

"I'm here on orders from your boss, the Chief of Detectives. He wants you to sign this 57," Paddy said placing the form on the desk in front of the chief.

"Are you out of your fucking mind? I'm not signing that."

"Yes you are. You've been ordered by your bosses to sign it. And we all know what a good German you are. You follow orders. Besides, this is a Joe Pos contract. So, it's getting done."

"How the hell do you know Joe Pos?" the chief demanded.

"It turns out we're both cops. That's a rare thing and a big deal. So sign the fucking paper like a good functionary, and you'll never see me again."

Pasquale signed the 57, and threw it back at Paddy. Before he told him to get the hell out of his office, the chief reminded him.

"You're still never making detective."

"Never is a long time, boss. There's a mayoral election in November. It's not looking too good for your boy. You know what happens to the guys at the top when the administration changes? It's like the Russian Army under Stalin. They kill all the old Generals and make new ones. Enjoy your retirement."

Paddy was at the 83rd Precinct a half hour later. He gave Joe Pos the completed transfer request. Joe told Paddy he would take care of the rest, but he should pack his things at the 108. Moving day was at hand. Paddy was now a believer. Joe Pos really had that kind of juice. What he couldn't figure out was how. The rank of full inspector in the NYPD is an elite and prestigious rank, but it doesn't usually afford the holder the ability to make chiefs and deputy commissioners jump through hoops. So Paddy had to know how Joe Pos could get something like this done.

Joe tried to explain the art of the contract, as he practiced it. He told Paddy he recognized early in his career that ninety-five percent of the cops on the job were disinterested bystanders. But, things still had to get done. A capable young officer can distinguish himself quickly in such an environment. Joe did that, but he took it one step further. When asked to do something, he did it and then did a little more to exceed expectations. He never met a challenge he didn't think he could master. And he never refused anyone. He made himself the *go-to guy*.

After consistently demonstrating his ability and making his bosses look good, Joe Pos started collecting gratitude in the form of owed favors. He didn't need the favors for himself. He knew his competence was going to get him where he wanted to be. But by using those favors on behalf of friends, who were also competent, he could shape his environment, and have many more hands who wanted to get things done, just like him. Success breeds success.

Thus, Paddy learned the art of the contract at the knee of the master. He started to take note of who benefited from his work, instead of just doing it because it was the right thing to do. It wasn't long before Paddy had amassed an impressive list of people in high places who owed him favors. He had been practicing the art ever since.

Two weeks later the order came down from Personnel that he was transferred to the 83 Squad. Paddy informed Lieutenant Patterson he was leaving forthwith. He signed out in the blotter of the 108 Squad for the final time. He left a personalized note before doing so.

To all my dear "Friends" in the 108 Squad, Alpha-Mike-Foxtrot!

This was the military alphabet acronym for "Adios, Mother-Fuckers." Then Paddy left. He had taken the opportunity over the last two days to clean out both of his lockers and his desk. The contents of which were now in the trunk of his car. He wanted to be able to put Queens in his rear-view mirror as soon as he could. He did that, not bothering to check the mirror to watch the bad experiment of the 108 Squad receding behind him. As far as Paddy was concerned, Queens was already in the past. And, the past is prologue.

CHAPTER SEVENTY-SEVEN

November, 2013
Brooklyn

When Paddy got into the 83 Squad on that dreary Monday, he got right to work before he could wallow further in his own misery. He checked his messages. There was no news from Sean Gilmartin in Bridgeport. Ronnie Kingsbury had nothing on his dumps. The whereabouts of *Casper's* specific location in Bridgeport remained a mystery. So Paddy figured he would try to further solidify his evidence in expectation of eventually finding him.

Paddy called his friend in SAFIS, Technician Rosemary Falcinetti. She was unquestionably the best fingerprint examiner in the NYPD. Her work was timely, efficient, and beautifully reported. She had become every DA's favorite expert witness on fingerprint analysis. Paddy loved working with her. She anticipated his evidentiary needs and provided them most times before he could even ask. She was also one of the kindest, nicest people Paddy had met in the department. Paddy steered all his homicide work to Rosemary, and she was the only one in SAFIS with whom Paddy would work.

"Hi Paddy, I thought you would have called by now. Didn't you get my message?"

"Did you give it to the PAA?"

"A week ago," she confirmed.

"Unfortunately, that's a black hole for messages. She takes them and they disappear into the void, without a trace. But that's my problem. What have you got for me, Rosemary?"

"The four prints on the outside of the gun all belong to the comparison prints you sent down. I ran them through SAFIS anyway, and there was no record."

"That figures. The guy who recovered the gun is a solid citizen. What about the lifts from the shell casings?"

"They all come back to one guy. I ran his NYSID number through BCI. He is decidedly not a solid citizen. Does the name Erik Vasquez ring a bell?"

"Like a four alarm fire."

"Is he your doer?"

"He's not my shooter, but he's culpable. He's going down. Could you fax me your report?"

"Check your mail. It should already be there."

After recovering the fingerprint report from his mailbox, Paddy sat down to type the *fives*. Joe Furio came over and sat down at the next desk. He looked uncomfortable and seemed to be chewing something over, trying to decide if he really wanted to mention it. Paddy prodded him along.

"Whatever is on your mind, Joe, out with it."

"I didn't want to say anything with what you're dealing with right now, but are you aware that Thursday is Thanksgiving?"

"No. Somehow that got past me. What do you and Armando want to do?"

"Armando is taking his kids to the parade, and then he's going to his parent's house in Whitestone. I was looking to spend the day with Luciana and Mario at her sister's house."

"That's terrific. You guys should do that. I'll cover the office."

"What are you going to do about dinner?"

"I just told you. I'm going to cover the office. I'm pretty sure I won't starve."

Joe wanted to say more, but he didn't know if there was anything he could that would help him. Joe was gravely concerned about his friend's state of mind. Absent anything else to discuss, he just thanked him.

CHAPTER SEVENTY-EIGHT

1995
Brooklyn

Paddy's time in the 83 Squad began like a breath of fresh air. To begin with, it was busy. In 1995, the year he got there, there were eighty-four homicides in the precinct. Given the command was the size of a postage stamp, the bodies seemed to be literally falling from the sky. In addition, the cops and detectives protected each other like family. It reminded Paddy of the comradery he once enjoyed in the *three four*. He didn't realize how much he had missed it in the three years he was forced to waste in Queens. The 83 Squad was fertile ground to build his skills as a detective, while he waited for that elusive *Gold Shield*.

In January of the next year, a new mayor took the oath of office. Unlike the previous resident of Gracie Mansion, this mayor was a law and order advocate of the cops. He was determined to get the crime rate, which had hit a historic high, under control. The quality of life in New York over the previous four years had crumbled under the weight of the unprecedented violence and depravity.

The new mayor's first priority was to clean out the desiccated functionaries and politicians who were running the department under the previous administration. He appointed a strong police commissioner who assembled a young, vibrant, and visionary staff of up-and-comers to facilitate the mayor's will. As such, Joe Pos was promoted to two star chief and given command of the Boro of Brooklyn North.

A month later, a short list of promotions to detective came out. Paddy had to read it three times before he would believe his name was on it. A day later, another order came down backdating his promotion by a year. He was to be awarded back pay and seniority commensurate with his originally scheduled promotion date. That took all the sting out of being passed over.

The good fortune continued for the Durr's in February the following year, when their daughter Katelyn arrived. She was named after, and in honor of Katelyn Crowe at the insistence of Mairead, who found her as extraordinary as Paddy did. Mairead understood that Katelyn, through her gentle coaxing, had put Paddy on the road that brought them together. Katelyn Crowe was delighted to stand in as her namesake's Godmother.

Paddy continued to catch homicides and hone his chosen craft. Two years later, Mairead gave birth to their daughter Casey. This birth was difficult. During the labor, Mairead started hemorrhaging from her uterus, possibly from an undetected aneurism. Her blood pressure plummeted. To his horror, Paddy almost lost her. After Mairead was out of the woods, she and Paddy agreed that three healthy children constituted a full enough house. Mairead was going to have her tubes tied, until Paddy researched the procedure and vetoed it due to the risk. He wasn't taking any chances on losing Mairead again. So, Paddy cowboyed up, and got a vasectomy.

A month later Paddy was promoted to Detective 2nd Grade. Life was good. They were happy. They had plenty to do between running the kids everywhere and holding down their various jobs. Mairead had started picking up nursing shifts at Long Island Jewish Hospital, working around Paddy's schedule. In the course of attending the gym with an almost religious devotion, (she was determined to get her pre-pregnancy body back) she was offered the opportunity to teach some of the exercise classes. She accepted. Paddy was making a lot of overtime at this point. As such, they were spending less time together. They still managed to make sparks fly, just not as frequently as before. Paddy rationalized that this was the natural trajectory of a marriage and a busy family, but the lost intimacy started to affect him. He resented it a little. Not enough to do anything stupid yet, but enough.

Paddy's misfortune was that his formative years were spent devoid of any affection or intimacy whatsoever. His first near encounter with it was his disastrous affair with Inez Vasconcellos. Because of that, Paddy had a hard time differentiating between Intimacy and sex. Much of his sense of self-worth was derived from his sex life. Being sexually desired by women was the only source of validation Paddy understood. By the time he met Mairead and experienced true intimacy for the first time, he was already an adult. As Paddy understood it, sex and intimacy went together. You couldn't have one exclusive of the other. He would later find out how wrong he was, but for now this was operating on him as if it were unassailable fact.

In 1999, before the new millennium, Paddy was promoted to the prestigious rank of Detective 1st Grade. Very few detectives ever ascend to that rank. Paddy got there in thirteen short years on the job. The pay was good. The autonomy was better. The bosses tended to leave 1st grade detectives alone. So Paddy had the ability to run his investigations as he saw fit, unencumbered by supervisors suggesting how to re-invent the wheel. He happily pursued murderers in the 83rd Precinct for the next couple of years.

Joe Pos had since been promoted again. He was now the Chief of the Department, the highest ranking uniform member of the service, truly *the Boss*. He kept asking Paddy if he needed anything, but in Paddy's estimation he had already achieved the pinnacle of his profession. He worked with terrific detectives and supervisors, in a great command, and the department would have to invent a rank to promote him again. He would go to Joe Pos to facilitate a contract for a friend from time to time, but other than that, there was nothing he needed.

September 11th, 2001 changed everything. The carnage, the loss, the terrible waste of it all, filled Paddy with an unappeasable rage, exacerbated by his sense of absolute hopelessness. Suddenly a Brooklyn street murder didn't have the allure or importance it once did. In the days and the weeks after the Trade Center attacks, Paddy and the other detectives and cops would trek down to Ground Zero after their regular tours and volunteer to dig for a couple of hours. Collectively, they felt like they had to do something. But it would never feel like enough. The work, even as necessary and selfless as it was, did nothing to alleviate the frustration and helplessness they all were feeling.

The city and the nation as a whole needed to heal this great wound. There was a re-birth of patriotism and respect for first responders. Regular citizens would man the barricades at the outskirts of Ground Zero. They would thank or applaud the cops and firefighters as they entered and left the cordoned off area. Frequently, they provided water or other beverages for the filthy, ash and grime covered rescue workers.

Paddy understood their need to do it, but he didn't like it. He was embarrassed. He didn't feel he deserved any of it. In his view he wasn't doing anything to justify their adulation or even gratitude. Paddy felt impotent. He wanted to strike a blow, and take a piece out of the terrorists who had so wounded his city. Two months later he got his chance.

The Joint Terrorist Taskforce had been created in the wake of the FALN bombings of the 1970s. It was an elite and important detective assignment. But, it was largely a surveillance and monitoring gig. As a result, the unit had identified a lot of terrorists in the New York metropolitan area. These were people who had direct knowledge of on-going terrorist activity in the city and abroad. They were already considered deportable, but prior to the attacks, nobody had bothered to round them up and question them. They needed rounding up and questioning now.

When the call for volunteers went out for detectives to beef up the JTTF, Paddy jumped at the chance. The new detectives were grouped together with FBI agents, federal marshals, and immigration and customs enforcement agents. They spent the next eleven months rounding up known terrorists and delivering them to the bowels of 26 Federal Plaza, never to be seen in New York again. A CIA agent who had been liaising with the Taskforce intimated that every one of the terrorists they were apprehending ended up in Guantanamo Prison. Paddy was alright with that.

It was during this time Paddy encountered the informant who gave him the subway bombing plot. Rolling up that operation before the cell could hurt anyone was his signature accomplishment in his time in the Taskforce. Unfortunately, after eleven months of proactive terrorist abatement, the powers that be decided to revert the unit back to the surveillance operation it had once been. The plan was to keep the manpower at its present strength. To do that, the newer detectives would have to pass their background checks, before getting a *top secret* security clearance. Paddy wanted no part of a surveillance gig. He made his desire to return to the 83 Squad known in the office. The leader of his group in

JTTF was a Special Agent Connor Fox. Fox was the son of a retired NYPD detective. Unlike most of the FBI agents, he had the soul and sensibilities of a cop. He tried to talk Paddy out of leaving the Taskforce.

"Connor, you can talk till you're blue in the face, but there is no way I'm passing that background check."

"What the hell are you talking about, Paddy?"

"I was indicted in Federal court in 1994. It got vacated three days later, but that's not going to placate the State Department and the CIA. It's going to automatically disqualify me."

"How the hell did you even get this far?" Connor wondered.

"After 911, nobody asked."

So Paddy parted company with the JTTF and returned to the 83 Squad. His life started to normalize for the first time since the terrorist attacks. But the long hours of separation between he and Mairead seemed to have engendered a distance between them. Neither one of them took a breath from their hectic lives to do anything about it. If anything, they got busier.

It was during this time Paddy started coaching at the high school. Football helped, but it couldn't fill the void left by the distance in his marriage. He became resentful, considering perhaps Mairead no longer loved him. It would not be his first experience with abandonment. Before Mairead, it was all he ever knew. Now he was living with that dreadful sense of alienation again. He could have spoken up. If he had voiced his feelings and concerns to Mairead. She would have responded. But, she had no idea he felt this way. Mairead loved him with all her heart. If he had only opened his mouth, she would have readily bridged the gulf between them. But he didn't do that. Instead, he sulked like a petulant child. This was Paddy's state of mind. This was the environment he had created. It was a laboratory of his own haphazard design that would allow Roxanne Barcellos to become the toxic time-bomb she was destined to be.

CHAPTER SEVENTY-NINE

2005-2011
Plainedge

For the first several years at Plainedge High School, Paddy had little trouble keeping his distance from Roxanne. They had no real business together. Paddy had the great satisfaction of coaching his son Patrick for four years, winning two Long Island Championships, and seeing Patrick win the Piner award as the best linebacker in Nassau County his junior and senior years. When Patrick graduated and went on to play at Sacred Heart, Paddy continued to coach at the high school. He continued to avoid Roxanne as diligently as before. But soon enough, Katelyn was playing varsity soccer. Even as a freshman, she was the best player on the team. Roxanne began trying to get Paddy to come to her office to pick up training DVDs for his daughter. Paddy knew a trap when he saw one. He was able to sidestep this one, for a while.

It was in Katelyn's sophomore year when Big Bill got sick. All the years of working with asbestos in the roofing business had caught up with him. In the end, the big man was felled by a little cell that insisted upon replicating itself, until he became more cancer than not.

In the face of this tragedy, Mairead did what any daughter would do. She saw that her father was as comfortable as he could be, so her parents could spend what was left of Bill's diminishing time together. In this, she was heroic. But to Paddy, she was just gone.

The demands of caring for her sick father created a situation where Paddy and Mairead could go days without seeing each other. Paddy's rational self accepted this was as it needed to be. Sacrifices had to be made for family. But his emotional self was not in accord. Paddy's ego and id had long since agreed to a non-disclosure pact. Because he could not reconcile his emotions with what his reason told him should, and must happen, Paddy was left with nothing to feel but loss. The feelings of abandonment and alienation again descended over his psyche like a shroud.

Paddy tried to pitch in and help with Big Bill, but Mairead and her sisters had things so well in hand he was left to feel like he was in the way. For the first time since Paddy had been embraced by this family, he began to feel like an outsider. Paddy arranged to visit his father-in-law in the evenings when he was at work. Mairead would not be there at those times. This was intentional on Paddy's part. He was having a hard time dealing with what he perceived as Mairead's distracted, impatient, and peremptory treatment of him. He had started to feel like an anachronism in his own home. So he receded into himself.

This went on until Big Bill got too sick to remain at home. By the time Bill had to be transferred to Sloan-Kettering, Paddy's marriage had started to feel like a rumor to him. Given that the very foundation he had built his life upon had turned into shifting sand, it shouldn't have been a surprise when he lost his footing.

Katelyn's senior year of high school had arrived. She was rated as one of the top soccer players in New York State. Colleges began recruiting her in earnest. If not for her father's illness, Mairead would have handled the recruiting process for her daughter. She had been through it herself when she was in high school. But caring for her father was so time consuming, Mairead readily accepted Coach Barcellos' offer to shepherd Katelyn through the process. Of course Mairead had no idea Roxanne also had designs on her husband. She never would have believed Paddy could fall for such shallow enticements. But, her absence from Paddy had prevented her from seeing the emotional, needy wreck he had become.

When Roxanne next approached Paddy outside the gym, she had a new tactic. Her involvement with Katelyn's recruiting process created the illusion of a common goal with Paddy. She would exploit it.

"Why don't you come down to my office, Paddy? I have some highlight DVD's of Katelyn that Mairead wanted to send out to some schools."

The look on her face was anything but innocent. It was pure hunger. It turned to surprise when Paddy told her he would be down in five minutes.

When Paddy let himself into Roxanne's office, he was immediately overcome with a sense of foreboding, but he couldn't put his finger on it. The office was enormous, maybe seventy feet square. The walls were decorated evenly between mirrors and soccer posters. The desk was in the center of the room, facing the far corner where the door was. Roxanne was seated at her desk doing something on her desk-top computer. She deftly locked the screen as she got up and brought several DVD's over to Paddy.

"Yeah Roxanne, that's why we're here," Paddy said acidly.

Roxanne took his meaning as an invitation, and she grabbed the back of his neck and kissed him hungrily. But Paddy thought kissing Roxanne felt unnatural, and he wasn't there to kiss. They started tearing at each other's clothes. Paddy picked Roxanne up and frog carried her over to the desk. He dropped her right on her legendary ass. In one deft move, Paddy removed her running shorts and thong underwear, and threw them on the floor. Then he was in her.

The sex was furious, even manic. He pounded into Roxanne as if he could expunge all of his anxiety and loneliness with the act. But even as he was thrusting into her, Paddy got the sense again that something was not quite right about the room. At this point Roxanne was screaming as she was grinding herself against him. Paddy put his fingers in her mouth to try and quiet her. It was of no use, and he needn't have bothered. The room had been soundproofed.

When Paddy dismounted Roxanne, flipped her over, and pushed her face down over the desk, he noticed the wall clock. Its twin was on the wall behind him. He thought it odd. Who needed two of the same clock? If he had looked a little closer, he might have seen the pinholes in the clock faces, behind which the digital cameras were recording them. But he didn't look. He was preoccupied, as he drove deeply into Roxanne from behind. His thrusting went from frenzied, to animalistic, to almost brutal. Roxanne was crying out in ecstasy when he let go inside of her with a grunt.

In that moment, Paddy was enveloped with a sense of self-loathing he hadn't known since his childhood. He discovered unhappily, nothing will give you post-coital depression like the sex you shouldn't be having. He wanted to will himself away from this place, and forget he ever met Roxanne Barcellos. But it was a little late for that now. So he busied himself with bringing his breathing under control, and getting dressed.

"I've never been fucked like that in all my life," Roxanne said.

"Don't get used to it. There won't be a return engagement."

"Oh, yes there will," Roxanne said with confidence.

When Paddy got home, he was so full of his own misery he didn't even notice the note left by Casey on the kitchen table. It said Big Bill was having a bad night, and Mairead would be staying at the hospital. After he showered and got into his empty bed, all Paddy knew was that he was utterly and fundamentally alone. He started to accept that this was to be his natural condition.

As bad as Paddy felt, it didn't stop him from returning to that office four more times. Roxanne had predicted as much. She knew what her allure was worth. But the attraction, as shallow as it was, was already starting to fade for Paddy. By their fifth encounter, Paddy got bored and distracted in the middle of it, and couldn't even finish. Roxanne took that surprisingly well. She attributed Paddy's preoccupation to fatigue and stress. She thought this liaison was a thing that would continue. She didn't realize it had already run its course. This would be the last time they would see each other like this.

CHAPTER EIGHTY

December, 2011
Plainedge

It was a week later, when Paddy had the emotional confrontation with his dying father-in-law at the hospital. Big Bill knew instinctively that Paddy had been poisoned inside. He begged his son-in-law not to infect his daughter. Even though he lied to Bill about his damaged state of mind, Paddy silently promised them both that he would end this dreadful thing, and never visit it again.

Two weeks later, Big Bill Dunleavy was dead. Every hour and attention shifted to settling the affairs of, and burying a beloved family patriarch. In the end, Bill had gone on to meet his God as content and grateful for his life as any man ever had. He was ready to go. He told Sinead not to hurry. He would wait for her. His whole family was around him, having all said goodbye, when the big man closed his eyes for the final time.

The days and weeks after Bill's passing were an adjustment for Paddy and Mairead. They found themselves in each other's company more so than at any time in the last several years. It was as if they were rediscovering each other, having forgotten how much they relished being together. There was a tenderness between them that hadn't been there for a long time. Paddy was supportive of Mairead's grief, but she knew Paddy's sense of loss was just as palpable. She knew how much he had loved and revered her father. So they supported each other. But Mairead couldn't help but feel that something else was eating at her husband. She had no idea of the guilt and self-recrimination Paddy was beating himself up with. But she sensed something.

For a while Paddy considered admitting the affair, and begging Mairead to forgive him. But he didn't think he could bear to subject her to more heartbreak in the wake of her father's death. So he packed it down, and continued to just hump the guilt.

Two months later Roxanne Barcellos took that option off the table. She confronted Paddy out on the field at school.

"It's been weeks, Paddy. Meet me in my office. I need to have you."

"Roxanne, we're done. This is not what I want. It's not who I am. You have to leave me alone."

"That's bullshit, Paddy! You know you want this as much as I do. We have something special together."

"Special!" Paddy scoffed. "We are awful together. We're two terrible, selfish people who just get worse when we're even near each other. I can't do this anymore, Roxanne. Mairead doesn't deserve this."

"I wonder what she'll do when I tell her about us," Roxanne threatened. Paddy knew in an instant she was serious.

"Do you really think blowing up my marriage could ever result in us being together? You can't be that naïve. If you do this, I will hate you forever."

"I don't care. I just want you to hurt."

Paddy knew what he had to do. There was no way he would let Mairead hear about this affair from anyone but him. He owed her that much.

When he got home that night, Paddy grabbed Mairead in the kitchen. Mairead didn't like the look of concern on his face. When he told her he needed to talk to her about something, a wave of dread washed over her. Paddy insisted they take a ride.

They drove to a remote, wooded parking lot at Bethpage State Park. There Paddy disclosed to Mairead the affair with Roxanne. He watched as her face morphed from disbelief into abject pain. When she fell apart emotionally, he lost it with her. She got angry and slapped him in the face. Paddy offered his other cheek, feeling deserving of every blow. But instead of hitting him again, she apologized for doing so. Then she composed herself enough to ask him.

"Are you in love with her?"

"No, never," Paddy said.

"Are you leaving me?"

"Oh God, no. I don't ever want that."

"How could you do this to us?" Mairead finally beseeched him.

That one drove him to his knees. After prostrating himself at her feet, he looked up through his tears and begged for all he was worth.

"I will do anything. I'll go to counseling. I will give you space and time, if that's what you want. But please, don't give up on me. I will move heaven and hell to fix this. I don't even expect you to forgive me. I'll never forgive myself. But I don't think I can live without you, Mairead. So I'm begging you, please give me a chance."

She let him kneel there for a while. Then she moved closer and pressed his head to her midriff. They stayed like that for a while. Then Mairead asked Paddy to take her home.

"We'll talk more about this tomorrow. For now I just need to be alone with my thoughts. If I have questions, will you answer them honestly?"

"Of course. Whatever you want to know."

"No more lies?"

"Baby, I'm at rock bottom here. What could be worse, that I would lie about it?"

When they went home, Paddy set a bed up for himself on the futon in the family room. Mairead secluded herself with her thoughts in their bedroom. As promised, she had questions. She came down the stairs to ask them.

"Why did you tell me about the affair, Paddy?"

"Roxanne was going to confront you with it. I couldn't let you hear about it from her. But to be honest, I don't think I could have carried the guilt for much longer. I think I would have told you about it eventually, Roxanne notwithstanding."

"Is that what's been bothering you recently?"

"You mean torturing me? Yeah, that was it."

"How do you feel now?" she asked.

"Right now all I can feel is shame for having betrayed you. I'll never find the words to express how sorry I am."

"I know. But you'll try," she said, before going back upstairs.

They went on like that for three days, Mairead coming to him to ask specific questions. Paddy answering with absolute candor. When Mairead asked Paddy to describe the sex, he shuddered but soldiered ahead. He told her there were five total encounters, all in her office. He wanted Mairead to understand, they did not otherwise see each other socially. He stressed it was strictly intercourse. It was quick, it was angry, and it was never more meaningful than that. He related that by the fifth encounter, he had grown sick with himself and couldn't even finish. Mairead seemed to take comfort in that.

After the three days, Mairead came down to the family room and asked Paddy to come back to bed with her. When she let him hold her, Paddy hung on to her desperately. As they lay there breathing each other in, their hands wandered to those natural places they always did. It was Mairead who asked Paddy to make love to her. He did, with as much tenderness and passion as he ever had. He devoured her. With his face buried in her, he breathed her in, trying to inhale the very essence of her. He felt her buck and shudder, but she firmly held his head in place, not wanting him to stop. While down there Paddy started to castigate himself again. How, he wondered, could he have ever jeopardized this? This was the only place he ever needed to be.

When Paddy came up for air and entered Mairead, she gasped and locked her legs around his waist, pulling him deeply into her. His hot tears mixed with her own. They made love and wept until they collapsed into each other. What followed was eight hours of the best sleep Paddy would ever know.

CHAPTER EIGHTY-ONE

December, 2011
Plainedge

For days after, Paddy and Mairead stayed in each other's space with a need they had forgotten they had. Paddy arranged to take a week of vacation, telling Lieutenant Martino he had to deal with a family crisis. The lieutenant was concerned, but he let his detective remain cryptic. He didn't ask for specifics, he just wanted to know if Paddy and Mairead needed anything. Paddy assured him they just needed some time together. That week off was followed by another.

They used the time well. Mairead would have questions for Paddy. He would answer them without hesitation, even the revelations which caused Mairead pain. It killed him to do it, but he would not lie to her again. Only one inquiry put Paddy in a quandary.

When Mairead asked Paddy why he would seek comfort outside their marriage, from someone other than her, Paddy blanched. Mairead sensed he didn't want to answer.

"Just tell me, Paddy. I can't fix anything if I don't know what it is, no matter how bad it hurts."

"It's not that I don't want to tell you, Mairead. It's just that I need you to understand. None of this was your fault. You didn't do anything to cause this. This was all on me."

"Then, why can't you tell me?"

"I can. I will. I'm just trying to figure out how to express it without sounding like some justification or excuse for hurting you. It's the worst thing I've ever done. I'm having a hard enough time trying to live with it, without trying to explain it."

"But, I need you to explain it."

"I promise I'll try. I'm still struggling with it, but here's what I have so far. Do you remember when we first started dating? Do you remember how amazing it was?"

"Of course I remember. I fell so in love with you."

"That was the first and only time I ever felt that way with anyone, ever. You were an emotional epiphany for me. I never wanted to be without that feeling ever again."

"You didn't have to be without it. You know how much I love you."

"No, Mairead. I don't know anything. That's my problem. I'm not emotionally constructed as soundly as you. I spent my childhood being told I was unworthy of love. I didn't experience it until I met you. I want to believe you love me, but I have to be convinced. I have to be reminded. I have to be reassured constantly. Before you, I had grown so used to being unwanted, discarded, and ultimately abandoned, I never wholly trust anything else is even possible for me. I live in constant fear that one day you will come to your senses, and kick me to the curb."

"Paddy, you know that's not true. I told you so many times. You are my forever. You know that."

"I know it in a rational sense, Mairead. But this insidious thing doesn't reside in my head. The sickness is in my heart. It won't ever allow me to believe I'm worthy of you. I sure don't feel worthy now."

"How can I convince you otherwise, Paddy?"

"You shouldn't have to. I have to learn to accept it."

"Can you?" she asked.

"It's easy when we're like this. I have to learn to do it when it's hard."

"Oh Paddy, what happened to us?"

"It didn't happen to us, Mairead. It happened to me. I'm trying to make you see none of this was your doing. For the last few years, through circumstances beyond our control, we've been so busy taking care of everything else, we forgot to take care of each other. That was okay for you. Between the kids, our jobs and responsibilities, and then your father getting sick, it's no wonder we got distracted. You were secure enough in yourself to endure that. I wasn't. I'm not just emotionally dysfunctional, Mairead. I'm the fucking poster child. When you drifted away from me, it started to feel like I had died. I should have told you I was hurting. But I didn't. I turned in on myself. It just got worse, until I convinced myself you were done with me. Then I told myself you wouldn't care what I did. I thought you gave up on me. Once I got to that point, I reverted back to the animal I was before I met you. I let myself believe sex with Roxanne could somehow make up for the love and intimacy I thought I lost with you. It was the worst decision of my life. It was awful. If I could change anything, that would be it. If God gave *mulligans* that would be mine."

Their sexual reawakening for each other continued. But it had taken on a desperation and intensity which was probably unhealthy. They were getting at each other two and three times a day. They made love to each other like every time could be the last. It was a comfort at first. But it couldn't last. Paddy thanked God it was Mairead who first tapped out. It wasn't a matter of pride for him. He just couldn't bear the idea she might suspect it was something other than fatigue. He didn't want her to ever entertain the thought he didn't desire her. When the breakdown came, they still went to bed together, but every once in a while, they just held each other. Paddy found it almost as satisfying.

They started couples therapy that week. Mairead had chosen the psychologist. Paddy was surprised when Doctor James Cregan turned out to be a guy not very different from himself. He made a point of informing them both that he had personally blown his own life up more than once, before he fixed himself, with help and many hundreds of hours of therapy. He now wanted to share the secret with everybody. Cregan listened to their story. He told them he was encouraged. The biggest hurdle to healing was never an issue for them. It was obvious how much they loved each other.

So they were making progress. They were trying to heal. They had found each other again, and were determined to hold on. It started to look like they would survive this, until *Hurricane Roxanne* blew into town.

CHAPTER EIGHTY-TWO

February, 2012
Plainedge

Mairead was upstairs, making the bed when she saw Roxanne pull into their driveway in that red Jaguar convertible she was always tooling around in. Mairead looked from the dormer window to the digital clock on her night table. She noted the time was 09:00 A.M. *Misery is prompt*, she thought as she came downstairs to meet her nemesis at the door. Paddy was out buying groceries for the breakfast he had planned for the two of them. Mairead wasn't sure if that was a blessing or not. She was a little afraid if the ensuing confrontation with Roxanne got heated, she wouldn't be able to stop beating that whore until she had killed her. Paddy would have at least stopped her short of that.

As Roxanne got to the front porch, Mairead swung the front door open. She stood defiantly in the threshold with her arms folded across her chest.

"You shouldn't have bothered to come, Roxanne. There's nothing for you here. Paddy already told me about the affair."

That stopped Roxanne abruptly. She didn't imagine Paddy would blow himself up so readily. Still, she was here to make someone hurt. She wasn't leaving until she did

"I just wanted you to know that your 'perfect' husband was a snake like every other man."

"I don't love Paddy because he's perfect. He's as flawed as most men. But he's a good man down deep, and he loves me. You might have poisoned his mind for a while, but that's over now. He's mine. We're fixing this thing. The last thing we need is any input from you."

"You think you're better than me," Roxanne said.

"I know I'm better than you, you awful, treacherous bitch. You ingratiated yourself into my family. You pretended to be my friend. You offered to help our daughter with her scholarship offers. Meanwhile, you were just trying to get your claws into my husband. You managed to smudge him up a little, but you didn't ruin him. And you don't get to have him. So, why don't you turn around and slither back to whatever rock you crawled out from under? That's just a suggestion. This is an order. Stay away from my family, Roxanne. Or I'll kick your bony ass back to Brazil."

Roxanne was not prepared to be on the defensive. But, Mairead took the initiative from her and never relinquished it. Something in Roxanne snapped. Her eyes took on a feral quality. Her face twisted into a sneer.

"Oh, I'm not done with you by a sight," Roxanne spit.

"That sounded like a threat. Don't do that," Mairead cautioned her. "If you come anywhere near my family again, the police will never find your body."

Mairead stood there on the porch, with her arms folded. She glared intently at Roxanne, as she watched her peel out of their driveway in her little Jag. She patched out and fishtailed, before her tires found purchase and she sped off.

Paddy came in the door with an armful of groceries less than a minute later. Mairead was obviously jacked up. Her green eyes had an intense vibrant gleam to them. Paddy had seen the Jaguar tearing off the block, so he already had an idea why.

"Roxanne was here?"

"Oh, yes."

"How did it go?"

"I made it clear that if she bothered this family again, I would kill her. I wasn't joking, and she knows it."

"I'm sorry I put you in this position, along with everything else I did."

"No," Mairead stopped him. "This had to happen. I needed it. I feel strong for the first time since this broke. I feel like I reclaimed a piece of myself today. I want to enjoy it."

"Okay, baby," was all he said.

Mairead was bouncing around, all adrenaline and nervous energy. The thrill of confronting her enemy had infused her with an intense feeling of power. She flashed on Paddy again with those amazing green eyes.

"I feel so good. Take me upstairs and make love to me right now."

"Yes, ma'am," Paddy said, as he hoisted her over his shoulder, and secured her there with one big hand clamped onto her perfect ass. Mairead was giggling as Paddy fireman carried her up to the bedroom.

After they got done making a mess of the bed and themselves, they laid there languidly enjoying each other's company. Mairead was confident they were rid of Roxanne Barcellos. When she shared this with Paddy, he told her he hoped it was so. But Paddy knew how diabolically evil Roxanne could be. She was committed and insidious. He did not believe she would go away so easily.

CHAPTER EIGHTY-THREE

February, 2012
Plainedge

The first phone call the next day came from Buster Melnick. It was 0800 hours. Buster seldom called Paddy at home, and never before noon. So Paddy had a bad feeling about the call even before he picked it up.

"Good morning, Buster."

"Paddy, did you by any chance look at your email this morning?" Buster asked, obviously upset about something. The edge in his voice spelled trouble.

"I'm not even out of bed yet."

"Oh, Jesus!" Buster exclaimed.

"Just tell me what happened, Buster."

"The cops just broke down Roxanne's office door. She was dead in there. She had overdosed on a shit-load of phenobarbital and Xanax. She washed it all down with a fifth of vodka sometime last night."

"That's horrible. But why are you telling *me*?"

"Paddy, it's bad. I don't know how to say it. So I'm just going to say it. A little after midnight, Roxanne sent out a group email to every email address in the school district."

"What was on it?" Paddy asked, already dreading the answer.

"Her video suicide note. She was quaffing those pills and washing them down with the vodka like they were a salad. She went on a rant about how you seduced her and kicked her to the curb. She said you ruined her reputation, and that's why she was killing herself."

"That's bad. But we both know it's not true. You were there. You saw how she was after me since I first showed up at the school. I mean for Christ's sake, she already fucked the whole athletic department and half the school board. What reputation could I have ruined?"

"That's not all. There were five other videos attached to the email. They were all of you and Roxanne having sex in her office. They left nothing to the imagination."

"Do the cops have the video?" Paddy asked.

"I don't think you understand, this went out over the internet. It's about to go viral. *Everybody* has the video."

Paddy sat up in bed. His brain had already started to pound at the inside of his skull. In spite of just waking up, Paddy felt exhausted.

"Are the cops looking to talk to me?"

"Yeah, Paddy."

"Did you tell them I'm a detective in the city?"

"They know who you are. I don't think they want to hurt you. They seem sympathetic, but they have a few questions."

"Tell them I'll be at the school within the half hour."

Paddy got up and got dressed. Throwing on jeans, running shoes, a tee-shirt and a Plainedge Football hoodie, his first order of business was to break this horrible turn of the screw to Mairead. When Paddy got downstairs and heard her crying at the computer terminal in the family room, he knew he had been beaten to the punch.

What filled the screen sickened him. Mairead turned around and looked at Paddy with the most hopeless and forlorn expression he had ever seen. That he had to see it on his wife's face, and know he had been the cause of it, was nearly more than he could bear. He wanted her to stop looking at the awful video, before it became all she could see when she looked at him.

"Please, Mairead, don't look at that anymore. There isn't anything on those videos I haven't already discussed with you. You won't find anything new, and looking at it will only scar you."

Mairead's whole body was trembling as she spoke through her heaves and sobs.

"I don't want to look at it, Paddy. But people are sending it to me. It's as if they want me to see it. Who are these people? How did they even get my email address?"

"They are people who are going to claim they're your friends. But they're not. They're just cruel. They relish in the suffering of others, secretly delighted it's not them. And they got your email from the header. It was a *send all* message. They had to look through a few thousand names to find it. But your email is your name. It wasn't that hard. Now, baby, please, turn it off. I have so much already to atone for. Don't let these people poison your mind any further."

Mairead just stared at him for a moment through her tears. But she didn't turn it off. She let it play. The sound was audible and clear. Roxanne's screaming could be heard, coupled with Paddy's animalistic grunting. The affect was like a rhythmic, primitive drumbeat. The sound of it turned Paddy's stomach. But Mairead wouldn't turn it off.

"You know, Paddy?" she said. "I hate Roxanne for doing this to us. But I can't help but feel like I should be hating you as well."

When Paddy got to the crime scene, he was ushered into Roxanne's office by Detective Al Crawford from the Nassau County Homicide Squad. The room smelled like vomit, vodka, and the beginning stages of putrefying flesh. Paddy surmised from that, and the lividity which was forming at the bottom of Roxanne's body, she had died at least six hours earlier. He estimated her time of death at approximately 0200 hours, or about two hours after she had sent out the accursed emails. Crawford's partner, Detective Pamela Yodice was directing the crime scene photographer as he carefully walked around the desk with Roxanne's dead body splayed out across the top. Paddy knew and respected both of these detectives. He had numerous occasions to confer with them about possible perps in common. A few years ago, Paddy got to collaborate with them on a murderous drug gang from Hempstead who had done a double homicide during a drug rip in the 83rd Precinct. Crawford and Yodice used Paddy's homicide case as the centerpiece of their RICO prosecution on Long Island. They took down the whole gang together, clearing numerous murders on both sides of the border. The fact they were in the Homicide Squad didn't concern Paddy. He knew homicide handled all death investigations in Nassau, including accidents and suicides. They greeted Paddy cordially, if a little awkwardly.

"Have you seen all the videos yet?" Crawford asked him.

"Just a brief glimpse. My wife was watching it when I left the house."

"Oh, Paddy. I'm so sorry," Yodice said.

"That's alright, Pam. I did this to myself."

"We've got some questions. Given the situation, the cringe factor is going to be kinda high. Are you up for this now?" Crawford asked.

"Ask me what you need to know."

"The obvious question is, who recorded the video?" Pam asked.

"I think it was remotely recorded. There was no third party in the room, if that was what you were thinking. But I would have to see the video to gauge the camera angles to know more."

So the Nassau detectives cued up the videos for him on Roxanne's desktop computer. The first video was of Roxanne's drunken, pilled-up tirade against Paddy, obviously shot by the camera at the top of Roxanne's computer monitor. It was as bad as Buster had described. The next five videos were all of Paddy having sex with Roxanne. Paddy's first impression was the videos looked like they were professionally edited. There were two camera angles. All the images were shot from opposite sides of the room, taken from an elevated position. *The clocks!* Paddy thought. Whoever edited the video kept shifting back and forth from the rear view to the full frontal. The effect was dramatic, and *very* pornographic. When he was done watching the last video, Paddy stepped away from the computer.

"Any questions?"

"We didn't find any cameras in the room, other than the one on top of her monitor. Any ideas?" Pam asked.

"I've only been in this room a total of five times, but right from the jump, those twin clocks struck me as odd. I mean, who needs two of the same clock? It doesn't even make any sense as a décor consideration. Based upon the camera angles from the videos, I'm guessing the cameras might be behind those clock faces."

When the detectives got a ladder and examined the clock faces closely they could see a pin-hole camera in each clock face, positioned consistent with where a rivet should have been. The rivets had been replaced with the tiny camera lenses. The fact that the clocks were mounted high on the wall, and on opposite sides of the room was the only reason they weren't readily noticeable. When the detectives removed the clocks, they found two digital recorders in the void in the wall, behind the clocks. These turned out to be wirelessly linked to Roxanne's desktop computer.

The detectives were satisfied Paddy had not engaged in any criminal wrongdoing. There were no loose ends to tie up. This was a straight suicide. The toxicology report would verify the cause of death to be from an overdose of prescription barbiturates and alcohol.

"Just to give you a heads-up, our lieutenant notified your Internal Affairs when he found out you were involved with the victim. I have no idea how your department will handle the adultery thing," Pamela said.

"They're not going to touch it," Paddy predicted.

"No?"

"Half of the chiefs and deputy commissioners in the NYPD have *rolodexes* full of girlfriends and mistresses. They can't afford to have that particular can of worms opened."

"So, you're in the clear," Al Crawford observed.

"I don't think my wife would agree," Paddy said.

Mairead most certainly did not agree. Paddy found himself on the futon again. Mairead didn't overtly signal she was giving up. But, she already had. She continued to go to counseling with Paddy for a while. But she could get no traction in the healing process. The problem was the video. It kept resurfacing and recirculating. It's hard enough getting past your own imagined vision of an unfaithful spouse. It's impossible when you are forced to see it occur on video, day after day. What was worse was the false empathy Mairead was shown by people, strangers really, who in truth delighted in her discomfort and misfortune. She saw right through it, but it made her feel weak, worthless, somehow less of a person.

The other problem was she couldn't stop herself from looking at the video when it popped up. She would stare at it intently for hours, trying to derive some sense of reason or meaning from it. She obsessed over it until all she could see was Paddy's betrayal whenever she looked at him.

She stopped going to counseling soon after, reasoning the issues and problems were his alone. Paddy understood. It was a hard point to argue. He continued to see Jim Cregan on his own, but the sessions seemed to morph into something more akin to grief counseling than anything related to saving his marriage.

Mairead briefly let Paddy back into the bed, but it was only because his back had started to bother him from sleeping on the futon. She wasn't talking to him. She wasn't touching him, and she would not permit him to touch her. She turned her back on him, and hugged her side of the bed. The few inches separating them in the king-size bed might as well have been a bottomless chasm. Paddy had started to feel as lonely in Mairead's presence as he had ever been in his whole, miserable life.

When Mairead told him a few weeks later she needed space to figure out what she wanted, she asked him to move out. Paddy wasn't surprised, but that didn't make it any easier.

"Mairead, I'll do anything. I'll leave, if that's what you want me to do. But I don't want to give up on us. I'll retire.. We'll sell the house and move. We can go anywhere. Just please, don't give up on us."

"Oh Paddy," she said wearily. "There is no us. I seriously doubt there ever was. All along, it's been you and your propensity for self-destruction. You insist on spinning off the rails, no matter who it hurts. You were impulsive and selfish when I met you. I don't think that's ever changed. I can't live like this anymore, and I need to not see you to figure out what I want. So please, just go."

A week later, Paddy was living in the apartment by the Farmingdale train station. His scandalized family wanted no part of him. The football program he had helped to build into a perennial championship contender had dismissed him without ceremony. He was informed he wasn't to step foot on the school grounds. He couldn't even attend their games as a spectator. Paddy could relate. He wanted no part of himself either. The idea, when Mairead asked him to leave, was that it would be a temporary arrangement, but it had a certain finality to it.

CHAPTER EIGHTY-FOUR

Thanksgiving, 2013
Farmingdale

Paddy did a double shift at the 83 Squad. He covered the office alone for the day tour and four to one. He hadn't heard from his family. So he had no idea what they were doing. The kids had thawed a little since he moved out. They accepted his texts, and occasionally texted him back. So that morning, a little after eleven he group texted his children.

Happy Thanksgiving. I love you all, and I miss you.

A little while later, his daughter Katelyn of all people, texted him back.

What are you doing today?

Working all day.

We are at Grandma's. She said to wish you a Happy Thanksgiving. We miss you too.

Paddy texted back a heart sticker, but he wouldn't go any further than that. What he wanted, was desperate for in fact, was to hear Mairead's voice, just to hear her say she was okay. But he didn't dare call. At this point, Paddy was walking a ragged edge emotionally. He wouldn't risk more disappointment right now. It might well put him over the brink, and cast him into the abyss.

Paddy got home to his apartment around 0200 hours. He took a quick shower, wrapped a towel around his waist, and sat down in front of the TV in the living room to watch the football games from this afternoon. He had recorded them on his DVR. Paddy had his Thanksgiving feast arrayed before him on the coffee table. It consisted of a half a pound of Boar's Head turkey, a head of romaine lettuce and a squirt-bottle of French's yellow mustard. To the right incongruously, was his .38 special five-shot revolver.

Paddy was wrapping the lettuce around the turkey, adding a squirt of mustard and trying to eat it as fast as he could. He found the taste of food to be like sawdust in his mouth. He was trying to watch the Detroit Lions crush the Dallas Cowboys. Paddy was a lifelong Giants fan. As happy as he was to see Dallas lose, he was unable to pay attention to the game. His concentration was diverted. He was wholly occupied with the decision of whether to put the gun under his chin, or in his mouth. Paddy thought about the two scenarios. In the end he didn't like either of them. His demise might end his agony and simplify his families' lives, but they would be horrified he had descended to such depths. In the end it would just cause them more pain. He didn't want to be the source of anymore of that.

So he put the food away, threw on exercise clothes and dragged himself to the gym. He burned off his negative energy with a three hour grueling workout. By the time he left the gym, it was five in the morning. There was a line outside the brightly lit Best Buy next door to the fitness center. Paddy approached the security guard.

"What gives?"

"Black Friday."

They had started letting people into the store, so Paddy spontaneously decided he needed a laptop computer. He went in and bought one. He thought perhaps if he could get some of this twisted shit in his head down on paper, he might be able to make some sense of it. He determined then and there to write a novel.

When Paddy got home, the sun was coming up. He opened the computer and started writing. He took his title from a description of him his father had been fond of using. *A Thing of No Particular Worth* began on his kitchen table that Friday morning.

CHAPTER EIGHTY-FIVE

November 29, 2013
Brooklyn

That Monday, November 29th, 2013 began in the 83 Squad like most Monday mornings following a long holiday weekend. No one really wanted to be there.

Paddy called Ronnie Kingsbury at TARU to see if he made any progress on the dumps he had requested. Ronnie came on the phone in an excited state.

"I got *Casper's* Grandma's address in Connecticut for you."

"How did you do that, Ron?"

"I went back over his mother's calls on her home phone, just checking to see if I missed something. Sure enough, there were calls every two days from the same 518 area code. I checked the subscriber. It came back to an Yvette Moreno at 160 Saint Stephens Road, in Bridgeport. That's right where *Casper's* cell phone has been pinging."

"Fax that over. It looks like I'm going back to Connecticut."

Romeo Amodeo came over from the Homicide Squad. Paddy brought him up to speed about the new information. They started to reach out for permission to leave the city. Paddy called Sergeant Sean Gilmartin on his cell phone.

"Holy shit, Paddy! Do you have ESP or something?"

"What do you mean?"

"I was just going to call you. I got your guy in the back seat of my patrol car."

"You've got Oscar Nieto in your car? How the hell did you manage that?"

"After the feds shined me on about the tenant list, I was doing surveillance over by those HUD projects under the cell tower. I saw Oscar, and who I assumed was his grandmother come out of one of the townhouses. When the guy climbed into the trunk and they tried to drive away, I had to stop them."

"Let me guess, Yvette Moreno from 160 Saint Stephens Road?"

"How did you know?"

"Sometimes the shit comes down so heavy, Sean, I think I should wear a hat. Did he say where he was headed?"

"He said he was going to Brooklyn to talk to you. He had your business card."

"That was never gonna happen. The trunk of a Corolla is no way to get to Brooklyn. You don't have him handcuffed, do you?"

"He's sitting comfortably in my caged and locked backseat. He hasn't tried the doors yet, so he doesn't know he's not free to leave. He said he would wait for you. How quickly can you get here?"

"What does it usually take, an hour and a half? I'll be there in forty-five minutes."

Paddy and Romeo tore up I-95, with the lights and sirens blaring the whole way. They pulled into the parking lot of 160 Saint Stephens Road forty-three minutes later.

Paddy and Romeo pulled up to Sean's squad car.

"Did you guys fly here?" Sean asked.

"Practically. Has he said anything?"

"He's been sitting there listening to his ipod, not a care in the world."

"Did you toss him good? I don't want to search him and risk raising him up."

"No worries. I rubbed him good. He's clean as a whistle."

"His composure suggests three possibilities," Paddy said. "The first is that he's a total moron. The second, he's so smart, he thinks he can talk himself out from under a murder rap. That's the same as being a moron.

The third possibility is he's as guilty as hell, and just doesn't care about what happens next. Either scenario works for me."

"He's all yours, Detective."

"Thanks, Sean. I will call you later to get some names and mailing addresses. My lieutenant wants to send a letter of commendation to your job. I want to make sure it gets cc'd to all of your bosses."

Paddy walked over to the cruiser and opened the rear passenger door. Nieto looked up and smiled. He took the earphones off before Paddy addressed him.

"Hello, *Casper*," Paddy said.

"Oh, so you know who I am," *Casper* said, confirming his nickname, and already incriminating himself.

"Do you know who I am?"

"I guess you're Detective Durr. My *moms* said you were looking to talk to me. What's this all about?"

"The day you left for Connecticut, a guy named *Negro* got himself smoked. Your name comes up in that investigation. We heard you had drama with him. So, now we have to talk. Will you come back to Brooklyn with me and my partner so we can get this out of the way? I'll take you to your mom's place on Willoughby when I'm done with you."

"I could meet you there. I was on my way down to see you when I got pulled over."

"I'm sure you were. But I would prefer you ride with me. You can't drive as fast as I'm going to. I've got a lot to do today. I wanna finish with you quickly, so I can get to that other stuff."

"Okay," *Casper* agreed.

On the ride south on I-95, Paddy and Romeo casually chatted *Casper* up. Since the subject of his beef with *Negro* had already come up, they talked about that.

"That beef with *Negro* got squashed," *Casper* insisted.

"Well, what was it about?" Romeo asked.

"I used go out with his cousin, Beatriz. We had an argument and her phone broke. He wanted me to pay for the phone. But I already bought her a new one. When I told *Negro* that, he said '*Ah-ite, we good.*'"

"What about Beatriz, are you still good with her?" Paddy asked.

"I had to get rid of her. She's a *puta sucia*. You know what that is, Detective?"

"Oh yeah," Paddy assured him. "I know what that is."

Romeo had to suppress a laugh. He got the reference.

"So, that's all it was, just a disagreement about the phone?" Romeo asked.

"Yeah. Me and *Negro* were cool. I liked him. It hurt my heart when I heard he got *kilt*."

A few minutes later Paddy pulled into the rest stop on the New York side of the border with Connecticut, in Rye. Paddy explained they were taking a bathroom break. When he pulled over, *Casper* climbed out of the backseat. Paddy told him to turn around. When *Casper* asked why, Paddy told him he was arresting him for the murder of *Negro*. *Casper* calmly turned and placed his hands behind his back. Paddy hand-cuffed him and put him back in the car.

"Why did you wait till now to arrest me?" *Casper* asked.

"Because I have no powers of arrest in the state of Connecticut," Paddy admitted.

"Oh," was all he said for the rest of the ride to the 83 Squad.

When they got back to Bushwick, Paddy cuffed his prisoner to the rail in the interview room. He told *Casper* he would be back in a little bit, so they could talk.

"What if I don't want to?"

"You don't have to. But when you hear what I have on you, you're going to want to tell your side of it. In fact, your life may depend on it."

Paddy locked the room and went to his desk. He called Tommy Crowe on his cell phone.

"What's up?" Tommy answered.

"Are you working right now?"

"Yeah, we're on Irving and Hart. We're looking for a gun to walk off the block."

"I got a sure thing for you, if you want it."

"Absolutely, what have you got?"

"I have probable cause on EB for the *Negro* homicide. Pick him up for me. He should be on Knickerbocker and Starr. If he's by that van, and the passenger side door is open, there is a trap under the carpet on the floor there. Whatever is in there you can charge him with, but I'm taking him down for this murder. Can you do that for me, *Boyo?* Paddy asked, not forgetting for a minute that Tommy's father used to call only his good friends *Boyo.*

"I'm on it, Paddy."

When Tommy dragged EB into the 83 Squad, he was kicking and screaming. He kept protesting the guns and body armor found in his van weren't his, even though he was sitting on the trap in the open door of the van when Tommy grabbed him. When EB saw Paddy glaring at him from his desk, EB closed his eyes and stamped his foot.

"Not this motherfucker again!" EB exclaimed.

"This motherfucker, for the very last time, EB."

Paddy had Tommy put EB on the rail in the other interview room. When Tommy locked his prisoner in the room, he told Paddy EB must have been expecting trouble. In the trap were two loaded nine millimeters, sixteen additional magazines and two bulletproof vests.

"The Latin Kings are looking for him."

"I thought he was a Latin King," Tommy said.

"He is no longer in good standing. He owes the Kings from the Bronx a ton of money and dope. And, he is in default. His life isn't worth three cents right now."

"Wow, sucks to be him. So, what do I do now?"

"Tell your boss we are charging your prisoner with murder. I'll explain to him you have to process your case with ours. Then you come up here and be a fly on the wall. Watch everything. Listen to everyone. You want to observe the interrogation, you can do it through the mirror. When the DA gets here later tonight, you gotta tell her about your collar."

"That's a lot of work."

"You wanted to be kept informed. You wanted to be involved. You still want that?"

"Absolutely. I was just making an observation. I'm all in."

"Good, because it's gonna be a wild ride. And you get a front row ticket. Welcome to the big time, Boyo."

CHAPTER EIGHTY-SIX

November 29, 2013
Brooklyn

Paddy walked into the interview room carrying a cardboard box full of documents, folders, photographs, and computer printouts. The outside of the box had writing on it in black permanent marker. It said on all four sides; *People of the State of New York vs. Oscar Nieto.* Paddy had just written those words a minute earlier. He needed *Casper* to focus on the very real peril he was in. This was what his case folder had become. It was intimidating to look at, if you were a suspect. That was the point of letting *Casper* see it. During the ensuing interview, Paddy wouldn't need to refer to any of it. He had every minutia of fact on this case committed to memory. He just left the box there for *Casper* to think about. It dangled over his head like the Sword of Damocles.

Romeo had set *Casper* up at the interview table, opposite the two comfortable chairs where the detectives were meant to sit. After Paddy came in the room and plopped that monstrosity of a case file on the table, he shoved the table against the side wall, and out of his way. Rather than taking a plush chair, he grabbed one of the hard backed line-up chairs and placed it two feet in front of *Casper*. Paddy sat there.

After Romeo had handled the background and pedigree information, he read *Casper* the Miranda Warnings from a pre-printed sheet everybody in the room got to sign. Paddy leaned in and began without preamble.

"We detectives like to refer to this space here as the *truth room*. That's because nothing is supposed to emerge from it but the absolute and unvarnished truth. Unfortunately, a lot of lying gets done in here. I would advise you not to do that. You can't tell a lie I won't recognize as such. I'll know, because I'm not going to ask you anything I don't already know the answer to. I got a box full of witness and informant statements, and physical evidence that tell this story better than you can. In truth, I don't need you to say a thing. I've got you cold for shooting *Negro*. I don't need another ounce of proof to convict you of this crime. We call a case like this a *slam dunk*. Prosecutors pray for a case like this every night before they go to bed. You, as it stands, are now a prosecutor's wet dream. And if the legislature can get out of their own way and rewrite the death penalty, you might get the needle for this."

"If you've already got me, why should I talk to you?" *Casper* asked.

"That is an excellent question, *Casper*. Your motivation for talking to me is so I can present your side of the story to the DA. If we leave it based solely on the evidence, you come off as a cold-blooded murderer. You got punked by the guy who stole your girl. He shook you down for three hundred bucks for Beatriz' cell phone. He was going after yours' and the Latin King's drug spots. *EB* found out about it, and ordered you to take care of him. He gave you the gun, and sent you down to Angela's diner to kill him. He told you, 'Don't come back unless it's done.' You ambushed *Negro* and shot him till your gun was out of bullets. We know all of this because *EB* is in the next room telling us all about it. You smoked this guy because you didn't want to look like a punk. I mean, hell, he already made a *cabron* out of you."

At the mention of being a cabron, Paddy noticed a crack in *Casper's* composure. It was a twitch and a brief narrowing of his eyes, but it was there. Paddy thought he might have found *Casper's* tender spot. He had definitely hit a nerve. When the time was right, he would go back and bang away at that. First though, he knew he had to listen to some lies.

"You got it wrong, Detective. I was in Connecticut when *Negro* got shot. So it couldn't be me," was *Casper's* attempt at an alibi.

"I've been up on your phone since this murder went down," Durr said. "I pulled the cell tower report. That tells us where and when the phone signal was hitting the nearest cell tower. Your phone didn't start hitting in Connecticut until two days after the murder. Prior to that, it showed you were in the vicinity of Starr Street and Knickerbocker. In the early morning hours of October eleventh, it puts you in the vicinity of Wilson Avenue and George Street. I don't have to tell you what was happening there at that time."

"I ditched that phone days earlier. I go through phones like other people change their underwear. So, somebody else had that phone."

"That's what I heard about you. You change phones a lot. But for some reason, you kept this one. We know because two days later, we can track it all the way up I-95. It's been hitting the cell tower underneath your *Abuelita's* house ever since. It was pinging there right up until the time I had Sergeant Gilmartin recover it for me. It was sitting on your grandmother's kitchen counter, where you had been charging the battery. So, nobody else had the phone."

Paddy spent the next couple of hours chipping away at *Casper's* lies. Paddy decided to tell a few himself. He told *Casper* his fingerprints were recovered from the gun, along with *EB's* on the shell casings, a half-truth. That troubled *Casper* a little, but not enough to exploit. Paddy told him his mistake was letting the two guys with *Negro* live. They looked him right in the face. They already identified him from photos. There was no question how the line-ups would go. *Casper* shrugged this off.

Paddy decided it was time to re-address the Beatriz angle. He asked *Casper* if he had spoken to her recently. When he said no, Paddy told him he had spoken to Beatriz a couple of weeks ago, when she got locked up in Manhattan for selling stolen Metro Cards.

"She told me all about you and *Negro*. She wasn't his cousin. She was fucking him, even while she was supposed to be your girl. That had to hurt. What I'm sure was worse was when he punked you on the street. He was going to chase you out of Bushwick and take your drug spots. Why not? He already took your girl. A *cabron* and a punk, all in one week, how do you deal with something like that?"

Paddy watched *Casper* grow hotter and more agitated every time he referred to him in those terms. His ego and street cred wouldn't allow him to concede the point. He would not think of himself like that. He was all wound up now. Paddy knew he was ready to explode. He just needed one more little push. So Paddy pushed.

"The only thing I'm curious about, *Casper*, is why you shot him in the dick. I thought that was a Dominican thing. Aren't you Puerto Rican?"

Casper jumped out of his seat and screamed at Paddy.

"I didn't shoot that motherfucker in the dick! I shot him in his fat, fucking face! Then I emptied the gun in his back! I ain't no *cabron*, and I ain't nobody's punk!" *Casper* said, before collapsing back into his chair.

The rest of the interrogation became a mere formality. Paddy convinced *Casper* telling the truth was in his best interest. So they went over the story from the beginning, this time with no lies. He told Paddy all about *EB's* involvement. He told him all about the drug operation on Starr Street. After he broke, *Casper* would have given up the man on the grassy knoll. "Hell yes!" was his response when Paddy asked him if he wanted to tell the DA his story on video.

When Paddy came out to his desk to call the DA, Tommy Crowe was waiting for him. He had watched and listened to the entire interrogation from the viewing glass.

"How did you know he would break like that?"

"Interrogations are all preparation and intuition. If you're going to ask a guy about the murder he committed, you have to know everything about the crime. You also have to know everything about your subject. You can't let him have any secrets. Then just talk to him. Scratch the surface. Poke here, poke there, until you hit a nerve. Then bang on that until he snaps. *Casper* cared only about how he was perceived in the street. His ego mandated he defend himself. In the end, he wanted me to know that he wasn't a punk. Point conceded. *Negro* is cold in the ground. But *Casper's* still a *cabron*. We just don't need to tell him that."

"So, what now?" Tommy asked.

"First we do the line-ups. Then we call the DA down with a video guy, and you get to tell your story. Melissa Chen is the DA. She's gonna love you, *Boyo*. She's got a thing for young, pretty-boy cops."

The line-ups were a formality, as Paddy had anticipated. With the assistance of his partners, Joe Furio and Armando Gigante, they got them done quickly. All of the witnesses identified *Casper* as the shooter, even Miguel Baez, the car thief.

Melissa Chen came down with her videographer. She got *Casper* to reiterate his statement on video. Before she interviewed Tommy, she made him blush by remarking to Paddy how cute he was. Tommy survived this, and gave the DA a statement a veteran cop could be proud of.

Finally, Paddy had Dave Molinari bring in *Clambake* to give his testimony. That cemented *EB's* culpability. Melissa charged both defendant's with murder in the second degree. Three days later, they were indicted for that by the grand jury, and remanded into custody pending trial. The only question at this point, was whether the Latin Kings would ever let *EB* see the inside of a courtroom. Paddy didn't like his odds.

CHAPTER EIGHTY-SEVEN

December 14, 2013
Farmingdale

The second week of December brought a surprise visitor to Paddy's apartment. His son Patrick was home for the Christmas break. So he came over to see his dad. Paddy answered the door wearing nothing but a towel around his waist and his reading glasses. The two hugged it out for a bit, before Patrick came inside and Paddy took his coat. Patrick noticed the open lap-top on the kitchen table.

"What are you doing there, pop?"

"I'm writing a novel."

"What's it about?"

"Police shit. You gotta stick with what you know, right?"

"How is it coming along?"

"I'm almost done with it."

"How does it end?"

"I haven't figured out the ending, but badly I think."

"Why no happy ending?"

"Happy endings are just stories that haven't finished yet, *Boyo*," Paddy said, grinning at his son, but they both knew he meant every word of it.

"Can I read some of it?"

"Sure, have at it."

Patrick read for a while. He found the story gripping, but a little frightening. Much of what was in the book were stories he had grown up hearing from his father and his partners. They scared the shit out of him when he was little. Now he was just troubled. This was a novel in name only, he realized. Only the names were changed to protect the guilty. The casual violence, the brutality and the abuse, Patrick knew his father had been carrying around for years. Now, they were poured out in detail, in black and white. Patrick felt like a voyeur. It was like looking at a train wreck as it was unfolding, but being unable to look away.

"Do you think you could send me this so I could read the rest tonight?" Patrick asked.

"Sure. I'll email it to you."

Paddy offered Patrick something to drink, as he went in to the bedroom to get dressed. He asked his dad what he had. Patrick wasn't surprised he had nothing in the fridge but a half empty gallon of milk and a case of bottled water. Other than condiments, there was no food. Patrick took a water and surreptitiously checked the freezer. He was gratified to see chicken cutlets and a few boxes of frozen spinach in there. So at least he was eating something. Paddy noticed his son's curiosity.

"What are you doing, a child welfare check on me?"

"You look thin. I wanted to make sure you were eating. I remember if mom wasn't around to make you eat, sometimes you would forget."

"I'm just trying to get lean."

"You're already lean. You look tired. Are you sleeping?"

"Like a baby," Paddy lied. "I'm just tired. I've been busy."

"I'm sure that's what it is."

Patrick finished his water while he caught his father up on how he was doing in school. He would graduate in May with the same degree as his father, comparative literature. He was going to tell Paddy he decided to join the Police Department. He had called his investigator, and he was now on track to enter the Police Academy in July. But he decided not to tell him. After reading some of his novel, Patrick didn't think his father would want him joining the family business. His plate was already full. So he sat on the information.

Paddy had the look about him like he needed to say something, but wasn't sure if he should. Patrick noticed.

"Is something bothering you?"

"I want to ask you something, but you have to promise not to tell your mother I asked."

"Why?"

"Because I promised her I would leave her alone. I don't want her to think I'm checking up on her. She wants me out of her life. Fair enough. I ruined everything for her. I broke every promise I ever made. The least I can do at this point is to honor this one. So, promise."

"All right, I promise. What do you want to know?"

"Just how she is. Is she well? Is she any happier?"

"Mostly, she's sad. But she's keeping busy. Between the nursing shifts and teaching classes at the gym, she doesn't have much time for anything else."

"Please take care of her for me. Take her and the girls out to dinner. You can put it on the American Express card I gave you. Get her out of the house and, make her laugh. You always could. She thinks you're hysterical."

"I'll do that," Patrick said, as he hugged his father before leaving. He turned around at the door. He had a question of his own.

"How come you didn't ask if she asks about you? Don't you want to know?"

Paddy grinned at his son with an expression in his eyes of absolute defeat. His attempt at a brave face failed utterly.

"I'm afraid, Boyo," he said. "That is no longer any of my fucking business."

CHAPTER EIGHTY-EIGHT

December 14, 2013
Plainedge

Patrick got home that night and checked his email. As promised, his father had sent him the entire novel. He stayed up through the night to read it all. Not that sleep would have been possible after glimpsing the horror that was his father's state of mind. He knew he would break his promise now. He thought his mother should at least know the shape he was in.

He broached the subject with her the next morning. She offered to make breakfast for him. Patrick just wanted coffee. He sat down to drink it with Mairead at the kitchen table.

"I saw Dad yesterday."

"How is he?" Mairead asked, in spite of herself.

"Thin," Patrick offered.

"He's never been heavy."

"I mean painfully thin. Like he's not eating. He looks haggard, too. I don't think he sleeps."

"Your father is a big boy. He's been taking care of himself for a long time. I'm sure he's fine," Mairead said, but the worried look on her face said something else.

"No, he's not," Patrick said. "Did you know he's writing a novel? I read it last night. It's gut- wrenching."

"What's it about?"

"He changed all the names, but, I think it's about you, him, us, and everything. He spans his whole career in it. There's also a murder story in there somewhere. But it reads more like an expiation of his sins than a novel."

"I'm sure he'll do well with it. He could always write."

"At the rate he's going, he won't live to see it published."

"What are you talking about?"

"That man hates himself. The title of the book is *A Thing of No Particular Worth*."

"I remember him telling me that was something his father used to call him. He used to joke about it."

"I think he's bought into the central premise of it now. He isn't joking anymore."

"Your father doesn't believe in suicide, if that's what you're worried about. He views it as cowardice, and that's something he could never be."

"I understand that. But he's not himself anymore. He's lost his center. I just don't think he gives a shit about what happens to him now. I can see him walking into a bullet."

"What do you want me to do, Patrick?"

"You could call him. Just let him know you're alright. It might help."

"He could call me."

"You asked him not to. You know he won't."

Patrick was at the tipping point of whether or not to break his promise to his father. In the end, he couldn't in good conscience keep it any longer.

"He made me promise not to tell you, but he asked how you were doing."

"What did you tell him?"

"The truth."

"Did he ask anything else?"

"No. He just expressed concern for you. He wants me to take you and the girls to dinner. He wants me to make you laugh. I'd like to, but I don't feel very funny right now."

"Did he want to know if I ask about him?"

"I could tell he wanted to, but he wouldn't. He said he broke every promise he ever made to you. He said you asked him to leave you alone. He said he was keeping that one, that it was the very least he could do for you. When I asked him if he wanted to know if you asked about him. He said he didn't think it was any of his business anymore. I'm telling you, Ma, he's a shot unit. He's lost without you."

"Am I supposed to just forget what he did to us?"

"No. But you could forgive him. You know he won't forgive himself."

"It's not that easy, Patrick. Not with that video that keeps popping up. How am I supposed to get past that?"

"You could stop watching it every day for starters. You'll never get the picture out of your head if you keep looking at it. Especially since you're not seeing it for what it was."

"You have special insight all of a sudden?" Mairead snapped.

"No, but I looked at every second of those tapes, several times. That wasn't love. It wasn't an affair. It wasn't even sex. It was self-abuse. The man in those videos was not happy. He hated himself for what he was doing, and he couldn't be done with it quickly enough. If you have to look at it, next time focus on his face. Every second, it was a mask of pain and disgust. Then ask yourself honestly, has he ever looked that way with you? My guess is never."

Mairead took her son's advice. She watched the video again. It wasn't long before she was crying. But this time she wasn't crying for herself. When she was done, she asked Patrick to send her Paddy's novel. She read it that night. Patrick could hear her weeping forlornly from his bedroom down the hall. He had no idea where this was going, but the status quo was unacceptable.

CHAPTER EIGHTY-NINE

December 18, 2013
Farmingdale

A week before Christmas, Paddy was just getting out of the shower when he heard his cell phone ringing. His reading glasses weren't nearby, so he couldn't read the caller ID. So he answered it the way he always answered the phone.

"Durr."

"Hello, Paddy," said Mairead. His heart almost stopped.

"Is everything alright?" he asked, worried. He had leapt right to the worst-case scenario. Other than an emergency, he couldn't imagine any other reason Mairead would be calling.

"I just called to see how you were doing."

"You know me," he said, calming down. "I'm tactical. I'm doing alright."

"That's not what I heard."

"Has Patrick been telling tales out of school?"

"He was concerned about you. Frankly, so am I. I read your novel. It's disturbing."

"Well, it's a novel. You know, fiction."

"Except that it isn't. I'm sorry you had to endure all of that, Paddy. I'm sorry you couldn't talk to me about it."

"Don't do that, Mairead. You've never done anything to me to be sorry for."

"I'm still sorry."

"You don't have to worry about me. I'm really okay. I just want you to be happy."

Paddy had misread Mairead's concern for pity. He wanted to distance himself from that as quickly as possible. So he diverted the conversation from himself.

"I've been waiting for a package. It hasn't come. It was almost a month ago I left it for you. I can't imagine why you haven't filed it with the court. Is there a problem with the terms?"

"As a matter of fact, there are. I don't like the terms at all."

"I don't know what else you want, Mairead. I'm giving you everything already."

"I don't want it," she told him. "I want you. I need you here with me, Paddy. I want you home for Christmas. No, I mean right fucking now. I don't know what I was thinking, but I don't want a life without you in it."

"Are you sure?" Paddy asked, praying she wouldn't change her mind.

"I'm sure," Mairead said. "It's time for you to come home now, Paddy Durr."

EPILOGUE

December 25, 2013
Plainedge

Christmas saw the Durr family together again. The house was full and festive. Paddy had put back on five healthy pounds from Mairead's cooking. He looked rested. He was content and fit. Mairead was happy again for the first time in a long time. The two of them were rediscovering each other, all over again. They had a difficult time being in a room together without giving in to the need to touch each other. They had a lot of work to do, but they were doing it. They resumed couples therapy. Mairead wanted to throw out the signed and sealed, but not filed divorce papers. Paddy asked her to hold onto them. He wanted a constant and tangible reminder of how close he came to shit-canning his entire life, just in case he ever got the urge to get stupid again.

In July, Patrick Durr entered the Police Academy. When he graduates in January, Paddy intends to have him assigned to the 75th Precinct. Still in Brooklyn North, it is close enough for Paddy to keep an eye on him, but far enough away to allow Patrick to learn the job and become his own kind of cop. Police Officer Tommy Crowe has evinced a desire to transfer to the 75 to work with him. Paddy already vetoed it. Tommy's stepfather, Ed Morrissey would have a heart attack if Paddy sent Tommy to work in East New York.

In August, Erik Vasquez, AKA *Elephant Boy,* or *EB* to his friends, of which he had very few, was found stabbed one hundred and thirty-three times, and stuffed face first into a high capacity dryer in the laundry room of the Anna M. Cross Center on Rikers' Island. He was a pre-trial detainee the Latin Kings wouldn't let see the inside of a courtroom. They wrote the word *Insecto* on *EB's* back, with his own blood.

After *EB* died, all the sexiness of Dave Molinari's RICO drained out of the case. He took the Latin Kings down anyway, dismantling what was left of the drug operation on Starr Street.

In September, Oscar Nieto, AKA *Casper* went on trial for the murder of Euripides Luis Betances, known as *Negro* to his friends, of which he also had very few. It was a one week trial. The case was so strong, the only defense *Casper's* attorney could mount was the victim was a worse scumbag than the defendant, and he deserved every bullet. The jury didn't buy it. Neither did the judge. He sentenced Nieto to forty years to life, ostensibly burying him under the jail.

Paddy is still holding things down in the C Team at the 83 Squad, with Joe Furio and Armando Gigante. But he's not making as much overtime as he used to, and that's his choice. Paddy didn't miss coaching football as much as he thought he would. The extra free time he spends with Mairead. Occasionally, he drops into one of her exercise classes. If you've never seen a six foot, two hundred and ten pound man doing a Zumba class amidst a sea of middle-aged women, then you haven't lived.

Paddy and Mairead have learned to tune the haters out. The video would still resurface from time to time, but they would just delete it, and block the sender forever. Every once in a while, Mairead would catch someone staring critically at them. Whenever it happened, she would reach up, pull Paddy's head down to her own, and kiss him deeply and tenderly, a fine fuck you very much. They knew who they were. They knew what they wanted, and they were determined to never let anyone or anything come between them again. And, Paddy finally found a happy ending for his novel.

ACKNOWLEDGMENTS

An undertaking of this magnitude could not occur without the assistance of a lot of people. Especially given the fact that I was unfamiliar with the process of creating a book. I discovered pretty quickly that preparing DD5s and Unusuals are a far cry from writing a novel. So I have many people to thank for guiding me through to completion.

I would be remiss if I failed to thank the men and women of the old 34th Precinct. The cops and supervisors were instrumental in protecting me, more often than not from myself, and keeping me from spinning of the rails, as was my wont to do. Along the way, we got some hellified police work accomplished. I want to thank the detectives from the 34 Squad who gave me my first glimpse of the kind of cop I wanted to be, and hopefully eventually became.

There are far too many people to mention individually, but this book is a homage to all the incredible cops who survived a crazy era in an insane environment, while never forgetting those of us who did not survive, particularly Police Officer Michael J Buczek. A gifted and committed young cop with limitless potential, he was cut down tragically on October 18th, 1988. He was and remains an inspiration and a guardian angel to us all.

I want to specifically recognize my old Anti-Crime team, several of whom are my dearest friends, and contributed their memories, which inspired some of the stories in the book. John Moynihan, Tom McPartland, Artie Barragan, Pat Duffy and Pat Regan were a wealth of knowledge and support, and were the greatest gun guys I ever saw. Most especially I want to recognize Pat Regan, who literally took one for the team and emerged afterwards, stronger and greater than us all. These were the toughest, craziest, smartest and bravest cops I ever met. I would not be breathing out of the right end if not for their care and protection.

I need to thank Dave Hunt and Pete Walsh, the owners of Coogan's Pub and Irish Restaurant in Washington Heights. They allowed me to use their wonderful establishment as the setting where Paddy meets and falls in love with Mairead. They are two of the most loyal friends and supporters of the cops in the 34th and 33rd Precincts, and the Washington Heights community as a whole.

Finally, I need to recognize the family of Michael Buczek. I dearly miss his wonderful parents, Ted and Josephine. Their sacrifice was immeasurable, but they never lost their sense of purpose or connection to the cops and the community. Mr. B was a staunch advocate of the police, and me in particular, in my time of crisis. They were both honored guests at my wedding, and my wife and I miss them terribly. A special thank you goes out to Mike's sister, Mary Jo Buczek, who runs the Michael J. Buczek Foundation and Little League along with John Moynihan. The little League has served the youth of the Washington Heights community for more than two decades. Many of the ball players from over the years have since become members of the NYPD. This is a fitting tribute to Mike's memory and ensures that his service, and the family's sacrifice will never be forgotten. In addition, Mary Jo was one of my early readers. Her criticisms were concise, insightful and very helpful in the editing process.

In the novel I seem to give harsh treatment to the cops and detectives in Queens. This was done solely as a plot device and for dramatic effect. It in no way reflects my true sentiments. I had the opportunity to work with some wonderful and gifted detectives while assigned to Queens. Mark Valencia and Bob Matera were two of my partners, and were indicative of the great detectives and cops I was blessed enough to work with in my three years there.

I spent the majority of my career as a detective in the 83 Squad in Brooklyn North. I was also fortunate enough to work closely with the amazing detectives and supervisors of the Brooklyn North Homicide Squad. There is no way I could name everyone I need to thank for their help and guidance during this most rewarding time of my life. They are legion. I could randomly pick almost anyone from that time, and have an inexhaustible source of material for my fiction. Deeply felt gratitude and admiration goes out to you all. Special mention goes out to my former partners in the C-Team, Joe Tallarine, Artie Barragan and Geoff Hernandez. They are great detectives, and were an endless source of hilarity. Their expertise and assistance were crucial to crafting the story of the murder detailed in the book.

Though not quite as chaotic as the career of Paddy Durr, my own was still very eventful and at times tumultuous. I had a penchant for being my own worst enemy. You don't survive a hectic life like that without some terrific support. My DEA trustees, George Fahrbach and Mike Zeller were instrumental in pulling my ass out of the fire more than once. They protected me from myself and helped me to become the kind of detective I wanted to be.

I would be greatly remiss if I failed to thank my old PBA Trustee in Manhattan North. One tough Marine, Eddie Mahoney was a godsend to me during the worst crisis of my life. When the world was tumbling down around my shoulders, Eddie pulled me from the wreckage and reminded me that I had thirty-thousand brothers and sisters that believed in me and had my back. None of what followed could have been possible without his care and guidance, and I will love him forever for it.

I reserve immeasurable gratitude and esteem for Chief Joseph Esposito. "The Boss", Chief Esposito was the longest serving Chief of the Department in the long history of the NYPD. I met him when he was a Deputy Inspector and I was a snot-nosed rookie Detective. He "rescued" me from Queens, and brought me back to the *barrio*, arranging my assignment to the 83 Squad. His stewardship over my and my wife's careers was instrumental to our ultimate success. With his help, we were very successful. One of my proudest titles achieved on the job was to be known as an "Espo Guy". I was honored to be that, and still identify myself as such when the subject comes up. Anyone who had the privilege to work for the Chief will recognize the character *Joe Pos* as a loving homage to the best boss any cop ever worked for.

I need to thank my early readers. They took the time to endure this book from it's earliest iterations, starting from the first unedited manuscript. Their input, advice and criticism had much to do with the finished product. Thanks go out to Lisa Banke. My friend since grade school, she was a long time resident of Bushwick, and gave her stamp of approval for the authenticity of my descriptions. Special shout out to my sister-in-law Christine Mayer and Joan Santoli. They both finished the manuscript in a fortnight and were specific in their criticism as well as their praise. They were my first, and biggest fans.

I would hate myself if I didn't thank a man who has been like a second father to me for my entire life. Thomas Anderle was a firm and caring hand for me through a tumultuous childhood. He was a shining example for me of what a man was supposed to be. I have tried to emulate him as best as I could. I don't think I ever quite achieved that level, but following his example has always served me well. As a particular reader of the genre I'm trying to write in, Tom was one of my early readers. His advice and encouragement gave me the fortitude to see this project to completion. It's not like I had a choice after that. You don't disappoint a man like Tom Anderle.

I must thank my friends from X-Sport Fitness in Massapequa. Ben Grieve, Sinead Kinney, Deanna Miller and Corianne Banks. They were kind enough to let me sound out my plot ideas to them. They patiently listened and made recommendations. Those recommendations went into the finished product, which they also read and advised me on. They demonstrated the latent natural talents to be excellent literary critics and editors.

I want to thank Thomas Easley, Robert Jackall and Linda Fairstein, three extraordinary writers who took the time to advise me with respect to this industry. Their experience and guidance were very helpful in completing this project.

Thanks go out to Angela Delodi Campo. As a former Transit cop, her expertise and advice about the doings underground were essential to the story-line. She also served as the muse and inspiration for the character, Transit Police Officer Anita Devry. In the same chapter I did a little shameless name dropping. Detective 1st Grade Caroline Shabunia, NYPD Retired, was kind enough to let me refer to her by name. As she is a long-time friend, and unquestionably the best Special Frauds Detective I had the good fortune to work with, I really enjoyed writing about her. I feel that mentioning her in the book gave that chapter an authenticity that wouldn't have been there without her.

I want to thank my colleagues at the Farmingdale Creative Writers Group, who were kind enough to let me share my manuscript with them, one chapter at a time. Their critiques and support were beyond helpful. Especially Ann Lettal, who carefully read the entire manuscript and dutifully "red-penned" where applicable. Her observations were far more intuitive than spell-check, and she is a *Grammar-Cop* of the first order.

I need to extend my deepest gratitude to my dear friend and mentor, Judy Turek. Known professionally as J R Turek, she is a wonderful poet and an extraordinary editor. She is also the moderator of the Farmingdale Creative Writers Group, as well as being creatively involved with several other Long Island Poetry and Prose societies and publications. She has been instrumental in finding and developing numerous new voices and encouraging their writing careers, mine being one of them. If not for her gentle insistence and expert advice and guidance, this manuscript would have gone into a drawer, never to see the light again. Her stewardship has allowed me to realize my dream.

Lastly, I need to thank my family. They have patiently endured, and yet encouraged this arduous birthing process. Their indulgence of me, as I commandeered the kitchen table to write upon, allowed me to create this story. Their support through this process sustained me. To my children Ryan and Kelly and my beloved wife Janet, thank you so very much. I love you.